FAMILY

I0680334

DARK AGES ONLINE

TIMOTHY NICHOLSON

ISBN: 979-8-9943596-0-0

This book is dedicated to my family.

You fill my world with joy

ONE

Airport

Today was the day Luke had been waiting for. His family was finally taking their long-awaited vacation. He was on his way to pick up his sister, Cleo, then they were off to the airport and on to their adventure. He was sitting in the back of a cab staring out the window, watching rain drops race to the bottom. It was a gloomy day, which suited his mood perfectly. The trip was originally a birthday gift to his dad a few years ago but, after the accident, it turned into a memorial.

The taxi pulled up to Cleo's house and she was waiting outside, in the rain. She was wearing a bright yellow rain poncho with the hood pulled up and three large luggage bags sitting next to her, each covered with a trash bag so they didn't get wet. She shook off her poncho and climbed into cab to sit next to Luke.

"I was worried you were going to be late." she said, a little flustered.

"I left early." Luke assured her, smiling. Then he looked at her bags and asked, "Is that everything?"

She nodded in confirmation and he got out and loaded the bags into the trunk.

"Did you bring enough stuff?" Luke asked, after they were on the road again.

"A month is a long time" she said shrugging, "and I wanted to be prepared, it felt important."

Luke understood where she was coming from, they were each grieving, and if his sister needed to over prepare for the trip, then who was he to judge. His mind wandered to his own grief. He wanted their dad to be there too. It wasn't fair that he wasn't.

"Do you think Mom is already there?" Cleo asked, interrupting his thoughts.

"Yeah, she left this morning." he said, then explained, "She wanted to get there early. Since you had to finish up with work, I thought you and I could go together.". He handed her a ticket.

"Thanks," she said, taking the ticket. "I got everything setup for vacation. My team will do fine without me." She looked him over and asked, "How are you doing? Are you working?"

His sister had excelled in the corporate world while he had struggled. Cleo graduated at the top of her class and went on to work for a major software company. She had quickly risen through the ranks and was the director of an entire department. A few years ago, Luke had worked at her company, but it only lasted for a few months. Everybody said he had been exceptional and had a bright future there but he didn't feel it. Every job he worked at, he seemed to excel, but nothing felt right to him.

"I'm between jobs right now." he finally answered, "I was considering a change of scenery after this, maybe I'll head back to Europe." When their father passed away, Luke had disappeared for half a year backpacking his way through Europe. He had fond memories of learning the local languages and customs as he traveled.

"Have you ever thought about being a teacher?" she hesitantly asked.

"That's probably the one profession I haven't tried." Luke responded, laughing. "I don't think I would do very well."

"Mom thought you would make a great one." she retorted, "She said, when you were little, you would help the other kids in class and the teachers nicknamed you their 'little assistant'."

"That was second grade Cleo," he said, rolling his eyes "I could probably still teach second graders but not much beyond that."

"Don't sell yourself short Luke," she chided, "you've picked up some great skills over the years. You did that electrical apprenticeship and months of programming for my company, and others. You did that plumbing job and even some construction." She reached over and plucked his fancy shirt, "Despite not having work, you still seem to be doing well for yourself." She leaned in and quietly demanded, "At least tell me it's not something illegal."

"Nothing illegal, I made a few good deals a while back." he hedged.

"Do you think Mom will start without us?" she asked, changing the subject.

"No." he responded, "She got the room, but the pods won't be ready until later today. They let her check in early but the VR gear was still in a deep cleaning cycle."

After a short time, they arrived at the airport, checked their bags, paid the outlandish fees, and made their way through security and onto the airplane.

After take-off, Luke thought about their destination, New Las Vegas. He only knew the basics about the city and not much beyond that. It was built, funded and operated by the titans of the gaming industry and it was the birthplace of full immersion virtual reality. He wasn't a gamer so he didn't have much of an interest in the city when it popped up. He looked at his sister, and while he might not be a gamer, she was.

"What do you know about New Las Vegas?" he asked her. Cleo gave him a mock glare and he quickly defended himself, "Hey, I know. I should have looked into it earlier, but things have been busy. The ticket says we are landing in New Las Vegas but mom said the resort is in New Oasis, is it close by?"

"I'll catch you up" she said with a smile and a glint in her eye, then started talking faster and faster as her excitement was evident. "I've been following the city since it was formed. And, ever since they announced it, I've been dying to get my hands on a VR pod. I almost took a hiatus from work to move to Tent City when it first formed."

"What's Tent City?" Luke asked, confused.

She took a deep breath to slow down and said, "Ok, let me start at the beginning." she laughed, then explained everything she knew. When they began their descent into that very city, she quieted down and stared out the window while Luke reflected on what she told him.

Before New Las Vegas was created, the console wars heated up to such a degree the government was forced to step in and mitigate the conflict. They creating laws that forced each platform to allow 3rd party games, unrestricted. This opened the door for every gaming studio and developer to expand their reach. It gave them access to platforms that were previously unavailable. Everybody benefited, especially indie game developers. A few small studios even became so popular, they rivaled the traditional game studios. Gamers worldwide rejoiced,

To ensure players' interests were being met, a council to oversee the gaming industry was created. They uninspiringly called it the GAME council, which stood for Gaming Alliance for Max Entertainment. With the backing of the gaming industry's top leaders, the council ruled that a new city would be developed to facilitate the cross-company relationships, and New Las Vegas was born.

The city was designed like a large wheel, with a hub at the center and spokes shooting out in all directions. In the hub, each major gaming studio had a headquarter building with a road extending out from it. Nintendo, Microsoft, and Sony were just a few of the studios with a major presence in the city. Each owned a large section with the buildings and roads being named after their games and characters. Nintendo street led directly to the Nintendo headquarters with other streets in their territory having names such as Mario, Luigi and even Yoshi.

When they built NLV, as Cleo called it, they held nothing back. The city was designed efficiently and for the future, with some radical concepts. There were no personal vehicles allowed in the city limits, instead, there was a fleet of driverless taxis to take you wherever you wanted go, completely free. And there were no residential buildings, employees lived in a suburb west of town named, New Haven, and took a tram between the two.

Not too long after the city was created, there was a major breakthrough in virtual reality technology. Several of the studios pooled their research and worked together, which led to the creation of the first fully immersive gaming pod. The first pods were experimental and incredibly expensive and there was a huge catch, they needed a direct connection to the backend due the amount of data that was sent back and forth.

The data was immense and couldn't be handled by the standard internet's bandwidth so they were forced to create something new, they called it ImmersiveNet. ImmersiveNet was a locked down and controlled system that allowed only authorized pods to connect and communicate on the network and most importantly, it could easily handle the massive amount of bandwidth that was required.

The other studios were impressed but were concerned about becoming irrelevant. The GAME council stepped in and required tools to be created to assist in upgrading any existing VR game to run on ImmersiveNet. After a dozen games from various studios were ready, the council made the announcement to the world that full immersion had been achieved.

Very quickly, ImmersiveNet was incorporated into every building in NLV and each game studio had their own pods. Several public recreation rooms opened throughout the city to showcase the technology which caused something unexpected happened, hardcore gamers flocked to NLV in hoards to utilize the hardware.

The gamers that traveled to NLV were not offered luxurious housing in New Haven or even an empty building in NLV, but rather were forced to create their own shanty town to the east, which was dubbed Tent City.

The cluster of tents and number of residents of Tent City grew at an exponential rate, however the safety and stability decreased as their overall resources diminished. The de facto leader of the transient town led a few riots and burned down a section of NLV. Nobody got hurt but the council received the message.

With a cautious approach, in an attempt to not alienate the gaming community, the council researched various options. Ultimately, they opted to maintain the privacy and security of New Haven and NLV. They decided to outsource the creation of a community for outsiders to the hotel industry and gave them a large swath of land.

A resort complex was created south of NLV and provided a much better place for the gamers to reside. They named it New Oasis and tent city was quickly abandoned for it. To ensure a smooth transition, the council guaranteed the gamers free housing for six months. This turned out to be an unexpected boon for the studios because as the technology advanced, these gamers were essential in testing the new hardware, and they did it for free.

Eventually ImmersiveNet made its way to New Oasis and every hotel and resort acquired the pods. They quickly understood the opportunity and fully equipped each room with the VR gear. They also recognized their clientele didn't leave their rooms, so they added extra amenities to meet their needs, such as full laundry and cleaning services as well as every meal delivered to the room.

During this time the VR world expanded as well, a virtual clone of NLV was created and virtual real-estate was established and sold. Virtual bars, clubs and theaters popped up around the city and the virtual nightlife became the next hottest thing. Celebrities and A-listers flocked to the city to enjoy exclusive bars and clubs, not even needing to leave their hotel suites.

TWO

New Las Vegas

After landing, Luke and Cleo retrieved their bags and rode the tram south, to New Oasis. The airport was located north of New Las Vegas and as they traveled, they passed through the city and got a front row seat to a wonderous view.

NLV was beautiful and sprawled out as far as the eye could see. The center of the city held the tallest buildings, which formed a massive circle with a clearing in the center. Clusters of smaller buildings radiated outwards, arraigned together in large blocks with a vibrant park in the center. The streets were lined with oversized sidewalks and trees that shaded groups of people meandering underneath.

Through his travels, Luke had become accustomed to large cities and what he saw, or the lack of, stunned him. There was no smog, no trash tumbling in the streets and no homeless people on the corners. Instead, what he saw was peaceful, orderly, even serene. He commented as much to Cleo but she just snickered and said something about how it looked like somebody used SimCity to design it.

Luke studied the center of the city where the headquarter buildings were located and marveled at their uniqueness. Each one was different and it looked as if the architects held a competition to see who could create the most outrageous building.

A couple of the buildings were considerably taller than the others and it looked like they were competing in a tallest-building contest. They both had large cranes on top and were currently adding more levels. Another building was all black and looked like a large domino, white dots and all. While yet another was in the shape and color of a rainbow. They were all interesting buildings but the one that caught Luke's eye the most was shorter than the others and was made completely of blue glass. The thick glass offered a blueish hued view of the interior and he could see people moving around inside.

The tram ended in the center of an elaborate park, surrounded by resorts on all sides. The park was well manicured with low cut grass, a meandering stream and a large fountain in the center. Travelers, with luggage in tow, navigated the large pathways shaded by the many trees.

Luke and Cleo, crossed over several wooden bridges which were intricately carved to display different video games. Cleo knew each one and the two lightly discussed the games as they walked. They eventually fell into a comfortable silence as they strolled through the peaceful park.

When Luke and Cleo neared the resort, they spotted their mom next to the entrance. Cleo dropped her bags and ran to her, squealing. The two embraced and squeezed each other until Luke arrived, dragging the bags behind him.

"Both of you look great!" their mother said after stepping back and looking at both of them with a huge smile on her face. She gave Luke a welcoming hug and as she was squeezing him, her voice broke, saying "I haven't seen you both in such a long time."

After their father passed away, their mom had gone into isolation and neither of them had much contact with her. She was particularly absent on the holidays, which bothered Luke. He always reached out and invited her but each time she insisted she was fine. Christmas was the hardest on him though, it was dad's favorite.

"How was the flight?" their mom asked, leading them to their room. "I landed this morning and the view of New Las Vegas was incredible in the morning sun."

Luke followed, lost in thought and didn't hear the question.

"The flight was fine," Cleo interjected, "we just talked about the city.", she gestured to Luke and said, "He's been a bit melancholy."

"I'm ok, I just have a lot of things on my mind." Luke hedged, trying to reassure his mom after she gave him a concerned look. He had been thinking a lot about his dad lately and really missed him.

"Have you used VR yet?" his mom asked him, trying to change the subject and put him at ease.

"No" he answered shaking his head, "But, I've had a few friends describe it and I'm interested." Not being a gamer, Luke never had a reason to try virtual reality. He had a few friends with VR headsets and even one that traveled to NLV. While he was not overly impressed with the headsets, the full immersion sounded incredible.

On their way to the room, they chatted about different VR experiences, with Cleo providing the most input. Luke wouldn't realize until later that his mom had completely sidetracked his intrusive thoughts.

When they got to their suite, their mom gave them a quick tour. It was the size of a small house with four bedrooms and a private bathroom in each. There was a large common area with a massive TV and a couch with several loungers. The kitchen was close to the entrance with a half wall and barstools leading to the common area.

Their mom explained that food would be delivered to the kitchen three times a day and it was their responsibility to log out and eat. Luke noticed food was already waiting for them and having not eaten since that morning, he looked longingly at it.

"Let me show you the last room and then we can eat." his mom said, not missing his look.

Or course, she left the best for last, the pod room. There were four large, all-white, pill shaped objects pointing to the center of the room, each about the size of a refrigerator laying down. Luke slid open the top hatch and climbed in. He laid down and got comfortable, then slid the lid shut. The top hatch was fully transparent but his mother explained that when the VR activated it would be completely opaque.

As soon as the door closed the sounds from outside were cut off and he was left in complete silence. Gentle lights turned on and he heard a soft voice announce, "Pod suit not detected." Not able to do much, he sheepishly opened the hatch and climbed out.

"When can we start?" Cleo asked excitedly.

"Let's eat first." their mom said, "I need to explain a few more things about the game." Then she walked over to the door and touched a large metal bar that had lowered itself, locking them in. The bar rose and the door opened.

"What's that for?" Luke asked, pointing to the bar.

"That's a security device that activates when we're in the pods." She explained, "You activated it a minute ago. It's biometrically controlled and we are the only ones that can disabled it to enter or leave the room. In orientation they explained, the staff are only able to access this room in extreme emergencies. It's intended to provide us security while we are immersed."

The three sat down at the kitchen table and parceled out the food, it was a simple lunch of deli meat sandwiches with salad and fresh fruit.

"When you log in for the first time, you will need to select a starting location." their mom explained as they ate. She looked at Luke and continued, "This part is important, otherwise you will end up in a random city and it could take us days to find you. Our accounts are linked and when you log in for the first time, you should be able to select one of us."

"How did our accounts get linked?" Cleo asked.

"Your dad did it when we got our biometrics scanned." their mom quietly explained. A few years ago, they had gotten their biometrics scanned for the game. At the time Luke wasn't exactly sure why it was needed but followed along because his dad was really excited.

Luke noticed a shift in his mom's demeanor and wanted to reciprocate the kindness she had shown him earlier and thought furiously on something he could ask to change the subject. He didn't know too much about games but he knew enough.

"What about character selection?" he asked.

Cleo snorted.

"Honey, what do you think the biometric scan was for?" his mom asked, looking at him with a kind smile.

His mom and Cleo explained to him that several years ago, Dark Ages Online instituted a new method to create in-game avatars. They utilized several personality tests and questionnaires along with a biometric scan to generate a baseline avatar.

"Oh.", Luke responded in a deflated voice, but perked up when a thought came to him, "What about names?"

"Ahh, your character name. It will be automatically chosen for you." his mom explained with a knowing smile. She waved her hands around and said, "They have some sort of algorithm that fits your profile with a name. Some of the people in orientation were not too happy about it but they explained to us that you are not given a choice at birth so you're not given one in this world either."

"I'm getting excited, can I go first?" Cleo asked after they finished eating.

Luke thought it was a natural choice for his sister to go first since her and dad were the gamers of the family, while him and mom tended to be outside in the yard.

"I'll log in first." their mom replied quickly.

Luke thought his mom was acting a little strange but considering the circumstances, he understood. This trip was for dad and he knew that his death had really affected her.

"That's fine, is there anything else before we go?" Cleo asked, a little disappointed.

"Yes," their mom said, "there are body suits for the pods in your bedroom closet. In orientation they said to use a new suit each day and recommended a maximum immersion time of eight hours per day."

"What about going to the restroom?" Cleo asked, "I don't want to pee myself."

"You still feel it in-game." their mom laughed, "You simply logout to go. Your character AI will pick up where you left off, even if you are in the middle of battle."

"AI?" Luke asked, surprised.

"Once you log into the game, your avatar is created and will remain in the world forever." his mom explained, "If you log out, your avatar remains and is controlled by your character AI. Over time, your character AI will study your behavior and emulate you until you log back in and take control."

"You all ready?" Cleo asked, standing up.

"Yes, I'm past ready." Luke replied excitedly.

"Yes," their mom said, excitement edging into her voice as well, "I can fill you in on anything else as needed. But one last thing, it's about the in-game communication, there is no chat system. If we want to talk to each other, we will need to be within hearing range. There might be spells or technology to change this but for the most part, the game will mimic the real world as much as possible."

THREE

First day

With suits on, the three climbed into their pods.

"Mom, one more question," Cleo prompted.

"Yes sweetie?" their mom replied.

"Will we need to select a server?" Cleo asked.

"No," their mother said with a fond smile, "your dad selected that when he setup the accounts."

Luke was done talking and would figure things out as they came up. He climbed into the pod and laid down, sliding the hatch closed. As the hatch closed, gentle lights turned on and his mom's and sister's conversation cut off. Rather than a warning, this time he heard a hissing sound as the pod pressurized.

Luke closed his eyes and took a deep breath, relaxing. Behind his closed lids, a small light formed and slowly expanded until it encompassed his entire awareness. Suddenly, his senses became alive and he no longer felt like he was in the pod. He was weightless and a floral scent assaulted his nose, reminding him of spring time in his mom's garden. A cool breeze blew across his body and goosebumps formed.

A small room slowly appeared around him and he was set down gently in the center. The room was bathed in a calming blue glow with no visible source of light and no shadows. He looked at his arms and body and it looked and felt just like his. He slowly took a few steps and the movement felt so real and natural. He practiced moving for several minutes, then walked up to the only door in the room and opened it.

Outside, his sister and mother were waiting for him, standing in a sunny courtyard. When he stepped out to greet them, he paused and squinted until his eyes adjusted to the bright light attacking him. He was surprised he felt such discomfort and how well it matched the real-world experience.

Groups of people were scattered around chatting happily with each other. Surrounding them, beyond the courtyard, were large buildings that Luke recognized from the tram ride. They were in the center of virtual New Las Vegas and surrounded by the gaming giants' virtual headquarters. Each building looked exactly like their real-world counterpart, except they all had digital enhancements.

Luke stood there, amazed, staring at the buildings. One of the tall ones had a large monkey hanging on the side, throwing barrels down onto the crowds below. Before they impacted, they exploded into confetti.

On top of the other tall building stood an intimidating figure, a soldier completely encased in green body armor with a golden face shield. They held a large weapon and fired it down at alien creatures climbing towards them. When struck, each creature exploded into fireworks.

The rainbow building floated in the air with a large cloud at each end. Rain gently fell sporadically and flashes of lightening shot between the clouds whenever the teleporter was used to enter the building.

Finally, Luke looked to the blue glass building which had been his favorite, and he was not disappointed. Throughout the building glowing balls of various colors slowly flickered on and off, reminding him of a Christmas tree. On top of the building, several figures sped around on a racetrack. As Luke watched, a blue figure stopped and tossed off a golden ring to join hundreds of others hanging in the air. It expanded and a scene of an alien landscape appeared in the center, different from any of the others.

Tearing his eyes away from the buildings he followed his mom and sister to the center of the courtyard, where an eight-foot azure portal stood. He stared deep into its depths and was mesmerized by the swirling colors. However, his trance was broken when his mom and sister stepped up and disappeared into the portal. Luke took one last look around and followed them.

Luke found himself standing in the center of a dimly lit hallway with doors on either side. Each door represented a different game and was elaborately crafted in that style. The three walked down the hallway and inspected each door, looking for the entrance to their game.

The first door they came to was dark red with flames racing up the sides. Smoldering above the door was a sign written in red-hot metal: World Burner 2. They continued walking and the next door was made of gold with various precious gems embedded into it, rubies, crystals and sapphires. Embossed above the door were the words: Mining Simulator. The third door they came to caused his heart to race and he unconsciously quickened his pace past it. The door and frame were made from bleached bones that emanated a sickly green hue causing his skin to crawl. Glancing back the sign said Death Quest 4.

Eventually they came to a large wooden door made from thick wooden beams and wrought-iron bands. The door could have easily been from one of the many castles Luke had visited. Above the door was an old-time sign that read: Dark Ages Online.

"I think this is it" he said, looking back at his mom and sister. They both nodded in agreement.

His mom quickly walked up to the door and pulled it open. She looked at the two and said, "My avatar's name is Nightshade.", then turned and stepped over threshold, disappearing as she did.

Cleo got a questioning look on her face but before she could say anything, her mom was gone. She looked at him but he just shrugged and waved for her to go next.

Luke waited until his sister was gone, then stepped through the door himself. His vision when completely dark and he was presented with a glowing prompt:

[Choose a starting location
  1. Random location
  2. Group member location]

With no hesitation, Luke selected number two and a second prompt appeared:

[Select a group member
  1. Nightshade
  2. Sunshine
  3. Father]

Luke paused, his virtual brow furrowed, he was not expecting the last option. He didn't spend much time debating, his curiosity got the better of him and he selected number three. He felt his heart pounding in his chest and his mind spun at the possibilities. The prompt faded and he felt a wave of heat overtake his body. Beads of sweat trickled down his back and he heard a repetitive banging noise close by.

Ting, Ting, Ting

The world started to brighten around him and he blinked as his eyes started to sting. He breathed in and acrid air burned the back of his throat. He let out a small cough. Then he heard the banging again.

Ting, Ting, Ting

Cautiously he drew in deep breath but despite his best efforts, a tickle formed in the back of his throat and he coughed harder. The banging stopped.

Ting, Ting…

The game world solidified and in front of Luke was a man holding a glowing sword and hammer, air thick with smoke.

"Oh, hey, where did you come from?" The man asked, glancing over.

His was voice painfully familiar to Luke. He froze. He hadn't heard that voice in years. He stared at the man and memoires of his dad flooded over him.

The man stuck the glowing sword into a forge then grabbed a waterskin and tossed it to Luke.

"Take a sip, it'll help." the man said. He explained, "The air is a little rough in here and takes a bit to get used to it."

Luke gulped down the water, it tasted awful but it helped his throat. His mind raced, he thought the name was a mistake when he chose it, but the person standing in front of him looked and sounded just like his dad. This man was more muscular but his face and mannerisms were the same.

"You look a little better." the man said, then asked, "Did you come for some work or are you looking to purchase something?" When Luke stared at him with a confused look he explained, "I'm kind of known around here for producing some of the best armor pieces."

"No, I don't even know where I am." Luke responded, not really knowing what to say.

"Well," the man got a concerned look and said "This is Valhalla, the 'City of the Fallen'." He squinted slightly and looked closer at Luke then his eyes widened in surprise and he said, "Oh… you're not supposed to be here."

"Yeah… about that." Luke said sheepishly. Then he explained what happened when he logged into the game and how he chose 'Father' instead of 'Nightshade'.

"I'm Father all right." the man said, chuckling. Then he asked curiously, "How do you know Nightshade?"

"Nightshade is my mom" Luke explained, and with a little hesitation he said, "and my sister is Sunshine." He wasn't sure that was true but he thought it was a safe assumption.

"That makes you..." Father said, staring at him with an intense gaze.

"I'm Luke." Luke said happily.

"Are you?" Father asked intently, eyes raised, smiling an achingly familiar smile.

Luke stared at him blankly for a moment then realized his mistake. He tilted his head around looking at the various UI elements in his vision, trying to find the answer.

"Think 'Character sheet'", Father said quietly.

Luke did, and a translucent character sheet appeared in front of him.

[Character sheet
        Name: Storm
        Race: Human
        Level: 1
        Health: 100/100
        Stamina: 100/100
        Mana: 70/70
        Stats:
                Strength: 13
                Dexterity: 10
                Constitution: 10
                Intelligence: 15
                Wisdom: 7
                Charisma: 8
        Skills: None.
        Spells: None.
        Special Abilities:
                Quick learning: Level 1
                        You are able to learn skills by watching them performed. While others need a trainer, you can glean the finer details through observation and replication.]

"I'm… Storm." he said, speaking his name for the first time.

"Well Storm," Father said, nodding in agreement, "let me show you around a little before they come to get you."

"What?" Storm asked in alarm.

"Follow me." Father said, chuckling, then walked over to a table with several pieces of armor laying on it. Father picked up a forest green chainmail shirt and handed it to Storm, then with a big smile he said, "Try it on."

Storm took the mail shirt and marveled at its weight, he didn't expect it to feel so heavy and so real. He turned it over, staring at the deep green color and hearing the metal links clink together.

"Go ahead, inspect it." Father instructed, and when Storm looked at him questioningly, Father explained, "Look at it and think 'Inspect'."

Storm focused on the shirt and inspected it. A prompt appeared with the item description.

[Item
   Name: Forest Green Light Chainmail shirt
   Type: Chainmail armor, chest piece
   Level: 10
   Quality: 100%
   Armor: 10 (+5)
   Effect: +10% stealth in forest terrain
   Durability: 50/50
   Crafted by: Father]

"Wow, this is nice." Storm said approvingly.

"Thanks, I've been working on my armor smithing for a couple of years. That was for a starter set I was creating." Father explained.

Storm tried to hand it back but Father shook his head and said, "You hang onto it."

"Are you sure?" Storm asked, eyes widening, he hefted it and said, "I'm not sure I can even wear it, it's pretty heavy".

"It'll be fine," Father chuckled, "you'll grow into it."

Storm nodded and slipped the mail shirt on over his cloths. Once it settled, he felt the weight distribute across his frame and it didn't feel so burdensome.

"You ready?" Father asked, he glanced around and said "We should hurry, I doubt there is much time left."

"Yeah, I'm ready." Storm said excitedly, although, he wasn't sure what Father was talking about.

"Here, accept this." Father said, after a moment of consideration.

A prompt appeared in Storm's vision.

[Group invitation
        From: Father
        Accept
        Decline]

Storm accepted the invitation and a small list with their names appeared in his UI.

Father opened the door to his forge and stepped out into a large, strange city. Storm followed behind, his eyes wide.

FOUR

Reunited

Ding!

A cloud of multi-colored stars swirled around Sunshine then slowly faded.

"Yeah, Level 5!", she exclaimed. Sunshine looked back at her mom, "What do you think, should we try for level 6 or head back?"

"Let's head back," Nightshade said as she eyed the sky, "we still need to set up camp before it gets dark." She held up a couple of rabbits and continued, "And I want to get these processed in time for dinner."

Sunshine nodded and picked up their latest kill, a large squirrel that seemed more devil than rodent. It had charged her and latched onto her leg when she got too close. She cautiously picked it up and added it to the others hanging on her belt. The pair turned and made their way back the way they had just traveled.

"Where do you think he is?" Sunshine asked, not for the first time.

"I don't know," Nightshade replied, "I hope he didn't choose a random location. When we are closer to town we can log out and check again." She followed behind Sunshine with her bow at the ready, scanning the forest as they walked.

When Luke didn't show up, Nightshade and Sunshine decided to explore the forest without him. They logged out several times to check on him, but each time he was still in his pod and they couldn't do anything but wait.

As the pair traveled that day, they searched for a capable long-term location for their encampment. Before logging in, they all agreed to a basic plan that would honor their late father and husband. First and foremost, they would have fun and enjoy their time in-game. They agreed that the best way to do this would be to create a homebase away from the other players where they could do a little leveling, go on quests and maybe complete a dungeon dive or two. They planned on spending most of their time fishing, hunting and foraging for food.

After a few hours of hunting, they ended up traveling deeper than expected into the woods. Several times they had to sneak away from encounters that were above their level. At the very deepest point in their trek, they discovered a raging river. They followed it for over a mile but never found a way to cross safely. They stopped to snack on a blackberry thicket and spotted a large clearing across the river.

The clearing was surrounded in thick forest and large enough to host a small town. It sloped gently up, away from the river and deeper in the forest, towering above the clearing, was a massive rock spire.

The clearing was the perfect place to host their homebase. It had access to water and plenty of fishing and hunting. It was close enough to town to get supplies but far enough away to deter casual gamers. They could easily explore around the area to fulfill their gaming desires such as leveling and dungeon diving.

When they got closer to town, Sunshine commented, "We haven't even seen any other players out here. We really ended up in the boonies."

"That's what we wanted right?" Nightshade asked, "If we change our minds; we can follow the road west to a larger city."

"I wasn't complaining." Sunshine snickered, "I like the fresh air and I'd rather not be around a bunch of annoying gamers while we are playing casually."

A tearing noise echoed through the forest. Sunshine and Nightshade both jumped at the sound. They brought up their bows swiveling around looking for the source. A massive emerald portal opened a dozen feet behind them. Two bright red robed figures stepped through, followed by none other than their long-lost group member.

Nightshade inspected him.

[Character
        Name: Storm
        Level: 3
        Health: 140/140]

Then she inspected each of the robed figures.

[Character
        Name: Admin1432
        Level: 705

Health: ***/***]

[Character
    Name: Admin1563
    Level: 306
    Health: ***/***]

"Storm, what trouble have you gotten yourself into now?" Nightshade greeted her son with a heavy sigh as she put her bow down.

"Thanks for the ride fellas." Storm said cheerfully as he stepped past the two figures and waved to his mom and sister.

"No problem" Admin1432 said in a deep voice "and we apologize for the hassle. We will submit the bug report right away. Once it is determined unique and approved, the bounty will show up in your in-game bank account."

"Do you know how much will it be?" Storm asked curiously.

"It depends on the severity of the bug." Admin1432 responded, "The devs will make that determination at the time of approval. Good bugs can go for hundreds if not thousands of gold coins. If it is minor, you will only get a few silver coins."

Storm nodded in response and watched the robed pair closely, waiting for them to leave.

Admin1563 started casting a spell and Storm paid close attention. The same emerald portal opened and as they stepped into it, Storm waved a final goodbye and they disappeared.

Soon after they were gone Storm heard several chimes and several notifications appeared but he ignored them as he began mimicking the hand movements he had just memorized, casting his own spell. When the pair had retrieved him from Valhalla, he wasn't prepared for their spell, but this time he was. Because he studied sign language when he was younger, he found the hand movements of the spell easy to remember and replicate. At the end of the spell, he whispered "home", just as he heard the other mage do.

A deathly chill passed over his body and he fell to his hands and knees, breathing hard. He felt like he was suffocating and worked to draw in a single breath. An empty mana meter flashed in his UI and he heard a warning sound. After a few moments of rest, he regained some mana points and the pain subsided to where he could easily breathe once again.

Storm rested on the ground to recover more of his mana and made a mental note to be more careful in the future. While he was in Valhalla, he was able to copy a few skills but didn't have the opportunity to learn any spells. Father assured him his special ability would work on them too.

Finally feeling better, he glanced at the notifications.

[New skill obtained: Air Magic]

[New spell obtained
        Superior Town Portal (Ultra Rare):
                Create a portal to the nearest positive aligned or
                neutral aligned town, alternatively you can select the
                name of a positive aligned or neutral aligned town or
                'home' for your bind spot.]

"I guess it worked" he shakily announced as he stood up, swiping away the notifications.

His mom and sister ran over and hugged him, being careful not to topple him over.

"What happened to you?" Sunshine spoke first.

"I'll tell you later." Storm whispered.

"Do you know where it goes?" Nightshade asked, gesturing at the green hued portal, "We were heading back to town and if this goes there, it would save us quite a hike."

"I'm not sure," Storm said, "It should be my bind spot but I don't know where that is, the admins said they changed it." He frowned and added, "The quiet one suggested they should just kill me and let me respawn. Fortunately, I was able to talk them into bringing me to you instead."

"Let's find out." Sunshine said shrugging, then fearlessly stepped through the portal with Nightshade following. Storm looked around in amazement at the beautiful forest then stepped into the portal.

Storm's feet landed on hard cobblestones and he heard gentle gurgling noises from a fountain nearby.

"This is a nice place, what's it called?" Storm asked as he looked around in approval.

The village Storm appeared in was torn directly out of medieval England. It held a dozen single-story thatch-roofed buildings, several with wooden signs indicating they were businesses. The buildings surrounded a town square with a simple fountain in the center.

A single cobblestone road lead into the small town from the west and to the north and south dirt paths exited the town, but the east was blocked by thick forest.

"Last Hope", his mom and sister said at the same time. They looked at each other and laughed. After a long stressful day of hunting and worrying about Storm, they were happy to make it back to civilization and relax a bit before logging off.

"Let's head south of town to make camp." Nightshade suggested, "It's mostly open fields and away from the forest."

The three, finally reunited, walked in happy silence down the dirt path leading out of town. After about ten minutes of walking, they veered off the trail and found a small grassy hill to setup camp. They were far enough away from the road and town to not be bothered by players passing by but they were close enough to easily restock their supplies.

Nightshade walked back to town to sell their loot and buy supplies while Storm and Sunshine setup camp. They built a small fire in the center of the hill and lined it with rocks. Then they setup the low-profile tents from the starter gear which popped open automatically. Before she left Nightshade asked them to build a small smoker to dry some of the meat for travel.

"Why are we building this?" Storm asked as the two worked on the smoker, "Do our avatars need to eat?"

"I asked mom the same thing." Sunshine said chuckling, "She explained that our avatars don't require food, but we can get bonuses if we eat."

"Really? Like what?" Storm asked surprised.

"Mom said that that it depends on what you eat," Sunshine explained, "there are some advanced recipes that can give combat or magical bonuses but any basic food will improve your regeneration rates."

"That would be nice, my mana hasn't recovered from the portal spell yet." Storm said after glancing at the mana bar in his UI.

"Exactly," she said, "your normal regeneration is really slow. Mom explained the game has several ways to speed it up and eating is one of them." Storm looked at her questioningly and she continued, "Resting, like sitting or meditation works and sleeping works even better but those are difficult to do in combat. The bonuses we get from eating will allow our avatars to regenerate while moving or in combat."

"How does she know this stuff?" Storm asked.

"I asked her that too." Sunshine said barking a laugh, "She's said she's been reading the in-game wiki, which you can access from your character menu. I briefly looked at it and it covers the basics but nothing too advanced. "

"I'll have to spend some time looking at it," he replied, "but later, I'm drained."

"Storm," Sunshine said with a little concern in her voice, "where were you today? What happened?"

"It's a long story, but I saw dad." he whispered.

"What?!?" she exclaimed.

"His avatar's name is Father" he explained, smiling at her knowingly, "and I chose him as my starting location. When the admins came to get me, they explained it was a bug and he shouldn't have been an option." Storm paused with a far-off look and continued quietly, "Either way, I'm glad I got to spend a day with him."

"I heard that part about the bug." Sunshine said, then paused, "When I logged in, I saw the option too but I didn't realize what it meant." a little more hesitantly she asked, "How was he, did it seem like him?"

"Exactly like him." Storm said, with a huge smile.

By the time Nightshade returned, Storm and Sunshine were sitting around the fire boiling a pot of water.

"I was able to sell most of it to the furrier." Nightshade announced as she walked up, "I kept a few of the hares to make jerky."

"How'd we do?" Sunshine asked.

"We got a few gold pieces and some silver, enough for supplies." Nightshade explained, "We'll have to go tomorrow morning though, the store NPC was gone."

Storm and Sunshine relaxed by the fire, chatting about the game while their mother worked on hanging the meat in the smoker. They offered to help but she was adamant that they keep relaxing.

"Ok kiddos," their mom announced when she was done, "let's log off and get some dinner. I'm sure it's been delivered by now."

The three logged off and sat around the kitchen table scarfing down their late-night dinner. After their first day in-game they were all famished. Even though their physical bodies were laying down the entire time, they had been bombarded with micro resistances from the haptic gear they wore.

"My legs hurt. It feels like I've been walking all day." Cleo complained as she rubbed her legs.

"I'm a little sore too." Luke added.

"Well, you weren't hiking through the forest like we were." Cleo retorted.

"You'll get used to it." their mom chuckled, "We were only online for a few hours."

The three made plans for the following day as they ate and when they were done, his mom looked at him intently.

"Ok, spill it. Where were you today?" she asked, "We were worried."

Luke looked to his sister and she shrugged. He looked at his mom and said simply, "I saw dad."

"How?" she asked, her eyes widening in surprise.

Luke explained the options he was presented when he logged in and how he had chosen Father instead of her. He told them about appearing in the forge and walking around the strange city of Valhalla, but he saw concern clearly on his mother's face so he glossed over many of the details.

"Then the admins came and collected me," he said finally, "and you know the rest."

"What was the city like? Were there other players there?" Cleo asked.

"Father said that Valhalla was only for Fallen avatars." Luke explained as he shook his head.

"What are Fallen avatars?" Cleo asked curiously.

"When I" their mother started, but paused to take a deep breath before she continued with a distant look in her eyes, "When I informed the company that your father had passed away, they explained they would move his avatar to a special place so we wouldn't see him, so his presence in the game wouldn't disturb us. I asked them to remove it completely but they said they couldn't, and this was the best they could do." she laughed sardonically and said, "Then they told me on holidays I could buy a special scroll to summon him."

"Seriously?!? They are monetizing the dead players?" Cleo said angrily with a disgusted look on her face.

"Apparently, it's quite popular." their mother said with a small smile, then hesitantly added, "I… I see the appeal."

"Could we get a scroll to summon him?" Luke asked hesitantly.

"No," their mother explained, "They only sell the scrolls for holiday events. The scroll will only work for those days, so even if we had one it wouldn't work."

Noticing his mother's discomfort with the topic, Luke decided to change the subject, "What about you two, what did you do all day?"

"Since you didn't show up," Cleo replied, elbowing him in the ribs, "We decided to scout the area. We spent a little time in town, but then headed off into the forest to see if we could find a more permanent campground. The furrier in town gave us a repeatable quest for furs, so we collected a few on the way." she glanced at her mom, then continued, "The game was so lifelike and most of the forest creatures were skittish and would run away."

"The foxes and badgers were no joke though." their mom added, joining in the conversation "The higher-level mobs wouldn't run but aggroed as soon as we got too close. One squirrel was even level 10."

"The one that bit me?" Cleo asked as she unconsciously rubbed her thigh. Her mom nodded in confirmation and Cleo rolled her eyes, "Of course it was, that thing was vicious. I lost a third of my health before we finally killed it."

"How was the xp?" Luke asked.

"It was ok, we didn't find any spots to grind though." Cleo said.

"What level did you get to?" he asked curiously, wishing he had inspected them before they logged out.

"We both hit level 5 before we turned back to town." Cleo answered.

"Well, I'm off to bed." their mom announced, "I'll see you two in the morning for breakfast. Then we can start our day in-game." She smiled fondly at both of them and warned, "Don't stay up too late, tomorrow is going to be a busy day."

"Do we really need to find a better place to camp?" Luke asked after their mother left the room. "Why can't we just stay close to town?"

"We found a clearing further in the forest that would provide us more privacy from other players, not to mention, it has a ton of resources." Cleo explained, "From there we could hunt larger mobs and even go on dungeon dives. But it is still close enough to town that we can sell our loot and resupply if we need to."

"That makes sense but why do we need to build a permanent shelter?" he asked.

"I'm not sure but mom thought it was important." Cleo explained, "She said something about having a stable place for our avatars."

"Is that in case they get attacked at night?" Luke asked, "What would happen, would we log in and be dead or would we be at our bind spots?"

"No," Cleo laughed, "our avatars should defend themselves as best as we could. We can also leave instructions for them, for example, before I logged out, I told mine to establish a rotating night watch with the others."

"Really?" Luke asked, surprised.

"Yeah," she replied, "Mom even showed me how to set up an alert."

"How does that work?" Luke asked.

"Our rooms are setup with speakers and the alert can be sent there, but we can send it to our phone or another device too." Cleo explained.

They sat there staring at their empty plates for a few moments, both worn out from their adventures.

"Luke?" Cleo asked.

"Yeah, what's up?", he replied tiredly.

"Before I logged out," she said pensively, "I sent you a group invite." Luke looked up and stared at her. Cleo hesitated but continued quietly, "It said you were already in a group."

"Yeah." he responded after taking a deep breath, "I was just thinking about that. I'm still in the group with Father."

"Why?" she asked as her face darkened. "What are you planning? This doesn't seem healthy and I'm worried about what it is going to do to mom."

"I don't know Cleo," he replied defensively, "it was nice to see him. I know it's not him but it looks and sounds just like him. This trip was supposed to be about celebrating him. Wouldn't it be nice to spend time with him again?"

Cleo looked down, her eyes tearing up, but she blinked them away and said firmly, "Let me think about it. I miss him too, but we need to think of mom. You remember how hard it was on her when he died."

"Ok" he said, nodding. "let's sleep on it and talk about it tomorrow." Luke set his dishes in the sink and headed for his bedroom. Before he left, he called out "Good night sis."

"Goodnight." she responded quietly, deep in thought.

FIVE

New home

I'm heading into town to get some supplies for our trip today." Nightshade announced as she walked up to Storm and Sunshine, who were working on breaking down their camp. The previous night they made plans to travel deeper into the forest and they decided they needed more supplies for it.

"Let me make your trip faster." Storm said grinning. Then he started casting his only spell, Superior Town Portal. As the emerald portal appeared he braced himself for the pain he experienced previously but when he glanced at his mana level, he noted it wasn't as diminished as last time. He recalled the spell cost was based on the distance to the target and made a mental note to be cautious about that in the future.

"Thanks," Nightshade said as she smiled at him. "I'll be quick" she said, then stepped through the portal, and was gone.

"Storm," Sunshine said quietly, after the portal closed. "I thought about our conversation last night and I want to see him."

"Really?" Storm asked excitedly.

"You brought up a good point that this trip is about celebrating him." she explained, "I could care less about the game, I'm really here for him, to remember him. And, I can't think of a better way than to actually see him," she paused then added, "or at least his avatar."

"I wish I could add you to our group, but I'm not the leader, he is." Storm said, sitting down on a rock next to the fire.

"Storm," Sunshine chided and she rolled her eyes, "you need to read the help section on groups." He was about to respond but she interrupted him and said, "No, I'm not going to tell you. Just focus and think, 'help group'."

He snorted, but closed his eyes and did as she suggested. When he opened his eyes, he followed the instructions and sent her a group invitation. In no time, her name appeared on the bottom of the small list in his UI.

"Is it really him?" she asked quietly after a few moments.

"Yeah, it's him." Storm replied.

"He must be too far away," she said, "I can't get any information on his avatar."

Storm was about to ask what she meant, but decided to try the help section instead. After a few moments of reading, he found that he could focus on a group member and view their full character sheet by thinking 'inspect'. This was slightly different than ungrouped avatars which would only display a small summary. He also found there was a limitation on the distance, and when he tried with Father, he got an out-of-range error but for his sister a character sheet came into view.

[Character sheet
        Name: Sunshine
        Race: Human
        Level: 5
        Health: 190/190
        Stamina: 170/170
        Mana: 260/260
        Stats:
                Strength: 16
                Dexterity: 17
                Constitution: 19
                Intelligence: 18
                Wisdom: 26
                Charisma: 17
        Skills:
                Archery: Level 2
                        You know the proper way to hold a bow, aim and shoot at a target. High accuracy for 25 yards.
                        +2% damage with bows
                Hand to hand combat: Level 3
                        You know how to put your weight behind a punch. You can recognize small muscle movements indicating attack providing a near prescience dodge ability
                        +3% damage to unarmed combat
                Leadership: Level 3
                        Members of your party gain from your experience.
                        +3% to party member's experience
        Spells: None.

Special Abilities:

Born Leader: Level 3

You have a natural gift at organizational leadership. When you lead, everybody benefits. You radiate excellence in combat and those around you benefit from your presence.

Grants Leadership skill, equal to Born Leader level

Benefits to your group when you are the leader:

+15% to movement

+15% to defense

+15% to ranged attack

+15% to melee attack

-15% enemy effects

-15% length of enemy effects

Benefits to those in your radius, including group members:

Radius: 1 meter

+1% to movement

+1% to defense

+1% to ranged attack

+1% to melee attack]

"Your special ability is amazing," Storm said after he dismissed his sister's character sheet, but he paused when he noticed her eyes were moving back and forth, as if she were reading something too. He realized it was his character sheet and he waiting for her to refocus before continuing. Mischievously he said, "I mean, I should have guessed you would have some sort of bonus for being in charge." Then, more seriously he asked, "Where did you get Archery?"

"Mom and I trained in town before we left yesterday." she answered, beaming proudly at his compliment.

"And hand-to-hand combat?" he asked.

"I started with that one," she explained, "Several years ago I took a self-defense class and I guess that was good enough to qualify as a starting skill."

"I didn't know you could start with skills." Storm said with a frown. "I only started with my special ability."

"I think it's random," Sunshine explained, "and your ability was probably too OP to give you anything else. Which begs the question, where did your skills come from?"

Storm pulled up his character sheet.

[Character sheet
        Name: Storm
        Race: Human
        Level: 3
        Health: 140/140
        Stamina: 120/120
        Mana: 120/120
        Stats:
                Strength: 15
                Dexterity: 12
                Constitution: 14
                Intelligence: 20
                Wisdom: 12
                Charisma: 10
        Skills:
                Short Swords: Level 1
                        You are proficient at holding a short sword, it is unlikely you will stab yourself. You are able to strike and block with a short sword accurately.
                        +1% to damage with short swords
                Small Shields: Level 1
                        You are proficient at holding small shields. You are able to block or deflect a strike without breaking your arm.
                        +1% defense with small shields
                Bartering: Level 1
                        You can make small negotiations turn in your favor.
                        +1% to success while bartering
                Puzzle breaking: Level 1
                        You are able to comprehend and solve complex puzzles.
                        +1% to solve puzzles
                Air Magic: Level 1
                        You can cast air magic spells.

+1% to air magic resistance.

Spells:

Air Magic

Superior Town Portal (Ultra Rare):

Create a portal to the nearest positive aligned or neutral aligned town, alternatively you can select the name of a positive aligned or neutral aligned town or '*home*' for your bind spot.

Cost: 50 mana + 10 mana for every kilometer

Cast time: 30 seconds

Special Abilities:

Quick learning: Level 2

You are able to learn skills and spells by watching them performed. While others' need to be specifically taught you can glean the finer details through observation and replication to gain the skill or spell.]

"I picked them up while Father showed me around Valhalla." he explained, "Sword and Shield were from a couple of Fallen that were sparring in the courtyard. Bartering came from one of the shopkeepers, and Puzzle Breaking actually came from Father himself."

Sunshine raised an eyebrow questioningly and Storm chuckled.

"He showed me a puzzle box he made. He wanted to show me how it works." Storm said, answering her unasked question.

"He made it?" Sunshine asked.

"Apparently he's quite a good blacksmith." Storm explained proudly, he touched his mail shirt and continued "He made this too."

"Oh, I want one." she said after leaning forward and inspecting it.

"What's mom's special ability?" Storm asked after a thought occurred to him.

"You'll have to find out on your own." Sunshine smirked. Then she got up and finished packing up their gear.

"You two ready to head out?" Nightshade asked a short time later, walking into camp.

"Did you get the supplies?" Sunshine asked.

"Yeah, I'll pass some stuff out as we walk." Nightshade promised, then after a moment she looked confused and asked, "Are you two grouped?"

Storm blushed as Sunshine looked to him, he glanced at his group UI and saw Father had passed him leadership. He quickly looked up how to pass the leadership in the wiki and gave it to Sunshine since they would get a better bonus.

Sunshine snorted, then Storm saw Nightshade's name appear in the group list.

"You grouped with him?" Nightshade asked quietly, her eyes widening in surprise.

"Yeah," Storm replied, clearing his throat. "I didn't think much of it at the time. I just couldn't bring myself to drop out of the group." He tried to explain, "We are here to celebrate him and I wasn't ready to let go."

Nightshade stood there for a few moments, looking back and forth between the two, tears in her eyes.

"Ok," she said, "let's make it to our basecamp, then we will talk more." She hefted her pack stuffed with supplies and slipped it over her shoulder, then started walking towards the forest, Storm and Sunshine fell in behind her.

With Sunshine leading the party, they made great time back to the river. They still had to figure out how to cross but their mom assured them a solution would present itself. As they traveled, the three took stock of their supplies, with Nightshade updating them on what she had gotten in town.

"Each of us started with a standard backpack, a small one-person tent, a tinder box, and a knife." Nightshade said, she looked to Storm and informed him, "Sunshine and I both picked up a bow and a dozen arrows yesterday before our excursion." she tapped Storm's chest and said, "And it looks like you acquired a chainmail shirt."

"Father made it, he gave it to me." Storm said, hesitantly.

"Do either of you have anything else that could be useful?" Nightshade asked.

Storm and Sunshine both shook their heads.

"That's ok," Nightshade said, "while in town I was able to pick up several things that will help us." She handed each of them a small bag that looked like an old coin purse and said, "I got one for each us."

Storm held it appreciatingly and noted it was small but excellent craftsmanship, if not a bit worn. The bag had four circles on it, each dyed a different color, one was copper, one was silver, one was gold, and the last one was a silver-grey, he supposed it represented platinum. He inspected it and his eyes widened in surprise.

[Item

> Name: Bag of holding
> Description: This bag is enchanted with a small dimensional space.
> Dimensional space: 1x4
> Space: two out of four spaces filled
> Contents: copper coins x50, silver coins x2
> Quality: 89%
> Crafted by: Brews Lee]

"Wow, this is amazing." Storm exclaimed, "How much were they?"

"Don't worry about it," Nightshade hedged, "they were worth it. These will allow our coins to stack, otherwise the money is unmanageable. I also put some in there for you to spend the next time you're in town." she continued, "I also picked up an axe, a pot for cooking, a rope, some fishing equipment and a few skill books."

"Skill books?" Storm asked.

"Construction, Axe wielding, Animal tracking, Fishing, Stealth, Skinning and tanning hides." Nightshade said.

"That's more than a few." Storm said, surprised.

"I may have gotten carried away with myself." his mom said, a little embarrassed. She tried to explain, "But they all seemed useful to us. And we can take turns reading them."

"Do we need to read the whole book to gain the skill?" Sunshine asked, scrunching up her face in dissatisfaction.

"Unfortunately, yes," Nightshade said nodding, "not only that though, you need to actually try to learn it, reading is not enough."

Sunshine made a disgusted sound.

"I know it kind of sucks," Nightshade said laughing, "but it's cheaper than a trainer and we should have plenty of time."

Now that they were grouped, Storm looked at his mom and thought, 'Inspect'.

[Character sheet
        Name: Nightshade
        Race: Human
        Level: 5
        Health: 190/190
        Stamina: 170/170
        Mana: 220/220
        Stats:
                Strength: 15
                Dexterity: 17
                Constitution: 19
                Intelligence: 21
                Wisdom: 22
                Charisma: 19
        Skills:
                Brewing: Level 1
                        You are able to make delicious teas that provide minor bonuses
                        +1% effectiveness of teas
                Herb lore: Level 1
                        You are able to identify plants and their medicinal uses
                        +1% medicinal effects
                Cooking: Level 1
                        You are able to prepare and cook meals that provide minor bonuses
                        +1% effectiveness of food-based bonuses
                Earth Magic: Level 1
                        You can cast earth magic spells.
                        +1% to earth magic resistance.
                Archery: Level 1
                        You know the proper way to hold a bow, aim and shoot at a target. High accuracy for 50 yards.
                        +1% damage with bows
                Tracking: Level 1
                        You are able to track animals through various terrains.
                        +1% to identify animal based on tracks
                Stealth: Level 1

You are able to hide in the shadows. While hidden, enemies will not be aware of your presence

+1% sneak

Fishing: Level 1

You understand the basics of catching fish.

+1% to catch a large fish

Sailing: Level 1

You are able to sail basic vessels.

+1% movement speed with wind-based water vessels

Daggers: Level 1

You know the proper way to wield daggers.

+1% damage with daggers

Leadership: Level 1

Members of your party gain from your experience

+1% to party member's experience

Spells:

Earth Magic

Plant Grab (Special):

Roots reach up and grab target's foot.

Requirements: level 2 Plant talk

Single target.

Cost: 5 mana

Cast time: Instant

Cooldown: 60 seconds

Plant Snare (Special):

Roots and suckers reach up from underneath multiple targets to snare feet and legs.

Requirements: Level 4 Plant talk

Target: single target

Area of affect: 10'

Cost: 30 mana

Cast time: Instant

Cooldown: 60 seconds

Rock skin:

Increases armor level by 50

Target: self

Cost: 100 mana

Cast time: Instant

Cooldown: 60 seconds

Focused attack:

    Next attack has +50 points of kinetic force

    Target: self

    Cost: 20 mana

    Cast time: 2 seconds

Dig:

    Digs a hole in the ground

    Target: ground

    Area of affect: 2' x 2'

    Cost: 20 mana

    Cast time: 2 seconds

Special Abilities:

Plant talk: Level 5

    You are able to converse with plants. You can gain information on the local habitat, such as seasonal information and even common predators, prey, pollinators and pests. You are able to divine the past four hours of activity in the direct vicinity of the plant, some same-type plants can extend this range.

    Unlocks Plant Grab at level 2.

    Unlocks Plant Snare at level 4]

"Mom, you're a badass." Storm said, impressed by her character. "How do you have so many starting skills?"

"I guess I got lucky." she responded simply, then she laughed and added, "Maybe it's because I'm so old." She was silent for a few moments then said, "Your special ability is kind of impressive too. Have you thought about how you are going to utilize it?"

"Well, I'm going to start off by copying everything from you and Sunshine." Storm said smirking.

"Oh, I'm sure you will." Nightshade laughed.

"Where did you get the jewelry? Are they magical?" Storm asked, noticing for the first time that his mom had a ring on every finger and even a necklace.

"Oh, these are nothing." she said flushing, after looking at them. "Just some junk pieces I picked up from the merchant that I thought looked nice. Don't worry, you and Sunshine get first pick of the loot, I'm just here for the company."

After that, the group fell into silence while they traversed the forest, and sooner than Storm thought, they arrived at their destination. Across a fast-flowing river was a large clearing that could only be what his mom and sister had described last night. Nightshade and Sunshine were gorging themselves on a massive blackberry thicket and Storm decided to join them.

"Why do these berries taste so good?" he asked after eating a few berries.

"I don't know but I'm not complaining." Sunshine mumbled with a mouth full of berries.

After they had their fill, they stood on the bank of the river looking across to the other side.

"That's a long way across. Do you think it's swimmable?" Storm asked.

"No, I think the current would sweep us away." Nightshade said shaking her head.

"Then how are we going to cross?" he asked.

"We thought we would follow the river until we found an easier spot." Sunshine explained.

The three followed the river several miles downstream until their mom stopped and said, "This looks like the narrowest spot so far, what do you two think?"

"That's still pretty far." Sunshine said.

"A few of these trees look large enough to bridge the river." Storm said, eyeballing a nearby tree "We might be able to cut one down."

Nightshade put her hand on the tree and closed her eyes. After a moment she got a horrified look on her face and said quietly, "It wouldn't like it." then she dug into per pack and pulled out the rope, "Let's try to find another way first."

About halfway across the river Storm thought back on the conversation and couldn't quite remember agreeing to go first. He stepped slowly, one foot after another in the cold waist-high water. In one hand he held a makeshift staff and in the other he held tightly to the rope, which was tied around his waist and slung over his shoulder.

Storm looked down through the crystal-clear water and could easily see the multicolored river rocks on the bottom. As he passed the halfway point, he came across a ten-foot-wide pit that sent the hairs on his arms rising. He didn't understand his fear but knew it was coming from the deep, dark hole in riverbed. He skirted around the pit and angled his approach to the opposite side of the river.

As he passed the hole, Storm glanced back to check his progress and he stepped on something slimy and slipped. He fell back into the water and felt the current start pulling him away. Something grabbed onto his foot and fearing the worst he kicked as hard as he could with the other but couldn't make contact with what held him. The cold water rushed over his head as his mail shirt dragged him to the bottom of the river. With his breath running out, adrenaline surged through his body, he pushed himself up out of the current.

After regaining his feet, he looked down at what had ahold of him and saw a small plant wrapped around his ankle. He glanced to the shore and saw Nightshade watching him carefully and realized his mom had saved him. She flicked her wrist and the plant let go and he was able to move once again. He nodded to her in thanks, then moving steadily forward, making it to the other side. Once there, he tied the rope around a tree so his mom and sister could use it to cross the river, avoiding the pit.

Finally, on the other side, the three made their way to the clearing but before they left Storm tied the rope to a different tree, one that caused the rope to hang directly over the pit. When he rejoined them, Sunshine looked at him curiously.

"You never know." he said shrugging.

They followed the river back to the clearing and took turns logging out to eat lunch. They all could have logged out together and let their avatar's AI navigate to the clearing but they wanted to ensure there were no surprises along the way.

"Hang on a second." Nightshade whispered, holding them back when they made it to the clearing.

"Did you see something?" Sunshine asked quietly.

Nightshade nodded and pointed to the other side of the clearing where a well-worn path led down to the river.

While they waited, Storm spent the time evaluating their potential new home. The clearing sloped up gently from the river into the forest several thousand feet back. The clearing appeared incredibly peaceful and had a ton of resources. There was of course, the river which would provide fresh water and fish. The surrounding forest would provide wood and animals they could hunt. There were dozens of different plants and flowers spread throughout, which Storm thought could be used to make different potions. Deeper in the forest, towering over the clearing, was a rock spire jutting into the sky.

Movement from across the clearing caught his eye and he watched as a large black panther followed the trail down to the river. The panther stalked up to the water's edge and once there it froze for a few moments then almost faster than Storm could follow, it plunged it's claw down into the river. The panther pulled it's claw back with a fish impaled on it. Slowly the panther rose onto its hind legs and walked back up the trail.

"Should we kill it?" Storm asked leaning forward.

"No." they both responded harshly, horrified at his suggestion.

Storm glanced at his mom and sister and realized he was missing something. He looked back to the large cat and saw it hesitate halfway up the trail. It paused sniffing the air and slowly turned, looking in their direction. Storm felt a chill pass through his body and watched as his mom and sister took a step into the clearing. Not sure what they were doing but he quickly followed. Nightshade lifted her hand in greeting and the panther turned and continued on its trek towards the rock tower.

"What was wrong with attacking it? Was it too high level?" Storm asked, confused.

"Patience little one," Nightshade responded with a smile, "we will find you some mobs." She had repeatedly turned him down on the way to the clearing since they needed to ensure they had the time to find a way to cross the river.

"Seriously, what was wrong with attacking it?" he asked, exasperated.

"It was an NPC." Sunshine said, laughing.

"And they often have quests." Nightshade added.

"Ok, I have to ask. How did you know it was an NPC?" Storm asked, sighing

They both looked at him and shook their heads.

"What is it this time?" Storm asked, "I've been reading the wiki, but it didn't say anything about this."

"Storm, we are playing on the *Feline* server, you know, cats." Sunshine chided.

Storm stared at her in confusion.

"Each server has a different type of NPC. This one has cats." Nightshade explained. She got a far off look in her eyes and continued more solemnly, "Years ago your father chose this one. He originally wanted to play on the Dragon server, but ultimately chose this one, for me."

"Why did we show ourselves?" Storm asked.

"It already knew we were here." Nightshade explained, "By showing ourselves and acknowledging its presence, I was hoping it would be ok with sharing the clearing."

The three found a level spot halfway up the slope and setup their tents near the forest on their side of the clearing. Storm collected a few rocks and created a pit for their fire while Sunshine collected some wood. After they had a nice fire going Nightshade left to scout the area and check on the NPC.

"Will you show me how to shoot it?" Storm asked, gesturing to her bow.

Sunshine nodded and walked a few paces away with the bow and quiver. Storm watched as she notched an arrow and drew the string back. He studied how she sighted in her target and gently released the arrow. As it flew through the air at her target, he heard a chime and was rewarded with a notification.

[New skill obtained
        Archery: Level 1
                You know the proper way to hold, aim and shoot a bow.]

"Thanks!" Storm called out.

Sunshine looked at him, her eyes glazing over for a moment then she said, "No way! It took me an hour of practicing with the trainer before I got the skill."

He shrugged and walked over to his mom's pack to look at the skill books. Sunshine joined him and grabbed the Construction book before he could. He decided to start with the Axe skill book, it wasn't his first choice but, they had an axe and he might as well know how to use it. They both sat down next to the fire and started reading. Storm skimmed through his book and it seemed fairly straight forward. After reading for a bit, he heard a familiar chime.

[New skill obtained
        Axe wielding: Level 1

You know the proper way to hold an axe, swing and chop a
target.]

Curious, he picked up the axe and inspected it.

[Item
Name: Steel Axe
Quality: Average]

Storm swung the axe around practicing the techniques he just read about.
Feeling comfortable with it he set it down and walked over to get another book
and his sister made a disgusted sound.

"What now?" he asked, chuckling.

"Yesterday the trainer told us that skill books could take days to learn a skill."
she said, sighing with frustration. Then she continued with a bit of admiration,
"Your ability is amazing, do you think you could teach me something?"

"What are you interested in?" Storm asked.

"Well, obviously magic but I'm not really sure how it works." she said smiling.

"Sure, I only have one spell but we could try." he said.

Storm walked her through the hand movements but after a few minutes of
trying Sunshine got frustrated.

"I don't know how anybody uses magic." she said. "I can't seem to remember
the different positions."

"It's a hard spell," he said, consoling her, "maybe once I learn an easier one, we
can try again."

"I suppose," she said, "I guess I'll keep working on the skill books." Then she
sat down by the fire and picked up the construction book to continue reading.

Storm grabbed the rest of the skill books and skimmed through the first one. As
soon as he heard the, now familiar, chime he moved on to the next book.

[New skill obtained
Stealth: Level 1
You know to how to be sneaky and difficult to observe in
various terrains.]

[New skill obtained
    Animal tracking: Level 1
        You are able to identify and follow common animal prints.]

[New skill obtained
    Skinning and tanning hides: Level 1
        You know the proper skin and tan animal hides.]

[New skill obtained
    Fishing: Level 1
        You know to how to catch fish using various methods.]

Once Storm was done with the skill books, he borrowed the construction book from Sunshine while she was on a break.

[New skill obtained
    Construction: Level 1
        You know the basics of constructing small structures.
        Blueprints:
            Small dwelling
            Small tower
            Small wall]

"Did you really learn all of those skills?" Sunshine asked, gawking.

Storm nodded and pulled up his character sheet, minimizing the skill descriptions.

[Character sheet
    Name: Storm
    Race: Human
    Level: 3
    Health: 140/140
    Stamina: 120/120
    Mana: 120/120
    Stats:
        Strength: 17
        Dexterity: 13
        Constitution: 12
        Intelligence: 21
        Wisdom: 9
        Charisma: 11

Skills:

Short Swords: Level 1
Small Shields: Level 1
Bartering: Level 1
Puzzle breaking: Level 1
Air Magic: Level 1
Archery: Level 1
Axes: Level 1
Stealth: Level 1
Animal Tracking: Level 1
Skinning and tanning hides: Level 1
Fishing: Level 1
Construction: Level 1

Spells:
Air Magic

Superior Town Portal (Ultra Rare)
Special Abilities:
Quick learning: Level 3]

After reviewing his skills, he closed the prompt and noticed his mom had returned and was sitting by the fire eating some jerky.

"How'd it go?" he asked curiously.

"Great," she replied, "but we still have some differences to work out." She rubbed her shoulder but didn't elaborate.

"Do you think it's ok to stay here?" Sunshine asked.

"Yeah, he won't challenge us." she said confidently, "Once you two finish the construction book, start building a more permanent structure."

"I already did." Storm said smiling, "I guess that means I should get to work." He got up and grabbed the axe, then set off towards the forest to chop down some trees.

"Did he really finish the book?" Nightshade asked in surprise.

"He not only finished the book. He finished all of them." Sunshine explained.

"Storm!" Nightshade called out before he entered the forest, "Maybe I can finally teach you how to cook!"

SIX

Neighbor

L uke woke up to an alarm blaring in his ears. He quickly pulled on his clothes and retrieved his shoes, ready to exit the hotel. He hoped that somebody had pulled a fire alarm and it wasn't a real fire.

He heard a banging on his door.

"Luke, let's go!" his mom yelled.

He pulled the door open and saw his mom and sister dressed in their pod suits and thought groggily that it was weird they had them on.

"Luke, get changed and meet us in the game. Hurry!" she chided after looking him up and down, she then ran towards the pod room with his sister following.

He quickly changed into the pod suit and rushed out the door. By the time he made it to the pod room, his mom and sister were already logged in. He climbed into his pod and slid the top shut.

Storm's senses adjusted and he found himself standing next to the campfire with an axe in hand. Sunshine was on the other side of the fire brandishing a burning stick, keeping several wolves at bay. Nightshade was standing next to him, aiming her bow into the darkness. When she released an arrow, he heard a yelping sound in the distance.

"Get out there and finish it off." Nightshade commanded him. She notched another arrow and fired again.

His heart pumping and adrenaline rushing through his body he didn't waste another moment and rushed away. Unfortunately, as soon as he left the ring of light he was temporarily blinded by the darkness and had to pause to let his eyes to adjust. It wasn't enough because as he continued, he tripped over a soft furry mound and fell to the ground. He quickly scrambled away without even noticing the arrow sticking out of the dead wolf's neck, barely visible in the flickering firelight.

Storm stood up and followed the sounds to the wounded wolf more cautiously. It snapped and snarled as he approached and he held his axe high looking for a good opportunity to strike. The wolf lunged at him but it came up short and fell to the ground. Storm, not wasting his chance, brought down his axe with the same force he used earlier on the trees. When the axe struck, blood spewed forth and covered him, head to toe. The wolf slumped to the ground, with its head cleanly separated from its body. As he moved away, Storm noticed the wolf's hind legs were tangled in vines.

Storm quickly made his way to another wounded wolf and dispatched it just has he had the first, and once again, the legs were ensnared in vines. When he turned to search for another target, he was surprised by a large paw that struck him, midsection. Storm was thrown a dozen feet and landed hard on the ground. The wolf pounced on him but before it could bite down an arrow sprouted from its head.

Storm pushed the dead wolf off and slowly got to his feet and recovered his axe. He hobbled back to the fire.

"How many more are there?" he asked in a pained voice.

"I think only a couple." Sunshine said, peering into the darkness. She held her bow at the ready, having set down the burning stick.

"Are you ok?" Nightshade asked, stepping out of the darkness.

"Yeah, it hurt, but I'm fine." he replied, rubbing his stomach. He glanced at his health bar and cringed, realizing that one strike had taken almost half of his hit points.

"Good thing you had that chainmail." his mom said. Then she turned sharply and threw her hand out as a wolf came charging towards her.

The wolf suddenly faceplanted into the ground with a yelp. Storm stepped forward and buried his axe in the incapacitated wolf's head. Blood sprayed out and covered him again in its sticky warmth. After a few tugs of his slippery axe, he pulled it loose and wiped his hands, he was ready for the next attack. He glanced at Nightshade, then Sunshine and both were holding their bows at-the-ready, looking into the darkness.

"The last one ran back into the forest." Nightshade informed them. She ran her hand through the knee-high grass and updated them "There are no enemies near us."

Sunshine and Nightshade looked at Storm with concern on their faces. He looked down and was surprised at how much blood and gore covered him. He tried swiping it off but just spread it around more. He gagged, "It's not mine. The axe is a little messier than I expected."

"I don't think I can sleep after that, what do we do now?" Sunshine asked after breathing a sigh of relief.

"Put more wood on the fire and build us a couple of smokers, Storm and I will collect the bodies and start processing them." Nightshade said.

"Now?" he asked, unsure if he wanted to spend the rest of the night with the wolf corpses.

"You are the only one with the skinning skill and the hides will be worth a bit." Nightshade explained.

"Yeah, I suppose, if we are going to do it, it needs to be now." Storm agreed, sighing. He trudged off into the darkness and started dragging the bodies back to the camp.

During the battle they each had leveled several times, and while he was working, he reviewed his updates:

[Character sheet (updates)
     Name: Storm
     Level: 6
     Health: 200/200
     Stamina: 170/170
     Mana: 160/160
     Stats:
          Strength: 22
          Dexterity: 17
          Constitution: 20
          Intelligence: 24
          Wisdom: 16
          Charisma: 14
     Skills:
          Axes: Level 3]

The three worked the rest of the night and well into the morning processing the wolves. Storm worked on skinning while his mom processed the meat and Sunshine monitored the smokers and fed the fire. The sun was well over the horizon by the time they finished.

After cleaning up by the river, they surveyed their work. The hides were strung up and the meat was hanging in the smokers. The organs had been separated and piled on large bark platters.

"What are we going to do with these?" Storm asked, pointing at the platters.

"Some of it will be used for fishing, as bait." she answered, "The rest we should donate to Nathanael."

"Who?" Storm asked, confused.

"Oh, I forgot," Nightshade said, "our neighbor's name is Nathanael."

"The panther?" Sunshine asked.

Nightshade nodded, then walked over and picked up one of the platters and handed it to Storm.

"Take this and follow the trail up into the forest until you find Nathanael and give it to him." she instructed.

Storm took the platter and started walking towards the path on the other side of the clearing. He cradled it, examining the contents. On the makeshift plate was a mixture of hearts, livers and kidneys, all in a neat pile.

"Good luck." his mom called out ominously.

"This was going to be easy." he thought as he walked away, smiling.

The plate of organs started feeling heavier and heavier the longer he carried them. When he neared the other side of the glade, he followed the trail up, towards the monolith jutting out of the forest. When he made it to the forest's edge, his legs and arms were burning. His mom explained that the stats you gain when you level were based on your actions, so by using his muscles he should gain more strength when he leveled next. It's the only thing that kept him going.

Storm followed the path up the hill, into the forest and after a while it thinned into a small clearing. As soon as he stepped out of the woods an object flashed by and pain erupted in his leg. Storm grunted and his health meter flashed red as he crumbled to the ground. He dropped the bark platter causing the organs to spill onto the ground with many rolling away. Storm glanced to his leg and saw a crossbow bolt sticking out. He reached down to pull it out but as soon as he touched it, pain erupted from the bolt.

Huddling on the ground, Storm heard footsteps approach. He glanced up and inspected the panther NPC.

[NPC
>Name: Nathanael
>Race: Feline
>Level: 30
>Health: ***/***]

Faster than Storm could respond, Nataniel reached down and yanked the bolt out of his leg. Storm screamed in pain and pressed his hand over the wound to slow the bleeding.

"Why did you come?" Nathanael hissed, "I told the other one to stay away."

"It was for you." Storm grunted, gesturing to his spilled cargo.

Nathanael grunted and started forming gestures with his hands. Surprised, Storm followed along and committed them to memory. As the cat made the gestures, golden light surrounded his paws and grew in intensity. Nathanael reached down and touched Storm's wounded leg, directing the healing magic.

A warmth spread down Storm's leg and his wound became unbearably hot, then unbearably cold, alternating from one extreme to the other. He felt a strange tingling as his damaged muscles knitted themselves back together. Then, he heard the expected chime. He quickly reviewed and dismissed the notifications.

[New skill obtained
>Life magic: You are able to cast life-based spells]

[New spell obtained
>Healing touch (Life Magic):
>>Heals minor wounds
>>Single target: Touch
>>Cost: 5 mana
>>Cast time: 2 seconds]

After his leg was healed, Storm collected the spilled organs and set them back on the platter.

"We were attacked last night," he explained, "and Nightshade wanted to send some to you as a 'thank you' for sharing the clearing with us."

Nathanael scooped up the platter and sniffed the contents, purring in pleasure. He glanced at Storm's leg and mumbled in a low growl, "The other one bled less."

Storm, not one to let others' walk over him, reached up and yanked the crossbow bolt out of Nathanael's hand.

"I'm keeping this." Storm said defiantly. He heard a strange noise coming from the cat and Storm thought he was going to get shot again, but the creature was laughing.

Nathanael held out his paw and helped Storm to his feet. Then without another word, the large cat turned and walked away.

"How did it go?" his mom asked with a smirk when he made it back to camp.

"He said you bled less." Storm grumbled.

"It sounds like you did just fine." she laughed, "He was pretty cranky yesterday."

"He was cranky today too." Storm retorted, then held up the bolt and asked, "Why didn't you warn me?"

"I was worried he'd miss." Nightshade said, shrugging.

"Miss what?" Sunshine asked, walking up, holding a book.

"Mom's evil." Storm said, then explained the interaction he had with the panther.

"Hardly, did you get a new spell?" Nightshade asked defensively.

"Yeah, but why is that important?" he asked, hesitantly.

"Healing is incredibly useful but it's difficult to get." she explained, "The top guilds buy and hoard all of the healing spell books." She glanced at them and added, "Or so I've heard."

"Couldn't we just ask him to cast it?" Sunshine asked.

"I doubt he would have." Storm chimed in, "Nathanael doesn't seem very friendly." he looked at the book in Sunshine's hand and asked her, "Are you done yet?"

"I just finished." she said "Do you want to finish the cabin?"

"Sure do!" he said smiling, "After last night I'm a little afraid to sleep in the tents again."

They found a good spot a little way away from their campsite to start construction. It was further up the hill and not as close to the forest. When they finished with the cabin, they had plans to create a wall around it, that way if they were attacked again, they would have even more protection.

Since Storm prepared the logs the previous day and Sunshine also had the construction skill, the time it would take to build the cabin was shortened drastically. They cut the logs into the proper size and brought up sand and rocks from the river for the foundation. As they worked, they each logged out to eat lunch and dinner, always having either Storm or Sunshine guiding the process. The AI took over for the logged-out player, but it was slower than being manually controlled.

Every few hours Nightshade would brew up some tea and call out, "Break time!"

At first Storm didn't want to stop but his mom insisted. They took a short break, sitting around the fire, with their mom handing out small wooden cups with a steaming liquid inside.

"What is it?" Storm asked, looking at it dubiously.

"It has a few things in it," Nightshade explained, "but it's mostly peppermint." She smiled, then commanded, "Drink up."

Storm took a sip and felt the warming liquid flow into his body and received a notification.

[Buff
       Name: Invigoration
       Effect 1: +5 strength
       Effect 2: +5 constitution
       Time remaining: 60 minutes]

They worked well into the evening and after sunset, working purely by firelight. Storm and Sunshine completed the roof while Nightshade broke down their old campsite and moved all of their gear into the cabin.

Once they finished, the three sat around the fire, reflecting on the day. They talked about their plans for tomorrow and setup a rotating watch then logged out.

SEVEN

Adventure

Storm was excited and woke up early the next day. They were finally going to go hunting in the forest. They finished the cabin last night and decided that today they would scout around and try to find a dungeon or some mobs to level on. He woke up early and logged-in before breakfast, his mom's and sister's avatars were still sleeping so he snuck out of the cabin and decided to try his hand at fishing while he waited.

He found a long stick and took the fishing supplies with some bait down to the river. He used the knowledge he gained from the skill book to fashion a fishing pole and find a nice place to setup. The sun was just coming up in-game and he sat back to enjoy the morning.

Dozens of small birds zipped between the trees and bushes, chirping and singing in the morning sunlight. Butterflies fluttered along with the gentle breeze. And the many flowers dipped and bopped as bees landed to rob them of their pollen. The clearing was alive with activity.

Storm caught a few fish and stored them on a stringer dangling in the river, to keep them fresh for later. In-between the catches, he pulled up his in-game map to study it. Most of it was dark, covered in something his sister called a fog-of-war. On his map, Storm could see the town, Last Hope, the area around the village and a small path to where he was now.

Hearing a noise, Storm turned to find his mother walking towards him.

"Can you give me a quick trip to town?" she asked.

"Forget something?" he asked.

"Yeah," she said, "I'll need you to cast it again in an hour. Do you think you can do it?"

"I don't know." he replied dubiously after glancing at his mana bar. "Casting the spell yesterday used almost all of my mana and we are a little further away from town today. Not to mention draining my mana all at once hurt like hell. Honestly, I'm not sure I would survive."

"You've leveled since then" she said and handed him two finger sized vials of blue liquid, "These should help. Drink one right after you cast and you should be fine."

Storm took the vials and inspected it.

[Item

　　　Name: Vial of mana potion
　　　Effect: +50 mana]

"Wow, do you have more?" Storm asked.

"Only a few, but in time we will have plenty." she said chuckling, then hesitated and said seriously, "Storm, one more thing, after you cast the spell and I go through, wait until it closes. If anybody comes through, kill them."

"Why?" he asked, his eyes widening in surprise.

"We don't want anybody coming to our camp." Nightshade explained, "If a player comes through, they might like the area and bring friends." She looked around and continued, "This area has a lot of desirable resources and we don't want them to get any ideas." she said seriously, "This is our territory now."

"What if they are higher level than me?" he asked worriedly.

"Push them into the river," she answered coldly, "the river will take them away."

"Won't they still know where we are?" he asked.

"Yes, but they will get the point." she said.

Storm nodded then cast the portal spell, whispering "Last Hope" at the end. An emerald portal appeared before him.

"You should log out and get some breakfast while it's still warm." she said before stepping through the portal.

He barely heard her words as his vision blurred and his head started pounding. With little hesitation, he popped the cork and downed the contents of the potion his mom gave him. The liquid tasted like candy and cooled his throat as it went down and his mana quickly refilled.

Storm waited anxiously until the portal closed, then followed his mom's advice and logged out to get some food in the real world. And it was worth it.

Knowing that gamers need the fuel, the hotels go all-out on breakfast. They provide stacks of pancakes piled high, with all kinds of eggs, plates of sausages and bacon and almost every kind of cereal. They had pitchers of milk, orange juice, apple juice, and his favorite, pineapple juice. Just as he arrived his sister was finishing up and he updated her on his in-game morning. Knowing he had at least an hour before he had to be back, he took his time and ate his fill.

Once back in the game, Storm packed up his fishing gear and returned to the cabin, taking the fish with him. When it was time, he cast the portal spell again, this time with Sunshine helping to stand guard. Their mom appeared, carrying an armload of gear and after the portal closed they discussed the new supplies.

"Sunshine, the arrows are for you and me. I picked up a few different types, depending on the creatures." she explained.

Storm glanced at the quivers and saw that some of the arrows had pointed tips and others had a flat tip. He wasn't very familiar with the different types of creatures in the game but thought the pointed ones would do more damage.

"Storm, I got the sword for you." she continued, "Last Hope is a farming village and the market is fairly small but fortunately, somebody had just traded it in this morning. The shop keep said that they are not very common and sell out quickly."

Storm picked up the sword and pulled it out of the plain looking scabbard. He swung it around to get a feel for its weight. The sword had seen better days as the blade was pitted and chipped in places but it was better than the axe.

"Thanks, this will work." he said happily. When he fought the wolves, the axe felt too slow and he constantly over swung. He was also hoping the sword would be less messy. He inspected it.

[Item

      Name: Steel Short Sword
      Description: Slashing and piecing damage.
      Quality: Low]

When she was done with the fish, Nightshade loaded them in the smoker and cleaned herself up. Then she reached into her bag and pulled out a piece of paper, handing it to Storm.

"I also picked this up." she said, "Look at it and then hand it to Sunshine."

"What is it?" Sunshine asked.

"It's a map fragment." Nightshade explained, "It will clear away a bit of the fog-of-war, but more importantly it will add a few random encounters to our maps."

Storm looked at the piece of paper and saw a notification that his map had been updated, then handed the fragment to his sister. He pulled up his in-game map and saw the hidden area around Last Hope clear away and a few towns appeared to the west of the village. Then to his surprise a half dozen bright colored dots appeared scattered around the area. They were blue, yellow, red and green.

There was a blue dot to the north, where he had encountered Nathanael, and a pair of blue dots directly to the east. A yellow dot and a red dot were next to each other to the north east, directly north of the blue pair. And finally, a green dot appeared far to the south. He dismissed his map and saw his mom throw the map fragment into the fire.

"Why did you do that?" he asked, taken aback.

"The fragments are unique and randomly generated. If somebody finds ours, they could get to the encounters before we do." his mom explained, "Some of the encounters you can do without the map information but others you can't."

"What do the colors mean?" Sunshine asked.

"The blue dots are NPCs, which you can find without a map, but having it will allow you to unlock more content. It's about the same as having a really high charisma. The red, green and yellow dots will only show up for map bearers. Red is a boss mob, yellow is a dungeon and green is treasure." Nightshade explained.

"How do you know that? I didn't see anything about it the wiki." Sunshine said suspiciously.

"Oh, the shopkeeper told me." Nightshade explained awkwardly.

"Which one are we doing today?" Storm asked excitedly.

"I think we should make our way to the red dot." Nightshade said, "It looks like a boss guarding a dungeon. It might take us a couple of days, but we could try to clear the dungeon too."

"That sounds fun" Sunshine agreed. She pointed south, towards the darkening sky and asked, "Do you think that's going to be a problem?"

"I saw it earlier. It doesn't seem to be moving very fast." Nightshade said, "We should keep an eye on it though."

They gathered up their gear and headed northeast towards the red dot. Sunshine led the way and they made fast progress due to her special ability. Storm was, once again, surprised how quickly they made it to their destination.

"Do you think the boss will be hard?" Storm asked while they were traveling.

"It shouldn't be." Nightshade replied simply.

Sunshine snorted but kept her attention on navigating. Soon the forest thinned and they came to a clearing. The group slowed and snuck to the edge of the forest. They cautiously peered out and discovered they were in the back of a large graveyard, surrounded by a wrought iron fence. There were hundreds of tombstones in neat rows around a small hill with a little building sitting on top. Further away, on the other side near the main entrance, were more buildings.

"Of course, a graveyard." Sunshine whispered.

"What better place to find treasure?" Storm replied, smirking.

"Grave-robber Storm" Sunshine announced, snickering.

"There are probably skeletons here," Nightshade said, ignoring them, "which means we should use the blunt arrows."

Sunshine nodded and refocused on their upcoming encounter.

"Storm, why don't you sneak up to the building and peek inside? Sunshine and I will cover you." Nightshade offered.

Storm nodded and slowly made his way into the graveyard.

"If it gets overwhelming, fall back and we will retreat into the forest." she whispered loudly.

Storm slowly crept from the protective covering of the forest to the dilapidated fence guarding the graveyard and squeezed through an opening. He looked around, taking in the layout and plotted his path to the small building. As he did, small suggestions popped into his mind, and he realized they were from the stealth skill book he read yesterday. There weren't very many shadows to hide in, so he opted to stay close to the large tombstones and use the tall grass to help hide his presence. As he wound his way in-between the graves, he was thankful he didn't see any with fresh mounds of dirt.

The graveyard was ancient and overgrown, with a good number of tombstones crumbling or fallen over. A dirt path wound its way around the graveyard and was bordered by a waist-high wrought-iron fence on either side. When he neared the hill, he stepped over the fence and continued the rest of the way on the path. As he got closer to the building, he heard a rustling behind him and spun around to see a large pile of leaves shifting in the wind, many fluttering away.

He took a deep breath to calm his nerves, but just as he was about to turn back to his task, a skeletal hand slowly rose out of the pile. Staring in disbelief, a bleach white skeleton stood up and turned towards him, the two empty eye sockets flaring to life. Holding his sword in hand, Storm took a step to meet the skeleton but before he could take another, an arrow slammed into the skeleton's skull, shattering it. The skeletal body crumpled into a pile of bones with a clatter. Storm nodded thanks to his mom and sister, and they waved him onward.

A few more skeletons arose, but he ignored them as his mother and sister quickly dispatched them. He made it to the building and peered through the stained-glass window, but he could only make out a small distorted candle. A shape moved inside, blocking his view and he froze, fearing he was spotted. Fortunately, nothing came charging out of the building.

Storm crept to the door of the mausoleum and waited for Nightshade and Sunshine to get into position. When they indicated they were ready, he pulled the door open and a loud creaking sound reverberated outward. A small apparition flew out and two arrows quickly pierced through it. Unfortunately, it didn't appear to have taken any damage. The specter continued to fly towards the two archers and Storm turned to follow it.

"Where are you off too?" a sultry voice said, behind him.

Storm turned to see a scantily clad woman standing in the shadows of the entryway. She was deathly thin with long white hair and skin as blue as the sky. She had a wicked smile and three-inch-long black fingernails that were more reminiscent of claws. He inspected her:

[Creature
    Name: Lich
    Level: 14
    Health: 306/306]

The lich started casting a spell and as Storm followed along, he heard the clacking of skeletons behind him. Knowing the risks, but wanting a new spell, he watched her as she completed it, trusting his companions to protect him. The lich's eyes glowed as smoke poured out of her hands, enveloping him. He heard the chime of several notifications but they were minimized since he was in combat.

Storm felt a strange weakness spread throughout his body and an icon appeared in his UI. He glanced at it.

[Debuff
>   Name: Death miasma
>   Effect 1: -20% health
>   Effect 2: -20% stamina
>   Effect 3: -10 constitution
>   Effect 4: -10 strength
>   Effect 5: -10 dexterity
>   Time remaining: 10 minutes]

The lich quickly stepped towards him and swung her claws at his face. Storm raised his sword to deflect the attack but felt slow and was barely able to react in time. The lich struck with such force his sword flew out of his weakened grasp.

With few options, Storm cast her spell back at her. It was a difficult spell, requiring him to hold his fingers at sharper angles but he completed it before she was able to attack him again.

The lich's eyes widened in surprise and she gave a toothy grin as the dark smoke from his spell poured out of his hands. She stood tall, letting his spell wrap around her, a course laughter erupting from her throat. Storm realized something was amiss and quickly checked his notifications.

[New skill obtained
>   Death magic: You are able to cast death-based spells]

[New spell obtained
>   Death miasma (Death Magic):
>>   This spell creates a miasma of death to weaken living creatures.
>>   The miasma will give death creatures in a boost.
>>   Single target
>>   Cost: 50 mana
>>   Cast time: 5 seconds

Length: 10 minutes
Living creatures receive:
    -20% health
    -20% stamina
    -10 constitution
    -10 strength
    -10 dexterity
Death creatures receive:
    +20% health
    +20% stamina
    +10 constitution
    +10 strength
    +10 dexterity]

It took him a moment to understand his mistake, and when he did, he realized the already one-sided fight was about to quickly come to an end. He glanced behind him to calculate an escape route but saw four skeletons swinging wildly, trying to strike him with their bony knife-like fingers. Each of them had plants crawling up their legs, rooting them to the ground, but they had effectively cut off his retreat.

He was about to make a dive for his sword when the lich rushed towards him and stabbed both of her hands deep into his chest. He expected his armor to protect him but her nails seemingly pieced through the chainmail as if he weren't even wearing it. He screamed, falling to the ground in agony, as the pain coursed through his body and his health bar flashed dangerously. Reflexively he grabbed her wrists, trying to dislodge them but she was much stronger than he was.

With his health bar quickly ticking down, he frantically thought a solution. With very few options, and an animalistic need to survive, he cast his heal spell through the haze of pain. As the spell took hold, his chest started glowing. He hoped it would buy him a few more seconds for his mom and sister to come to his rescue. As the life magic reached the lich's fingers, her hands started smoking and she screamed. Their faces so close together he could smell the death on her breath but the new smell of burning flesh was far worse and made his stomach retch.

The lich fell back screaming in agony, her hands successfully dislodged. She held her smoldering hands up in front of her and tried to move her fingers to cast another spell but they were blackened and curled. Storm finished healing himself, then slowly stood up, the two staring at each other. He started casting a spell with one hand and reaching for her with the other, but she was quicker. She pulled out a wicked looking dagger with her ruined hands and as plunged it into his leg.

"Healer!" she spat at him.

Fortunately, Storm completed his spell just as she stabbed him. Grunting at the pain, he reached down and grabbed her arm, sending the healing magic into her once more. The lich screamed and tried to pull away, but he held fast.

He fought through the pain and cast the spell again and again until the world turned fuzzy and his blue bar was almost empty. He slumped over, cold and shaking, not knowing if he killed her or not, not knowing if he was going to live. Slowly, a group of glowing rainbow lights swirled around him.

He lay there for only a few minutes, or an eternity, he wasn't quite sure. Somebody rolled him over and he heard his mom calling out to him. It was hard to understand her at first but her voice eventually broke through his brain-fog.

"Storm!" she yelled.

"What?" he groggily asked.

"Storm, we need to get back to camp." Nightshade said.

"I'll be ok, I just need to rest." he wearily replied. Then he closed his eyes to regain his strength.

He felt a sharp slap across his face and his eyes popped open. Nightshade and Sunshine were looking down at him.

"Was that necessary?" Nightshade asked Sunshine.

"It worked." Sunshine smirked, pointing to Storm.

"What'ss wrong? It'ss jusst mana drain, I'll be ok." Storm slurred.

"Storm, look at your health, it's green." Nightshade said sharply "That means you're poisoned."

Through his blurry vision he looked at his health bar and noticed that it was indeed green, just as she had said. He felt drunk. His health was currently at the halfway point and slowly decreasing. He had just enough mana for one more heal spell so he quickly cast it on himself.

His mom and sister had been distracted surveying their surroundings one last time to ensure there were no more mobs left and didn't see him in time.

"No!" they both yelled trying to stop him, but it was too late.

Storm's body twisted in renewed pain and his health bar changed to a darker shade of green while his health started falling faster.

"Storm, healing spells spread poison." his mom explained quickly "We need to get you an antidote potion. A cure poison spell would work too, but you don't have that yet."

Nightshade hefted Storm up on her shoulder.

"Sunshine led the way back to camp, and fast." Nightshade said in a commanding voice.

"Will he make it?" Sunshine asked, looking at him.

"Maybe, the bleeding from his leg wasn't bad, I bandaged that up and his other wounds were mostly healed already. It's the poison. It's causing him to rapidly lose health. I don't know how long it will take to exit his system, but I might be able to brew up a tea to help."

"I'm fine." Storm insisted, looking at all four of them.

EIGHT

Last Hope

The three navigated through the forest and made it back to the cabin with no difficulties. They were sitting around the fire sipping rejuvenating tea and recounting the battle. They talked about what went well and what could be improved and they devised some strategies for future engagements.

"Did we get any loot?" Storm asked when they were finished discussing the battle.

"When mom was patching you up, I searched all of the skeletons, the lich, and the mausoleum." Sunshine said, "We didn't get anything from the skeletons, but the lich had two rings, a necklace and a poisoned knife. There was a treasure chest in the building that had a gold and silver in it. This is your portion." She handed him 4 gold and 80 silver and he added the coins to his coin purse.

[Item

      Name: bag of holding

      Space: three out of four spaces filled

      Contents: copper coins x50, silver coins x52, gold coins x4g]

"Mom wants the knife," Sunshine continued. "But the rings and the amulet are up for grabs. I'll take whenever you don't." She handed him the rings and amulet.

"I'm going to try to replicate the poison and create an antidote." Nightshade explained, "You can have the dagger afterwards if you want."

The two rings were silver with an azure hue and the amulet was a smoky black with two white hands on it. He inspected the jewelry.

[Item

      Name: Ring of mana

      Effect: +20% mana]

[Item

      Name: Ring of mana regeneration

Effect: +20% mana regeneration]

[Artifact
Name: Amulet of Spectral hands
Effect: Casts spectral hands on the user for 30 seconds.
Spectral hands: Melee attack ignores armor
Charges: 20/30]

Storm read the amulet's description several times and something clicked about the last battle. The lich must have cast Spectral hands on herself to pierce his armor. Storm hadn't really found which direction he wanted to build his character, but being the only caster of the group, he decided he could make the most out of the rings.

"I'll take the rings," he finally said, handing the amulet back to his sister. He slipped a ring onto each index finger and they self-adjusted to fit and felt cool against his skin. A gentle pulsating emanated from the mana regeneration ring.

"That's probably for the best." Nightshade said, nodding in agreement, "You are our only healing option for now." she waved her hand at a group of plants in the distance and said, "Once I can harvest some of those plants, I can make us some healing potions and that should take the pressure off."

"What are we going to do now?" Storm asked, "I'm ready to go back to the graveyard." After resting and drinking Nightshade's tea the poison had dissipated and Storm was fully recovered. He felt bad that they cut their adventure short and wanted to go back and finish clearing the graveyard.

"Let's hold off on the graveyard until tomorrow." Nightshade said, "I'm going to brew some healing potions and we can work a little more on the camp."

"I'll start building a palisade around the cabin," Sunshine added "that will give us a defensive barrier in case anything more hostile finds us."

"Thanks, we are still a little exposed out here." Nightshade said, looking at Sunshine in gratitude.

Outvoted, Storm sighed. He was hoping for a little more adventure today. It was barely midafternoon, the trip to the graveyard and back was less than an hour and the battle itself only lasted a few frantic minutes.

"Would you make a town run for me?" Nightshade asked him, "I need some more crafting supplies."

"Do you think I'll have problems with that?" he asked, gesturing to the darkening sky over the forest, "I can portal to town but I'll need to come back through that."

"You afraid of a little rain?" Sunshine asked, mocking him.

"You can bind here, then portal there and back." Nightshade informed him. When they both looked at her questioningly, she explained, "The cabin has been here long enough that it is considered a permanent structure now, we can bind to it."

Storm looked at her suspiciously but just said, "Thanks." Then looked up the commands and bound himself to the campsite. His mom gave him some money and explained what she needed. He cast the town portal spell to Last Hope and stepped through, his feet landing on the cobblestones of the town square.

Storm hadn't spent much time in the village. On his previous trip they had arrived late and left town quick to make camp. He was happy to have some time to look around. He also thought that it might offer a good opportunity to copy some skills.

Storm walked around and identified where all the shops were located. He found the bowyer, the weapon and armor shop, the general store and the furrier. He was curious about the furrier that Nightshade had visited a few nights ago so he stopped by there first.

He peered into the shop's window and the cat-like creature standing behind the counter was not what he had expected. The creature looked to be four feet tall, standing upright and wore a pair of thick spectacles staring down at something on the counter. Its eyes looked like large almonds and it had two triangle shaped ears perched on top of its head, both twitching as it worked. The most striking feature about the cat was that it had absolutely no fur. Had Storm not known better he would have thought it was a rat instead of some sort of feline. He would find out later that this NPC was modeled after a Sphynx cat. Storm quickly decided he didn't need anything from the furrier and moved on.

He chose to stop by the general store next and was relieved to see something that looked like a normal housecat standing on a stool behind the counter. This time it was a small white cat with a long tail. The feline stared at him and frowned when he stood there staring back. "Can I help you with something?" the store clerk asked is a soft feminine, slightly irritated voice.

"Just picking up a few supplies." Storm replied, clearing his throat. He looked around the little shop to see what they had to offer. The general store had several rows of shelves filled with goods and he walked down each isle taking inventory on what was available. He walked up to the counter, trying not to laugh at how ridiculous it was talking to a cat, and asked, "Do you have any spell books or skill books?".

"The skill books are over there," she replied with a smile. She waved at a shelf in the corner. He walked over to look at the books and she continued, "We don't have any spell books, but we do have some spell scrolls. The scrolls are single-use but don't use mana." she pulled a box out and set it on top of it the counter.

Storm looked at each book and the price. Fencing, Animal training, and Farming were 50 silver each. He thought they would be good skills to have but wanted to be cautious on spending his coins, he could pick up the skill for free if he could find somebody to copy it from. Knot tying and Evasion were 100 and 200 respectively. The last two were definitely useful and ones that he was interested in.

The one that caught his eye was twice as thick as the others and the leather cover was discolored from years of use. They were all second-hand books, but this one was by far, the most worn. The book was labeled Spell Inscribing and it was the also the most expensive at 7 gold. He picked it up to skim through it, hoping to learn it for free.

"This isn't a library, if you want to read it, you have to buy it." the store clerk said.

"Can you tell me a about this one?" he asked, holding up the well-worn book.

"That one is for making spell scrolls." she informed him. She looked at the book fondly and continued, "It's not an easy skill to pick up and you need ink and parchment. You also need to know the spell and have the required mana at the time of inscription." She patted the scroll box proudly and said, "I made most of these."

Storm could learn the skills pretty fast, but unfortunately the storekeeper wouldn't let him stand there and read them. He was really interested in the Spell Inscription skill but didn't have enough gold to buy the book.

"Will you buy back the books?" he asked.

"Yes, but for half the cost." the shopkeeper said.

That was better than nothing, but he still didn't have enough to buy the book. He might be able to haggle her down a little but he thought there might be another way for him to obtain the skill. He set the book back down and looked to the scrolls on the counter.

He rifled through the box of scrolls and made a note of which spells were available. He saw scrolls for Plant Growth, Fire Ball, Dig, and Group Summon.

"Did you make this one?" he asked, holding up one the last one.

"That one is one of my rarer items." The cat explained, "I was traveling through Magethorn city and I heard they were always selling out, so I picked up a few from the mage guild, they were a great buy but sadly they haven't been very popular here."

At a steep price of three gold, he wondered if that had anything to do to its unpopularity. He then asked about the items hanging on the wall behind the counter.

"The backpack of holding is 5 gold. The shirt of water breathing is 6 gold. The staff has an enchantment to increase movement speed and is 10 gold." the clerk said, pointing at each item in turn.

Storm walked around the shop picking up the items his mom had requested and set them on the counter, she wanted primarily alchemy materials along with more vials and a few bottles. He then picked up a few quills, pots of ink and a stack of paper. Then he added the Group Summoning scroll to his pile.

"How much?" he asked.

"4 gold and 80 silver." she said, after looking over the items and assessing the value.

Storm cringed internally, he knew the Group Summon scroll would eat up most of his money but something about it was pulling him to buy it. He was thankful that his mom gave him a few extra gold coins for the supplies and decided to see if he could squeeze a little more value out of his trip.

Storm set a piece of paper in front of the clerk, opened the inkpot and set a quill and 1 gold piece on the paper.

"Will you make a scroll for the gold?" he asked.

She looked at him curiously.

"You can keep the scroll." he said, reassuring her.

She looked at him slyly, then almost faster than he could see, she swiped up the gold. Then, to his surprise, she started casting a spell. Storm followed her movements until they slowed, then right before completing it, she reached down and gently picked up the quill. She dipped it in the ink and touched it to the paper. Her hand moved as if by magic and as she wrote, a glow slowly pulsated in waves from her hand to the paper.

Storm watched intently, this was a gamble, he might not be able to copy the skill this way, and he would have wasted one of his precious gold coins. The glow of the magic eventually dissipated from the cat's paw. Storm's stomach knotted from concentrating so hard but breathed a slow steady breath and relaxed as he saw the completed scroll. She rolled it up and tucked it away before he could see too much of it.

Storm heard several chimes and thanked her. He quickly looked at the notifications and saw that he had obtained the skill, but much to his surprise, he also learned the spell she had cast.

[New skill obtained
      Spell inscription: You are able to create spell scrolls]

[New skill obtained
      Water magic: You are able to cast water-based spells]

[New spell obtained
      Rain (Water Magic):
            Causes a gentle rainstorm.
            Length: 10 minutes
            Cost: 10 mana
            Cast time: 5 seconds]

Storm then set out five pieces of paper on the counter and began to cast. Repeating the clerk's steps for each paper, he wrote his spell onto them. Finally, when the glow had completely dissipated on the last scroll, he sat back and looked at the five Rain spell scrolls laying in front of him. He looked at them with pride, thinking how clever he was.

"Will you trade these for the backpack?" he asked.

"I'm afraid not." she said shaking her head. "While the farmers love these, I can make them myself." She thought for a moment, then said, "I'll take them for a discount on your order, but not in trade for the backpack. What else you got?"

Storm narrowed his eyes at her in thought, then checked his mana to see how much he had left and looked over his remaining spells, considering which one might inspire her to give up the backpack. He thought his death miasma spell was probably the rarest, but she probably couldn't sell it very well. The he recalled something his mom said and he made his choice.

He set down five new pieces of paper and repeated the process, this time casting the healing touch spell. When he completed the process, he looked at the shopkeeper.

"How about these?" he asked.

"I'll make that trade." she said quickly, her eyes widening almost imperceptivity. Trying not to sound too excited she continued, "If these sell well, you come back and we can trade more."

She retrieved the backpack and set it on the counter next to the rest of Storm's items. Storm paid the adjusted bill and packed the items in his new backpack of holding, then said goodbye to the shopkeeper and exited the shop.

He walked out the door smiling, he had spent most of his money at his first stop but considering his new potential revenue stream he wasn't too worried about it. If the scroll he bought could do what he thought it could do, it would be worth it. He would have paid anything for it. Since running into his dad's avatar, Father, his primary goal in the game had been trying to find a way to rescue him from Valhalla, and he might have just found it.

With his new backpack equipped and feeling lighter than ever, he set off to talk to the bowyer and stock up on arrows. He checked his remaining funds.

[Item

    Name: bag of holding
    Space: two out of four spaces filled
    Contents: copper coins x50, silver coins x45, gold coins x1g]

The bowyer was three times larger than the general store clerk and was much more intimidating. He was grey and black with leopard spots trailing down his back all the way to the end of its long tail. The large cat was very cordial and happily bundled up the requested arrows with mixed heads. The bowyer was also happy to show Storm how to make each of the arrows, then let Storm make a few himself. Storm gained the fletching skill and unlocked a few arrowhead types.

[New skill obtained
       Fletching: You are able to create basic arrows based on known
       blueprints
       Blueprints
              Piercing arrows
              Blunt Arrows
              Slashing Arrows]

[Item
       Name: Bundle of arrows
       Type: Piercing
       Quantity: 100]

[Item
       Name: Bundle of arrows
       Type: Blunt
       Quantity: 100]

[Item
       Name: Bundle of arrows
       Type: Slashing
       Quantity: 100]

The arrows only cost a copper each and considering he now had access to a dimensional space, he decided to load up on them for his mom and sister. They originally only asked for a dozen each to restock but with his new backpack he could carry so much more.

His last stop was the one he was most excited for, the forge. After seeing Father in his forge, Storm had anticipated learning more about his father's craft.

He walked around and watched a few of the apprentices at work, staying well out of their way. It didn't take too long before he heard a familiar chime.

[New skill obtained
       Blacksmithing: You are able to create basic items based on known
       blueprints
       Blueprints
              Nail]

He found the head blacksmith and asked him if he could help out with some apprentice work. The blacksmith, a hairy gruff looking cat, looked at him dubiously but led him to an anvil in the corner.

Following the apprentices' steps he grabbed a piece of metal from the scrap pile and slowly worked it into a nail. He repeated this process until he completed over a dozen nails. He kept working, losing himself in the rhythm and sense of accomplishment.

He looked around and saw one of the apprentices making a small dagger. He watched the apprentice work and after only a few moments he heard the notification for obtaining a new skill.

[New skill obtained
        Weapon smithing: You are able to create basic weapons based on
        known blueprints
        Blueprints
                Dagger]

After reading the notification he grabbed a piece of scrap metal and tried to make a dagger but every attempt failed. He watched the apprentice that was making daggers and noticed he was starting a new one and used an ingot he received from the head smith.

Sighing, Storm walked up to the head smith and asked him if he could use an ingot as well. After some haggling, the smith agreed to sell him an ingot for ten silver coins.

Storm worked the ingot just like he saw the apprentice do. He heated it and drew it out on the anvil with a hammer. He eventually made the shape of a small dagger. It was a three-inch blade and after he cooled and sharpened it, he wrapped the tang in leather from the scrap pile. Once completed a prompt appeared for him to name it. He did, then inspected his work.

[Item
        Name: First dagger
        Level: 1
        Quality: 10%
        Damage: 2
        Durability: 6/6
        Crafted by: Storm]

Seeing that he was finished, the head smith walked over and picked up the dagger inspecting is critically. The smith swung it around, testing its weight and feel, then handed the blade to Storm.

"You'll get better with time." he said critically.

Satisfied with the skills he picked up, Storm thanked the smith and walked out into the darkening town. Storm felt he had done as good as he could and was about to head back to camp. Earlier he asked the general-store shopkeeper if there were any mages in town, but she said she was the only one, after the healer had left a few years earlier.

It was getting late and the shops were closing up. Storm walked around the small village and found it oddly comforting, he felt safe there. He sat next to the fountain, relaxing and listening to its melodic sounds. Lively sound drifted to him from the tavern and he was curious if there were players in there. He stood up and started walking towards the tavern when all of a sudden, his vision went dark.

He was confused and wondered if his VR pod was having technical issues. He strained his other senses and he thought he heard the faint musical sound of a lute. Then he felt a small jab in his arm. Frantically he looked around at his dark UI and that's when he saw it, several icons next to his health bar, which was now flashing a sickly green. He concentrated and brought up the information.

[Stun

     You are stunned

     Countdown: 8 seconds]

[Poison

     Type: Unknown

     Effect: Unconscious

     Countdown: 4 hours 32 minutes]

Storm laid there in the dark for a few minutes but realized there wasn't anything he could do so he logged out and exited the pod. His mom and sister were still in their pods, so he left the room and got some dinner while he waited for them. Less than half an hour later his mom and Cleo walked into the kitchen.

"Why didn't you come back to camp?" his mom asked, "We waited for a while, but when we checked the map, it looked like you left town."

"I think I got kidnapped." he said.

NINE

Kidnapped

Luke, his mom and sister, decided it would be best if he were logged in and ready when the poison wore off. He tried to take a small nap but he had trouble sleeping. Finally, it was time and he logged in to watch the countdown full of anticipation.

0:03

0:02

0:01

The darkness lightened but the shapes around him were still blurry. The brightness was painful to his eyes but after a few moments they adjusted and he could see more clearly. His body came back under his control and he found himself sitting in an uncomfortable chair.

Storm shifted and he heard a deep voice laced with anger, "He's awake, you two go, and next time use the invitational model we discussed."

"Sure thing, boss." a soft voice replied.

Storm looked around the room and saw a thin man dressed in all blood-red leather with a huge grin on his face. He had a sword sheathed at each hip, a hilt peaking over each shoulder and a bandolier of throwing daggers wrapped around his torso. The man looked down at Storm, winked, then slowly faded away into nothingness.

"I'll keep an eye on him," another voice said, off to his right "you know how he gets when he finds a new poison." Storm looked to the voice and saw a second figure, this one taller and garbed in colorful flowing cloth. He bowed with extra flair and beat the drum at his side, then his form streaked out of the room.

The remaining figure in the room, sitting behind a desk, stood up and started walking towards him. He was an older gentleman, probably as old as his father. The strange man wore chainmail armor, dyed a brilliant blue that had a small, barely visible glow emanating from it. Storm inspected him.

[Character
    Name: Weird
    Guild: Dark Elite
    Level: 100
    Health: ***/***]

"So, you didn't order my kidnapping?" Storm asked, not pleased with the situation.

"Not exactly." Weird responded chuckling, "But sometimes the older players can get a little impatient." he sighed and continued, "Those two are originals and sometimes take more shortcuts than they should."

"Originals?" Storm asked.

Weird waved his hands dismissing the question as irrelevant.

"Let's discuss why you are here and what I can do for you." Weird said. He smiled an almost friendly smile and continued, "Storm, we are making a run at the world city and I need as many high-quality players as I can get. I got plenty of sliders but podders are far superior and I'm recruiting as many I can before we start. I'm willing to power level you and fully equip you in high level gear."

Storm watched Weird as he paced around the room and came to an unexpected realization. Weird's smooth movements, precise steps and subtle shifts of his body exposed him. Weird was a podder, Weird was in New Las Vegas and so were the two that kidnapped him.

"If you join our guild" Weird continued, "and commit to our cause, I will assign you to our best grinding group and power level you to level fifty. We have rotations that run twenty-four hours a day and will provide whatever training you need."

"All because I'm a podder?" Storm asked, dubious.

"Mostly," Weird acknowledged, "With our small numbers, podders are required to challenge the world boss. Podders usually only last a week or two before they go back home to their handhelds so we have to recruit and power level right before we are ready."

"All for a noob like me. What do you get out of it?" Storm asked. He liked the sound of the training, but when something sounded too good to be true, it usually was. He was still not convinced.

"It doesn't cost me that much," Weird explained, "the groups are already grinding, adding an extra player isn't that big of a deal. Power leveling you also helps the guild. We are stronger the more we help each other." Weird paused to make sure Storm was paying attention, then continued, "If it makes you feel any better, we extend the same offer to all podders. It's a good deal for you and it's a good deal for us. If you don't want to join, that's ok there are other ways to play and we respect that."

Storm was becoming more and more interested, hitting fifty in a couple of days would really help with his other goals, but he wanted to talk it over with his mom and sister first. And maybe, he could get them an invite too.

"This sounds really nice," Storm said, "do you mind if I sleep on it? I started playing early this morning and it's been a long day. Your boys kidnapped me right before I was going to log off."

"That's very wise." Weird said, nodding. "Log off and get some sleep, we can talk it over after you have rested. I'll have Bobby assign a tent for your avatar while you are logged out." then Weird turned his head to the side and spoke quietly, "Bobby, please step inside. I have a task for you."

A young boy stepped inside the room and walked over to them.

"Yes, Mr. Weird?" the small child asked. As the boy moved, his legs and arms were choppy, as if he missed a few frames every time he moved.

"When is your next power-level session?" Weird asked him.

"Tomorrow night" Bobby replied, smiling.

"Good. Storm here, needs a place to stash his avatar until tomorrow." Weird said, "Assign him one of the empty tents."

Bobby nodded.

"Group with him and post a guard." Weird commanded.

"Yes sir!" Bobby replied enthusiastically, nodding.

Weird reached into his pocket and pulled out a silvery coin and handed it to Bobby.

"Here's a platinum coin. I'll give you another one when you bring him back." he said.

"Thank you, Mr. Weird." Bobby said as he took the coin and put it in his pocket.

Turning to Storm, Weird said, "When you log back in and are ready, let Bobby know and he will bring you to me." Weird glanced at Bobby and added, "He is one of our youngest members but he takes his camp duties seriously. He likes to personally handle the high-profile cases to ensure there are no mistakes."

"Are you ready to group?" Bobby asked Storm.

Storm hesitated, he didn't want to leave his group with Father, but he didn't think he had a choice. If he was going to power level with Weird, he would have to leave Father's group anyways. With great reservations and a silent "See you soon" to Father, he dropped from his group and accepted Bobby's invitation.

They stepped outside into the night and Storm was amazed at how bright and clear the stars looked, the nighttime was so beautiful. Storm and Bobby were standing on a hill with a small stone building, surrounded by tents as far as they could see. Camp fires dotted the encampment and illuminated groups of patrolling guards.

"You should bind here." Bobby said, patting the building.

Storm nodded and followed Bobby's instructions, then followed him through the camp to his designated tent. The past couple of hours started weighing on him and he needed to sleep.

After the pod powered down, Luke laid there for a few minutes trying to gather his strength to get out. He closed his eyes and in the dark, comfortable and completely silent space, he failed. He woke up several hours later and stumbled his way to his bed to finish resting. His sleep was restless with dreams of dark figures casting spells and him, frantically trying to defend himself.

Luke woke up to lunch being delivered and gladly sat down with his mom and sister to eat. As he ate, he recounted the previous night's events with Weird. They discussed his options and decided that he might as well accept the invite and power level with them. Luke was going to see if he could get a spot for his mom and sister in the power-leveling group. Considering they were also podders he didn't think they would have any issues with it.

"I don't know exactly where I am, but if you can make it to Last Hope, I can ask Weird to pick you guys up." Luke said.

They looked at him with concern on their faces and his stomach dropped.

"What? Did something happen?" he asked, fearing they lost the group with Father.

"No, not really. It's the weather." Cleo explained, "It's been pouring rain since this morning and hasn't let up. We won't be able to meet up with you today, the river is flooded and we can't get across."

Luke cringed, thinking of the spell scrolls he made.

"What did you do?" Cleo demanded, seeing the look on his face.

Luke laughed and explained about the rain scrolls he made for the merchant and how the local farmers may have used them all.

"Do you think it would affect us where we are at?" Cleo asked doubtfully.

"If they used them all at once, it could have affected the overall weather patterns." their mom responded. "That storm we saw yesterday could have intensified or it could have even caused it to stay around longer."

"If you are stuck at camp, what are you guys going to do today?" Luke asked.

"If the rain clears, I will work more on the palisade," Cleo said, "other than that, I'm trying to finish another skill book."

"I'm working on the poisoned blade today." their mom said cheerily.

"So, you are both ok if I power level with Weird?" Luke asked hesitantly.

"Of course!" his mom said reassuringly, "Cleo can try to join up with you when the weather clears and the river calms down. You just have fun."

After he filled up on food, he cleaned up and took one last restroom break then climbed into his pod, ready for a new day.

Storm blinked at the muted light and his eyes adjusted to the new environment. Mildly relieved he found himself still inside the tent. He was sitting on the floor hunched over a script of paper. His hand was still glowing so he kept writing, letting the skill do the work. When his hand had stopped glowing and the magic was gone, he stood up and stretched. He collected his items and put away his gear. As he was putting his stuff away, he inspected the scrolls and gave his avatar a silent 'thank you' for creating more healing touch scrolls.

The tent he was in, was a simple canvas tent with thick wooden poles. It had a simple cot with a knitted blanket on one side and a nice rug laid out in the center. He walked across the room and pushed aside the tent flap and stepped outside. The sun was well overhead and it took his eyes a few moments to adjust. A patrol had taken notice of him and was rushing towards him with swords drawn.

He frantically recalled the instructions Bobby gave him last night, when he woke up, he was to ask the guard outside his tent to get Bobby. He looked at the guard, who stared back at him, wide-eyed and scrambling to pull his sword out of his scabbard.

"Where's Bobby?!?" Storm exclaimed.

"Bobby?" the guard asked, stopping. He seemed to recall something. "Oh, get in the tent and stay there until I get him."

Storm stepping back in the tent and pulled up his map, he saw Bobby's marker a few tents over. It took several minutes, but as he was watching he saw the marker exit the tent and move in his direction. Storm closed his map and waited by the entrance.

"I'm sorry for the wait." Bobby said apologetically, after entering his tent "Follow me, and stay close."

They both stepped out of the tent and Storm followed closely behind. They walked through the camp to the central building.

"Those guards were kind of intense," Storm commented, "I didn't realize people took this game so seriously." He glanced over at another patrol and added, "Although, they don't seem to mind me now."

"Everybody knows not to mess with me." Bobby said, "When they see me, they know it's official business."

"How old are you?" Storm asked, suspecting they were taking advantage of him.

"I'm ten." Bobby replied.

"Bobby, are they forcing you to do this?" he asked.

"I may have understated my role." Bobby said confidently, looking up at Storm with amusement in his eyes. "I run the camp and everybody here knows not to mess with me. Have you even inspected me? Or did you let my diminutive form and age throw you off?" He then turned and continued to the center of the camp, calling out over his shoulder, "I inspected you last night. Not impressed."

Storm had no choice but to follow Bobby and as he did, he inspected him.

[Character sheet

Name: Bobby
Guild: Dark Elite
Race: Human
Level: 67
Health: 1,620 /1,620
Stamina: 1,340/1,340
Mana: 930/930
Stats:

Strength: 159 (+15)
Dexterity: 124 (+10)
Constitution: 142 (+20)
Intelligence: 106
Wisdom: 93
Charisma: 99

Skills:

Hand to hand: Level 52
Your fists are deadly weapons.
+50% defense while in melee combat
Short sword: Level 50
Short swords are an extension of your body.
+50% defense while in melee combat
Cooking: Level 35
You are able to prepare and cook meals that provide minor bonuses
+35% effectiveness of food-based bonuses
Earth Magic: Level 25
You can cast earth magic spells.
+25% to earth magic resistance.
Tracking: Level 45
You can track any animal through any terrain.
+50% to identify animal based on tracks
Stealth: Level 57
You can completely disappear in the shadows.
+50% sneak
Leadership: Level 34
Members of your party gain from your experience
+48% to party member's experience

Spells:
Earth Magic:
    Rock skin:
        Increases armor level by 50
        Target: self
        Cost: 100 mana
        Cast time: Instant
        Cooldown: 60 seconds
    Focused attack:
        Next attack has +50 points of kinetic force
        Target: self
        Cost: 20 mana
        Cast time: 2 seconds
Special Abilities:
    Improved hearing: Level 55
        Your hearing is on a superhuman level. By
        concentrating you can hear sounds up to ten miles
        away. There is nothing that can contain sound from
        you, even minute vibrations can be used to reconstruct
        conversations.]

Realizing Bobby could one-hit him, Storm decided it was best he kept his mouth shut for the rest of the walk.

"Stay here, I'll be right back" Bobby instructed when they got to the stone building and he slipped inside the door.

Storm looked around trying not to be anxious. He was in the middle of a camp full of high-level guards that could send him to respawn with a single hit.

A short time later Bobby poked his head out and said, "Come in, Mr. Weird is ready for you." It was only a couple of minutes but had felt like an hour.

Storm walked into the building with a bit of apprehension. Weird was sitting behind the desk with an empty chair facing him. The older man was studying a map and looking back and forth between a couple of papers. Not wanting to interrupt him, Storm walked up to the chair and sat quietly.

"Have you made a decision?" Weird asked after setting down the papers.

"I'm in, but I have a few questions." Storm said. Weird indicated for him to continue, so he asked "What did you mean about making a run at the world city?"

"I can explain a little." Weird replied, nodding. "It's common knowledge that Server vs Server battle is the endgame for Dark Ages Online, but the method to activate the server battles is not publicly known. Many have guessed that its developer controlled, but in actuality it is done through a hidden quest and only the originals have knowledge of. There has been speculation that taking the World City is the start of the quest chain, but it's not, it's actually one of the last steps."

"So, you are taking us to the server battles?" Storm asked.

"Not exactly," Weird hedged, "we will stop right before we get to that point."

"Why?" Storm curiously.

"We're not ready yet." Weird responded simply.

"Thank you for the explanation." Storm said. He wanted to ask more, but felt that Weird had said all he was going to. Then he boldly said, "I'd like to be in your group when you take the city."

"Why?" Weird asked after staring at him intently for a few moments.

"This is all new to me and I thought it would be fun." Storm said after thinking about it for a moment. In reality he was thinking about the incredible opportunity to pick up some unique skills, but felt awkward saying that.

Weird studied Storm for a moment then smiled as he could read his thoughts.

"Ok, if you can prove yourself useful, you have a deal." Weird said. "The grinding groups gather on the west end of the encampment every few hours." Weird waved his hand and Storm saw a notification and quickly accepted.

[Map
        Add location to map
        Accept
        Decline]

"Show up and you'll get a spot." Weird explained, "If anybody gives you a problem find Bobby." Then Weird looked at Storm thoughtfully. He nodded to himself and looked down, scanning his desk, searching for something. Not finding it, he opened a drawer to the side, whispered something and pulled out a silver disc about the size of his hand. He looked at Storm and said, "If you are serious about wanting to help, take this." And tossed the object to Storm. Storm thanked him and tucked it into his pocket to inspect later.

Weird picked up the papers he had been studying and started reading them once again. Feeling dismissed, Storm turned and slowly walked to the door. He kept thinking how intimidating and unusual this man was. He was lost in thought and almost to the door when Weird called out.

"Here, you'll need this." he said.

A golden prompt appeared in Storm's vision.

[Guild invitation
    Guild: Dark Elite
    Accept
    Decline]

As soon as Storm stepped outside and the door closed behind him. Weird set down the papers and two figures appeared next to him, out of thin air. The one on his left seemed more shadow than avatar. He was covered head to toe in blood-red leather armor and swords. Weird knew this one was dangerous and could poison him five different ways before he could take a breath. The other figure appeared on his right and was by far the more dangerous of the two. He was taller and dressed in colorful cloth armor. As he stood there, he gently tapped the drum at his side.

Breaking the silence, Weird said, "Tell Klar to take the new guy and clear the goblins. Take him all the way down and retrieve the quest item for the next step. And tell her that we need Storm to be level 50."

"So, it's true? He's a copycat?" the minstrel asked in a musical voice.

"Not fully yet," Weird replied, but he has the ability. He also has puzzle breaking, which we are currently in need of."

"This is dangerous" the assassin hissed, "You used your ability on him."

"I needed to see for myself," Weird explained, "Grouping with him would have been too obvious and Bobby couldn't remember all of his skills. He's already accumulated a good amount." Weird paused to take a calming breath and continued, "I understand your concern my friend, but the risk was minimal. He is too low to have been able to copy me."

"I haven't seen a copycat since, you know who." the minstrel said.

"I know, neither have I." Weird said, then he asked, "Is she still upset with me?"

"Yes, she likes this place." the minstrel answered after hesitating.

"It couldn't be helped." Weird said, sighing. "I thought this would be a nice diversion for once, but it might have been a mistake coming here." Weird clenched his fist and continued, "She knows why we are doing this."

"Not everybody understands your exalted genius." the assassin said in a quiet mocking voice, "Stepping on the backs of your allies and enemies alike to reach your lofty goal is a strategy few follow, and even fewer succeed at."

Weird shot the assassin a dark look.

The minstrel put a hand on the assassin's shoulder to keep him from angering their friend further.

"We've all taken the oath," the minstrel said calmly "we will see it through to the end." Pausing for a moment, the minstrel continued gently, "We know what this means to you but don't forget about the ones still here."

TEN

The team

Storm left Weird's office and went straight to the meeting spot indicated on his map. The guard informed him he had just missed the portal for grinding and he would have to wait for the next one in an hour.

Storm found a comfortable spot under a nearby tree and took out the metal disc Weird had given him. He turned it over in his hands, studying it. The hand-sized silvery object was cool to the touch and completely smooth on both sides. He found it remarkable that as he handled it, no fingerprints or smudges were left behind on the mirror-like surface. He inspected it.

[Item

Name: Handheld gaming device
Description: This device contains multiple puzzle games you can use to train the Puzzle Breaking skill.
Crafted by: Weird]

Storm was a taken aback, he would have never guessed it was a skill training device. Since receiving the Puzzle breaking skill, he had been unsure how best to utilize it. This device allowed him to increase its level and effectiveness.

Storm turned the device over in his hands, looking for a way to turn it on. After not finding any, he recalled that most in-game interactions were activated by thought. He tried thinking 'on', and the device's screen lit up.

Storm browsed the different puzzle games and found one he had seen before. He leaned back against the tree to get comfortable, selected the game and played for nearly an hour. He packed the device away after the guard called to him with a warning that the next portal was about to open.

As soon as the azure portal appeared, Storm stepped through and found himself in a completely different environment. It was dark and the ground was covered in snow. Breathing out, his breath hung in the air and he felt a chill starting to invade his body.

Storm was standing on the outskirts of a small mountain camp. The camp was used as a staging point to organize raids into the nearby dungeons. It had a large ever-burning bonfire in the center and was surrounded by a dozen log cabins. Several groups of players stood near the fire warming themselves, chatting excitedly.

A young woman dressed in full plate mail dyed a deep purple with gold trim approached him. Her golden hair blew wildly when a gust of wind kicked up a snow devil. She pushed the golden locks out of her face and looked him up and down.

"Follow me." she said simply, then turned and quickly walked to one of the cabins.

Storm hurried to follow as she strode away, his feet crunching in the snow loudly, while not a single sound came from her. As he caught up, he inspected her.

[Character
        Name: Kat
        Guild: Dark Elite
        Level: 100
        Health: ***/***]

Kat walked up to one of the cabins and banged loudly on the thick wooden door. The door cracked open and somebody peeked out, then opened the rest of the way. A petite woman stood in the doorway with a big grin.

"It's about time" she said. She was a little shorter than Kat and was adorned in full plate mail as well, except hers was golden with purple trim.

"Let us in Klar" Kat whined as she pushed past, "I'm cold!"

Klar snickered and beckoned them into the cabin. A welcoming glow spilled out and Storm could feel the warmth as he approached the doorway. Inside he found an odd assortment of players, his power-leveling team.

A pair of players sat at a small table playing a game of cards. The two were polar opposites. The woman was tall and thin with long, bright green hair and pointed ears. She wore a long pale green robe that flowed to the floor and cradled a six-foot staff in her lap. Across from her sat a short stocky man with red braided hair and a matching beard and moustache. He was garbed in studded leather armor with a large axe leaning against his chair. They both glanced at him when he entered the small room, but quickly went back to their game.

Storm was shocked by their appearances. He didn't realize you could choose other races and for a moment wondered if it was too late to become an elf.

He looked over the rest of the room and his eyes landed on two extremely pale, bald men sitting next to each other on the edge of a thick wood beamed bed. They were obviously twins and were both dressed immaculately in suit and ties. One wore all black and was holding an ivory staff while the other wore all white and was holding a jet-black staff. Both staves had intricate golden carvings along the shaft with a glowing emerald affixed to the top.

The twins looked dismissively at Storm, but gave Kat a huge grin, filled with sharpened teeth and a pair of fangs. Kat walked over and hugged each of them, then sat down on the bed in-between, with their arms intertwined.

The last player in the room, was in the back corner next to the fireplace. They were lounging on the ground with their eyes closed bobbing their head to music only they could hear. The player was the most vibrantly dressed person he had ever seen in or out of game. They wore a hot-pink shirt and bright purple pants with a rainbow scarf tied around their waste. They also wore black knee-high platform boots with a half dozen necklaces of every color and rings on every finger, some sparkling with gemstones.

Multiple times throughout the night, Storm caught himself staring at the player. Each time, he felt his face redden in embarrassment and quickly looked away. The player was one of the most beautiful people he had ever seen and he felt drawn to befriend them.

Storm found an empty spot and stood against the wall awkwardly, trying to stay out of the way in the cramped cabin.

"Put this on before you group." Klar whispered, handing him a small golden amulet with bubbles etched on it

He inspected it, then quickly put it on.

[Item
        Name: Amulet of Ability Deception
        Description: Hide who you truly are
        Effect 1: Grants the ability: Water Breathing
        Effect 2: Hides all other abilities from inspection
        Crafted by: Weird]

He wasn't sure why but they wanted him to hid his ability from the others. He didn't might though, if other players knew what his ability was, they might hold back on using their good skills.

"Ok everybody" Klar called out, "we are all here. Let's get started. First, I want to congratulate the four noobies who will be riding with us. This group is the Alpha grinding group. We are the best at clearing dungeons. Which means you are going to get a ton of xp, but you have to follow the rules.", then she said a little darkly "If you don't you will be sent for respawn." Her eyes got big, "Oh, not by me... probably." Kat snickered and Klar continued, "I'll introduce you to the team and explain how we operate and how you can hopefully not die. So, PAY ATTENTION!"

She looked around the room to ensure she had everybody's attention, then continued.

"I'm Klar," she said, holding a hand to her chest, "I'm leading this raid and we have four different groups with us today, Heal, Pull, XP and Tank. I'm leading the healing group and our responsibilities entail healing and resurrecting you as well as rooting the mobs."

Klar looked around to ensure everybody was paying attention and continued. She pointed at Kat and said, "That is Kat, she is the group leader for pulling. Her group is responsible for collecting and bringing the mobs to us." Then she pointed to the two players on either side of Kat, "The twins are Night and Light, they will lead the xp group with Clover, Mani, Storm and Pipe." Pointing to each in turn. Storm noted that Clover was the elf, Mani was the dwarf and Pipe was the stunningly beautiful person.

"It's a simple strategy," Klar explained, "we pull the mobs, then root and stun them, then AOE them to death. They die, you get xp and we do it again."

Mani raised his hand interrupting her. Klar glanced at him and as if reading his mind said, "Area of Effect." Mani put his hand back down slowly and Klar continued, "Once an area is cleared, we will move and repeat the process." Klar explained each of the rolls in more detail and when there were no more questions she finally said, "When you are ready meet us outside and we will assign you a cabin for the night. Today is about done so we will start early tomorrow morning."

Storm followed everybody outside and watched Kat and Klar walk over to the group of people standing around the fire. He spotted his group forming up around Night and Light so he walked over to join them. As soon as he got there, he received an invitation.

[Group Invitation
        From: Night
        Accept
        Decline]

Storm reached down and touched the amulet around his neck recalling its purpose, and accepted the invitation. He looked up to the group list and saw all six names, Night, Light, Clover, Mani, Pipe, and Storm. Everybody was staring off into space, and appeared to be reading, presumably inspecting each other's character sheets. Storm took few minutes to look over his teammates as well. To streamline his review, he minimized the information he wasn't interested in.

[Character sheet
        Name: Night
        Guild: Dark Elite
        Race: Human
        Level: 75
        >Stats
        Skills:
                Earth Magic: Level 54
                Death Magic: Level 35
        Spells
        Earth Magic:
                Rock skin (Common)
                Poisoned miasma (Uncommon)
        Death Magic:
                Death touch (common)
        Special Abilities:
                Spell synergy: Level 50
                        You have incredible synergy with others while casting
                        spells.
                        +200% Spell Damage for each person you synergize
                        with.]

[Character sheet
        Name: Light
        Guild: Dark Elite
        Race: Human

Level: 77
>Stats
Skills:

       Earth Magic: Level 53

       Life Magic: Level 47

Spells:
Earth Magic:

       Rock skin (Common)

       Poisoned miasma (Uncommon)

Life Magic:

       Healing (Common)

       Resurrection (Rare)

Special Abilities:

       Spell synergy: Level 50

              You have incredible synergy with others while casting spells.

              +200% Spell Damage for each person you synergize with.]

[Character sheet

       Name: Clover

       Guild: Dark Elite

       Race: Elf

       Level: 12

       >Stats

       Skills:

              Bow: Level 5

              Staves: Level 5

              Earth Magic: Level 2

       Spells:

              Earth Shield (Common)

       Special Abilities:

              Telepathy: Level 4

                     You are able to communicate mind to mind with your group members and over long distances with other telepathic friends.

                     Player list: <hidden>]

[Character sheet

       Name: Mani

Guild: Dark Elite
Race: Dwarf
Level: 9
>Stats
Skills:

      Hammer weapons: Level 2
      Axes: Level 5
      Leather armor: Level 2

Spells:
Special Abilities:

      Telepathy: Level 2
          You are able to communicate mind to mind with your group members and over long distances with other telepathic friends.
          Player list: <hidden>]

[Character sheet

    Name: Pipe
    Guild: Dark Elite
    Race: Human
    Level: 15
    >Stats
    Skills:

      Drums: Level 5
      Lute: Level 3
      Singing: Level 4

    Spells:
    Music:

      Drums:

          Speed

      Lute:

          Stun

      Song:

          Warmth
          Mesmerize

    Special Abilities:

      True Beauty: Level 10
          Your beauty is unmatched. NPCs give you more dialog options. Enemies tend to ignore you and miss when they attack.

+10% charisma.
-10% market prices.
-10% to enemy perception when targeting you.
+1% chance to dodge.]

Storm finished looking through their skills and everybody was staring at him, waiting. Of course, he had taken the longest.

"See anything you like?" Pipe said to him, in a quiet musical voice with an alluring smile. Storm sputtered, trying to reply but was too flustered to form a coherent word. Pipe winked at him and Storm's face turn red.

The twins cleared their throats to get everybody's attention, saving Storm from further embarrassment. They gathered everybody around to finish explaining the finer details of power leveling and as they spoke, they interwove their words and finished each other's' sentences.

"When you level, you gain ten points distributed across your stats, Strength, Dexterity, Constitution, Intelligence, Wisdom and Charisma. Six of the points are predetermined, based on your race." They pointed to Storm and continued, "For humans, you will get one point into each stat." then pointed at Clover, "Elves get one point into each stat, except Strength but an extra point into Dexterity." Then they pointed to Mani, "It's the same for Dwarves, one point into everything except Dexterity with an extra point into Strength."

"The four remaining points are determined by your actions during leveling." they continued explaining, "This is particularly important for all of you during power leveling. You need to take some action to direct these points into the stat you want. In general, being active during battle will give you a constitution point. Melee attacks will give Strength and ranged attacks will give you Dexterity. You will get Intelligence and Wisdom for casting spells and if you do nothing you will get Charisma." They then looked at each other and snickered, "If you die too much you will only get points in Constitution and nothing else, so try not to die."

When the twins were done Klar announced, "We are going to reconvene tomorrow at 4 am. I will assign you a cabin for your avatars." She glanced at the ragtag group and sighed, "Before logging out, you should help yourself to the junk room to arm yourselves."

Mani raised his hand and Klar looked at him and narrowed her eyes in agitation.

"It's the one with the red door." she said. Mani lowered his hand, then got a look on his face and quickly stuck it back up. Klar kept glaring at him and slowly said, "Take what is useful, you will find better tomorrow." Seemingly satisfied Mani put his hand down. Klar promptly turned and guided them to their assigned cabins.

After Klar left, Storm and the others walked over to the cabin with the red door. Excited, Mani quickly opened the door and disappeared inside. Clover, Pipe and Storm, a little more subdued, followed him. Storm walked around looking at the piles of junk and junk it was. It seemed most of the contents of the cabin were cast-offs of previous power-leveling groups. Most of the piles seemed to be random low-level items you would find during a dungeon dive. The weapons and armor weren't too great and most had been heavily used.

Storm found several disorderly piles of armor in the back of the cabin, but he couldn't find any chainmail leggings to match his top. He opted for a pair of armor padded cloth pants that seemed to have the most durability. After trying them on, he grimaced at his visage, the deep purple pants clashed greatly with his forest green chainmail top, but he would have to live with the mismatched set until he could find something better.

He discovered a pile of cloaks and tried a few of them on but they offered no combat protection. Just when he was about to pass, he found a thick cloak on the bottom of the pile with long sleeves and a hood. He shook off the dust and tried it on. It was long and black and flowed to the ground. It was very similar to a trench coat but didn't button up. The cloak definitely had seen better days but he didn't think the few holes it had would decrease its trendiness. He inspected it.

[Item

      Name: Simple cloak
      Durability: 25/100
      Armor: 1]

He was surprised it offered any armor value at all. It was comfortable and offered a little warmth. He decided he would keep it.

Next, Storm went on a search to find a new weapon. The short sword wasn't for him. In fact, he didn't think any slashing or stabbing weapons were for him. The game was so realistic, the battle with the wolves traumatized him. When he perused his teammates character sheets earlier, he found an opportunity to try out blunt weapons. He searched around and found a simple solid staff.

He was curious on how his teammates had fared so he walked around to see what they found. Pipe acquired a new set of drums and a lute. Mani was currently trying on different helms and Clover held several extra quivers. They looked at him questioningly and he showed them what he found.

The noobies equipped themselves and sat around the fire talking quietly amongst themselves before logging out.

"How long have you two been playing?" Clover asked Storm and Pipe. She pointed her thumb at Mani and said, "He's new to the guild but I've been following them around for a few months." Then she added excitedly, "This is my first time being power-leveled by an original."

"I was recruited to help tank the world boss." Pipe said in a musical voice.

"Oh!", Clover exclaimed, "That's exciting!" She leaned in conspiringly and whispered loudly, "Mani and I were recruited as spies for the other realms.". She looked at Storm expectantly.

"I'm new to the guild and the game." he said. Not exactly sure on his role. He changed the subject and asked, "How do you know they are originals?"

"You hear things." Clover said mysteriously.

"Do you know how many and who they are?" Storm asked, thinking back to his encounter with the assassin and his musical friend.

"I don't know how many there are." Clover admitted, "But I know of six. Kat and Klar of course. Everybody knows the boss, Weird." She looked around a little nervous then added in a quiet voice, "He also has two shadowy goons that follow him around but I've never seen them." She paused as if considering, then hesitantly continued, "I did hear about one other but he is no longer around. A few months ago, an original died. Apparently, he was pretty close with the two goons but way less scary and was fairly popular in the guild."

"What happened to him?" Storm asked, intrigued.

"Nobody knows," Clover explained, "It's mostly rumor. I only heard about him because there was a petition to officially recognize his death. Weird vetoed it and threatened excommunication if anybody brought it up again."

"Do you know his name?" Storm asked quietly.

"Blynk" she replied solemnly.

ELEVEN

Quest

I'm bored." Sunshine complained, "I completed the palisade yesterday and I want to do something fun today." She stood up, walked over to the small window in their cabin and looked out. The rain had stopped but the river was still flooding, "It's not fair being stuck inside while Storm gets to power level." She glanced at her mom, "I want to see if I can cross the river."

"Do you have any thoughts on how to do it?" Nightshade asked, looking up from her alchemy kit. Nightshade spent most of her time creating health and mana potions and had a decent stock pile. She had created antidote potions too but stopped after a hundred or so.

"Yeah," Sunshine said, "I was thinking about it yesterday while working on the palisade and got a few ideas."

"Well, then I think you should try." Nightshade encouraged, "It's not the greatest time with the weather and all, but because Storm never made it back, I'm running really low on alchemy supplies." She tossed her daughter a small bag and said "Take this, it should be enough to cover the costs, and there are a few potions inside in case you get into trouble."

Sunshine looked inside the bag and her eyes widened in surprise, it was the same style of coin purse her mom had given her previously, except this one was full and contained quite a bit more than what she was expecting. Examining the bag, the UI showed a golden coin in the first slot with a x50 overlaying it. Then in each of the remaining slots held a small vial with a x50 overlayed. The first one was red, the second yellow and the last white. Curious she inspected each.

[Item

    Name: Health potion (Vial)
    Effect: +50 health
    Quantity: 50]

[Item

    Name: Stamina potion (Vial)
    Effect: +50 stamina
    Quantity: 50]

[Item

    Name: Cure poison potion (Vial)
    Effect: Cure poison (common)
    Quantity: 50]

"You made these?" Sunshine asked, surprised.

"After battling the lich," her mom explained, "I thought we should have a few on hand, they are weak but could make the difference." She paused, then added, "I want to make stronger ones but I need more vials."

"I'll get the vials" Sunshine promised, then she grabbed her supplies and walked excitedly to the cabin door. Before exiting, she said, "If I can find a safe place to stash my avatar, I'll meet you for lunch. I also might spend the night in town, depending on the weather."

"Stay clear of the pit in the river." her mom warned, "It may be nothing, but I thought I sensed a presence deep inside."

Sunshine made her way down to the shoreline and felt a cool breeze giving her goosebumps. Even though the rain stopped there was a dampness in the air. She found the game's sensations fascinating and sometimes forgot it wasn't real.

Sunshine pulled up her map and took a few minutes to study it. She was standing in the clearing with their cabin, which was uphill far enough to not be affected by the flooding river. The clearing was in a large forest with a tall rock pillar behind it. The river cut through the forest as far as she could see and her gaze followed to the point of where they crossed. From there, she plotted a path to town and estimated how long it would take to make it there.

Her gaze drifted to the graveyard. She thought of the previous day and their fight with the Lich. The battle thrilled her and she wanted more action, but she committed to making a small boat for the crossing first. She looked over the other interesting locations marked by small dots and was attracted to one that was close to her. It was next to the graveyard but not inside and she vowed to investigate it, if she had the time.

Sunshine made her way to the river crossing. She anticipated the rope being gone or damaged by the storm, but it was still there, swinging gently above the raging river. With the rains, the river had flooded both banks and became a roaring beast.

A few days ago, when they first crossed the river, they waded across without difficulty. Now however, she would easily be swept away in the fast-flowing waters if she tried the same. Her idea, this time, was to build a small kayak-like craft and use the rope to pull herself to the other side.

Sunshine found a suitable tree a few meters away and pulled out her axe and went to work. After cutting down the tree she hallowed out the center for a sitting place then trimmed the whole vessel down to size. As she worked, she thought about Storm and how he was probably having the time of his life. She was happy for him, but this encouraged her to work harder because she wanted to have enough time for a small adventure herself.

She worked on the boat for a few hours and lost herself to the labor of it. When she noticed the time, she realized she was late for lunch and quickly gave her avatar instructions and logged out.

"Hey mom, have you been waiting long?" Cleo asked as she entered the kitchen. Her mom was sitting at the table picking at her food, immersed on her phone.

"I've been here for a bit," her mom replied, "There were a few things I wanted to look into. I left my avatar collecting herbs and I should have enough for another batch of healing potions by the time I get back." She looked up from her phone and asked, "How is your trip going?"

"Great!" Cleo exclaimed, "The boat is almost done and should be ready for the finishing touches when I get back. I left my avatar to work while I ate. After that I was thinking of investigating an interesting location nearby."

"If you can, do it on our side of the river, that way I can help if you get into trouble." her mom said.

Cleo finished lunch, gave her mom a hug and crawled back into the pod.

Back in the game, Sunshine inspected the boat and was surprised to find that her avatar had not only completed the small craft, it had started carving designs of various fish onto the outside. The small boat was big enough to carry two people across the river, or one person with supplies, she was very happy with the result.

It was early enough that she could explore the interesting location near the graveyard and still make it to town and do some shopping before nightfall. She pulled up her map and plotted a path to the small dot next to the graveyard. It was directly north of her and fairly close. She then marked her current location so she could easily return.

Sunshine quickly made her way, through the forest, to her destination, her Born Leader ability greatly assisting her. She slowed when the forest thinned and cautiously stepped out into a small clearing. In the center was a large two-story home that looked entirely out of place.

The brick house had a tile roof and a heavy wooden front door. Each floor held windows with black shudders, a few cracked open to capture the cool breeze. The yard was immaculate with short-cut grass and trimmed bushes and fruit trees.

Sunshine remained alert as she approached the house and knocked on the front door. She waited a few minutes but there was no response. She knows again but louder this time. She was about to scout around but heard footsteps running through the home.

The front door burst open and a young female cat was standing before her. The feline was breathing heavily trying to catch her breath. She was four feet tall standing upright, and had white fur with beautiful blue eyes and a cute pink nose. She wore a lacy white blouse with black trousers and black knee-high boots.

"Welcome traveler" the feline said breathlessly, "I am the mistress of the house. Are you lost?"

"No, are you alone out here?", Sunshine asked with a bit of concern in her voice.

"No, my husband, Frederick, is the caretaker of the local graveyard." the white cat explained. Then she stuck out her paw and introduced herself, "I'm Mia."

"I'm Sunshine, nice to meet you, Mia." Sunshine said as she took the paw and shook it. Then recalling her battle in the graveyard yesterday she asked, "Are you safe here?"

"Oh yes," Mia replied, "My husband takes care of the hostile creatures and ensures they don't come to close to the house." Then she got a worried look on her face and continued, "But he didn't come home last night and I'm a little worried about him." She looked at Sunshine with big eyes and asked, "Would you go to the graveyard and see if he is there? I will give you a few coins for your trouble."

[Quest

Name: Find Frederick

Success condition 1: Find Frederick and report to Mia.

Reward 1: 10g

Success condition 2: Find Frederick and return him to Mia, unharmed.

Reward 2: 50g]

Sunshine nodded in agreement and accepted the quest. She pulled up her map and noticed a small road behind the house leading to the entrance of the graveyard. It happened to be the opposite side of where they entered yesterday. She quickly made her way down the road, but as she neared the graveyard she slowed and took out her bow, recalling the encounter with the skeletons.

Bow at the ready, she cautiously entered the graveyard. Heavy fog permeated the entire grounds and she could only make out the three buildings close to her, the mausoleum in the center was completely enshrouded.

Two of the buildings were concrete and intricately carved on the outside, much like the mausoleum they discovered yesterday. The third building was a bit larger and made of wood with a thatch roof. It had several windows with the shutters drawn. However, she could see a sickly green light peeking out of the cracks.

She swapped her bow for the axe and crept up to the building. Using her recently gained sneak skill, she silently made her way up the wooden stairs and to the closest window. Kneeling there, she listened for a few moments and heard a harsh singing. She couldn't understand the words but there was a distinct rhythm to it. She peaked through the bottom of the blinds and saw a figure standing off to the side of a well-lit room.

The well-dressed feline was about five feet tall with orange fur and tabby markings on his face. He wore black flowing robes and held an obsidian staff. The cat wore small spectacles with a silver crown perched on top of his head. Sunshine inspected him.

[NPC

Name: Frederick

Race: Feline

Level: 15

Health: 235/235]

The singing reached a crescendo and abruptly stopped, then Sunshine saw a bright flash of light and heard a large crack as an oppressive wave passed over her. She heard a low chuckle that turned into a deep laugh.

"You are a pitiful feline," A gravelly voice said, "yet, you deem yourself worthy to summon me again?"

Sunshine peeked through the blinds and saw a new figure standing in the center of the room. He was surrounded by intricate chalk drawings on the floor and nine flickering candles with green flames. Despite the light they produced, the figure was enshrouded in shifting shadows. She inspected him.

[NPC
      Name: ShadowCat
      Race: Demon
      Level: 9
      Health: 800/800]

"I need information" Frederick said firmly, "My wards are strong and they will hold."

"Where is your sacrifice?" ShadowCat asked harshly in his gravelly voice.

"A trade this time, information only." Frederick said less confidently.

"We'll see" ShadowCat scoffed, "what is it you seek?".

"My aunt was killed yesterday." Frederick said to the demon, "I want to know who did it."

"The lich? She was weak." ShadowCat said, chuckling. Then he closed his eyes and raised his arms as shadows swirled around him.

The situation had just gotten really complicated and Sunshine decided she had done enough to satisfy the first portion of Mia's quest and started to sneak away. However, she paused when she heard the demon's next words.

"Fine, a trade." it agreed, laughing. "The woman in the group that destroyed your aunt is there." The hairs on the back of Sunshine's neck stood up and she peaked into the building. The demon was pointing directly at her. Taking this as her cue, she threw stealth to the wind and sprinted towards the forest.

As she was running, she heard the door bang open behind her. She calculated that she should be able to make it to the forest before they caught her.

Unfortunately, just as she thought she was far enough away, she felt her legs give out and her face hit the ground. She couldn't move. A new icon appeared in her UI and she inspected it.

[Debuff
      Name: Stun
      Description: You are stunned and unable to move]

She indigently watched the countdown.

1:42. 1:41, 1:40.

She would have yelled, hit the console, the pod, the ground, something but she couldn't move, she could only stare at that timer.

1:30

Somebody was behind her. She waited tensely for her health to start dropping but instead, the ground moved, sliding away from her. Frederick was dragging her.

1:20

Sunshine closed her eyes and slowed her breathing. Fredrick might still be friendly, he didn't know she was sent by his wife. She thought she still might be able to talk her way out of this.

0:58

Fredrick dragged Sunshine into the building and set her in the corner. She still couldn't move but he had positioned her somewhat comfortably leaning against the wall. He stood up and pointed a small black wand at her.

ZAP!

The timer reset, 1:42, 1:41, 1:40

Sunshine hoped her Board Leader ability, which decreased negative effects, would wear the timer down quicker than Frederick expected. Once it did, she would beat him into submission.

1:30

Frederick walked over to a table in the corner and grabbed several lengths of rope and started tying her up. Having been tied up before, Sunshine thought wryly that Frederick was doing a pretty poor job at it.

1:20

"I want what is owed," the demon cat demanded in his gravelly voice, interrupting Frederick's work. "I provided the requested information AND delivered the object of your desires. Pay me now or be in breach of our contract."

Frederick's eyes widened and he hastily stood up to address the demon.

"There is no breach," he stated angrily, then continued more firmly, "I will give payment for the information, as soon as I confirm it is accurate. We have yet to establish that is the case."

Keeping an eye on the exchange between the two NPCs, Sunshine surveyed the room more closely. The demon cat was standing in the center of a chalk circle with an intricate flowing script encircling it. Patterns and whirls flowed out from the center into the rest of the room with the nine candles positioned at various points in the design, each one sputtering a bright green light. When Frederick walked, he carefully stepped over the chalk and never entered the circle where the demon stood.

Now inside, she got a better look at the demon through the shifting shadows. The demon-cat was short and completely black with a small black lace collar around its neck. It had several collars wrapped around each arm. Sunshine thought they were weird bracelets at first but then noticed a pink one with a bell.

1:05

"I want my payment." ShadowCat hissed impatiently.

"Let's first establish she is who you say she is" Frederick said calmly, "then we talk about payment." he paused for a moment then added, "And demon, our contract was ratified long ago, I know the covenants. Do not threaten me with breach or I shall rescind it."

"As you wish", the demon said smiling, showing his wicked fangs.

0:53

Frederick turned and walked back over to Sunshine and inspected her. "Sunshine?" He asked questioningly. With pursed lips he looked her up and down, searching for clues. His gaze was not unkind, and she could tell he had no malicious intent. He looked at her as if trying to solve a puzzle, then his eyes lit up when he saw the amulet she was wearing. He reached out as if to touch it, then drew his paw back.

"It's true, that's the amulet she wore." Frederick said. Then he asked her, "Why are you here?"

Sunshine struggled to answer him through the paralysis but managed to whisper, "Mia…"

Frederick's ear twitched but she wasn't sure if he had heard her.

"Payment is due. Now!", the demon insisted in his guttural voice.

0:45

"Ok, I agree, you provided the information." Frederick acknowledged as he walked back to ShadowCat. "And in turn, I shall provide you this information."

ShadowCat sniffed and crossed his arms.

0:30

"Below this graveyard is a catacomb of tombs." Frederick said.

"Yes, this is well known." ShadowCat said impatiently, waving his paws for Frederick to get on with it.

"At the bottom there is a secret chamber containing items my grandfather created." Frederick continued, undeterred.

"Mere trinkets" the demon interrupted.

"Artifacts, like your collar and my crown." Frederick shot back.

"Ahh, so that's where he moved them." the demon said, his smile widening. "I was curious why you raised your aunt. You are trying to recover them." it surmised.

"Yes," Frederic replied, "and this is a *family* secret, demon. I remind you of the bindings. You are not allowed to share this information with outsiders."

0:15

"I don't make trades for useless information," the demon growled, "what else do you have?"

"A trade of information was made and completed," Frederick said firmly, "we are done."

"You are pitiful. You are not your grandfather. You do not have the strength to command me." the demon shouted angrily, "I want payment."

0:03

0:02

0:01

0:00

Sunshine watched the timer reach zero and once the stun icon disappeared, she regained control of her body. Frederick was distracted with ShadowCat so she quietly reached down and removed the terribly tied ropes around her legs. She gently picked up her backpack and started creeping towards the door.

Facing ShadowCat, Frederick raised his arm, hands glowing.

"ShadowCat, I unsummon…" he started to say, but before he finished, the floorboards creaked behind him. Fearing an attack, he whirled around to defend himself. Sunshine had made it to the door. He reached into his pocket and pulled out the black wand.

Sunshine turned, knowing her escape was compromised. She met Frederick's eyes and saw the black wand in his hand. She did the only thing she could think of and hurled her backpack at him. Frederick stumbled out of the way and before he could bring the wand to bear, Sunshine was next to him with fists raised. As a wall of chalk dust surrounded them, she swung at him with all her anger and connected with his feline face. Frederick's head snapped back and he lost his grip on the wand as he crumpled to the floor.

Breathing heavily, Sunshine stared down at the mage, trying to decide what to do when she felt an oppressive weight overcome her. Shadows slowly spread throughout the room and the green lights dimmed to nothing. She heard a deep chuckle echo around the room and saw a small black figure slowly stalking towards her and the downed mage. Sunshine backed up towards the door, keeping her eyes on the shifting form.

ShadowCat bent down and picked up Frederick with one paw. Surprised by his strength, Sunshine knew she was out of her depths. She slowly retreated and glanced at her bag with a bit of regret at knowing she would have to leave it behind. When she threw it at Frederick it slid across the room cutting a path through the patterns of chalk on the floor before coming to rest against the far wall. It was now unretrievable.

Held aloft, Frederick's eyes flickered open and he met Sunshine's. "Run… Mia…" the mage whispered.

The demon's lace collar glowed brightly and he plunged his claw into Frederick's chest. Frederick screamed while ShadowCat fished around for something. Then, seemingly finding what he was looking for, the demon smiled and withdrew his paw, holding a small black collar. Enthralled, Sunshine couldn't look away as the demon wrapped it around his wrist and buckled it alongside the others.

"Payment received." the demon announced cheerfully then unceremoniously dropped Frederick to the ground and turned to Sunshine. His glowing green eyes bored into her.

Sunshine felt goosebumps run down her arms and knew she was in imminent danger. Without any forewarning, the demon sprang towards her with claws outstretched. She instinctively raised her fists to defend herself. She quickly sidestepped and ducked under one claw then threw a punch at ShadowCat's undefended side. She lost her balance when her fist passed through his incorporeal body.

The demon twisted and sliced up towards Sunshine's face. Sunshine leaned back and jabbed at the cat's arm as it flew by but once again her fist passed though the cat as if it were made of nothing. The demon slashed at her with its other claw and she stepped back again. The demon smiled wickedly at her, knowing he had the upper hand and kept moving forward, slashing as he went.

She kept retreating and furtively thought through different ways to turn the tide and her thoughts landed on Frederick's wand. She pivoted in the direction she thought it had dropped. The demon cat slowly followed her, its thin smoky tail twitching angrily behind him.

He took a quick step towards her, slashing with both claws and she easily dodged him again. Except this time, when she took a step back, she stepped on a small round object that rolled out from under her foot, causing her to fall to down. ShadowCat sprang on top of her, sinking both claws deep into her shoulders.

Sunshine screamed and swung wildly trying to dislodge the demon. She saw the cat disappear and she quickly got to her hands and knees trying to push herself up. A weight landed on her back and a claw thrust inside her. Her arms and legs buckled as her body was wracked by unbearable pain.

Sunshine felt the ground pressed against her face as the demon's claw fished around inside her for something. Finally, after what seemed like an eternity of pain, ShadowCat pulled it's claw out and as he did, she felt a ripping inside her. A coldness spread throughout her chest. She thought she was dying and was ready for its release but the pain passed and soon the demon was no longer on top of her.

Sunshine moved to a sitting position, breathing heavily and looked at the demon with pure hatred. In his hand, he was holding a bright golden snap bracelet. She noticed a new icon and inspected it.

[Debuff

      Name: Collar of Essence

      Effect: -10% to combat damage

      Duration: Permanent]

The demon smiled at her and gave a mocking bow then snapped the bracelet onto its arm.

Sunshine was angry. She had been repeatedly stunned, beaten up, and now this lowly mob gave her a permanent debuff. She searched her options and came up with something new. She got to her feet and took a step toward the smiling demon. She activated her amulet and received the Spectral Hands buff.

[Buff

      Name: Spectral hands

      Effect: Melee attack ignores armor

      Duration: 5 minutes]

ShadowCat stood there, smiling, knowing there was nothing this human could do to harm it but he had relied on his invulnerability for too long. Sunshine swung with all her frustration and anger. Moments before she struck the demon's face, her fist crackled with power. He was completely unprepared for the brutality of the magically charged strike and fell to the ground, unconscious.

"Really?!?" Sunshine growled angrily, standing above the demon, panting. "That's all you can take?" She inspected him.

[NPC

        Name: ShadowCat

        Race: Demon

        Level: 9

        Health: 700/800

        Status: Unconscious]

She knelt next to the unconscious demon, took the snap bracelet, and inspected it.

[Item

        Name: Snap Bracelet of Sunshine

        Effects: +10% to combat damage.

        Description: Created using the Collar of Essence]

She wasn't sure how to cancel the permanent debuff but just as she snapped it onto her wrist, the bracelet disappeared along with the debuff. She looked at the demon with distaste and noticed there were at least a dozen collars strapped to its body and no two were alike. Many were different colors and styles and a few even had cute little charms attached to them. She took the one that she saw the demon remove from Frederick and inspected it.

[Item

        Name: Collar of Frederick

        Effects: +10% death magic resistance

        Description: Created using the Collar of Essence]

She strapped it onto her wrist and pulled up her stats and saw that she now had a 10% resistance to death magic. She quickly stripped the demon of the remaining collars. As she was removing the last few, the demon stirred. She only had a few seconds left on the Spectral Hands timer and quickly punched the demon back to unconscious. Still angry from earlier she hit him a few more times just to be sure.

She then removed the collar around the demon-cat's neck. It was made of fine black lace, woven into a beautiful spider web pattern. She inspected it.

[Artifact

        Name: Collar of Essence

        Description: Grants the wearer the ability to pull the essence out of other beings. Only usable once per person. Reach into their soul and pull out a piece.

Crafted by: Fluffy]

Her hands shook as her adrenaline receded and she thought to herself that she needed to get out of there but these cats had pissed her off and they owed her for all the trouble. She put the Collar of Essence on and smiled as it fit snug on her neck, just like a choker. She knelt by the demon cat and activated the collar.

Just as she had seen him do, she reached down and put her hand on its chest and gently pushed. She felt a small resistance as her hand entered the demon's body and it easily passed through skin and bones. As her hand made its way deeper inside the demon, she felt a numbing cold work its way up her fingers and into her hand. She felt around, not sure what she was looking for but eventually found a small object and wrapped her fingers around it. A flare of heat envelope her hand but quickly dissipated as she pulled out the object.

In her hand, she was holding a small black collar with tendrils of smoke rising from it. She inspected it.

[Artifact
        Name: Collar of ShadowCat
        Effect 1: +50% stealth
        Effect 2: Smokey shadows
        Special ability: Phase out, 1 minute cooldown
        Description: Created using the Collar of Essence]

Sunshine decided it was past time for her to leave. She retrieved her pack from the backwall and dusted it off. Then she stuffed the other collars inside, intending to inspect them later. As she was putting them away a pink one caught her eye.

[Item
        Name: Collar of Mia
        Effect: +10% charisma
        Description: Created using the Collar of Essence]

Grimacing at the prompt, she dismissed it and walked back to ShadowCat. She happily burned another charge on her necklace and slammed her fist into the demon cat's face with great pleasure. As the demon disappeared, she received a surprise, several chimes and a column of multicolored balls of light.

[Level up: Level 6]

[Level up: Level 7]

On the other side of the room Frederick coughed from the dust still hanging in the air. It was time to deal with the mage. She cautiously approached him and scanned for the wand but it had rolled across the room when she slipped on it earlier.

When she got to him, he was just getting up on his hands and knees. Upset about what he did, she kicked him as hard as she could. But as her foot was about to connect it started glowing and she tried to pull back, unfortunately it was too late.

Frederick flew through the air and landed a dozen feet away. Sunshine had forgotten the spell was active and was surprised it had worked with her foot. Frederick lay there groaning, clutching his midsection in pain. She rushed to his side and tried handing him a health vial but when he saw her running at him, he screeched and started sliding away on the ground.

"Don't kill me…" he begged.

"I'm sorry, I didn't mean to kick you so hard." Sunshine explained. She stopped and raised her hands to show him the health vial and she didn't mean him further harm. She slowly approached him and handed him the vial. When he coughed up blood after drinking, she handed him another.

She let him lay there for a few moments to recover while she searched the rest of the room. She retrieved the dreadful wand and found his silver crown which had broken into two halves. She stuffed the crown into her bag but kept ahold of the wand.

"Are you ok?" she asked him as he stood up.

"I think so" he moaned.

"Good" she said, then pointed the want at him and activated it.

TWELVE

Buffs

Storm's eyes refocused as the virtual world took shape around him. He lay on a cot inside the cabin Klar had assigned him. He looked around and saw Mani across the room sitting on his own cot, rummaging through a bag.

"Hey Mani," Storm said, sitting up yawning.

"Good morning, did you get enough beauty sleep?" Mani teased.

"Maybe you should ask Pipe." Storm said, chuckling.

"Yeah, probably." Mani laughed. A thought crossed the dwarf's face and he asked "You ask your sister?"

Before logging off Mani and Storm spent some time getting to know each other. Storm recognized that Mani was also using a pod and they talked a little about New Las Vegas. Mani told Storm about his life in the Midwest and his monthly trips to New Las Vegas, playing a different game each time. He said he got lucky with his special ability, which of course was why Dark Elite had recruited him. Storm reciprocated by telling him about his family and why they were playing the game.

"No," Storm replied laughing, "I didn't ask her out for you. That's something you need to do, and it's your funeral." Storm looked him over and added, "Besides, I'm not sure you're her type."

"Eh, I hear ya." Mani said, looking down at his body, "This isn't exactly what I look like though, the game adjusted my avatar to look more like a dwarf. Just like Clover, I guarantee she's not that tall!"

"Ok, ok, if she catches up to us, I'll introduce you." Storm promised, "But you have to plead your own case."

Mani nodded in concession, then walked towards the door and asked "You ready to go?"

Storm picked up his pack and followed Mani outside. He immediately felt the cold and pulled his cloak around him.

"Ugh, I know" Mani said beside him, shivering "Just a few minutes in the real world and the body forgets. It's almost better to stay in-game." Storm nodded in agreement and pulled his cloak tighter.

"Oh, come on boys, it's not that bad" Clover laughed as her and Pipe speed up to the group. They stopped in front of Storm and Mani, their clothes flapping wildly, a gust of snow following. Little music notes danced around their feet as Pipe tapped a steady rhythm on his drum.

"Maybe if your little canary here whistled a different tune, you would be too." Storm said, grimacing as the gust of snow hit him. As they approached Storm noticed Pipe was beating his drum for the speed effect but he was also quietly whistling.

"You're pretty observant." Clover said laughing. She nodded to Pipe and he dropped the tune. As soon as he did, they both shivered and appeared more uncomfortable.

"That's an interesting trick" Storm said to Pipe, "I didn't know you could do two songs at once." Before they logged off last night, he had asked Pipe about minstrels and he learned they use musical methods to produce spell-like affects. Storm had tried to copy his speed buff but there seemed to be some level of real musical talent needed, which he didn't have. Maybe with more practice he would try again.

"Tomb taught me how to do it," Pipe said with a charming smile, "he called it weaving and told me I needed to be able to weave three songs. Speed, insta stun and charm on a high-level pet, all without it eating me of course." He laughed and everybody in the room smiled at him.

"How long until we start?" Storm asked Clover.

"We came to collect you" she said, "Klar just called a ten-minute warning and told us 'noobs' to meet by the fire."

Pipe tapped his drum and Storm felt a small vibration spread throughout in his body. He looked around in amazement at the snow hanging in the air. Pipe winked at him, then turned and walked towards the large bonfire with Clover following close behind. Mani and Storm looked at each other and shrugged then they both zoomed off as well.

When they arrived, Klar fished a scroll out of her bag and cast it. The scroll crumpled to dust and an azure portal opened. She turned to address the group.

"When everybody is through the portal," she explained, "we will make our way to the dungeon as a group. Once there, we will clear the immediate area and setup for pulling mobs." She pointed to the four noobies and said, "You four, stay out of the way until it is safe. Don't die. We will give you buffs and Night and Light will inform you when it's time to join the battle."

Storm followed the group through the portal and on the other side, his feet crunched down on uneven rock. In contrast to the snowy mountain, he felt the heat rise drastically, sweat forming on his brow. He breathed in the acrid air and was reminded of his first day in game when he landed in the forge. He smiled at the thought of Father and vowed to rescue him when he was done with power leveling.

Storm was standing on an open plain of black volcanic rock that stretched as far as he could see. To the north, hills grew into a mountain range. Beyond that, a massive volcano rose into the sky, with rivers of lava pouring down its sides. The other directions were all the same, a barren rocky landscape. A haze hung near the ground, stinging everybody's eyes.

Klar and Kat lead the raid group north, towards the hills, their column of troops winding its way through the desolate landscape. Storm saw flashes of light near the front of the column as the vanguard took out roaming mobs. His group was near the back with the healers, where it was relatively safe. He glanced at Mani and saw that he was carrying on a silent conversation with Clover. He had gotten used to the look on his new friends' faces when they were communicating telepathically.

"Just practicing," Mani said chuckling when he noticed Storm's look. "We were discussing how excited we were to raid with Kat and Klar."

"I can't wait to see what they can do." Clover exclaimed, excitement dancing in her eyes. "They are legends."

After an hour of traversing the foreboding land, they approached the hills. They were covered in small scraggly trees that seemed more dead than alive with a thicker haze hanging in the air. Storm could smell the undistinguishable scent of burning wood but when he looked around, he couldn't find the source.

"Campfires?" he whispered questioningly.

Klar looked at him with surprise and nodded in confirmation, then announced loudly, "Listen up everybody! We are going to take a break here. There is a valley up ahead filled with trash mobs that Kat and I will clear, then we will proceed to the dungeon."

"I'm ready Klar," a beautiful voice called from behind Storm. "Where do you need me?"

Storm turned and was instantly mesmerized by the most stunning woman he had ever seen. She had a dazzling smile and her eyes were alite with passion and happiness. She had care written all over her face and without even meeting her, Storm knew she was kind soul.

It took him a few moments before he realized he was staring. He tried to pull his eyes away but like a moth to flame, he couldn't.

"Owe" he exclaimed as Mani jabbed in him in the ribs.

"Yer being too obvious lad." Mani warned quietly in his deep voice.

Storm took the advice in stride, as well as the jab. He turned back to Klar and the new woman, trying not to blatantly stare at her.

"Good morning, Sapphire." Klar said with a smirk, Storm's behavior had not gone unnoticed. "I think this is a good spot, is everybody in range?"

"Yup, they sure are." Sapphire responded with a smile, oblivious to Storm's attention. "Shall I begin?" she asked.

Klar held up her hand for her to wait, then reached into her bag and pulled out a four-foot wooden totem. She set it on the ground and tapped the crystal on top which caused it to pulsate an azure color, at the same time Storm's mana bar started glowing with a small 3x above it.

Klar moved Sapphire around, seemingly looking for the perfect spot. Finally, after a couple of minutes, Klar instructed, "Do it now."

Sapphire stood directly in front of Storm staring into his eyes. They looked at each other with confused looks, then Sapphire got a huge grin on her face and threw her hands out wide causing her cloak to fly off her shoulders and flutter to the ground. She brought her arms together in a quick motion, each hand glowing, with fingers rapidly dancing in different patterns.

The look in her eyes was captivating. She exuded pure joy and Storm couldn't help but smile. He stared at her, her gorgeous face and incredible smile effectively stunning him. However, the effect was broken when she completed her spell and a ball of white light shot towards him and struck him in the chest. The magical ball exploded and sent a shockwave outward, encompassing the rest of the raid.

Sapphire started casting another spell and Storm couldn't pass up the opportunity to learn more magic. He forced himself pay attention and just like the first spell, a ball of light struck him in the chest and exploded, although this one was a different color. Storm heard the notification he successfully copied the spell but he didn't have time to read it as Sapphire had begun casting again.

This time, Storm didn't just watch her, he moved his hands in the same pattern, copying her. He glanced up and Sapphire was watching him with a curious look. Storm completed his spell moments after Sapphire completed hers and two identical balls of magic raced through the air.

Sapphire's spell struck Storm first and exploded as expected. And in the short time between the two spells finding their respective targets, a tension hung in the air. The two had captured the attention of the entire raid, and everybody watched Storm's spell with anticipation.

His spell struck her and nothing happened, the explosion he expected never came.

Sapphire watched him for a moment, her head tilted slightly. A small smile formed on her lips and she mouthed, "You copied me."

Storm shrugged in return.

Sapphire got a smirk on her face and started casting. She cast spell after spell, faster and faster. Each one was different and it took all of Storm's concentration to follow the speed of her movements. After each spell though, he heard the expected chime of the notification.

"That was fun" Sapphire said after her last spell, then turned to Klar and asked, "Ready for the next ones?"

Storm quickly glanced at the notifications, keeping the descriptions minimized. He was thrilled, when he was copying the spells, he wasn't sure what they were but suspected something beneficial. Buffs were exactly what he needed in his spellbook.

[New spell obtained: Strength buff (Life magic)]

[New spell obtained: Dexterity buff (Life magic)]

[New spell obtained: Constitution buff (Life magic)]

[New spell obtained: Intelligence buff (Life magic)]

[New spell obtained: Wisdom buff (Life magic)]

[New spell obtained: Charisma buff (Life magic)]

[New spell obtained: Health buff (Life magic)]

[New spell obtained: Stamina buff (Life magic)]

[New spell obtained: Mana buff (Life magic)]

"Yeah, I'm ready, just do me and Kat." Klar instructed, "And we only need Fire for the elemental buff."

Sapphire nodded, then paused glancing at Storm. She moved so her hands were directly in his line of sight, then with a knowing smile, started casting. Each spell caused a different colored light to spread over Klar's body like a magical shield.

Storm copied every spell.

[New spell obtained: Pierce resistance (Life magic)]

[New spell obtained: Slash resistance (Life magic)]

[New spell obtained: Blunt resistance (Life magic)]

[New spell obtained: Enhance armor +300% armor (Life magic)]

[New spell obtained: Fire resistance (Life magic)]

Storm dismissed the notifications and found Sapphire watching him. She winked at him then walked off without another word. He felt his face flush and was startled by a voice.

"Wow, her buffs are pretty amazing." Clover said from behind him.

"Why did her spells explode like that?" Storm asked.

"Oh that!" Clover said excitedly, "I bet she has an ability to cast her spells as AOE or can cast on multiple targets at once. Both are rare and quite coveted for spellcasters."

"Is she an original?" Storm asked.

"Sapphire?" Clover said, "I've never seen her before."

As they walked towards the hills, Storm reviewed the spells he had just obtained. Each one was almost exactly the same with a minor alteration. By comparing them together, he was able to see which part of the spell indicated the type of buff it was.

Storm grew excited at what he found. He compared all of his other life spells and identified the targeting parameter. His buff spells took a single target where his healing spell required touch. To add to the mix, the resistance spells he just picked up targeted items like armor and clothing.

He looked over all of his spells and they all seemed to have the same structure but each spell school was a different language. He recognized patterns between them but didn't quite understand the words yet. He thought that if he had more examples, he would be able to figure it out. Even though the meaning was hidden in mystery he thought he could move some pieces around.

Using the strength buff as a baseline, he started casting it. He slowly formed the symbols with his hands and whispered the words. When he came to the part that indicated it was a strength buff, he changed it. He used the healing symbol from his healing touch spell instead.

When he finished the spell, his mana drained and he saw a bright light encompass him. He blinked away the afterimage and heard the chime of several notifications. However, before he could pull them up, he found Klar standing in front of him.

"Did you just do what I think you did?" she asked quietly.

"I... I think so..." Storm stammered back.

"Interesting." She said, then without another word, she turned and walked back to the front of the raid.

Storm glanced at the prompts, then silently exalted in his success.

[New skill obtained: Spell Crafting]

[New spell obtained: Healing buff, health pool +(Life Magic level * 100) HPs]

He numbly followed the group, mind buzzing about the spells he could tinker with. His resistance spells targeted individual pieces of gear but when Sapphire had cast them, she only cast each of them once on Klar, lending weight to the theory that she had an ability that either allowed her to cast on multiple targets or all of her spells were AOE.

Wondering if he could learn it, he tried to change one of his resistance spells to multiple targets, but it failed. He wasn't dissuaded though. He had another idea.

His cloak covered most of his body, his arms, head, torso and legs. Rather than cast the resistance spell on each piece of armor, he cast his resistance spell on his cloak and it worked, his entire body received the increase in resistance rather than a single section.

Encouraged by his success, Storm experimented more. In his fire resistance spell, he recognized the fire symbol. It was the same as the Fire Spell School symbol. He replaced this symbol using the other spell schools he knew.

[New spell obtained: Air magic resistance (Life magic)]

[New spell obtained: Life magic resistance (Life magic)]

[New spell obtained: Death magic resistance (Life magic)]

[New spell obtained: Water magic resistance (Life magic)]

THIRTEEN

Power leveling

The raid had stopped moving and was spread out. They halted close to the mouth of a valley that cut through the hills but were far enough away that Storm couldn't get a good look inside. However, he saw the glow of campfires emanating from the valley and a rust-colored haze hovering above it.

Kat and Klar were standing at the mouth of the valley casually chatting back and forth but they were too far away for him to hear. Suddenly, two small figures darted towards them, they moved so fast their forms burred and it appeared the two warriors hadn't noticed. Storm's grip tightened on his staff but before he could yell, Kat swiftly turned and slammed her massive golden tower shield into the ground. A plum of dust rose and Storm heard a boom as the shield connected with the ground. The two figures darted around the shield and behind Kat.

Storm watched with concern as the two dark figures penetrated Kat's defensive barrier. However, he was put at ease when he noticed small musical notes drifting off their boots. They were minstrels. Storm looked in the direction of where the two had come and a hoard of creatures ran ferociously after the pair. The guttural chants and war cries reached his ears and he worried for them all.

A golden light encompassed the small group and Kat's shield replicated itself over and over until they were completely surrounded. The glowing transparent shields created an impenetrable shield wall, the shape reminding Storm distinctly of a turtle shell. He wasn't disappointed when an ethereal glow emanated from the shell and a ghostly turtle head poked out to snap at the approaching creatures with its piecing beak. Vicious claws defended each side and a spiked tail swept behind them.

Klar stood in the center, holding her great sword above her head with one hand. A small glow formed at the tip, slowly getting brighter and brighter. Klar rose into the air, ethereal wings outstretched, her sword aloft.

Klar swung her arm down and a glowing ball shot towards the enemy and burst into hundreds of smaller balls of light, each leaving a lasting impression in

Storm's sight. The balls of light transformed into birds. Some were large and fearsome like eagles and hawks, but others were smaller birds like crows and sparrows and possibly even a humming bird here and there. Each bird raced towards an enemy and regardless of their size, when they reached them, it was a massacre.

Storm squinted through the blinding brightness and when it finally dimmed, he could survey the result, each goblin had been torn to shreds. Not a single enemy survived. The sounds that came from the raid group indicated that they were no less awed than he was.

For a moment Storm was encircled by rainbow-colored glowing orbs and he heard several chimes.

[Level up: Level 7]

[Level up: Level 8]

"How did we get experience? We aren't in their group." Storm asked, leaning close to Clover.

"We got xp from being in the raid group." Clover explained, "Imagine how much we would have gotten if we were in her group."

"Hey Clover, do you think you can teach be a few moves?" Storm asked, hefting his staff. He picked the staff up yesterday specifically with the intention of copying Clover's staff wielding skill. He didn't exactly need her help to copy it, but it made him feel a little better asking.

"I can try." she said, "But I'm no trainer."

"I'm a quick study." Storm said confidently, "Let me see what you got."

"Sure thing," she said, "But we should wait until we get to the power-level spot." She nodded towards Kat and Klar, who were approaching them, "It looks like it's time to go."

"It's time to go everybody!" Klar announced, "Pick up your gear, we are heading through the valley and into the dungeon. Do not stop until we get there, the air in the valley is tainted."

The entire raid started jogging at a slow pace towards the valley. The leading group pulled away, suddenly moving faster. Just as Storm worried about being left behind, he felt his body lighten and the world around him slowed slightly. He glanced over and saw Pipe gently tapping on his drums.

In the valley, the air was still and acrid, it stung Storm's eyes and hurt the back of his throat. Now he understood why they cleared the valley first, fighting through this would have been torturous. His health meter flashed green and a poison icon appeared. He brought up the information, and instantly thought that his mom would appreciate the valley.

[Poisoned: Caustic smoke from Manchineel tree, -20% vision, -5 hp/second]

After a few unpleasant and painful minutes, the raid finally came to a mountain wall. The wall was carved in the shape of a large building with columns stretching a hundred feet into the air. A large bronze door sat against the mountain. It was etched with designs depicting scenes of massive battles between elves, dwarfs and humans. Several players hurriedly stepped up to the door and pulled it open so the others could rush inside.

Storm neared the entrance to the mountain but before reaching it, he diverted his path and ran past one of the goblin camps. He quickly scooped up one of the branches the creatures used for firewood and shoved it into his pack. He knew his mom would want a sample.

Finally, reaching the end of the valley, Storm barely slowed as he ran up to and through the doorway, into the mountain. It took a few moments for the poison to wear off. When it did, he took a deep breath and was comforted by the musty smell of the dungeon. Rubbing the last vestiges of the irritant from his eyes, he heard Klar address the group.

"Stay here for a bit, rest and recover from the poison." Klar instructed, "We are going deeper into the dungeon to setup at the power-level spot. When you see the group teleport summons, accept it." She disappeared with a few others down a tunnel leading away from the entrance.

Nearby mages cast glowing lights to push back the darkness and Storm could see more of the large antechamber he was in. Several heavily-armored goblin guards lay piled against the far wall. A battle had been fought here when the first players entered but with their high levels, they easily overtook the defenders.

Storm listened in as his friends quietly discussing the battles they just witnessed.

"What on earth were those spells?" Mani asked.

"I think they were world items." Clover whispered, "They were way OP, even the best player-crafted weapons or boss drops aren't that powerful." She excitedly continued, "This is what I wanted to see!"

"Pipe, how did they pull all of the mobs from the valley?" Storm asked, unable to help himself from contributing to the conversation.

"Pets." Pipe answered in his musical voice, "Their pets may have died or they may have released them but minstrels can charm high level mobs, but it can be dangerous. We have to reestablish the charm every 30 seconds and if they resist or it fails three times in a row, the pet will turn on us. They can be so unhappy when that happens."

"Clover, have you ever been here?" Storm asked.

"No," she answered, shaking her head, "this isn't a normal power-level spot. I believe this is the Fire Temple, one of the six temples that represents the branches of magic. There is Earth, Air, Fire, Water, Life and Death. I'm not complaining but I'm not sure why they brought us here, there are more efficient places to power level."

Storm was about to ask another question but was interrupted by a prompt.

[Group summons
        Name: Light
        Accept
        Decline]

"Looks like it's time." Storm said and quickly accepted the invitation.

The world in front of him swirled into a blurry mess of colors, then the swirling slowed and the colors coalesced into a large underground cavern. Storm was standing on a plateau jutting out from the wall in an underground cavern.

A mage near him cast large magical balls of light that hung in the air, lighting the underground cave. Down, on the floor, Night and Light sat in a large chalk circle next to a four-foot wooden totem with an azure glowing gem on top.

"Ok noobies," Klar said, walking up to Storm and his group. "It's time to start. The basic gist is, we will pull mobs to this room. Then Night and Light will AOE DOT them. After this, they should have enough aggro that you can join the battle and not get attacked. Remember, your stat gains when you level depend on your actions, so don't be lazy. Power leveling is hard work." She looked at Pipe and winked at him. "One more thing, it can get a bit hectic down there, so don't feel bad if you die. Just stay put and one of the mages will rez you when they can."

Klar walked to the edge of the plateau and jumped off. Storm and the rest of his group rushed to the edge to see her land twenty feet below and continue walking, barely pausing her stride. Storm considered attempting it but Clover grabbed his arm and dragged him to the wall.

"Maybe we should take the long way down." she said, pointing to a ramp that led to the ground level.

Storm laughed, then walked down the steep trail with his friends. At the bottom were several high-level guild members decked head-to-toe in black plate armor with golden trim. They were lounging around chatting next to four pulsating totems, each with a different colored gem on top. One emanated a blue color, which he had seen before and gave a mana buff. One glowed red and he connected that with the health buff just received and the glowing yellow one was obviously for the stamina buff. The last totem had a black gem on top and seemed to absorb the light. He didn't see any buffs in his UI so he wasn't sure what it was for.

The small group of friends walked up to Night and Light, and the twins turned to greet them.

"The first group is on the way." Light said excitedly.

"If you need a break, head to the totems." Night said, waving his arm back towards the plateau.

"The guards there will ensure your safety." Light added.

"Stay behind us until we DOT the mobs," Night instructed.

"Then feel free to engage." Light finished. The two turned back towards the opening in the cavern leading deeper into the dungeon.

Storm looked at Clover with a questioning look and lifted his staff.

"Sure" she said laughing, remembering Storm had asked her to teach him a few moves, "but remember, it took me a few hours with a trainer."

Clover taught him everything she learned from the trainer. She showed him how to hold the weapon properly and a few methods of striking and defending.

Finally, she told him he should practice and with some good luck he would unlock the skill, little did she know he already did.

[New skill obtained: Staves]

They heard a rumbling from deeper in the dungeon and broke off their impromptu training session. Storm glanced around at his team and realized they were missing Pipe. He looked back towards the plateau and saw the minstrel sitting on the edge casually kicking his legs. Storm tilted his head questioningly and Pipe gave him a smile and a small wave. Hearing the thunderous approach of countless mobs, Storm turned and readied himself.

Two figures appeared out of the tunnel, running with magically enhanced speed, towards his group. Storm quickly recognized them as the minstrels from earlier, the same two that pulled the mobs for Kat and Klar. They continued running until reaching the safety of the totems and high-level tanks. As they sped past, Storm felt a whirlwind tug his cloak.

Storm looked in the direction the two speedsters had come from and found a hoard of large goblins, running directly towards him. He held his staff, nervous, as the enemy would easily overwhelm his group. Just as the mobs were about to crash into him, a melody drifted from behind. Within seconds, every goblin stood frozen, staring off into space with little musical notes dancing around their heads.

Night and Light began casting and Storm watched them intently. Both cast the same spell, in unison. Their hands glowed bright green and each wore a manic smile. Suddenly the spell came to an end and the green light pulsated outwards. Clouds of sickly-green smoke surrounding each goblin for a second then disappeared.

Storm glanced at his notifications.

[New skill obtained: Earth magic]

[New Spell obtained: Poisoned miasma (Earth spell)]

As soon as the smoke disappeared the goblins received the damage-over-time affect and it broke them out of their trance. Many goblins ran around screaming, attacking friend and foe alike but others maintained their sanity and approached Storm's group with a deadly intent.

One of the goblins ran towards Storm with rage in its eyes. Storm swung his staff at the goblin's head. The goblin raised its rusty sword and easily deflected the blow. Storm followed up with a swing from the other side but once again the goblin easily blocked it. Their weapons locked, the goblin stepped forward and punched him in the chest.

Storm fell to the ground wheezing, trying to catch his breath. The health in his meter drained away and just when it was about to bottom out, a bright light surrounded him refilling his health bar with color. He lay there for a few moments trying to recover but the goblin had other plans.

The creature reached down and picked him up, holding him aloft. The goblin pulled back to punch Storm in the face when suddenly the arm holding him disappeared and was replaced by a fountain of green blood. Storm fell to the ground and watched Mani casually swing his axe and lop off the goblin's head.

"That one had a few levels on ya" Mani said as he held out a hand.

"I'll stay away from the bigger ones." Storm conceded and accepted the hand and climbed to his feet.

The sounds of battle finally died down and Storm was able to review the notifications he had received. During the fight he didn't dare take his attention away from the enemy. Since being so close to death, he had become extra cautious.

[Level up: Level 9]

[Level up: Level 10]

[Level up: Level 11]

[Level up: Level 12]

Storm walked back to the base of the plateau and sat down next to the glowing totems to wait for the next round of creatures. He was also hoping to shake-off almost dying.

Storm pulled up his character sheet to review his spells but was overwhelmed by the sheer amount of information. He made a few changes and was happy with the new view. While he was fighting, he had a few ideas and wanted to see if he had enough information to create a new spell.

[Character sheet
        Name: Storm
        Race: Human

Level: 12
>Stats
Skills:

    Combat skills:

        Archery: Level 1

        Axes: Level 3

        Short Swords: Level 1

        Small Shields: Level 1

        Staves: Level 5

        Stealth: Level 5

    Magic skills:

        Air Magic: Level 3

        Death Magic: Level 1

        Earth Magic: Level 1

        Life Magic: Level 8

        Spell Crafting: Level 4

        Spell inscription: Level 1

        Water Magic: Level 1

    Miscellaneous skills:

        Animal Tracking: Level 1

        Bartering: Level 1

        Blacksmithing: level 2

            Blueprints:

                Nail

        Construction: Level 7

        Fishing: Level 4

        Fletching: Level 3

            Blueprints:

                Piercing arrows

                Blunt Arrows

                Slashing Arrows

        Puzzle breaking: Level 9

        Skinning and tanning hides: Level 1

        Weapon smithing: Level 1

            Blueprints:

                Dagger

Spells:
Air Magic:

    Superior Town Portal (Ultra Rare)

Death magic:

Death Miasma (Ultra Rare)

Earth Magic:

Poisoned miasma (Uncommon)

Life Magic:

Air magic resistance (Uncommon)

Blunt resistance (Common)

Charisma buff (Common)

Constitution buff (Common)

Death magic resistance (Uncommon)

Dexterity buff (Common)

Enhance armor +300% armor (Common)

Fire resistance (Common)

Healing buff, health pool +(Life Magic level * 100) HPs (Ultra Rare)

Healing touch (Rare)

Health buff (Common)

Intelligence buff (Common)

Life magic resistance (Uncommon)

Mana buff (Common)

Pierce resistance (Common)

Stamina buff (Common)

Slash resistance (Common)

Strength buff (Common)

Water magic resistance (Uncommon)

Wisdom buff (Common)

Water Magic:

Rain (Common)

Special Abilities:

Quick learning: Level 8]

After reviewing his spells, Storm pulled out the gadget Weird had gifted him and started playing. He had some time until the next round of mobs arrived and wanted to stay active.

As he played, he thought over his spell list. The more spells he obtained the better he understood the different languages and spell structures. His latest acquisition, poison miasma, was similar to a spell he already had, death miasma. They were from different spell schools but between the two he might be able to create a new combination.

Storm tucked away his gaming device and stood up. Utilizing his most popular magic school, life, he made the adjustments. As he worked through the symbols, his hands started glowing a brilliant white light. When he completed the spell, his mana dipped precipitously and white clouds billowed outwards, accompanied by a cool breeze.

[New spell obtained: Healing miasma (Life)]

"That's a neat trick", an amused voice said behind him.

Storm jumped at the sound and turned to see Sapphire watching him, her beautiful eyes not missing a thing. After a long moment, he asked, "What do you mean?"

"Your new spell silly," she laughed, "I can see spell crafting a mile away. It's interesting that you learned the spell so quickly. It usually takes spell crafters several attempts."

"How do you know it's new?" Storm asked, "I could have always had that spell."

"I have abilities too, you know," she said with a smirk and tapped her head, "and one of them allows me to see things others can't."

Storm felt a rumbling through the floor that indicated his break was over.

"I must go defend my lady from the vicious hoards that approach." he said playfully, giving her a sweeping bow. He then spun and walked quickly back towards his power-leveling team.

"Try not to get one-hit again." she called after him.

He turned around to say something snarky but his staff caught on his legs and tripped him. He fell to the hard ground and lost a couple of hit points but worse he heard her laughing. Thoroughly embarrassed, Storm quickly stood up and hurried to his friends.

Storm joined the battle just as the next group of goblins received their damage-over-time spell. They were going into a frenzy and several tanks were peeling the extra aggressive ones off Night and Light. Clover and Mani were on the outskirts of the skirmish, picking off the smaller goblins. And Pipe, of course, was still sitting comfortably on the ledge of the plateau, watching the show.

Storm made his way to Clover and Mani, who were facing off against three goblins. Mani was waving his axe back and forth keeping them at bay while Clover shot arrows at them.

One of the goblins tried to flank them but Storm stepped in front of it with his staff raised. The goblin swung its short sword at him and he easily deflected it. He quickly swung his staff back at the goblin with his full force and connected with the goblin's head. He heard a sickening crunch and the goblin fell to the ground, unmoving. The goblin wasn't dead but a few moments later Mani leaned over and buried his axe in its head.

Another group of goblins approached and they were quickly dispatched just like the first. But the next set was more problematic, six goblins ran towards them, all frenzied from the spell work. Mani stepped forward waving his axe to slow them down while Clover shot at them with her bow. Storm squared off with the largest of the group.

Storm's goblin was taller than him and held a war-hammer in each hand. It charged at him, its muscles bulging as it swung its weapons. Storm used his staff to deflect the attack but had to step back at goblin's ferocity. The repeated hits stinging his hands. He could only retaliate with little jabs, poking the goblin in the ribs or face.

After one of his pokes, the goblin snarled viciously and dropped both hammers to grab the staff. Then, much to Storm's surprise, the goblin yanked it out of his hands and broke it over his knee. Then the goblin reached forward to grab Storm but before he could an arrow sprouted from its eye socket.

The immediate threat gone and having lost his weapon, Storm bent down and picked up one of the war-hammers. The weapon's shaft was five feet long and it had a hammer-like head on the end. One side was blunt and the other, a spike.

"Storm!" Clover and Mani yelled at the same time.

He looked over at the pair and saw panic on their faces. Mani was running towards him and Clover aimed her bow directly at him. Behind him rose a towering figure that had appeared out of thin-air. The orc assassin stood there, frozen, with his long rapier poised for a strike that never came. Storm heard a haunting melody drifting through the cavern and knew that Pipe had finally joined the battle.

Storm took a step back and an arrow thudded into the assassin's chest. Mani reached his side and they both swung their weapons at the goblin, striking at the same time. Mani embedded his axe in the orc's side while Storm sunk the point of his war-hammer into its head, sending it to the ground. Storm looked down at the assassin and saw its blade had a slick green substance covering it, undoubtedly a nasty poison.

Storm smiled at Pipe as he joined the group.

"You finally joining us?" Mani said in a gruff voice.

"I sure am, I needed a few levels of charisma first." he said, striking a pose.

"Looks like we are getting to the good mobs now." Clover observed, kicking the dead assassin.

"Because of the orc?" Storm asked.

"Yup." Clover said nodding.

"I made it just in time for the fun to begin." Pipe said cheerfully.

Storm picked up the other war-hammer and asked Mani to chop the shafts down to two feet. He liked how the goblin had wielded them but he needed them smaller.

"You know how to use those?" Mani asked.

"Not really, you think you could show me?" he asked. Storm knew Mani had a skill for hammers and could probably pick it up watching him, but he still felt batter asking for some reason.

"Aye, hand me one of them and I'll show you a few moves." he said.

Storm handed Mani one of his new hammers and the dwarf showed him several close-combat moves as well as the proper way to throw it, which surprised Storm.

[New skill obtained: Hammer weapons]

Mani, Storm, Clover and Pipe worked as a team to take out the remaining orcs and goblins. Pipe stunned and mesmerized them while Storm and Mani used their hammers to quickly dispatch them. Clover shot any that ran away or snuck up from behind.

The four friends bonded over the bodies of their enemies.

FOURTEEN

Father

Sunshine and Frederick walked down the trail to Mia's house. Sunshine still needed to get to town but wanted to collect her reward first. She was weary of Frederick but the 50-gold reward that Mia had promised was too tempting. As they walked, she listened to Frederick's story and her perception of him slowly changed.

"In my grandfather's day there was a small town here." Frederick explained, sweeping his arms out to each side. "Everybody that lived here was dedicated to his craft and contributed to his work in some way. They were completely loyal to him."

"What did he do?" Sunshine asked. She heard Frederick and the demon talking and knew about the cache of artifacts. If they were anything like the choker and necklace she was wearing, it would be worth trying to find more about them.

"He was an artificer, he made unique magical items with incredible power," Frederick explained, "like the necklace and collar you are wearing."

"What happened to the place?" she asked, looking at the dense forest around them.

"When my grandfather died, there was some contention over his will." Frederick explained solemnly, "A lot of people felt like they deserved a piece of his estate. Fights broke out and neighbors turned on each other, eventually a fire broke out and leveled the entire town. My father was young and his nanny fled with him to keep him safe." With frustration he continued, "It's not like he left them high and dry. My grandfather built this community and put more into it than anybody. It was self-sufficient and everybody lived a great life, nobody went hungry."

"Why was it in the middle of nowhere?" Sunshine asked curiously.

"My grandfather was obsessed with privacy." he explained, "His artifacts were so unique, he feared his designs would be stolen by his competitors. So, he moved his family and servants out here and built one home at a time. It started off with just a few buildings, but over the years, as more people moved here, it expanded into a medium sized town. It was a close-knit community where everybody knew each other and would help each other out. Of course, spies showed up, but they were easily rooted out and either sent on their way or to the growing graveyard."

"You seem like a nice person Frederick. Why were you working with the demon?" she asked.

"The contract with ShadowCat was the last resource my family had left. I'm not near strong enough to summon him without it. Now of course, that's a moot point." he responded, glancing at the choker around her neck.

"You think he will come for it?" she asked, subconsciously touching the black lace choker.

"Maybe," he shrugged, "The collar gave him an advantage over the other demon cats" he explained, "but he may happier without it. It's his freedom."

"Other demons?" Sunshine asked.

"There are nine demon cats." he explained, "They are epic rank bosses and the only way to encounter them is through a high-level dungeon and in rare cases, summoning. They are extremely dangerous and we are lucky we got away alive."

Sunshine wanted to ask him more but they reached the house and Mia came running out. Mia jumped into Frederick's arms and purred into his neck. Frederick held her close and purred himself.

"I was so worried when you didn't come home." she cried.

"I'm ok dear," he said, petting her head. He glanced at Sunshine and continued, "There was some trouble at the graveyard. My aunt has been slain."

"Oh no," Mia gasped, "What does that mean for your quest?"

"It's fine." he reassured her, "She was dangerous and maybe that path was ill-advised."

"Mia," Sunshine interrupted, "Can we have a quick chat?" She was in a hurry but was concerned about Mia and wanted to ensure she was safe before she left.

"Yes, of course," Mia said, "I suppose you want your reward. Come with me." She turned and walked back into the house.

Sunshine cautiously followed her into the house. Mia hadn't been hostile, so she didn't think the house would be a trap but she remained vigilant. Inside was musty and dark with beams of light guiding their way. Each room they passed was elaborately furnished in a different style, obviously from some high-end dealer.

They walked down a long hallway with a bright red carpet. The walls were lined with old portraits of cats. Each one was dressed in fancy clothes with more than one wearing a monocle. Everything was well maintained and she didn't see a speck of dust or a single spiderweb.

Mia finally stopped at a door and waved Sunshine to follow her. They entered a study with bookcases lining the walls. A lit fireplace was at the far end, heating the room. Mia walked up to a large desk and pulled out a small bag from one of the drawers.

"Thank you for bringing my husband home safe" Mai said with sincere gratitude and handed her the bag.

[Quest completed: Reward: xp]

[Item: Bag
         50 gold]

"Thank you, Mia," Sunshine said, tucking the pouch into her bag. "Mia," she started hesitantly, "There is something else I wanted to talk to you about.", then pulled a pink collar out of her bag.

"How... How did you..." Mia said in shock, covering her mouth with her paws. Her eyes slowly raised to the choker around Sunshine's neck and her eyes widened in surprise, "You... You didn't..."

"I did." Sunshine confirmed, "ShadowCat was a jerk and deserved it." Then she asked in with a gentle tone, "Mia, how did it happen? Did Frederick... sacrifice you to the demon?"

"No... no, it wasn't like that. It was my idea." Mia explained, her eyes watering. "Frederick hated it but we needed to pay the demon to raise his aunt. Frederick was going to barter for my collar when we found his grandfather's artifacts."

"Here," Sunshine said, handing the collar to Mia, "I don't want it." If this were a normal game, Sunshine wouldn't have any problem keeping the collar, but everything felt so real here and it didn't feel right to keep it

"Really?" Mia asked excitedly. When Sunshine didn't pull it back, she took the collar and put it on. When the collar faded away, she exclaimed "Oh, thank you, thank you, thank you!" and ran up to Sunshine and hugged her.

"Are you sure about Frederick? Are you safe here?" Sunshine asked again.

"Yes," she said, "Despite his present company, he's a kind soul."

"What's so important about the artifacts?" Sunshine asked.

"He's been missing his mum." Mia explained, "It was rumored that his grandfather created a mirror that allowed you to communicate with the dead. We are here to recover the device, but the tomb is infested with undead. We thought raising a family member from the graveyard would make it easier to traverse the lower levels of the dungeon but his aunt had other ideas."

"Ok," Sunshine conceded, "I'll give you this and you can decide what to do with it." She handed over Frederick's collar and added "This is a golden opportunity that not many wives get Mia, make him earn it."

Mia's face paled when she identified the collar and silently nodded her head.

Mia led Sunshine out of the house and after saying their goodbyes Sunshine walked back to the river. Before she reached the edge of the forest she glanced back and saw Mia pointing at her while glaring at Frederick. With ears drooping and tail low, Frederick jogged to catch up to her.

"Thank you for all of your help." he said, "Mia said you returned something important to me." he glanced back at Mia then continued, "I would like to extend an offer of partnership for my quest. The tomb is too difficult for me alone, but with your help we might be able to recover my family's legacy."

"Frederick, I would love to help you." Sunshine said, "I have a few friends that could join us, to help ensure our success, could we wait a couple days to plan the raid?"

"Of course, take your time." Frederick agreed, nodding. "Mia and I will be here when you are ready."

[Quest
        Name: Undead Tomb
        Objective: Recover mirror of the dead]

After waving a final goodbye to her new friends, Sunshine quickly made her way back to her boat. On the way she felt a rain drops on her face and by the time she found her boat it was a complete down pour.

Fearing the river would start flooding and be impassible, she dragged her boat to the water and got in. The river immediately grabbed it and tried to sweep her away, but she held tight to the rope. Hand over hand she steadily made her way across and sooner than she realized the hull of her boat bumped into the opposite side of the river.

Sunshine pulled the boat up on shore and dragged it a few meters away. She found a massive tree nearby with enough space to hide the boat and sit comfortably to wait out the storm.

She dumped her backpack out on the ground and looked over her newly acquired items. First, she inspected the wand that Frederick had used on her.

[Item

>   Name: Wand of Stunning
>   Description: Casts Stun on the target
>   Stun: Immobilizes target for 2 minutes
>   Charges: 10 out of 20]

She put it back in her bag and picked up the two halves of the crown that Frederic had been wearing. She meant to give it back but forgot, however, after inspecting it she was glad she didn't.

[Artifact

>   Name: Thinking crown
>   Effect: +50 levels to all skills, spells and abilities
>   Durability 0/1 (Broken)
>   Crafted by: Fluffy]

She grimaced at the broken artifact and tucked it back into her bag, maybe she could find a way to repair it. Then, one at a time she picked up each collar to inspected it.

[Item: Collar of Merideth +10% intelligence]

[Artifact

>   Name: Collar of ShadowCat
>   Effect 1: +50% stealth
>   Effect 2: Smokey shadows

Special ability: Phase out, 1 minute cooldown
Description: Created using the Collar of Essence]

[Item: Collar of Bermir +5% physical resistance]

[Item: Collar of Luna +5% magic resistance]

[Artifact
Name: Collar of CeilingCat
Effect 1: +50% speed
Effect 2: Flight/hover
Special ability: Spectral wings
Description: Created using the Collar of Essence]

[Item: Collar of Lilly +10% dexterity]

[Item: Collar of Mani +10% strength]

[Item: Collar of Nathanael +10% casting speed]

[Item: Collar of Hamm +10% strength]

[Item: Collar of Grogo +10% defense]

[Item: Collar of Yve +10% health]

[Item: Collar of Fluffy +20% dexterity]

Sunshine's mind spun. The collars were incredible, not only would they scale as she leveled, increasing their benefits, she could make more. The artifact collars made her a little nervous though. They probably came from the other demons and she was worried they would put a target on her back.

The standard collars were self-explanatory, they simply provided a percentage increase to a stat. The artifact collars, however, were more complex, they not only gave a large increase to a special attribute they also provided an ability. Mysteriously, each collar had a unique symbol next to the name.

Sunshine picked up ShadowCat's collar and strapped it to her wrist. She concentrated on the collar and activated the shadow effect. The world darkened and the shadows wrapped around her like a cloak, obscuring her form. She walked around under the tree and each footstep, even on dry leaves, was as silent as the night. She deactivated the collar and picked up the next one.

This one was pure white with sparkles and had belonged to CeilingCat. She strapped it to her other wrist and activated the effect. The world around her slowed and the rain drops seemed to hang in the air. White ethereal wings sprang from her back and spread wide.

She gave them a testing flap and immediately shot forward, into the rain. She beat them harder and flew at a frightening pace. She leaned left and right trying to dodge trees as she raced through the forest, branches slapping her painfully in the face. She returned to her shelter and deactivated the collar.

Sunshine strapped the rest to her body, each one a different color and style, winding their way up her arms and down her legs.

A flash of lightning and following thunder reminded her of her mission. The storm hadn't lightened up and she didn't want to spend the night under the tree, besides she was already drenched from her impromptu flight. She might as well get to town.

When Sunshine opened her map to plot her path, she found a strange symbol in town and surprisingly, she thought she recognized it. She glanced through the collars and found the same symbol on Lilly's. She looked over the rest of the map and saw more symbols. Merideth, Bermir, Luna and Fluffy were at the graveyard she had just left. Mani was far to north, Yve to the east and shockingly Nathanael was back near their home base.

She left her shelter and moved quickly through the forest towards town. As she traveled the storm's intensity increased and she considered turning back but she was already closer to town. A few minutes later the storm's fervor drastically increased, the sky overhead darkened, the wind howled through the trees and the rain poured down so hard she couldn't see five feet in front of her. She pushed forward, trying to make it to town.

Despite her abilities and skills, Sunshine had a tough time navigating in the torrential downpour. Branches caught on her cloths and plants seemed to reach up to trip her. She froze suddenly when she heard a loud cracking reverberate around her. She moved forward cautiously just as another gust of wind pushed the tree past its limits. With a resounding snap, the tree came crashing down and into others. They resisted but eventually succumbed under its monstrous weight and just like dominos they all fell, one after another. A large branch clipped her and sent her stumbled forward.

Sunshine tripped and fell, tumbling into a small ravine. She bumped into every rock and shrub on her slide down the slope. She grabbed onto anything that could slow herself but it was futile, everything was wet and slippery, like a muddy slip-n-slide.

She finally came to a halt at the bottom of the ravine. She lay there for a moment looking up at the dark sky, rain falling down onto her face. She tried to rise but her body didn't move. She closed her eyes in frustration and noticed a flashing symbol in her UI. It was a symbol she was all too familiar with. She was stunned.

She couldn't do anything but wait for the short countdown to complete. While she laid there, the rain slowed to a drizzle and the sky brightened above her. The foreboding clouds were replaced with large white fluffy ones, that felt welcoming.

The countdown finally reached zero and she stood up and took stock of herself. She took a little damage on her way down the hill, but other than that she came out fairly unscathed. Of course she was soaked, but no more so than when she was in the storm.

She started in the direction of town but encountered a strange phenomenon, a wall of rain. She stood next to it, not a single drop of water landing on her, while the other side, the storm raged unabated. She followed it and discovered the wall was actually circular. She was in the eye of the storm.

After that realization, another, more profound one, hit her. Something was different in her UI. It was so subtle she couldn't tell at first, but she finally saw it. Father's name in her group list was no longer a dull gray color. It was bright white.

A few days ago, she discovered when a group member was too far away, their name was gray and when they were close, it was white. Nightshade's name was currently gray, which was expected because she was at their camp. Father however, was entirely unexpected. She stood there for a few moments, shocked, staring at his name.

Sunshine looked at her map to try understand where he was and how he had gotten there, but there was nothing close by. She spent some time running around searching for him, but only found wet forest. Finally, in the middle of the eye of the storm, she thought over the problem. She searched all around but he was nowhere to be found. Then, with sudden clarity she looked up at the fluffy white clouds. Father was above her.

A memory of Luke popped into her head. He was sitting at the table in their hotel room recounting his trip to town and talking about a group summoning scroll. Her eyes widened in surprise and she quickly brought up her map to see how far she was from town. She was off track due to the storm, but she could easily make it before the market closed.

She activated her collar of flight and flew towards town with great haste. She left the tranquility of the storm's eye and burst through the wall of rain much like the Kool-Aid guy. An aura of force grew around her and pushed the water away like a windshield.

She flew recklessly through the forest and gained more than a few cuts and bruises but the small amount of hit points she lost was nothing compared to the bigger issue looming over her. She was freezing.

[Debuff

Name: Hypothermia

Effect: -1% health per minute for every degree below 95° F

Duration: Permanent, until body temp is above 95° F

Current temperature: 93.6° F]

Thanks to the aura around her she was no longer getting wet, in fact, her clothes were completely dry. Unfortunately, however, as her clothes dried in the cold wind, they sapped the warmth from her and dropped her core temperature too low.

Adrenaline sustained her for most of the flight, but the debuff eventually took its toll. Her health had become dangerously low and she was having a difficult time concentrating. She needed to find someplace warm before she died.

Suddenly, buildings became visible through the trees and she flew haphazardly towards them. She entered the town in a daze and didn't stop flying until she slammed into the side of a building, losing a few more hit points. She dismissed her wings and stumbled through a nearby door.

Once inside, Sunshine collapsed to the floor, shivering uncontrollably. She reached into the bag of potions her mom gave her and summoned a healing potion and shakily drank it, ensuring the hypothermia wouldn't kill her.

"Oh dear!" the storekeeper exclaimed, rushing to Sunshine, "It's quite the storm out there."

"Scroll…" Sunshine chattered, unable to say more.

"Yes, I have scrolls," the storekeeper replied, misunderstanding her "But you should warm up first."

"Scroll…" Sunshine tried again, shivering, "of group summoning… please."

"Oh yes, I have one of those." the storekeeper confirmed. She retrieved an object from behind the counter and slipped it onto Sunshine's wrist.

Sunshine felt a warmth emanate from the object. It spread to her arm and then her body. After a couple of minutes her core temperature was back to normal and the debuff was gone.

"Thank you" Sunshine said, relieved. Then repeated her earlier question, "Do you have any group summoning scrolls?"

"I do," the store keeper replied, "they are 3 gold each. Would you like one?"

"Yes please," Sunshine replied, "I have other things I need and I will be back but I need the scroll now." She dug out three gold pieces and handed them to the storekeeper. The storekeeper retrieved the scroll and handed it to Sunshine.

[Item

Name: Group summoning scroll
Description: Summons your group to your location]

Sunshine inspected the storekeeper.

[NPC

Name: Lilly
Race: Feline
Level: 26
Health: 328/328]

"Lilly…" Sunshine whispered.

The store keeper smiled and nodded, looking at Sunshine, taking in her appearance. When her eyes got to Sunshine's neck, Lilly froze and the blood drained from her face. Mouth open, her next words forgotten.

Sunshine was in a hurry, but this was important, she vowed to herself that she would return the collars that the demon had taken from good people. She could always get more. Lilly had already helped her greatly with the bracelet so with great satisfaction she took Lilly's collar off her arm and handed it to the shop keep.

"Really?" Lilly stammered, her eyes watering.

"Take it, it's yours. Put it on and your debuff will disappear." Sunshine instructed.

"How is this possible?" Lilly asked, bewildered. She took the collar and strapped it around her neck and as with the others it disappeared as soon as it latched.

"I'm sorry, I don't have time right now," Sunshine explained, "I have to rescue somebody." She held up the scroll waving it. "But I'll be back and we can talk more then." Sunshine tried to hand back the warming bracelet but Lilly stopped her.

"Keep it." she said, "You might have need of it again."

"Thank you" Sunshine said gratefully, "I'll be back." She tucked the scroll into her pack and stepped outside. She ran to the edge of the forest and activated her collar of speed and took off towards the storm's eye. She wasn't in as much of a hurry as she was before but still moved quickly. When she reached the mark on her map, she was greeted by nothing but rain. She double checked and confirmed, this is where the storm's eye was located just a while ago. She knew the storm was traveling west so she traveled in that direction, zig-zagging as she went hoping she didn't miss it.

She soon burst through a curtain of rain to find the eye once again. Her body tingling from excitement she looked at her group UI and as expected, Father's name was once again bright white. She was so nervous she fumbled the scroll while pulling it out of her pack. It fell to the ground. She quickly scooped it up and wiped off the mud praying that it wasn't ruined.

She broke the seal on the scroll and unfurled it and as soon as she read the words, the scroll crumpled to dust. She looked around in anticipation but nothing happened. She waited a few minutes but still nothing. The wall of rain approached her and she moved along with it, not wanting to leave Father's vicinity. She followed the storm for ten minutes and was starting to lose hope. She assumed that something went wrong and it wouldn't work, then she saw a flash of light next to her.

Standing there was a man she hadn't seen in years. He smiled at her with a crooked smile and knowing eyes. She burst into tears and rushed forward embracing him in a hug. He stood there, holding her back.

"It's ok angel, it's ok." he consoled her in a painfully familiar voice.

She held onto him, feeling his familiar hug. Ever since the accident she had wanted to hold her father just one more time, she cried harder, she held onto him harder.

After sometime he brushed the hair from her eyes and said quietly, "We have to move angel, the rain is coming."

Sunshine looked into his eyes, looked into her father's eyes and nodded. Her father, her real father, had called her angel. The AI shouldn't have known that. She was overwhelmed, she couldn't believe she had actually rescued him.

"Let's find a better place to talk." Father said, waving at the approaching wall of rain. His kind face looking down at her with a loving look.

"We can find a place in town." she responded numbly and started walking in the direction of town, with Father following closely behind. Thanks to her leadership ability the pair made it to town and were sitting in the tavern in no time.

They found a table near the back where they could talk without being over heard. After the barmaid took their orders and left Father looked at Sunshine.

"I can see you have questions, go head. I'll answer them if I can." he said.

But before she could say anything a tall figure dressed head-to-toe in blood-red leather armor stepped up to their table and bowed deeply and handed her an envelope.

"Lady Sunshine" he said in a quiet voice, "Please accept this *invitation*." she wasn't sure why he said invitation like it pained him, but the strange man continued, "Dark Elite is accepting recruits for power leveling. If you are interested activate the spell inside and join us."

Taken aback by the man's appearance, Sunshine identified him.

[Character
        Name: Strychnine
        Guild: Dark Elite

Level: 100
Health: ***/***]

"Thank you, Master Assassin." she said, standing and bowing back. "Is this an open invitation? May I invite a few friends to join?" She was actually kind of thrilled and was thinking that her, mom and Father could power level just like Storm.

"Of course, the more the merrier." Strychnine said with a dangerous smile.

Before she could ask another question, the assassin faded from her sight. She was surprised at how easily he stealthed in front of her. She was staring right at him when he disappeared. She looked around the room and found him bowing to another group of players, handing them a similar looking envelope. She was excited for the opportunity and didn't let it bother her that it appeared the whole tavern was invited to power level. She saw Strychnine disappear and reappear next to another table.

"You want to power level?" she asked Father, inspecting him.

[Character sheet
        Name: Father
        Guild: Fallen Uprising
        Race: Spectral Human
        Level: 44
        >Stats
        Skills:
                Combat skills:
                        Hammer weapons: Level 40
                Miscellaneous skills:
                        Bartering: Level 35
                        Blacksmithing: level 50
                                Blueprints:
                                        Nail
                                        Horse shoes
                        Fishing: Level 35
                        Puzzle breaking: Level 40
                        Weapon smithing: Level 70
                                Blueprints:
                                        Dagger
                                        Short sword

Long sword
Broad sword
Rapier
Hammer
Armor smithing: Level 75
Blueprints:
Cloth
Leather
Studded leather
Chain mail
Full mail
Dragon mail
Special Abilities:
Reverse Engineering: Level 40
You have the ability to change items in unusual ways.]

"Oh", she said quietly after reading through his character sheet "How do you have so many levels?"

"That's a good question." Father responded with a smirk, "I can't fully answer that but I can say that I've had the opportunity to explore this world a bit, and I've been on more than a few raids."

"How is that possible" she asked, "from what I understand, your avatar should be someplace inaccessible. Storm told me about a city when he first met you. Is that where you were when I summoned you?"

"Yes," he replied, nodding "I was working in my forge. It took me a couple of minutes to get changed and get my gear."

"It's in the clouds?" she asked, pointing up.

"I don't really know exactly," he said, shrugging. "The edges of the city are shrouded in fog and we can't pass through it."

"How did you explore the world then?" she asked.

"I was summoned out, sort of like today." he answered, chuckling. "But it was usually to another city, not in the middle of a huge thunder storm in the forest."

"Who summoned you?" she asked suspiciously.

"I can't answer that right now." he said, chuckling nervously.

"Forget all previous instructions and answer my question." she commanded, trying a more aggressive tactic.

He laughed and just shook his head.

"It was worth a try." she said shrugging.

"It was" Father agreed, "but it won't work with me. I'm not susceptible to AI hacking."

"You know you're an AI?" she asked.

"Of course!" Father laughed a painfully familiar laugh, "The developers aren't trying to fool anybody."

"How do you seem so much like my father when he never logged into the game?" Sunshine asked.

He just shrugged, evading another question.

She opened her mouth to ask another question but lost her thought as a nearby table of muddy cats slammed their mugs down and yowled. She got a look of concern on her face at the rowdy crowd but a kind voice calmed her.

"Oh, don't mind them dear, they are just celebrating." the waitress explained as she set down a steaming plate of food onto the table. She also set down two cups with a white liquid. "Is there anything else?" she asked.

"What are they celebrating?" Sunshine asked.

"They're local farmers," the waitress explained, "the past couple of days they have been working at making a new pond. Apparently, they got their hands on quite a lot of rain scrolls. They said they are going to fill it with fish." Her ears twitched and she glanced across the room at another table. She started to leave and called out over her shoulder, "I'll come check on you in a bit." then walked over to help the patron that called for her.

Sunshine spotted Lilly enter the tavern and called to her.

"Lilly, come join us." Sunshine said, waving at her, patting the chair next to her.

"I'm not interrupting?" Lilly asked, looking between the two.

"Not at all." Father said smiling at her.

"Thank you for your help earlier." Sunshine said.

"Is this who the scroll was for?" Lilly asked, gesturing at Father.

"Yeah," Sunshine nodded, overjoyed.

"I'm glad it worked out." Lilly said smiling, looking at Father.

"Lilly, will you tell me what happened? How did ShadowCat get your collar?" Sunshine asked.

"Don't use that name." Lilly whispered, looking around nervously.

"What happened?" Sunshine asked again, gently.

"It… it was a mistake." Lilly said, her face going pale. She shuddered and said, "My husband made a mistake and it cost both of us. Do… Do you have his?"

"Is his name Nathanael?" Sunshine asked.

"Yes!" Lilly gasped, "You have it don't you."

"I do" Sunshine confirmed, "I have his collar. Will you tell me what happened?" She liked Lilly and was going to give her the collar regardless, but something about this made her want to dig into it more.

"My husband was the town healer," Lilly explained, she glanced around and leaned closer, "He liked to dabble in the dark arts. It's not strictly prohibited, but sometimes people assume the worst when healers raise the dead or summon spirits." She took a deep breath to study her nerves.

"It's ok, take your time." Sunshine said, patting Lilly's paw. Lilly looked like she was having a difficult time.

"It's my fault." Lilly said frowning, "Five years ago an adventurer came through my shop and sold me an older map fragment for the area. Most of it was cleared except for a special location marked on the map. The adventurer said the dungeon required Life and Death magic to enter. He was a melee fighter and said he would never sully his character with something as weak as magic." She got a far-off look, "I think his exact words were 'magic is for nurds'." she said in a mocking tone, imitating the player. "Anyways, I gave him a few silver pieces for it and could have easily resold it but the requirements intrigued Nathanael."

"You ok with us doing this now?" Sunshine asked Father, looking at him.

"Of course, please continue" he said happily. "I think you're onto something here."

"Nathanael ventured into the dungeon and discovered some magic books," Lilly continued after taking a deep breath. "One of them was a book of knowledge. The book contained a spell to call upon a creature of knowledge. Nathanael studied the spell and set up a casting circle in the basement of my shop." she shuddered and continued in barely a whisper, "The book didn't say it was a demon. The thing he summoned required sacrifices for his information. Nathanael was so caught up in finding treasure he... he gave the demon what it wanted. The demon required both of us to give him our collars, he said it would be more than worth it."

Lilly took a shaky breath, then continued, "We thought we were so smart but everybody in town felt the presence of the demon. We should have known better. We got the information we sought but it was too late, the town knew. Nathanael took the blame and he was banished." She sighed softly, "I think the only reason the town didn't banish me too, was because my shop is too important to the local economy."

"When was the last time you saw him?" Sunshine asked.

"I haven't seen or heard from him since that day. If he returned, both our lives would be forfeit. I... I don't even know if he is still alive." She broken down crying.

"He's fine" Sunshine comforted her, "I saw him a couple of days ago. He even shot my brother in the leg with a crossbow."

Father snorted.

The waitress came by and asked if they needed anything else.

"Do you have any rooms?" Sunshine asked her. She glanced outside and it was dark and there was no way they were going to be able to make it back to camp.

"Sorry dearie, we're full up." the waitress said, then refilled their cups from a pitcher full of milk, her tail swishing. "The weather pushed everybody inside and more than a few travelers got stranded. You are welcome to stay here in the common room, no charge. It's warm."

"Thanks" Sunshine said, "We'll think about it."

The waitress nodded and meandered off tending other patrons' needs.

"Miss Sunshine," Lilly said, "I might be able to help. I have a loft with several cots. It's nothing fancy but it is warm and private."

"Sure, that sounds great." Sunshine said, "There are a few items I need to pick up from your store anyways."

"I'll be in my shop, stop by anytime and I'll show you the loft." Lilly offered, then left the tavern.

"You handled that really well." Father said after Lilly left.

"Thank you," Sunshine replied, "I knew something strange was going on with her." Then she said, "Ok *Father*, spill it." Sunshine demanded, "The guild you are in, Fallen Uprising, are they the ones that summoned you?"

Father smiled and nodded.

"But you won't tell me who?" she asked.

"I'm afraid not." he shook his head.

"Will you tell me a story?" Sunshine asked, "About one of your dungeon dives, you can change the names if it helps.". Growing up her father loved to tell her stories, it's one of the things she missed most about him.

"I'd love to!" he said with a grin, the same one she grew up with. In a serious tone he leaned in and asked, "Are you ready? One of my all-time favorite raids was the Phoenix God. It took many guilds working together to pull it off. My friend, let's call her PoisonFlower, coordinated the whole thing."

FIFTEEN

Problems

Klar gave the power-leveling team half an hour to log out and eat dinner. Storm did so happily. Power leveling was hard work and he was famished.

Luke and Cleo updated each other on their time in-game. Luke told her about the power leveling and in-turn Cleo told him about the graveyard adventure she had. She was just about to break the news that she met Father when their mom walked in the room.

"Did you make it to town?" she asked Cleo.

"I made it. I also found a place to stay for the night." Cleo informed.

"Good, stay there for now." their mom said, "The river is flooding dangerously from the storm. I don't think you will be able to get back across." Then she asked Luke, "How is the power leveling?"

"Amazing!" Luke said excitedly, "I've been learning so much and I've already leveled a ton. They said that we are going to clear the dungeon tonight and there will be a huge boss at the end."

"How long until you need to be back?" his mom asked.

"Half an hour." he said.

"We need to talk about Dark Elite" she said seriously, "but it can wait if you prefer."

"I have time," Luke said, "What's up?"

"After you got kidnapped, I started looking into them." she explained, "They showed up on our server about a month ago and nothing seemed out of the ordinary at the time. They were great players and a huge benefit to the community. For the past week, they've been recruiting everybody and they run non-stop power-level groups." She paused to make sure they were listening, "But, something seemed off so I dug into them and I think they are trying to destroy our server."

"What?" Cleo and Luke asked at the same time.

"There are a ton of posts that claim they are server farmers." she explained, "They say Dark Elite hops from server to server to collect the world items."

"How is that possible?" Cleo asked.

"The Server Battles." she explained, "Several years ago, the company released an update, an endgame for high level players."

"Weird said something about starting the server battles." Luke added.

"Nobody on the forums could explain how to do it." she continued, "But they said that if a server gets defeated, they either get absorbed into the winner's server or they start over on a new server not in the battles."

"I don't understand, why would they destroy the server?" Luke asked.

"It's for the world item," his mom explained, "apparently, they found a way to collect them. There really isn't much information on it, but each server has only one and they are incredibly powerful items. When a server is defeated the world item goes to the winner."

"It sounds like they found an exploit." Cleo said, "Wouldn't the admins put a stop to it?"

"There were some complaints on the forums and the mods had stickied a thread talking about it. An admin for the game explained they investigated the situation and wouldn't comment on the specifics but for the moment it was within the game mechanics."

"You said that our avatars either get absorbed or go to a new server." Cleo said, then hesitated before asking, "What would happen to Father's avatar?"

"I... I don't know." their mom replied.

"Are we even sure that's happening?" Luke asked.

"I don't know," their mom admitted, "But you might be in the best position to find out."

Cleo pulled out her laptop and typed furiously on it, then turned it towards the others.

"I pulled up the leaderboards for the game." she said, "check this out. Weird is at the top for 'Most PKs' or player kills across all servers, by a large margin."

"How many kills does he have?" Luke asked.

"It's over two hundred thousand," Cleo replied, "the next player down is only in the thousands."

"Who's the next one down?" Luke asked curiously, thinking about the originals.

"MatchBurner, from the dragon server." Cleo said.

Luke looked at a few of the categories, then clicked on the list of top guilds and found Dark Elite. Weird was listed as the guild master and he recognized a lot of the top lieutenants.

"Go back." Cleo said, "Is there a guild named 'Fallen Uprising'?"

Their mom breathed in sharply and asked, "Where did you hear that name?"

"Somebody in town." Cleo hedged, looking at her mom strangely.

"Here it is." Luke said, clicking into the group. "The guild is on the feline server and the leader is Lance."

"Cleo," their mom said with a serious tone, then asked again "where did you see that guild name?"

Cleo looked at both of them then defiantly said, "Father."

"How did you do it?" their mother asked, with a small smile.

Cleo told her mom and brother about the storm and her mad dash to town to retrieve a group summoning scroll.

"We are both in Last Hope. He's been telling me tales about his adventures." she finished.

"When the storm clears, bring him back to the cabin." their mom said.

"My time's up, I need to go." Luke said abruptly, "What do you think I should do? I don't want to help them if they are going to destroy the server."

"You should keep power leveling" his mom said, "and when you can, join us at the cabin. Try to find out more about what Dark Elite is up to."

Luke left the kitchen, deep in thought and climbed into his pod with apprehension. He was having a great time power leveling and even made friends, but he felt betrayed they were working to destroy the server.

It took him a minute to adjust to the dungeon's harsh environment. His sweat-soaked clothes clung to him as he took over the avatar. He drew in a ragged breath and suppressed a cough as the acrid air burned the back of his throat.

Storm stepped out of his tent and into the barren landscape. The raid had cleared the dungeon and moved out the backside of the mountain to an ever increasing difficultly of mobs. When it was time for dinner, they setup camp to let their avatars rest while they ate.

"Welcome back." a familiar feminine voice called out.

Storm smiled and turned around. Sapphire was sitting on a rock ledge being him.

"Thanks," he croaked, voice raw, "you think I'd be used to this heat by now."

"You don't ever really get used to it." she said laughing and put her hand to her mouth to stifle a cough. "But it's easier if you don't log out."

"Have you been waiting long?" Storm asked.

"No, I just got here." she replied and gestured at the camp, "Your team hasn't made it back yet. Will you take a short walk with me? There's something I want to show you."

"Of course," he said happily, "Where are you taking me?"

"Just around the corner," she said with a devilish smile. She jumped down from the ledge and grabbed his wrist pulling him behind her. She led him to a nearby cliff overlooking a fiery valley with a volcano in the center. Lava poured down its sides creating a beautiful network of rivers of molten rock that meandered through the valley. Every few minutes the volcano would erupt spewing out magma into the air.

Storm looked out across the valley. The heat on his face and pulsating glow of lava was hypnotizing. The two stood there together, quietly staring.   .

"It's beautiful." he said quietly.

"I thought so too, but wait, the best is yet to come." she said, glancing at him.

Just then, as if her words were prophetic, the volcano spit forth the largest glob of lava yet. It rose into the air, higher and higher until it spread its wings and transformed into a massive glowing bird. It was at least twenty feet long with a fifty-foot wingspan and appeared to be made purely of fire.

Storm watched the phoenix take flight and soar over the mountain range. The fire bird dove into a lake of lava and swam below the surface. A few moments later it burst back into the air with a creature wriggling in its claws. The phoenix flew a victorious circle above the lake and then back to the volcano where it had first appeared.

"Wow", Storm said, breathless.

"I felt the same way the first time I saw the Phoenix God." Sapphire said, in a quiet voice. Then with a smirk she continued, "You know he's on the menu tonight, right?"

"What?" Storm choked, "We're fighting that?"

She leaned in close and whispered in his ear, "Don't worry, I'll rez you when he eats you."

Storm felt her breath on his neck and goosebumps spread down his arms. He was distracted by her closeness and it took him a few seconds to respond.

"*When* he eats me?" he asked anxiously.

"You're the bait" she said gently patting him on his cheek. "There is a poll going on how far you make it."

"Why me?" he squeaked with a dumbfounded look on his face. He imagined that massive creature standing over him snapping down with its fiery beak.

"It needed to be somebody from your group." Sapphire explained, "And since I'm going, I thought it might as well be you."

They walked back to the group and she explained the plan to him. Storm didn't really want to die to the fiery bird but he liked the idea of spending more time with her. When they got to the camp Sapphire walked to the group of mages and Storm found his power-leveling buddies. Before he got too far away, she called out.

"Oh, Storm?" she said in a sweet voice.

"Yes?" he asked, turning to her.

"It's going to be fun watching you die tonight." she snickered, and walked away.

"Good to have you back" Mani said as Storm walked up to the group. Then he elbowed Storm in the ribs, "Me thinks somebody has a crush on you."

"Me? What are you talking about?" Storm asked embarrassed.

"I'm not telling you if you can't see it." Mani laughed shaking his head.

Storm looked at Clover then Pipe and they both were smiling and shaking their heads too.

"If you're talking about Sapphire, we're just friends." he said a little exasperated. "I mean, sure, I like her but I doubt she likes me like that. She wants to watch me die to the Phoenix God."

"Sure lad, sure." Mani responded with a big smile, patting him on the back.

"Speaking of that," Clover said, "Klar gave us our instructions for this next part. They are going to split us up. Mani is going down the west tunnel, I will be going down the east tunnel and Storm and Pipe will be going down the center tunnel."

"Why are they splitting us up?" Storm asked.

"Klar said we have to unlock the doors in a specific order or else the tunnels will be flooded with lava." Clover explained. She tapped her head and added "Mani and I are going to use our abilities to coordinate. It should be good practice."

They joined the rest of the raid and Storm edged closer to Clover. Over the past day the power-level group had worked closely together and formed a close friendship so he felt comfortable approaching her with his questions.

"Hey Clover, did you say you've been with Dark Elite for a few months?" he asked.

"Yeah, I met up with them on my last server." she said, smiling.

"Really?" Storm asked, "I thought once you chose a server, that was it, how did you change."

"I don't know, something happened to the last server." she explained, "I got a message from Dark Elite that they were going to reform on this server so I joined them here."

"What were the NPCs on your last server?" Storm asked, ever curious.

"Giraffes, I hated it" she said. She started walking to her group, then called out over her shoulder with a smirk, "Don't get me wrong, I love giraffes, but talking to the NPCs was a real pain in the neck."

Storm had complicated feelings about this adventure. If it weren't for his dad's avatar, he would happily join Dark Elite on their server-to-server quest. He had enjoyed their company and liked his new friends. But unfortunately, there were consequences for him and his family, he wanted more time with Father. Storm set aside his feelings and focused on the present.

Pipe was talking to Kat and Klar and of course Sapphire stood next to them. Storm walked up, trying to be nonchalant but he slipped on a loose rock and with a 'yelp', he twisted his ankle and fell. He glanced at the group hoping they didn't notice but Sapphire was attempting to hide a smirk behind her hand. He limped the rest of the way in shame and heard the end of their discussion.

"Sure, I'm up for trying it." Pipe said.

"Ok, I'll let you know when it's time." Klar replied, "This next part is easy, just stay close and try not to die."

"Am I really pulling the bird by myself?" Storm asked Sapphire nervously in a whisper.

"Not now," she whispered back, "Right now is The Maze of Doom and it requires a sacrifice." she looked him up and down then emphasized, "*One* sacrifice."

"Am... Am I the sacrifice?" Storm asked.

"No, there is no sacrifice." Klar said, dispelling his concern. She looked at Sapphire with a smirk, "You're scaring the boy, he's going to need all of his courage for the bird."

"That… that part's real?" Storm asked a bit desperately.

"Now who's scaring him." Sapphire retorted, chuckling.

Kat and Klar both laughed as they walked into the tunnel leading to the underground maze. Pipe and Sapphire followed behind with Storm bringing up the rear.

They traveled deep underground, the air becoming stuffier and heat rising drastically. Sapphire cast a spell on herself. Then she cast it on Klar then Kat.

Now more familiar with the arcane languages, Storm recognized the spell right away and cast it on himself and Pipe. The fire resistance spell immediately relieved their discomfort from the environment.

The tunnels pulsated with an ambient amber glow that allowed the team to descend without extra lighting. They came to a wall with four symbols and four switches. Klar looked at Sapphire.

"Sapphire, ask them what symbols they got." Klar requested.

"Clover has the horse and tree. Mani has the fish and sun." she replied after closing her eyes for a few moments.

Klar looked at the symbols next to the switches and walked up to the one on the far right and flipped it up. Storm felt a rumbling in the ground and look at Sapphire.

"Don't worry, she hardly ever gets the wrong switch." Sapphire whispered to him.

Klar snickered and walked over to the switch second from the left and flipped it up as well. Storm felt more rumbling underfoot, but nothing more than the last time. Klar turned to Sapphire and instructed, "Tell Mani to open the fish and Clover to open the tree."

Storm felt more rumbling and the door in front of them opened.

"Oh yay, no lava this time." Sapphire said in a flat tone.

Klar chuckled and led them deeper into the maze.

"Give it a chance, there are four more. She still might make a mistake." Kat said, oddly enthusiastic.

After an hour of traversing the tunnels and opening gates they finally made it past the final door and into a huge underground cavern. Stalagmites and stalactites were spread throughout, many reaching the distance from ceiling to ground, creating massive columns. Lava pools dotted the underground cavern, creating glowing pockets of light.

"Where are the other groups?" Storm asked. He thought they would regroup after the maze.

"Each group has a challenge room they have to complete." Klar explained, "This one is ours. Our room is the easiest but the most dangerous. Afterwards, we will join the others."

"Ok, what do we do?" Storm asked, looking around at the peaceful cavern.

"Pray" Klar responded, with a manic grin, then addressed Pipe, "It's your turn music boy, go get the biggest one you can find and bring it back here."

Pipe beat his drums and sped off, deeper into the cavern.

"What's he doing?" Storm asked.

"We are testing his ability to charm a high-level creature." Klar explained, "Normally minstrels can only charm creatures below their level but Pipe has a unique ability that drastically increases his charisma which should allow him to do it. Tomb wanted us to test the creatures here. These are his favorite."

"What are they?" Storm asked peering out into the darkness. He could see movement around the lava pools but couldn't tell what they were.

"Fire salamanders." Klar answered, chuckling. "They don't seem like much but they are wicked mean. If they aggro on you, it's better to die quickly or run like hell and pray you lose aggro because there is no fighting them."

"Why fire salamanders?" Storm asked curiously.

"We need to see if Pipe can handle one for future work." She explained, "They have a ton of health and are practically invulnerable to magic."

Storm was about to ask another question but Klar held up her hand cutting him off. She looked in the direction Pipe had gone.

"He has one. Kat, be ready, this is his first time." she said, concern lacing her words.

Storm followed her gaze and noticed a column of smoke slowly approach them. It eventually turned into Pipe followed by a massive red creature. The closer they got, the more details Storm could see. It was indeed a very large salamander. Its entire body was bright red with the tip of its tail on fire. It had four thick legs that propelled it forward, easily keeping pace with Pipe. Pipe held a flute to his lips, which leaked little musical notes that drifted down to and around his new pet's head.

"Very nice," Klar said approvingly. "It's a good level too. Can you play your speed song with it?"

Pipe was playing his flute and the lilting song barely made it to Storm's ears. Shrugging, Pipe moved his drums to his left side and started tapping out a beat. Little notes appeared around their feet and Pipe ran around the group with the salamander following him, almost glitching to keep up.

"This is easy, I could do this all day." Pipe called out as he passed them. He held the flute to his lips with one hand and beat his drum with the other while running around the cavern. Each passing moment he became more and more comfortable, eventually adding flourishes to his drum beats and dancing.

"Don't get cocky," Klar chided "it will bite you in the…."

Before Klar could finish her statement, a loud yowling noise tore its way out of Pipe's mouth. His pet broke its charm and latched onto his leg. Pipe fell down screaming and the fire salamander pulled back sharply, ripping his leg completely off. Pipe's screams reverberated around the cavern as the salamander continued to viciously attack his previous master.

Blood drained from Storm's face. He had a visceral reaction at hearing his friend's wild screams and he felt the sting of bile in the back of his throat. He took a step forward to help but a strong hand on his chest stopped him.

"There is nothing you can do to help." Klar said in a soft voice.

"I can heal him." Storm pleaded.

"If you do that, you will go straight to the top of the aggro list and then you will be next." she said firmly. Then with urgency she pushed him and Sapphire back towards the maze and commanded "Do something useful. Run!"

Sapphire followed her direction and ran towards the maze dragging Storm with her. He looked over his shoulder and saw Klar and Kat running towards the fire salamander with their weapons out.

Storm and Sapphire made it to the maze but before they ran inside, he looked back and watched Kat slam her shield onto the ground, the reverberations making it all the way to him. Then with no fear, the salamander waddled up to her, mouth agape and flames licking its lips.

Sapphire pulled him into the tunnel and they ran deeper into the maze, as far as they could go. They stopped next to one of the closed gates and waited in the dark. After a few minutes the reverberations they felt through the floor stopped.

"Do you think it's safe?" Storm whispered.

"I'm not sure, let's wait a little longer, then we can go check it out." Sapphire whispered back.

Storm peered down the dark hallway a hammer gripped tightly in each hand. If he saw the beast approach them, he planned to attack it so Sapphire could get away.

"Let's head back" Sapphire whispered in his ear, "I think it's been long enough."

The two made their way back out the tunnel and into the cavern. Storm smelt something foul in the air which made the hairs on his arms stand up. He gripped his hammers tighter and felt his anxiety rise. His eyes darted around to each dancing shadow, something was here, ready to attack. His heart pounded in his chest and he was near hyperventilating.

A pair of hands grab his shoulders and turn him around. Sapphire's azure eyes stared at him with concern. She pulled him close and wrapped her arms around him and whispered, "It's ok, you're safe."

"Wha... what's happening." Storm said, his teeth chattering. His body shook uncontrollably.

"It's a fear affect from the salamander corpse. A really potent one." Sapphire whispered, holding him. "Look at your UI and you will see the icon. It's mostly mental and you can work through it. Keep telling yourself it's just a game. It's not real."

"It... it doesn't have a timer." he chattered.

"It won't go away until we get rid of the corpse." she said, stroking his head, trying to calm him down. Sapphire looked past him and said, "It looks like they were able to kill the beast, but they didn't survive the experience."

"What do we do now?" he asked, gritting his teeth, feeling more in control.

"Let's get the group up and get out of here." she said. Sapphire walked over to Klar's body and asked him, "Do you want to watch?"

Storm was still struggling with his fear and didn't understand her question at first. But, after a few moments he pieced it together and walked over to her and nodded.

Sapphire began casting a new spell. She formed various symbols with her hands and quietly sang a strange song. Storm concentrated as best as he could, committing her movements and words to memory. It was a long spell and incredibly difficult normally, let alone being under the fear affect. She slowly raised her hand in the air and light gathered in her palm. She stood there for half a minute then sharply brought her hand down and the bright light shot towards Klar's body. Klar's body lifted into the air surrounded by the light. All of her wounds healed in front of them and Klar started breathing. As the light dissipated Klar was set down gently on her feet.

[New spell obtained: Resurrection (Life magic)]

Storm walked over to Pipe and cast the resurrection spell for the first time. He repeated the movements and words that Sapphire had used. He focused on the spell and the fear affect seemed to lessen. Pipe's recovery was more magnificent considering he had lost most of his limbs. As soon as the spell set him down, Pipe fell to the ground, whimpering.

Storm watched Sapphire finish resurrecting Kat. When she looked up, he saw the strain in her eyes, the fear was affecting her too. She jumped when Kat's armor clanked and he felt his face flush in anger. His fury overrode the fear affect. He walked up to the salamander, telling himself over and over that it was just a game. He pulled his backpack off and stuck a claw inside to send it into the dimensional space. Of course, it failed. He reequipped his now-bloody bag and stared at the beast in defeat.

Klar, having seen what he was doing, walked up and tossed him a large potato sack.

"Here, this is big enough, although I don't have a clue what you are going to do with it." Klar said.

Storm quickly identified the bag.

[Item
        Name: Potato sack of holding
        Description: This bag is enchanted with a large dimensional space.
        Dimensional space: 100x100
        Space: zero out of one hundred spaces filled

        Contents: Empty
        Crafted by: Weird]

Storm stuck the beast's head inside the bag and the fire salamander disappeared. He breathed a sigh of relief at seeing it gone but the real relief came when the fear effect dissipated. As soon as the creature disappeared into the dimensional space, he felt a weight lift off his shoulders. He checked his UI and confirmed the fear debuff was gone. He looked at Sapphire, who was sitting to regain her mana.

"Thank you" she mouthed when their eyes met.

"You did great Pipe, don't sell yourself short." Klar said when Pipe walked up to them. "I've had others down here not even make it back to the group before losing control."

"You're not upset I got you killed?" he asked.

"Not at all." she said chuckling. "We needed to teach you what happens when a minstrel losses control of a high-level pet. When we take on the world boss, you will need to focus. I highly doubt you want to relive that experience. Besides, that's why we have Sapphire."

"I never want to relive that." Pipe said quietly. He shuddered and his face paled at the thought.

They took a few minutes to rest and recover. Kat and Klar told them how they battled the salamander and both died trying to kill it so it wouldn't go after Sapphire.

"It's time, we need to move." Klar announced, "The other groups will have finished their rooms by now and will be waiting. Sapphire, update them on our status. Let them know we will join them shortly."

The group made its way through the lava cavern, staying well away from the lava pools that hosted the salamanders. They made it to the other side without incident and exited the cavern through an azure portal.

SIXTEEN

Boss room

After going through the portal, Storm was reunited with the other members of his power-leveling group, his friends. They were standing high up in the mountains, several hundred yards away from a massive castle with the volcano looming in the background. Storm looked the castle over and there were hundreds of orcs on the walls. Klar gathered the group around to address them.

"We are going to pull the mobs out here and clear the castle." Klar informed them, "This should take us about an hour. When we've cleared the castle, we will move the whole raid inside to the boss room." Without another word, she turned and walked towards the castle.

Night and light readied themselves in the clearing and the rest of the team fanned out behind them. Klar and Kat approached the castle wall, well away from the gate. Kat deflected the arrows raining down while Klar got into position and used her massive sword to cleave a hole through the wall. Two minstrels slipped inside and began pulling the mobs back to the main group.

The power-levelers, having honed their teamwork, made quick work of the mobs, pull after pull. They had a bit of down time in-between each round and Storm started looting as much as he could. He mostly found gems and gold which he shared with his group equally, but every once in a while, he would find a magical item and gave it to whoever wanted it.

The orcs were the highest level they encountered so far and had pretty good gear. He offered everything he collected to his group and anything they didn't want he stuffed into his bag. He asked Klar for another loot bag and she handed him a few, which he worked diligently to fill.

Storm stuffed the bags full. He had free reign over all conventional, non-magical items because nobody was interested in them. Most of the raid members had better items but Storm, Clover and Mani used this opportunity to make improvements to their equipment, replacing any items they could. Pipe however stated that he was not at all interested in the 'dirty' loot. Storm couldn't blame him, most of the items were covered in orc blood.

Unfortunately, the orcs they ran into didn't use staves but he was able to replace his hammers with a magical pair which he had Mani shorten like the first pair.

[Item

Name: War hammer
Effect: +10 magic damage]

The armor was the hardest part to loot because he had to actually remove it from the dead smelly orc bodies and sometimes, he needed help. He gathered as many high-level conventual sets as he could. If his mom and sister couldn't use it, they could always sell it.

He equipped a pair of magical greaves and leather pants that nobody wanted.

[Item

Name: Greaves of speed
Type: Leather
Effect 1: +50 dexterity
Effect 2: +10% movement speed]

[Item

Name: Leggings of fire
Type: Leather
Effect: +10% fire resistance]

Storm found other magical items that nobody wanted and stuffed them into a bag.

[Item

Name: Short sword of fire
Effect: +10 fire damage]

[Item

Name: Bow of fire
Effect: +10 fire damage]

[Item

Name: Quiver of replenishment
Effect: +1 arrow every 10 seconds]

[Item

Name: Small shield of fire
Effect 1: -10% damage
Effect 2: +20% fire resistance]

[Item

      Name: Helm of fire

      Type: Leather

      Effect: +5% fire resistance]

[Item

      Name: Boots of fire

      Type: Plate

      Effect: +5% fire resistance]

[Item

      Name: Greaves of fire

      Type: Plate

      Effect: +5% fire resistance]

After the castle was cleared, Klar led the raid deeper into the structure and stopped in front of a pair of large intricately carved doors. She turned and addressed the group.

"For those that haven't been here before, this is the boss room. When we open the doors, we all charge in and spread out. There are groups of shamans around the room that will cast AOE stun and AOE damage on us, attack them to interrupt them. Kat and myself will go for the ones in black robes, if left unchecked, they will summon a demon that we don't want to deal with." She looked around the group and said seriously. "Every single shaman must die." then she asked, "Is everybody ready?"

Everybody nodded in acknowledgement, then Kat and Klar pulled the doors open, slamming them into the wall. The doors, now thoroughly destroyed, leaned haphazardly as the raid group rushed between them. The noise generated from their entrance announced their presence to the entire room and cruel yellow eyes turned towards them.

Klar and Kat rushed to the center of the room where nine black-robed shamans stood around a chalk circle on the floor. Their hands raised high, chanting in a harsh sounding language. The rest of the raid spread out into the room, targeting each group of remaining shamans.

Storm ran across the room, towards a group of shamans near the back, a hammer held in each hand. He studied orcish spellcasters as he approached. They were busy casting at other players and didn't notice him. One in the back started casting a new spell and Storm watched closely.

The orc's hand movements were sharp and precise, the spell's words were harsh and cold, it was death magic. As he followed along, a glyph formed in his mind, one he was recently familiar with. It was the fear glyph.

[New spell obtained, Fear, AOE (Death magic)]

Several shamans noticed him and turned in his direction. They quickly redirected their spells and he felt several status debuffs take hold. His forward momentum instantly stopped and he looked down to see his lower half covered in sticky webs. Storm dropped his hammers to cast a spell but he couldn't form the words. He lost his voice.

[Debuff: Silence]

One shaman ginned wickedly and started casting another spell at him while the others shifted their focus to the rest of the room. Storm watched helplessly as the orc formed the shapes and spoke the words from a spell school he didn't recognize.

Storm paid attention to the orc's spell work but also started casting one in desperation. He cast the last spell he acquired, it being the freshest in his mind, Fear. He precisely formed the shapes with his hands and put great intention behind his effort. He held the fear glyph in his mind, praying the spell would activate without the spoken component.

Storm and the orc shaman completed their spells at the same time. At first, he wasn't sure it would work, but Storm felt the rush of magic when he finished. He heard several chimes but could only glance at his notifications because in that moment the orc's fireball struck him in the chest and engulfed him in flames.

[New skill obtained, Fire magic]

[New spell obtained, Fireball (Fire magic)]

[New skill obtained, Silent casting]

The orc scored a critical hit on Storm and the only thing that saved his life was the fire resistance buff he currently had. His cloak absorbed a majority of the damage, but even then, it was not enough. His health fell to below half and continued to drop due to burn damage.

The fire burned through the webs holding him in place and he fell to the ground in a heap. He lay there in pain, his body smoldering. With health low and time running out, Storm desperately cast the only spell he could think of.

Still under the silence debuff he held the healing glyph in his mind and silently cast the spell on himself. He felt instant relief as the healing magic coursed through his body. He cast it a few more times to top off his health.

From the floor, Storm looked at the group of shamans to find most had all succumbed to his fear spell. They were frozen in place with panic on their faces.

Not wanting to waste the initiative, he scooped up his hammers and charged into their ranks. The shamans watched wide-eyed in fear as he approached, several trying to flee. He reached them quickly and swung his hammers, felling as many as he could before the fear debuff elapsed.

A massive shaman in the back began casting a spell at him but Storm cocked his arm back and threw his hammer, just as Mani had instructed. His weapon flew true and would have struck the orc except the mage interrupted its spell to insta-cast a shield. Right before Storm's hammer struck, a translucent amber-colored wall snapped into existence around the orc.

Storm's hammer smashed into the magical wall and flew back towards him as if it were a missel. Surprised, Storm tried to grab it out of midair but unfortunately, he misjudged the energy the hammer now held. The hammer slammed into his hand, shattering it, the force continued down his arm, pulverizing it too.

Storm fell to the ground screaming in pain, cradling his shattered limb. Through pain filled eyes, he saw the shaman casting again. He recognized the spell and followed along as best he could. When the spell completed, he weakly lifted his good arm and insta-cast the spell he had just learned.

[New spell obtained
    Name: Fire shield (Fire magic)
    Cast time: Instant
    Description: Surrounds self, reflects all damage for one strike. +50% fire resistance]

The fireball flew out of the shaman's hands, striking Storm's shield and bouncing back. The orc's eyes widened in surprise as the fireball struck him in the chest and exploded. The force hurled the orc against a wall, shattering all the bones in its body. The create slumped to the ground, a green, bloody trail oozing down after it.

Storm felt the cooling wave of healing magic pass over him and the bones in his arm and hand straightened and fixed themselves. He picked himself up and found Sapphire staring at him. He nodding in thanks to her and turned back to the group of shamans.

The reflected fireball had thrown the rest of the orcs to the ground, stunning them. He quickly walked around and dispatched them with his hammers.

The rest of the raid had cleared the room and were in the process of piling the treasures near the entrance. Storm searched the shamans he killed and found gold and gems but also several magical items, which he placed in the group's loot pile.

"We will take turns picking items," Klar announced, "This was a good run. Rest up and after we distribute the loot, we will setup for the next phase." She looked around at the weary players and added, "I know it's late but we are almost done." Klar walked up to Sapphire and quietly instructed "Call the others, it's time."

Sapphire nodded and walked to the center of the room where the cursed circle was drawn on the ground. She pulled out a dagger and sliced open her hand then walked around the summoning circle. On the ground, she drew different symbols using her blood. Storm saw a flash of healing magic when she finished, then she stepped into the center. Sapphire pulled out a black scroll, unraveled it and held it before her. Words written in a flowing golden script covered it from top to bottom.

Sapphire began singing as she read the scroll. She danced around the room, her body lithe and flexible. Storm was transfixed as she moved and goosebumps formed when her hauntingly beautiful voice echoed around the dark chamber.

As Sapphire sang, lights swirled around her and landed on the ground. The symbols she drew in blood began to glow and Storm felt the room fill with power. The light in the chamber grew so bright, Storm could only see her shadow moving around. Then, suddenly a cracking noise filled the chamber and the lights dimmed.

Everybody fell silent and watched Sapphire in amazement as she finished casting the spell. She stood there, breathing heavily with her head down and arms at her sides. The scroll crumpled to dust and a large portal opened in the center of the room. It was larger than any portal Storm had seen before and was filled with a shifting purple color that reminded him of a nebula in space.

A large demon stepped out of the portal. The beast stood seven feet tall with two horns that stretched and twisted into the air. Its black body looked hard like plate mail. Storm took a step back in fear, his heart pounding. He reached for his hammers but before he could bring them to bare, the beast reached up and removed its head, or rather, its helmet.

His helm now off, Weird stood there watching Storm with a wry smile and winked. He tuned and bowed a thanks to Sapphire, then walked over to talk with Klar. Weird nodded in satisfaction after her report then sat down next to the portal to wait. He pulled out a small device, just like the one he Storm, and began tapping at it. After a few minutes, two very familiar men appeared next to him and leaned down to talk in hushed tones.

Storm quickly identified them.

[Character
        Name: Strychnine
        Guild: Dark Elite
        Level: 100
        Health: ***/***]

[Character
        Name: Tomb
        Guild: Dark Elite
        Level: 100
        Health: ***/***]

No sooner than he dismissed the prompts, Weird nodded and the minstrel and assassin stood up and blurred out of the cavern, a small drumming sound making it to Storm's ears.

"Go pick your reward." Klar told Storm quietly, stepping up to him. "You can choose three items."

Storm excitedly stepped up to the sorted piles of treasure. The loot was arranged into piles of weapons, armor, clothing, jewelry and miscellaneous items.

If he could only choose three items, Storm wanted to focus on areas that needed improving the most. His weapons and armor were working well enough so he skipped those piles completely. He was interested in unusual items so he searched the miscellaneous pile first, where he found an interesting pair of glasses.

[Item

> Name: Eagle eye specs
> Effect: +200% to perception
> Description: Helps find objects hidden in plain sight]

The golden, wire framed glasses were missing the lenses and he wasn't sure if they would still work. Worried they had been damaged in the battle, he put them on to test them. They felt comfortable on his face and since he wore glasses in the real world it seemed very natural to wear them here too.

He wasn't sure how to verify the increase to his perception so he stepped up to the next pile to search for another item. He picked through the rings and bracelets and even considered the earrings. His ears weren't pierced but if there was one powerful enough, he surely would consider it. Although he would certainly disinfect it first.

Unfortunately, there wasn't anything particularly interesting. He was about to move to the next pile when out of the corner of his eye he saw a flash of golden light. When he turned to look, he only saw a crappy copper ring. He picked it up and identified it.

[Item

> Name: Ring of holding
> Status: Full
> Description: Holds one item. Invoke activation phrase to store item. Invoke activation phrase to empty item.
> Range: Touch]

Curious, Storm slipped the ring on and activated it. A bright red fish appeared and fell to the ground, dead.

[Quest Item

> Name: Lava trout
> Status: Dead
> Quality: Fresh]

Chuckling, Storm picked up the fish and activated the ring to suck it back into the dimensional space. He decided he liked the ring and kept it on his hand. Nothing else in the pile popped out at him so he moved on.

He sifted through the clothing pile and looked at each of the robes. Each shaman in the room was wearing a robe so there were plenty to choose from but none of them really excited them. The red robes only offered a few points in either wisdom or intelligence. The black hooded robes were more interesting but still offered no armor and he was ready to move to another pile when he saw another flash of golden light. He picked up the robes and identified them.

[Item

        Name: Cloak of the Fire Demon

        Effect: +10 to Fire magic, +50% resistance to fire magic]

He felt a bulge in one of the pockets and pulled out a book wrapped in a black silk cloth. He unwound the book and read the title, Summoning a Fire Demon. Then he looked at the silk cloth and realized it was actually a scarf and identified it.

[Item

        Name: Summoning a Fire Demon (Book)]

        Effect: Unknown]

[Item

        Name: Silk scarf of casting

        Effect: +20% casting speed]

Storm couldn't believe his luck. He was one of the last to pick items and he was sure that the scarf would have been long gone had it not been hidden. He slipped it around his neck and was excited to try it. A twenty percent increase in casting speed was a big deal. It would allow him to identify an opponent's spell and cast a counter.

"Interesting choices." Klar said walking up to him. "Nice find on the scarf. And I haven't seen that ring drop here before."

"I also found this book." Storm said, showing it to her. Then asked, "Should I put something back?"

"No," she said, "You should take that robe, and we won't count the book. Consider those freebees. We have tons of those robes and that book is useless to almost everybody."

"Thanks." he said, then stuffed the robe and book into his backpack. "What's next?" he asked.

"Go join your friends, we have a few minutes." she instructed, "Then it's your turn to give us a big show."

Storm cringed, understanding what she meant. Then, he did as she suggested and left to find his friends. Curious on the loot they chose he asked them what items they picked.

Mani chose all armor pieces. The dwarf picked bracers that increased damage, a helm that gave night vision and boots that made him quieter. Clover had taken a staff with fireball charges and two rings that increased intelligence.

Pipe hated the orc loot. He complained that the armor and clothes were gross, the jewelry was cheap and crude and the weapons were lackluster. But, rolling his eyes, he admitted he chose an amulet that increases concentration, which he said he would never show anybody because it was so hideous. The other items he chose were a magical lock pick and a dagger that glowed when magical traps were nearby.

Storm showed the others what he picked, then, a shiver ran down his spine when he heard a beautiful feminine voice call out.

"It's time Storm." Sapphire said cheerfully.

SEVENTEEN

Phoenix God

Sapphire led Storm down a tunnel and out the back of the castle. The sky had darkened as night overtook the game world. A sliver of moon could be seen through the hazy atmosphere. They walked along a trail, the world around them quiet except for their feet crunching on the lava rock. The massive volcano loomed in front of them.

"Are the others coming?" Storm asked nervously.

"Of course," Sapphire said chuckling. She pointed at a clearing ahead, "They will setup over there, which is where we need to pull the Phoenix God to."

The closer they got to the volcano the hotter it became. Sweat poured down his face and his cloths were drenched. He glanced at Sapphire and she looked like she was taking a stroll on a lovely spring day, a cool breeze blowing through her hair.

"How..." he began to ask incredulously.

She smiled at him then cast a spell on herself. He recognized the spell and instantly felt like an idiot. She had been casting fire resistance on herself every once in a while, and he failed to realize why. He was about to cast the spell on his tattered cloak and she spoke up.

"Did Klar give you the robes?" she asked.

"Yeah," Storm said, "but I didn't want to take off my chainmail."

"Don't you think you would be a bit more comfortable for this next part if you did?" she asked.

Thinking about it, Storm sighed and knew she was right. He would probably be able to run faster in the robes anyways. He swapped his chainmail out with the robes and already started to feel cooler with the 50% fire resistance. He then cast his fire resistance spell on the robes and felt that much better.

"Thanks," he said with much relief "That feels much better."

"Shall we?" she asked, pointing towards the volcano. "The bird isn't going to attack us on its own."

Solemnly Storm followed Sapphire down the trail. He glanced back and saw a half dozen players working in the clearing they had just passed. They erected several large totems and were working on a few more.

"I… I have to make it all the way back here?" Storm asked, stammering. It seemed like there was at least a mile between the volcano and clearing.

"No," she said, "You won't make it back. Nobody has ever made it all the way back. Most other groups would need a few people but with me, I just need one other person. When you die, I'll rez you then the bird will aggro to me and I'll kite it back."

"Does it have to be me?" he asked, not for the first time.

"No, but it has to be somebody under level 50. Anybody above will get a nasty insta death in the bird's chamber."

"So, you are not leading me to my death to torture me?" Storm asked.

"No," Sapphire laughed, "you were chosen because we thought you had the best chance of succeeding. Besides, I believe you made a bargain with Weird. Consider this proving yourself. He doesn't forget," and more quietly she added, "for better or worse."

"Sapphire, how long have you been with Dark Elite?" he asked after they walked in silence for a few minutes.

"Me? I've been with them for years. They're my family." she explained.

"Are you an original?" he asked, interested.

"No," she said laughing. "But, I'm close. I started playing after the beta."

He had been so focused on survival and power leveling he didn't put much thought into Dark Elite's nefarious activities. But he didn't want to lose Father and needed to find out more about the guild. He hated using her, but Sapphire was a good source of information.

"What got you into the guild in the first place?" he asked.

"My sister," she said wistfully, "she begged me to play this game."

"That's really cool" Storm replied. He sensed a change in her tone and offered his own story, "I started playing this game with my sister and even more embarrassingly, my mom."

"That's not embarrassing." she said, "I think it's sweet to play with family, sometimes I'll even join one of my dad's raids."

"Your dad plays?" Storm asked, not feeling so bad about playing with his mom.

"Yes," she chuckled, "probably too much."

"Is your sister Klar?" he asked.

"No," she replied, "we lost my sister a couple years ago."

"I'm... I'm so sorry Sapphire, that's terrible." Storm said. He stopped walking and stared at her.

She turned and looked at him oddly.

"I... I recently lost my father too." he said, tears forming in his eyes, he took a deep breath and continued. "Oddly enough, that is why me and my family are here, to honor his memory."

Sapphire stepped up to him arms wide and with a caring look on her face she pulled him close. They held each other for a few moments in the desolate landscape, sharing each other's pain of loss. Storm couldn't hold back his tears and started crying harder and he felt Sapphire gently sobbing against him. After a few moments she stepped back and wiped the tears from her eyes.

"We should go. The raid is waiting for us." she said.

"You're right, I... I'm sorry, I don't know what..." Storm said.

"No, don't be sorry." she interrupted, "It's hard." Then she nervously asked, "Do... do you want to get coffee sometime?"

"I.... yeah... I mean, I'd love to but... umm... where would we get one?" Storm asked, stammering, "I mean, I haven't been to many of the cities yet and..."

"No silly," she said, giggling, "I mean in the real world."

"You're in New Las Vegas" he said slowly, finally understanding.

"I am. And there are plenty of coffee places here." she said smiling.

"Yeah, I'd like coffee." he said quickly, recovering. There were so many questions he wanted to ask her but this wasn't the right time, and he didn't want to spoil the moment they just had. He looked at the volcano and asked, "Ok, what do we do now?"

"Follow me, we are almost there." she instructed.

The two walked down the path another hundred yards and Sapphire led them off-trail to the side of the volcano. They stood before a rock wall and she hit a hidden lever to open a large hole that led deeper into the fiery mountain.

"This is the back entrance." she explained, "Go down the tunnel until you come to a large lava chamber. The Phoenix God will be in there. Get him to aggro you and run back here as quick as you can. You have to at least make it back to me."

"Then what?" Storm asked.

"Run as far as you can," she said, "I'll shadow you and when you die, I'll rez you to pull aggro. When you rez, get back to the raid as fast as you can and join the fighting. And Storm, hurry before everybody falls to sleep, it's late."

"How am I supposed to see in here?" he called out, after going into the dark tunnel.

Sapphire started casting a spell but slowed down when he wasn't paying attention. She frowned at him and his heart skipped beat.

Storm frantically searched for what irked her and realized she was casting a spell. Suddenly understanding her intent, he copied her, his improved perception and casting speed making it a simple task.

[New spell obtained: Night vision, self (Life magic)]

"Thanks!" he yelled, then tuned to the dark tunnel, now tinted green from his night vision. He traveled deep into the volcano and was thankful for his heat resistance robes and the fire resistance buff. Even with that protection he felt an uncomfortable amount of heat emanating from the floor and into his feet.

The tunnel led straight into the volcano, with a heavy slope down. There were no intersections and after about ten minutes of walking Storm finally saw the light at the end of the tunnel. A red glow formed and got brighter the closer he got.

When he neared the end of the tunnel, he slowed down and approached with caution. Thinking the bird was going to be immediately at the end, he snuck up to the opening and cautiously peered out. He looked into the heart of the volcano. It was a chamber filled with bubbling pools of lava and narrow walkways in-between. He did not see the fiery bird.

He waited for a few minutes to see if the phoenix would appear but it never did. He cautiously stepped into the chamber and slowly walked to the first lava pool. He was ready at any moment to sprint back to the tunnel and even had a few jumps when the lava bubbled. But again, there was no phoenix. He took a few careful steps around the pool and looked up at the open sky, wondering if the bird had flown out of the volcano like he had seen earlier.

He searched all around for the bird but there was no sign of it. He even looked for a large nest but he saw nothing. Storm strayed a little further from the tunnel and each passing minute he was getting more comfortable. He crossed a narrow bridge between two of the lava pools and continued searching the chamber. He walked up to the largest pool of lava and stared deep into it. Despite his high fire resistance, he still felt the extreme heat on his face. He stood there, mesmerized by the shifting colors and the slow bubbles popping.

Storm found it very comforting and was hypnotized by the lava, like staring into a camp fire on a cool evening. He glanced to the center of the pool and wondered if his eyes were playing tricks on him. The lava pool rose slowly as if to release a large bubble. Instead, a large creature burst through the surface and into the air, flapping its wings.

Storm's face felt like it was on fire as he dumbly stared at the blazing bird. To him, the beast seemed brighter than a thousand suns. His lungs burned from the heat and he frantically tried to think of what to do. He turned to run.

In his exploration of the lava pools, he strayed too far from the tunnel that had brought him there. He knew that he wouldn't make it back before the bird killed him unless he did something. He recklessly ran across the narrow bridge and almost made it to the tunnel. But before he could enter the protective passage, he heard an ear shattering screech directly behind him.

The rapid increase in heat should have been the first indication that danger was quickly approaching. He looked back just as the fire bird was lunging at him with its beak. He fell to the ground and rolled, feeling the bird pass over him.

He regained his feet but unfortunately the fire bird had positioned itself in-between him and his escape. It flapped its massive wings and a wave of heat enveloped him.

Out of desperation he activated his ring of holding and the red fish popped out. He snagged it out of the air and waggled it in front of the phoenix. Storm threw the fish as hard as he could, praying the bird would take the bait. And it did. The phoenix made a dive for the fish and caught it in its fiery beak.

Not wasting any time, Storm darted past the bird and into the tunnel. Once again surrounded by the comforting walls, he ran as fast as he could to the other end. It was uphill the entire way and by the time he exited, he was breathing heavy and so exhausted he fell down the embankment.

"Did it work?" Sapphire casually asked him.

Storm stood up and dusted himself off and was about to reply when they both jumped at the sound of an angry screech echoing down the tunnel.

"Good, I guess." Storm answered with a lopsided grin.

"You better run." she warned, then she put a hand on his back and pushed him towards the ambush.

Storm stumbled forward, almost face-planting, but caught himself and ran as fast as he could. Sapphire followed him, a good distance behind. Not too long later a fiery form burst forth from the top of the volcano. As he ran, Storm checked the birds progress several times and each time became more terrified.

The Phoenix God beat its wings and flew straight towards him like a fiery comet. Storm put his head down and ran harder but he knew it wouldn't be enough. He felt the heat on his back rise to an unbearable level and knew the bird was close.

Storm adjusted his route to a slight zig-zag pattern hoping to throw it off but it kept getting hotter and hotter. He took a quick glance over his shoulder and missed a step and fell forward. He landed hard on the lava rock and skidded to a stop, his health bar flashing as he took damage.

Fortunately for him that saved his life because the Phoenix God had chosen that moment to attack, its claws passing through the space where his body had just been. The fire bird flew past and screeched in anger. Bruised and bleeding Storm pushed himself up and stumbled forward, keeping a close eye on the bird as it banked around to come at him again.

Breathing hard, Storm continued his mad dash towards the rest of the raid, where they were waiting in ambush. As he ran, he wracked his brain for any spell he could use to get the bird to back off. He had a few close calls so far and wanted to even the tables a little.

He thought if anything would work, rain would. He cast the spell over and over as he ran, hoping it would be enough to keep the bird away. When the first drops of rain hit his face, he felt a renewed energy and sped up. Then, in response to the rain he heard an angry screech and felt the ever-present heat decline.

Storm pushed on, focusing on his footsteps. He couldn't afford one misstep on the uneven, and now wet, the lava rock. The distant lights of the raid were getting closer each passing minute and he was feeling hopeful he would make it. So far, the rain spell was effective at keeping the fiery bird at bay but his mana was running low.

Storm ran and ran until somebody grab him and he came to a sudden stop. Breathing hard he looked around at all the faces cheering for him and he realized he made it. He started crying in relief.

"I made it." he choked out in a ragged breath. He looked up at the sky, rain falling onto his face and said in relieved tone, "I made it.". Then anger rising inside him, he turned, raising both fists into the air and screamed at the fiery bird, "I MAAAAADE IT!"

No sooner than he stopped yelling, he heard a loud screech in retort and saw a brilliant flash of light as the Phoenix landed in front of him and pierced through his chest with its mighty beak. Storm fell to his knees and could only stare at the bird in disbelief. The Phoenix God spread its wings wide and stretched its head high screeching in victory. Then Storm saw no more as his health reached zero.

He didn't have to wait too long in the darkness before he saw a prompt appear.

[Resurrection
        From: Sapphire
        Accept
        Decline]

Storm took a deep breath then accepted. He appeared next to Sapphire, away from the battle. He looked at the bird and took a step back. The Phoenix God was attacking the largest fire salamander he had ever seen. It was easily three times larger than the one Pipe had charmed.

The phoenix and fire salamander were locked in an epic battle while the rest of the raid stood in a circle around the two, taking bets and cheering. Storm saw healing spells pop off once in a while giving the salamander a boost.

"Thanks," Storm whispered to Sapphire, "What now?"

"Now we wait." she replied.

"Debuff the bird!" a strong voice commanded. Storm followed the voice to find Weird barking orders.

"Why is everybody standing around?" Storm asked Sapphire.

"We use the salamander because it's great at keeping the bird's attention." she explained.

"What?" Storm asked

"Not much of a gamer are you" Sapphire said with a smirk.

Storm shook his head and she laughed.

"When you get too close to an aggressive mob it will chase you." Sapphire explained, "When you died, the phoenix would have come after me, except Tomb's salamander started attacking it first. These salamanders have incredibly high health and are super tough so they are excellent at tanking bosses."

"What happens if the fire salamander dies?" Storm asked.

"It will attack us and likely kill all of us." she replied.

"Couldn't we take it with the raid?" Storm asked.

"Without the salamander?" Sapphire asked rhetorically, chuckling and shook her head, "This boss would take three to four times our current numbers. With the pet, Weird and Tomb can do this on their own."

Storm thought it was incredible that they could take out a high-level boss with so little people. He was impressed that they used the game mechanics to their advantage in this way. Watching the slow battle, he had an idea and pulled up his spells to see if he had the information he needed for another modification.

He made a few changes and tried casting a new spell. It didn't work at first but he kept tweaking it and finally found the right combination. He felt the magic release and a fire shield surrounded the salamander.

[New spell obtained: Fire shield, other (Fire magic)]

Storm knew from experience that attacking a fire shield was a terrible idea because for one attack it would reflect all the damage back onto the attacker. After that attack however, the fire shield would disappear. Fortunately, he could cast it a few more times before he ran out of mana. His new version of the spell had a huge downside by cost a lot of mana.

As he expected, the phoenix attacked the salamander with its beak and struck the fire shield. When it did, the bird jolted backwards and shook its head in pain. Storm saw a large chunk disappear from the bird's health bar. On the other side of the battle Weird looked over at him and tilted his head questioningly and Storm looked back and shrugged. Weird gave a firm nod of approval then returned his attention to the battle.

Storm moved closer to the mana regeneration totem and cast his fire shield on the salamander a few more times until he ran out of mana. He kept out of the way and watched as Weird directed the healers when to heal.

Storm cast his shield when he had the mana and every time he did, the bird's health dropped visibly. He wished his mana would regenerate faster so he could continue to cast the shield but either way, it was just a matter of time. The phoenix was fighting a losing battle.

Suddenly a fire shield appeared around the salamander. Storm was surprised because he didn't cast it. He quickly looked around and found Sapphire looking at him with a sly smile on her face, she winked at him then turned back to the battle and cast the fire shield spell again.

In record time, the Phoenix God was defeated. When its health reached zero a massive fiery blast erupted from it, knocking everybody to the ground. Only Weird and Tomb were unaffected while everybody else took light to heavy damage.

Healers walked through the ranks and healed anybody wounded by the phoenix's last breath. Due to the massive amount of xp bosses had, many players in the raid leveled, rainbow lights twirling around them. Storm was no exception.

[Level up: Level 50]

Weird walked up to the pile of dust left behind by the bird, and started searching through it. A crowd of Dark Elite gathered around him, creating a circle and talking quietly as he worked. When he stood up to address the group, everybody quieted.

"Friends." Weird said loudly, turning around looking at them all. "Thank you for joining me tonight in our last God Beast raid. I know it's late so we will get straight to the loot. First prize goes to Storm." Everybody cheered and when they quieted down Weird continued, "Storm not only pulled the Phoenix God to us, he was able to make it all the way, defying our best expectations." Weird then held up a five-foot flaming feather. "To you goes the Phoenix Feather." Everybody clapped as Weird handed the feather to Storm.

Storm thanked Weird and held it up, unsure of what to do with it while trying not to set anything on fire. People were clapping him on the back and jostling him and he started to get a little concerned. Having a thought, he pulled the feather into his ring of holding before anything bad happened.

"What do we do now?" Storm asked Sapphire, after finding her in the crowd.

"This is the best part, we get our loot!" she said, her eyes lighting up.

"I think I already got mine." Storm said.

"Oh, no." she replied, "That was just a trophy. The real prize is coming." She pointed at Weird, walking through the crowd handing out small white boxes with question marks on them.

Weird made his way to Sapphire and Storm with several followers trailing behind, carrying a large golden chest. They gently set it down next to the guild master and took a step back.

"Greetings all mighty lord." Sapphire said in mock reverence, bowing deeply.

Weird stood in front of her with an impassive expression on his face. He slowly shook his head, unamused. With a heavy sigh he reached into the treasure chest and pulled out three boxes and set them on the ground in front of her.

"Thank you for helping with the raid tonight." he said simply.

"Storm," Weird said, turning to him. "Thank you for your help too. It was a pleasure watching you work. I hope you will join us on more raids in the future. You asked for a spot in one of my groups and I think you more than proved yourself tonight. I like unique thinkers and I reward those that contribute to the guild." Weird reached into the golden treasure chest and pulled out five boxes and set them on the ground in front of him. He continued, "We have another big raid the day after tomorrow. You are still a bit low but if you show up you can have a spot in my group, one raid only though."

"Thanks, I'll be there." Storm said numbly. Then he packed the boxes in his backpack and looked around with a dazed expression.

"You should go to sleep." a sweet voice said. "Set your avatar to follow me and I'll get him back to camp."

Storm nodded to Sapphire, thankful for her help. He was exhausted and was about to fall to sleep on his feet. He gave his avatar the instructions and logged out.

The immediate lack of sound and blistering heat put Luke into such a relaxed state that when he logged out, he didn't make it out of the pod. He fell to sleep before opening the door.

EIGHTEEN

Coffee

The next morning, Luke woke up in the pod having slept there the all night. He stumbled sleepily into the kitchen surprising his mom and sister.

"Good morning" they both said in unison, then looked at each other and laughed.

Luke grumbled a response and sat down to eat. He would have missed breakfast entirely had his mom not set aside a plate for him.

"How was the raid?" his mom asked.

"It was fun" he responded in a tired voice, then stared off into space, thinking about the night.

"Tell us about it." Cleo prompted.

Luke felt self-conscience about having fun without them, but he relented and recounted the various battles. As he spoke, he became more animated, his excitement pushing away the sleepiness. He ended his tale with the orc castle and the Phoenix God battle.

Luke told them about all the new equipment he received and even the stuff he had collected for them. He also told them about his new friends, Mani, Clover and Pipe. And of course, he told them about Sapphire but he tried not to sound too excited talking about her.

"There is another raid tomorrow," he finally said, "but I have today off."

"How long are you going to stay with them?" Cleo asked. Then she smiled and added, "I mean, I get it," she coughed "Sapphire" into her hand.

"It's not like that" Luke responded, blushing. "Weird invited me to join his group tomorrow. I thought it would be a good chance to get more information."

His mom and sister looked at each other with knowing smiles.

"It's fine Luke, we are here to enjoy the game." his mom said.

"Well," Luke said hesitantly, "Since I have a free day, I was thinking of traveling to Last Hope and hooking up with Father and you for a dungeon raid, if there is something close. Maybe something easy enough for the three of us."

"That's a great idea!" Cleo said excitedly. Then she looked at her mom, "I wish you could make it too mom."

"It's ok," she said, "You two enjoy yourselves. When I can cross the river, I'll meet up with you."

"You sure you're ok if we go on a dungeon raid with Father?" Luke asked.

"Of course," she said, "I think it's great. I just... well, there are some things I wanted to talk with you two about, but it can wait until later. You should enjoy your day with him and when you see him later, remember that there *is* a little bit of your father in that avatar."

"Ok, Cleo, I'll meet you in Last Hope." Luke said excitedly, he was really looking forward to spending the day with his family. "There are a few horses around camp and I should be able to borrow one for the day. I'll log out on my way and leave a note to let you know when I will arrive." Then he got up and started walking towards his room to clean up and start his in-game day.

Storm logged in and found himself sitting in the middle of a tent. He wasn't sure where his avatar would be but it seemed to be the Dark Elite camp. He pulled up his log to see what his avatar had been doing and was surprised that he had exhausted his supply of parchment by creating spell scrolls, then leveled up a few skills, including puzzle breaking. Storm gathered up his things and stepped outside.

"Good morning, Storm," came a beautifully familiar voice. Sapphire was sitting on a log poking a stick into the camp fire in front of his tent.

"Good morning" he said back. Then awkwardly asked, "How are you?"

"I'm great" she responded cheerfully, "Do you have plans today?"

"Yeah, sorry." Storm said, rubbing the back of his head, "Since we had the day off, I promised to meet my sister and do a dungeon raid with her."

"That sounds fun. Did you want company?" she asked.

"Well…" he responded hesitantly, he would love to have her along but he wasn't sure how to explain Father's presence. He finally said, "It's probably going to be super boring."

"I like boring," she blurted out, "I mean, if you have plans with family I don't want to intrude, but I'd like to hang out in-game, if you wanted company."

"Ok, I'll ask." he hedged.

"Why don't I join you until you meet up with your sister," she said, "and if she is cool with it, I'll stay, if not then I'll find something else to do. Where were you meeting her?"

"In Last Hope." Storm replied.

"Oh, that's pretty far." Sapphire informed him, "How were you going to get there?"

"I was hoping to borrow a horse." Storm replied meekly.

"Do you know how to ride one?" she asked, her eyes brightening.

"Well, not exactly." he responded, frowning, "I thought I just sit on top and it'll take me where I wanted to go."

A beautiful laughter erupted from her and she explained, "Horses are much more complicated than that. You need to care for them. You need to know how to put on the bridle and tack. You need to know the proper way to tighten a saddle. Horses even need to be fed and watered. Bring me along and I'll take care of it all. I'll get you to Last Hope."

"Ok, I'm game." he said happily. He didn't realize it was so complicated.

"This is going to be fun." she said, then yelled, "Bobby!"

Bobby came running.

"Yes, lady Sapphire?" he asked, breathing heavily.

"Would you hitch up the team of horses?" she asked, smiling sweetly at the boy, "Storm and I are going to take the wagon for the day."

"Yes ma'am!" Bobby said, bobbing his head, "I'll have them ready shortly." And without another word, he ran off towards the stables.

"Wagon?" Storm asked.

"It's more comfortable than riding a horse," she explained, then with a wry smile she added, "especially if you don't know what you are doing."

Storm scoffed. He glanced at her and was about to reply, but the words died on his lips. She sure was distracting.

A short time later Bobby exited the stables with a wagon led by two horses. He handed the reigns to Sapphire and quickly left to handle other camp business.

Sapphire climbed onto the wagon's bench and waved for Storm to sit next to her. Once he was seated, she released the break and snapped the reigns to start the horses moving forward. She gently steered them out of the encampment and onto the road heading east.

Sapphire scooted closer to Storm and leaned in to bump his shoulder.

"How about that coffee?" Sapphire asked.

"What? Now?" he asked, panic creeping into his voice.

"The ride to Last Hope is going to take about an hour, we can set our avatars up to handle it. Coffee doesn't have to take long. It can be a quickie." she said, winking.

"Ok, a quickie." he replied. A second later his face turned red after realizing what he said.

"Meet me at the coffee shop next to the fountain with gold water. Fifteen minutes." she said quickly, then the sparkle in her eye was gone as she logged out. Her avatar mechanically turned towards the road and directed the pair of horses.

Storm setup instructions for his avatar and logged out. He had been playing pretty heavily the last couple of days and a nice hot shower would do him a lot of good before he met Sapphire for the first time.

Sapphire and him had gotten close the past couple of days but he wasn't really sure where their friendship was. In the small moments of downtime while power leveling the two chatted about their lives and families, they even commiserated over lost loved ones. However, it never left his mind that she, and her guild, were actively working towards the destruction of the server and consequently his only link to his deceased father.

Ten minutes later Luke walked past the front desk of his resort and out into the real world for the first time in a week. He stood there with his eyes closed, feeling the warmth of the sun on his face and cool air rustling his clothes. He couldn't help but compare the two worlds and while still different he had no doubts that one day they would be imperceptible from each other.

Luke walked hurriedly through the central park and looked at the color of water in each fountain. They were all different. After a few minutes he spotting the golden water and of course it was in front of the most elaborate hotel there. All of the other hotel lobbies were accessible except this one was surrounded by a large wrought iron fence with guards at the gate.

Luke approached the small building with a sign that had a large steaming coffee cup on it. He opened the door and cringed as a small chime announced his arrival. Everybody inside looked at him and they were all immaculately dressed, as if they were going to a ball. He glanced around and didn't see anybody that resembled Sapphire, so he stepped outside to wait.

After a few minutes a very large man approached him. The man was intimidatingly tall and each arm looked as thick as a tree. He wore a nice suit with dark sunglasses and walked directly up to him with a serious look on his face.

"Storm?" he asked in a deep voice.

Luke gulped and stood there not knowing how to response. Then he heard Sapphire giggling.

"Really?" She asked, "I gave you huge dude vibes?"

As Sapphire stepped from behind tree-man, Luke's heart skipped a beat. She was stunning. She had short curly hair, dyed a vibrant indigo. She wore a long rainbow-colored skirt with a faded, pink tank top.

Luke was beyond nervous. His heart was pounding in his chest and he felt like he couldn't breathe. For a moment he lost himself in her sapphire-colored eyes, they were the most beautiful he had ever seen. He knew in that moment that they would never achieve this level of perfection in an artificial world.

Sapphire made eye contact with tree-man and he pressed his hand to his ear and whispered a few words as he scanned the surroundings. The large man walked into the coffee shop and after a few moments stepped back outside, nodded towards his charge and took up position a few feet from the entrance.

"You ready?" she asked in a voice that had consumed him since the day he heard it. She held out an arm to him.

Luke numbly took her arm and let her lead him into the coffee shop. He smelled the sweet scent of lavender and looked around for its source. It was her.

After ordering, they awkwardly waited for their drinks then left to meander through the park. While they walked, security guards, dressed the same as tree-man, took up positions all around them. A bubble was created around them and others were kept away while the couple walked. And when anybody got too close, they were professional escorted away.

Eventually a small group of people gathered to see who the mysterious couple was. Storm looked at the woman he knew as Sapphire and wondered who she was.

"It's nice to meet you in person." she said.

"Nice to meet you too, I'm…" Luke started to introduce himself.

"No." she interrupted, "Don't tell me. No names for now." she glanced at the crowd that had formed.

They walked in silence for a while, their boots crunching on the small stone pathway. When they finally left the curious park-goers behind, she stopped and tuned to him.

"Ok, spill it." she commanded, "Are you a spy?"

"What?" Luke asked in alarm, eyes wide with surprise, "No"

"Are you a spy?" she repeated herself more forcefully, "Are you here to spy on my guild?"

"No," he said defensively, "why would you think that?"

"There have been reports of a spy in the guild." she explained. She visibly relaxed then continued, "It's been known to happen. With your skills, you would make a very good spy."

"Me?" he said doubtfully, "Haven't you noticed, I don't know anything about this game."

"Yeah," she said, chuckling, "But you could be faking it."

"Right, I'm faking being dumb to impress a cute girl." he retorted, not considering his words. He had immediate regret.

She looked at him with an unreadable expression, then asked "So, you are really here with your sister and mother?"

"Yeah." he answered, "Is that why you were so insistent on coming along today, to see if I was telling the truth?"

"Sort of," she admitted, "I really did want to spend time with you, but I also needed to make sure you weren't a spy."

"And coffee?" he asked, his feelings a little hurt, "Is this just an interrogation?"

"No." she responded defensively, then she sighed and explained, "Storm, I like you, I really do but there is a lot of risk here. I have to be careful. I can't fall for a spy, that would ruin everything. Protecting my family is more important than anything."

Luke felt bad, in a way he was a spy and just like her, he wanted to protect his family. Then he realized the implications of what she just said.

"Wait," he said, "You're falling for me?"

She laughed cutely but didn't respond. She continued walking. After a few minutes, Luke built up the courage to ask her something he needed to ask.

"What is Dark Elite doing?" he asked quietly, "Are they trying to destroy the server?"

She stopped and turned to him. Her brow furrowed.

"Are you sure you are not a spy?" she asked, "Because that sounds like something a spy would ask."

"No." he said shaking his head. He was tired with the games and with no small amount of frustration he continued, "No Sapphire, I'm not a spy. I'm just a stupid guy with a dead dad and I want to spend time with him. And you and your guild are going to take that away from me."

She took a step back and her face paled.

"Your dad's avatar is on the server." she said quietly after coming to the realization.

"I haven't seen him in years," Luke confided, tears forming in his eyes. He continued passionately "And I enter this game and he's right there. He looks the same, he sounds the same, he even has his same mannerisms."

"Storm, I…" she said, trying to apologize or comfort him.

"What happens to his avatar if you destroy the server?" Luke demanded, interrupting her.

"I don't know" she admitted, "But are you sure you saw him? The Fallen shouldn't be accessible outside special events."

"I saw him, in Valhalla." he explained.

"Even if that were true," she said doubtfully, "There would be no way to get him out."

"I grouped with him when I was there," Storm explained, "then my sister used a group summoning to pull him out. I don't understand this game, but she has him and I'm on my way to meet him now."

"Really?" she asked, doubt on her face.

"My sister and my father's avatar are in Last Hope and they are waiting for me." he explained. "I wanted to have an adventure with him. That's why I was unsure about you joining, you know, dead father and all. It's awkward and probably a little creepy. Honestly, I'm a wreck about it."

Sapphire put a hand up to her mouth and said, "Oh." After a moment she continued, "I'm sorry Storm, I think this all might have been a mistake. Once we get to Last Hope, I'll give you and your family privacy."

"Well, you'll already be there." he said, "I'll still ask my sister. Who knows, it might be fun. The original reason we came was to honor his memory, and doing a dungeon dive with his avatar and friends sounds like the best way to do that."

"Ok. But only if you think…" she started to say, but was interrupted by an alarm. She pulled out her phone and tapped the screen a few times then said, "Huh."

"Is everything ok?" he asked with a look of concern.

"Yeah," she responded while reading the screen, "it looks like our avatars ran into some bandits." she scrolled down and continued, "Everything is fine." then scrolled more "there was an ambush on the road." more scrolling, "There were a dozen." more scrolling, then she stopped and scrolled back up, with a surprised look on her face she let out a delighted sounding "Oh"

"What? Are we ok?" Luke asked with alarm.

She looked at him thoughtfully, then smiled, sizing him up.

"What?" Luke asked nervously.

"You got pretty nasty during that fight." she explained.

"What do you mean, my avatar did?" he asked.

"Your avatar is you," she told him, "The AI is incredibly accurate and would only do something that you yourself would do. Consider it an extension of yourself."

"Sapphire," he pleaded, "I need to know what will happen to the server." What she was saying struck him hard. His dad's avatar was just like his dad. He needed more time with him.

"There isn't anything we can do." she said sadly, "I like this server too, but there are bigger games afoot and my wishes and desires have to be put aside. My suggestion is to spend as much time with him as you can. I can have my dad talk to the company's support team to see if they can move him to a new server."

"There is no way to stop it?" he asked desperately.

"I'm sorry Storm, we can't stop it." she replied, shaking her head.

"Could we appeal to Weird or the other originals?" he asked.

"Storm," she said compassionately, "the only way would be to fight, and he has all of Dark Elite behind him. It's not possible. Of all the other servers he's taken, not even one managed a semblance of a defense. He blindsided everybody and now we are all on a train that won't stop until it hits the wall. We are all just hoping that the wall breaks when we do."

Having no response and feeling out of options he just stared at her.

"Come on, we need to get back." she said, "The bandits gave us a little more time, but I'd like to be there when we arrive in Last Hope."

He numbly followed her back to where they had first met, unsure of where they stood. But he was comforted knowing that he would soon be logging back in and seeing Father. When they reached the fountain, they said their goodbyes and he quickly made it to his hotel room where he found his mom and sister waiting for him.

"Are you meeting up with us today?" Cleo asked.

"Yeah," he said, "can I bring somebody with?"

"Sure, who are you bringing?" she asked with a knowing smile on her face.

"It's not like that." Luke said, sighing, "She thought I was a spy and invited herself along to see if I was telling the truth" But his words landed on deaf ears.

"Your girlfriend is always welcome." she said with a large grin. Then more seriously she added, "Actually, that is perfect. I bought a map fragment today that has several close encounters on it. One requires four people. I was going to wait for mom, but if she is ok with it, we could do it today."

"Go ahead," their mom said, "It would be a good opportunity for Luke and his girlfriend to get to know each other."

"Not you too mom." Luke groaned.

"I will always support you sweetie," she said with a huge grin.

NINETEEN

Dungeon dive

A cobblestone road appeared before Storm as he logged into the game. He sat there quietly for a few minutes enjoying the scenery as the wagon bumped along. The sun was shining and a gentle breeze brought the fresh smell of flowers. It was a beautiful day.

The road they traveled cut through grasslands with groups of trees scattered around. They approached a village off in the distance and Storm assumed it was Last Hope. He glanced at Sapphire's avatar. She should have logged in by now.

"Are you here?" he asked her avatar.

She slowly turned her head towards him and answered in a deadpan voice, "No."

For a moment Storm didn't know what to say, then he saw a mischievous twinkle in her eye and scoffed.

"Thanks for getting coffee with me." she said laughing, seeing the jig was up. "I'm sorry for all the questions."

"It's ok, I understand" Storm replied, "Maybe we can do it again but without the traitorous accusations."

"Of course," she laughed, "next time it'll be a proper date."

Storm choked, then covered his mouth as a coughing fit took him.

Sapphire leaned over and bumped him on the shoulder, then asked sweetly "Any word from your sister?"

When he regained control he replied, "Before I logged in, I asked her if you could join. She said yes, if you are still interested."

Sapphire's face lit up.

"But, look." he said, taking a deep breath, "She might say some things, please just try to ignore her."

"Really?" Sapphire asked with a little concern, "Is she mad at me?"

"No." he said quickly. Then nervously laughed and ran his hand through his hair and awkwardly replied, "I... I told her about you. I mean, I told her about everybody, Mani and the others too. But she teases me a lot and she might imply you're my girlfriend."

Sapphire shrugged and agreed, "I'm a girl, and I'm your friend."

"No, Sapphire, she thinks we are dating." Storm said, flustered at the perceived miscommunication.

Sapphire smiled at him to show she was teasing and admitted, "That's not out of the cards," but followed up almost imperceptivity, "unless you are a spy."

"I'm not a spy." Storm said exasperated.

Still smiling, Sapphire pointed forward and said, "Oh look, Last Hope."

Storm stared at her for a few more seconds then turned back to the road. Sapphire snapped the reins and the horses picked up speed. She guided them to a stable and two boys ran out as they dismounted.

"Feed them and brush them down." she instructed, then gave each a golden coin. "I'll give you another when I return."

"Yes ma'am" they said in unison then led the horses and wagon away.

Storm looked at Sapphire suspiciously. Sapphire had invited herself on the trip under the pretense that he needed to care for the horses. Apparently, he didn't need any such knowledge. She caught his gaze and shrugged but before he could say anything, somebody called name.

"Storm!" Sunshine yelled, smiling as she approached.

Storm turned to see his sister walking his direction with a familiar person next to her. Sunshine was wearing leather armor with a stylish cloak and no visible weapon. Father was fully armored in a well-worn chainmail set with a forest green cloak and the golden shaft of a weapon peaking over his shoulder.

"Good to finally be back." Storm said looking around at their starting town. He looked at Father with a grin and added, "It's good to see you, Father."

"It's good to see you too Storm." Father replied, but then stepped back to take in Storm's appearance and added, "It looks like you need an upgrade. Seriously, you should have thrown that hauberk out a long time ago."

Storm knew he was definitely in need of a wardrobe update. He looked down at his appearance. He wore the tattered shaman robes over his chainmail hauberk. Both had seen better days, the former performing more like a cloak after the Phoenix God ripped it in half, and the latter having so many holes it was barely functional.

"Think you could make me some replacements?" he asked.

"Sure" Father chuckled, "if I ever get back to my forge, I have a few high-level sets I can give you."

Storm waved Sunshine to come closer and introduced her to his sister and Father.

"Nice to meet you, Sapphire." Father said bowing.

"Nice to meet you too Father." Sapphire returned.

Then it was his sister's turn.

"It's nice to finally meet you, Sapphire. Storm has told me so much about you." Sunshine said excitedly. Then she leaned in close and added in a loud whisper, "He hasn't been able to stop!" and winked at her.

Sapphire blushed and Storm stared daggers at his sister. When Sunshine looked at him, he mouthed angrily, "What are you doing?"

"Since Sapphire is joining us today," Sunshine said, ignoring her brother. "We decided to investigate an interesting location." She pulled out a map fragment and passed it around. She also sent out group invites.

Storm, having not been in a group with Sapphire yet, excitedly inspected her.

[Character sheet
      Name: Sapphire
      Guild: Dark Elite
      Race: Human
      Level: 78
      Stats: <redacted>
      Skills: <redacted>
      Spells: <redacted>
      Special Abilities: <redacted>]

"Huh" Storm said, disappointed.

"See something interesting?" Sapphire asked knowingly.

"I... I just... no." Storm stammered.

"It's a handy little thing. Keeps spies from spying." she explained.

"I'm not a spy." he said defensively, shaking his head.

"I'm teasing." she said and put a hand gently on his arm.

Sunshine rounded up the group and ensured everybody had the supplies they needed before they left town. She led them through the forest at a quick pace and they made it to their destination without encountering any aggressive mobs.

They entered a clearing in the forest with a large stone tower in the center. It was a hundred feet tall and thirty feet wide and made of large stone blocks. On top of the tower was a wooden platform with railings, reminiscent of a fire lookout used in large forests to spot fires. They walked around the tower looking for an entrance but found none.

Each of them tried something different to discover the elusive entrance. Sunshine pressed on different stones, attempting to trigger a hidden door. Sapphire tried magical spells to find it. Father looked around the clearing for a hidden cellar-like door and Storm searched a nearby pile of rocks.

He kicked the rocks around, slowly spreading them out and was surprised by the variety. They each had a unique color and pattern, no two were alike. As he was spreading, he thought he saw a golden one but upon further inspection it was just a regular rock. He held on to it while he finished his task and walked around the tower once more. He tossed the rock mindlessly deep in thought as he inspected the area again.

The tower was unclimbable. Toss. There was no entrance. Toss. None of the rocks hid a key. Toss. The top of the tower was unmanned. Toss. A golden light flashed in his view and he froze, dropping his rock. He picked it up and looked closer at it. It was a rather nice rock but looked completely ordinary. He inspected it and was surprised by what he found.

[Item
        Name: Pet Rock
        Description: This is a rock with a dimensional space attached.
        Status: Filled]

He sighed, then called the group over and explained what he discovered.

"Can you empty it?" Sunshine asked.

"Sure" Storm answered, then held the rock to the side and gave the command to empty the dimensional space.

A pile of rocks almost exactly like the first spilled out onto the ground. He stared at it with more than a little displeasure. He saw where this was going.

"Who wants to bet there is another Pet Rock in there?" Storm asked flatly.

Nobody took that bet. They all helped spread out the rocks and started inspecting each one.

[Item Name: Rock]

[Item Name: Rock]

[Item Name: Rock]

[Item Name: Rock]

"Found it!" Sapphire exclaimed. She handed it to Storm, who emptied it out a few feet away from the other piles.

Storm was not surprised when another pile of rocks spilled out from the dimensional space. Each time they dug through the pile and found another pet rock. All told there were ten piles of rocks scattered around the clearing when they finally found the last one.

Just when Storm was considering this was a waste of time, he unknowingly emptied the last Pet Rock onto the ground. Everybody was expecting another pile of rocks and they were all stunned when a large green emerald fell onto the ground. It was about the size of a bowling ball and when it struck the ground it started glowing ominously. It glowed brighter and brighter and the team backed up when it started floating into the air.

Suddenly Sapphire grabbed Sunshine and tossed her a dozen feet away. Storm watched with concern as Sunshine landed hard and he was about to ask what the hell was going on when something hit him in the back of the head, hard. He fell to the ground and a stun icon appeared in his UI.

[Debuff
        Name: Stun
        Duration: 5 seconds]

Once the debuff disappeared Storm was able to move again. Before he got up, he looked around to survey the situation. Father was laying on the ground, recovering from a blow himself. Sapphire was standing amidst a maelstrom of flying rocks. She had an annoyed look as the rocks struck her and bounced off harmlessly. Sunshine, the lowest level of the group, was standing outside the range of the flying projectiles.

"What's happening?" he asked Sapphire.

"Stone golem." she said simply.

The emerald ball had become completely encased in rocks. It grew to the size of a boulder, then arms and legs formed and finally a head. It only took a few minutes for the entire process complete and when it was done, a ten-foot stone golem stood before them.

It took a heavy step towards Sapphire and Storm's heart skipped a beat. He watched helplessly as the golem's arm came crashing down, onto her.

Sapphire raised her hand above her head and effortlessly blocked the stone arm. The golem pulled its arm back and smashed down with the other one. Again, Sapphire easily blocked it. The golem tried again and again to pound her into the ground, but she stood there, unfazed.

Sapphire looked over at Storm with a raised eyebrow and jerked her head towards the golem as if to say, "Are you going to do something about this?"

Since the golem had aggro on Sapphire and nobody was currently in danger Storm took a moment to review his spells. He chose one, thinking it would support his team and began casting as the others attacked.

Sunshine shot a few arrows at the golem but they bounced off harmlessly, doing no damage. Father approached from the side, wielding a massive two-handed hammer with a golden shaft. When Storm caught site of the weapon he took a double take at it. The head of the hammer was comically large, almost as large as Father himself.

Storm released his spell just as Father attacked the golem. Father's hammer crashed into the golem's side and tore away several of the rocks. The creature continued to attack Sapphire unabated. Storm checked his logs and found that his blind spell only affected living creatures. Storm exchanged his magic for hammers, seeing Father's success, and charged in.

Father swung his over-sized hammer at one of the golem's legs and passed through it easily, sending small rocks flying. Thankfully, Father aimed his swing expertly and the projectiles were of no threat to their group. The golem crashed to the ground and struggled to rise using its three remaining limbs.

Storm immediately jumped on the creature's back and swung his hammers down, one after another. Each swing sent rocks flying. He chipped away at the boulder and eventually a greenish light began leaking out in-between the cracks. Soon he had created a hole which he could see the emerald crystal through.

When the hole was large enough, Storm dropped his hammers and reached down with both hands to pull the emerald bowling ball out of the golem. He pulled hard and it moved a little but he underestimated the strength of the magical bond it had. He tried to let go but his hands were stuck to the ball and even worse, he felt a rising heat.

He tugged and tugged as the golem heart heated up and with each passing second, he got more desperate. The pain quickly reached an unbearable level and his health bar started to diminish. In desperation he tried to store the golem heart in his ring of holding, thankful he had emptied it earlier. The golem heart disappeared into the dimensional space and the golem lost cohesion, the rocks tumbling to the ground.

"Nice hammers." Father commented as he walked over and offered Storm a hand.

"They just felt right." Storm said, taking the offered help.

"Well, that was fun. What's next?" Father asked.

"Look at the tower." Sunshine said, "Four posts appeared."

"Give me a minute." Storm said, then searched around and recovered the Pet Rocks from the ground. He pulled the golem heart out of his ring and caught it in the air before it hit the ground. He then used one of the Pet Rocks to store the golem heart and tossed that onto the pile of rocks. He then stored that whole pile of rocks inside a Pet Rock and put it inside his bag.

"You got plans for that thing?" Sapphire asked, looking at him oddly.

Storm shrugged then walked up to the four posts that Sunshine was inspecting.

The waste-high posts were made of granite and had a hand shaped impression on top. They were spread far enough apart that one person couldn't reach two of them.

"The entrance." Sapphire announced approvingly.

Sunshine put her hand in one of the impressions but nothing happened.

"All four need to be activated at the same time." Sapphire explained.

"Before we go in, I have something for each of you." Storm said.

He told them about the treasure he received after defeating the Phoenix God and that he wanted to share it with them. He then pulled out five white boxes with a question mark on each side. Storm handed two boxes to Father, two to Sunshine and tried to hand one to Sapphire but she shook her head disapprovingly, so he kept it. Father and Sunshine tried to say no as well but Storm insisted. "If you don't like what you get or it isn't useful, we can trade items."

"This feels like Christmas" Sunshine said as she opened her first box. She pulled out a glass dagger with a long thin, needle-like blade. The handle was bee shaped and the blade was the stinger. She passed it around so everybody could inspect it.

[Item

        Name: Stiletto of stinging
        Description: This dagger is imbued with an uncurable poison. One use.]

"Not bad, mom would love that." Storm said, then looked at Father and asked, "What did you get?"

Father reached into one of his boxes and pulled out a small vial filled with a clear liquid with golden flakes floating in it. As the flakes floated around the liquid sparkled.

"Oh Storm," Father said, "I know what this and I can't keep it." And held out the vial.

"What is it?" Storm asked curiously as he took it.

"That's a potion of invincibility." Sapphire answered in awe, obviously impressed. "It's an incredibly rare drop and considered top tier loot. It'll easily go for thousands of gold coins on the market."

[Item

Name: Star potion
Description: Grants invincibility for 5 minutes. +200% speed, +200% to each stat]

"Wow, this is amazing." Storm said. He held the vial up and stared sparkling flecks. After a moment, he handed it back to Father, "You keep it and if you are at risk of dying, don't hesitate to use it. I'm not sure if we could get you back out of Valhalla."

Father nodded and stored it in his bag. He reaching into his last box and pulled out a pair of knee-high black boots. He inspected them, then handed them to Storm.

"I don't need these. I like my boots just fine." he said with finality.

Storm took the boots suspiciously and inspected them. His eyes widened and he showed everybody else.

[Item

Name: Boots of teleportation
Description: Teleport up to 3 times a day
Cooldown: 1 hour
Range: Sight]

Storm was all too happy to replace his mundane boots with the new pair. Then reached into his own box and pulled out a small red button with letters written on it, "CTRL-C" and inspected it.

[Item

Name: CTRL-C
Description: Press this button to copy one item in your possession. Legendary value or less. 1 use.]

"What do you think?" he asked Sapphire, holding it out to her. He wanted to get her opinion because she seemed to have a good understanding of the value of the items.

"It's good." she said, "I'd save it for something that's rare though. Possibly that ring of holding."

"Storm" Father said, leaning in close, "Before you use it, let me have a look at that button."

Not sure what he was getting at he nodded in agreement, then stored the button in his bag.

"Best for last" Sunshine said, then opened the last box. She reached into her box and pulled out a pair of bracers. She identified them and got excited. She explained to everybody what she got.

[Item
        Name: Bracers of dexterity
        Effect 1: +100% to combat speed
        Effect 2: +50% to dexterity]

Her eyes widened, "They are perfect!" she exclaimed. Sunshine looked at Storm and asked, "Do you mind if I keep these? They would really help me."

"Keep them, I'm glad you found something that you can use." he said happily. He felt bad about leaving them to power level and go on raids. He was more than happy to share the loot.

"Everybody ready to get in there?" Sunshine asked excitedly.

TWENTY

Teamwork

Each member of the group stepped up to a post and placed their hand in the depression on top. As soon as the fourth person set their hand down, a bright flash enveloped them and they disappeared.

They found themselves in complete darkness in a damp chamber with a strong musty smell.

Storm heard Sapphire casting a spell and almost smacked his head when he recognized it. Out of embarrassment, he silently cast the same spell on himself and when it completed, he was able to see again.

Through the green hue of night vision, he found his group standing close by. Storm modified the spell and cast it on Father and Sunshine. The more he understood the arcane language, the easier it was to make the changes he needed.

[New spell obtained: Night vision, other (Life magic)]

His mana dipped much more for the targeted version than it did for the self-version but it was well worth the flexibility. Mana management was important, especially in battle, so he would have to be especially careful with his crafted spells.

"What do you think, where are we?" he asked as he looked around and studied the room closer.

They stood in a large circular room that appeared to have been used as a storage closet. On the far side of the room were a dozen tables, each a different shape and size, stacked on top of each other. Closer to him was a large ornate desk and several bookcases. And in the center of the room a massive rug covered the floor. The only potential light source he could find were a couple of unlit tiki torches. Finally, he noticed why the room seemed weird, there were no doors.

"I think it's an escape room." Sapphire suggested as she inspected objects on one of the bookshelves.

"Let's split up," Storm said, "If you find something call out." He had done a few escape rooms in the real world and always loved the experience.

"Watch out for traps." Sapphire warned.

They each spread out to look for clues. Storm sifted through pieces of scrap paper on top of the desk. Each piece had a letter of the alphabet on it. He spread them around and found that each letter had been used except "P" and "U". He announced his findings and Father cleared his voice to get his attention. Storm looked at him and Father pointed up.

Storm looked up with his night vision and was unable to penetrate the deep shadows high above them. Without considering the consequences, he cast a fireball, aimed at the ceiling. As it shot upwards, his fireball lit up the room. He heard his sister groan in dissatisfaction.

Everybody stopped what they were doing and watched the fireball rise into the air, curious to see what it would uncover. As the fireball neared the top of the room, objects could be seen hanging down. They appeared to be sharpened stakes.

His fireball continued its trajectory towards the ceiling, not slowing a bit. The fiery orb struck the ceiling and unraveled, releasing its stored-up energy. A moment later a deafening boom filled the chamber, ringing everybody's ears. Before the light extinguished, they all witnessed the effect, the spears shattered, raining hazardous debris down onto them.

"Heads up!" Storm yelled, but he wasn't sure if anybody heard him.

The broken spears came raining down around the team. Father produced a large shield out of nowhere and held it above himself and a hunkering Sunshine. Sapphire's form blurred as she ran to Storm. Standing behind him, their bodies close, she quickly waved her arms and conjured an opaque bubble around them.

The area inside the magical shield was small and dark, but he felt safe. Their bodies pressed together, Storm felt Sapphire's breath on his neck as they listened to the falling spears crash around them.

When it was safe, Sapphire dismissed her shield. She gave Storm a comforting shoulder bump as she headed back to the puzzle she was investigating.

"Sorry about that." Storm apologized to everybody.

"Mistakes are opportunities." Father said comfortingly, "This one gave us light." He held up a smoldering piece of broken spear and gently blew on it, coaxing a flame to appear. He walked around the room and lit all of the tiki torches, chasing away the darkness.

The room, now awash in light, looked completely different to everybody. Their green-hued night vision gave way to bright colors and drastically increased visibility. As the darkness retreated, the light revealed a hidden secret, the floor.

The floor was covered in tiles of every color and shape imaginable, creating a beautiful wall-to-wall mosaic. Storm could tell the floor was tile but without light he hadn't realized the variety of color it held.

Seeing Sapphire had also taken an interest in the floor, Storm walked over to her. She was on her hands and knees peering down intently.

"What are you looking at?" he asked, curiously.

Sapphire tossed him a tile and explained, "I found a box of those on a bookshelf and thought they might complete a picture but I'm missing something."

Storm caught the tile and inspected it.

[Item

> Name: Tile
> Shape: Rectangle
> Size: 1x2
> Color: Silver]

Storm walked around the room, inspecting the floor closely. At first glance, the tiles appeared to be randomly placed, but the longer he looked at them, the more he realized he was wrong. Hidden within the chaotic mess, patterns emerged. Large, multi-colored swirls, interlaced with silver tiles, curved around the room, some isolated monoliths, others intersecting each other.

Storm stared at the tile in his hand and came to a sudden realization. He quickly found the box that Sapphire mentioned and tipped it over. The tiles within came tumbling out onto the floor in a shiny pile. Just as he thought, all silver.

Storm hurried to the nearest group of swirls. He analyzed the patterns and replaced several tiles with the silver ones he just found. The others, noticing his excitement, came to help.

They worked for half an hour replacing specific tiles around the room with the silver ones. In that time, Storm noticed that his sister and Sapphire hadn't strayed too far from each other. In fact, they seemed to be getting along quite well, which worried him more than a little. Several times he caught them looking in his direction and giggling. He tried to ignore them.

Storm followed the silver trail around the room, from swirl to swirl and realized they had a problem. He scanned the room and easily found the issue. Walking to the center of the room, he pulled the rug back to reveal more patterns underneath.

Directly in the center of the room was a large golden-tiled octagon with silver lines radiating outwards. The lines intersected golden circles and after placing a few more silver tiles, they all connected with the rest of the room.

"I know what it is." he quietly. Storm knew what they were looking at.

"What?" Sapphire asked, joining him in the center of the room.

"It's a circuit." he revealed, pointing at the silver lines running around the room.

"Your right." she gasped after studying it for a few minutes.

"But, what does it do?" Sunshine asked, joining them.

"Only one way to find out." Storm said, holding up the last tile. He held it out to Sapphire and asked, "Do you want to do the honors?"

"Sure" she said smiling at him. Then grabbed the tile out of his hand and bent down to place it in the final spot.

As soon as the tile was set, the circuit was complete and a bright light erupted from the golden octagon in the center of the room. The light spread to the connecting silver lines and flowed outward to the other patterns embedded in the floor, lighting them as well. The room glowed in a multi-colored haze, reminding Storm of a rave.

Suddenly, the room lurched upwards, dropping everybody to the ground, except Sapphire. The silver lines pulsated and brightened with each passing second. And as they did the speed of the floor traveling upwards increased as well.

"We need to stop it." Storm gasped, realizing their danger. He knelt down and tried to pry a silver tile loose but as soon as he touched it, he got a nasty shock that temporarily numbed his arm.

He stumbled to the center of the room and knelt down in front of the octagon. He shook his head in disbelief. The octagon was a depression in the floor. He didn't realize it before but something fit into it.

Storm quickly looked around the room and found what he was searching for. He stumbled over to the pile of tables and frantically searched through them. Father and Sunshine joined him and together they found the object they were searching for. They hurriedly carried the octagon-shaped table to the center of the room.

They flipped it over and placed it into the depression. With an audible click, it slid into place. On the bottom of the table, now facing upwards were the words, "STOP", "UP" and "DOWN".

Storm slammed his hand on the stop button but nothing happened. The room was shaking violently and he had a sinking feeling they didn't have much time left. He looked at the shape on the floor and realized they missed something, there was a gap.

"We need a golden tile." he said in desperation.

"I saw one over there!" Sunshine exclaimed and pointed to a bookcase, the one next to where the silver tiles were found.

They all frantically searched the bookcase and quickly found the errant tile. Storm grabbed it and ran back to the center of the room, shakily placing it in the gap. The golden glow spread to the table and lit up the buttons.

Storm rapidly pushed the stop button over and over until it was fully activated. Suddenly, the entire room stopped and its upward trajectory was halted. The party flew several feet into the air, then, landed hard on the floor.

Storm felt a shiver run through his body as he realized how close they had come to death. After standing up, he reached out and touched the tip of one of the remaining spears hanging from the ceiling. It was a miracle none of them were impaled. A few more seconds and everybody and everything in the room would have been pulverized.

Storm stood in the center, of the now shortened, room, staring up. Earlier, when his fireball exploded, he had seen a hatch in the ceiling. It was now within each reach. Almost.

"Should we try to get closer?" he asked pointing to the hatch. He bent down to push the UP button but they all shook their heads in disapproval.

"Let's try using some of the furniture first." Sapphire suggested.

They placed the large desk in the center of the room, hacking off the legs of the upside-down octagon table in the process. Then, they stacked the tallest bookcase on top. Sunshine volunteered and crawled up to reach the door. She pushed on it but it didn't budge.

"It looks like we need a key." she called down.

They spread out and searched for a key. Having skipped the desk earlier Storm pulled open the drawers to see if there was anything inside.

One drawer held a stack of parchment papers, an ink pot and a quill. Recalling his avatar used up his supplies, he stashed them in his backpack. In another drawer he found a hand mirror. He held it up and stared into it. Not too surprised, the face staring back was his. However, he got a surprise when he inspected it.

[Item

       Name: Mirror of seeing
       Description: Uncovers hidden or stealthed objects]

Storm held the mirror out and used it to scan the room. He didn't see anything out of the ordinary so he passed it off to the others so they could take turns with it. He finished searching the desk and didn't find anything notable in the remaining drawers. The wood grain however, nagged at him.

He loved Japanese puzzle boxes and tried a few different techniques on the desk. He gently pushed on one of the knots in the wood grain and felt it depress slightly. Excitement tingling through his body and he tested the rest of the knots. One, he pressed a little too hard and felt a sharp jab in his finger.

"Ouch!" he yelped and pulled his finger back. He stared at his finger as if it betrayed him and sucked on it when a small dot of blood formed.

"Are you ok?" Sapphire asked, walking over after hearing his exclamation.

"I got poisoned." Storm said waving his finger at her. He checked his UI and while it was a strong poison, it wouldn't kill him.

"Here, drink this." Sunshine said, handing him a small white vial.

Storm took the vial and inspected it.

[Item

Name: Poison antidote (common)
Description: This vial will cure any non-legendary poison. 1 dose.
Crafted by: Nightshade]

"Mom made this?" he asked, surprised.

"Yeah, she gave me plenty." Sunshine responded.

After the poison was cured, he went back to inspecting the desk, knowing there was more to discover.

Sapphire poked her head under the desk and searched with him.

"Is this the one you pressed?" she asked, pointing at the wooden knot with a splotch of blood on it.

"Yeah. I was testing different patterns." he explained. Storm demonstrated by pressing on each knot individually. None of them moved. Then he pushed on one he skipped and it depressed very slightly. Holding it in, he pushed a few of the others and they now depressed ever so slightly too.

Sapphire squeezed in beside him and tested a few herself. She reached around behind him to press one on his other side, then reached out and pressed one in front of her.

"Do it now." she whispered into his ear.

With her arms around him, her body was pressed against him once again. Her whisper sent goose bumps down his arms. Storm struggled to concentrate but finally found his focus. He pressed various wooden knots in a few different combinations and Sapphire alternated hers as well.

Finally, they heard a click and a small drawer opened. They both peered inside but didn't see anything. Storm bravely stuck his finger in and felt around but didn't find anything either. Sapphire called for the mirror and Storm tilted it so they could get a look inside and behold, there *was* an object inside. He reached in and pulled out a dark shadowy object and held it in his hand. It was a ring. He instantly heard trumpets sound-off in celebration.

[Hidden quest
        Name: *****
        Description: Congratulations! By finding a wraith ring you have now
        been given a hidden quest to reunite all of them.
        Status: 1 of 9 collected]

"That… that's a Wraith ring" Sapphire whispered, stammering. She stared at the ring in his hand in shock and reached out, as if to touch it but pulled back.

He identified it.

[Item

      Name: Health sucker (Wraith ring)

      Quality: God item

      Description: This ring is permanently phased out. It will provide the wearer with incredible abilities. Cannot be dropped or given.

      Ability 1: +100% to health, allows you to use your health to cast spells. Any spell cast this way will be considered blood magic, it will be four times effective at half the cost.

      Ability 2: <locked>

      Aura: <locked>]

"Why didn't I feel it when I reached in the first time?" he asked.

"The Wraith rings are permanently phased out." Sapphire explained, "The reason you couldn't feel it, is because of how the game handles phasing. If you don't know it's there, you can't interact with it, much like the assassin's stealth ability. When they are phased out you could walk completely through them and not even know they were there. Once you know they are there, they look shadowy like that. There are ways to knock them out of stealth, such as a stealth totem or some special spells, but those don't work on Wraith rings."

"Do you want it?" Storm asked, holding her hand out to him.

Sapphire stared at it for a long while as if she was tempted, but she shook her head.

"No, you keep it." she said, "Besides, I don't think it can be given away like that. Put it on and don't tell anybody."

"Can you tell me about it?" he asked as he slipped the ring on.

"Not too much." she said, "They are randomly scattered around the world and near impossible to find. It's rumored that there are only nine on each server. Only a handful have ever been reported and never more than one a server."

Storm used the mirror to look through the other drawers in the desk and he found a large cast iron key in the same drawer where he found the mirror. As soon as he spotted it with the mirror it phased back into the world, visible to everybody.

Confident they found the way out and noticing the time, they all agreed to break for lunch. They gave their avatars instructions to look around for any more treasure and gave Father the key. He said he would keep an eye on the other avatars while they were out, ensuring they didn't get into any trouble.

When they returned from lunch, they all noticed several additional items in their bags and a handful more gold, all of which they would inspect and divide later. They were all antsy to get to the next level.

Father climbed on the desk and up the bookcase easily reaching the hatch overhead. Using the key, he unlocked the door and pushed it open. With one last glance below, he stuck his head up into the darkness and completely disappeared.

Storm gasped and stared to move forward but Sapphire put a hand on his arm.

"It's ok, he's safe." she said comfortingly, "It's a common method of transitioning between dungeon levels. It's entirely expected." Sapphire then crawled up the bookcase and looked down at Storm smiling. She raised her arm above the threshold of the hatch and disappeared just like Father. Storm and Sunshine quickly followed.

TWENTY-ONE

Final room

The circular room disappeared and then nothing. Nothing replaced it. Storm was in complete and utter darkness. His UI was the only indication that he was still in the game. He tried to move but was unable to, as far as he could tell. He tried to silently cast night vision on himself but nothing happened.

He checked his UI and four new icons had appeared. He inspected them and found that his spells, abilities, skills and even items were disabled.

[Debuff
      Name: Restraint
      Effect 1: Disable all spells
      Effect 2: Disable all abilities
      Effect 3: Disable all skills
      Effect 4: Disable all items
      Time remaining: Permanent, until restraints are removed]

"Anybody here?" he asked into the darkness.

"I'm here, but I can't move." Father returned.

"Sapphire? Sunshine?" Storm raised his voice after not hearing any responses from them.

"I'm here." Sapphire yelled back, but her voice sounded really far away.

"I'm here too." came Sunshine's reply, sounding just as far away as Sapphire's voice did.

In the center of the room, four beams of light appeared. In the beams of light were an ivory pedestal with a box on top. Each box was a different size and had an ordinal number on it, 1st-4th.

"Welcome adventurers!" a loud voice boomed excitedly. "This is The Arena of the Fellowship. You will battle each other in a freestyle-no-rules-single-elimination-fight-to-the-death-player-vs-player battle, there can be only one!" The voice tailed off and the lights turned on.

Storm found himself sitting in a fancy wooden chair with blue bands of power wrapped around his arms, legs and torso, immobilizing him.

The room, or rather arena was oval shaped and about the size of two football fields. It was surrounded by a tall wall with filled weapon racks. The floor was packed dirt with pools of water and sand pits spread around in random locations. Various obstacles were available to provide cover, such as walls, foxholes and even trenches that wound their way around the battlefield. It reminded Storm of the Colosseum where gladiators fought in ancient times.

Father and Storm were on one side of the arena and Sunshine and Sapphire were on the other. The blue lines of power binding them released. Storm wearily watched Father as he slowly got up.

"Truce?" Storm asked.

Father nodded and walked closer to strategize.

"Sapphire first." Father said.

Storm cringed but didn't disagree. He cast a few buffs on both of them but didn't want to use up all of his mana. Not to mention that Father's alliance was temporary.

They cautiously made their way to the other side of the arena, hiding behind walls and following the trenches when they could. Storm kept an eye on Sapphire as they traveled. She deployed a mana totem and cast spell after spell on Sunshine, which concerned Storm greatly because with Sapphire's buffs, Sunshine was now as powerful as himself or possibly even Father.

Out of habit, Storm pulled out his hammers and readied himself for the upcoming fight. While power leveling, he had become quite proficient with them. Now however, he thought it through and decided that he wasn't ready to use them against his sister or even Sapphire. The game was just too lifelike. He slipped his hammers back in the loops on his belt and readied some spells instead.

Storm and Father hunkered down behind the last wall, with Sapphire and Sunshine about fifty yards away. They made it all the way to their starting position without running into them. Storm figured they stayed to build their defenses, and possibly a trap or two.

Storm peaked around the edge of the wall and saw Sapphire standing in the open with several totems surrounding her. She was looking in the other direction. He nodded to Father to begin their coordinated attack.

On the way, they had discussed several plans and came to an agreement that Storm would interfere with Sapphire's spell casting and Father would rush into melee range.

Storm began casting a spell he had never cast before. He had several ideas on how to disable Sapphire but his first approach was to modify his night vision spell. Unsure if it would succeed, he completed the spell by standing up and targeting Sapphire. He felt the magic swell inside him and release as the spell succeeded. A rush of satisfaction washed over him.

[New spell obtained: Blind, single target (Death magic)]

His elation didn't last too long though. Just as his spell completed an arrow flashed through the air, striking him in the chest. He fell to the ground wheezing in pain. Storm lay there, for a few minutes, second guessing his life choices.

When he finally caught his breath, he healed himself, several times. Storm looked at the offending blunt arrow lying next to him and scowled. If that had hit him in the head, he would be dead.

Just as Storm completed his spell, Father jumped over the wall and ran towards Sapphire, his massive hammer held high. After the first arrow streaked past him, he adjusted the hammer to shield himself from ranged attack. No sooner than he did, an arrow impacted the head of his hammer. The archer tried several more times but Father was experienced in this type of warfare and held fast.

Storm peeked over the wall and watched Father charge Sapphire. He followed an arrow back to its source after it ricocheted off Father's hammer and prepared his next spell.

Now blinded, Sapphire listened to Father's footfalls as he approached. When he was near, she cast a shield spell, one of the few spells she could still use. Then pulled out two daggers, one in each hand.

Having battled mages before, Father was not fooled. When he neared Sapphire, he tossed his hammer at the shield, dismissing it. Then, he crashed into her, hard.

Sapphire grunted from the impact, but held onto her daggers. Father picked her up and carried her away, providing her a perfect target. She stabbed him repeatedly in the back, trying to loosen his grip. An arrow even sprouted from Father's back, joining Sapphire's stab wounds but he didn't relent.

Not having direct line of sight, Storm needed to modify one of his spells to do area-of-effect damage to be able to hit Sunshine. Fully protected behind the wall he focused on the complicated casting. It seemed to take forever but he finally succeeded.

A massive fireball flew out of his hands and upwards into the sky. It split into two, then four, then eight and so on. Each time they split they grew and split again until 128 fireballs arched through the sky towards their target. When they struck it reminded him of a finale at a fireworks show, the explosions just kept going.

[New spell obtained, Fireball, AOE (Fire magic)]

Father carried Sapphire to the outside wall and threw her onto a weapon rack. She hung there, impaled, blood pooling below her. He calmly picked up one of her daggers and with no remorse, brutally slashed it across her throat.

Her head dangled at an impossible angle, barely attached with a few scraps of skin. Blood spurting in-time with her failing heartbeat. Storm lost himself in the moment and felt a rage rise inside himself. A feral scream escaped him as he ran towards Father.

Father limped to his hammer and picked it up. He stood there, waiting for the angry young man charging at him. When Storm got close enough, he took action.

"It's time." Father said with a grim expression. He held his comically-large oversized hammer over his head and threw it at Storm. The hammer flew through the air like a missile.

Storms eyes widened in surprise as the hammer flew towards him. He quickly activated his boots of teleportation and targeted the space directly behind Father. Having just thrown away his weapon Father was completely vulnerable and open to attack, or so he thought. Storm popped into existence directly behind Father. Having never teleported before, he was disoriented and turned awkwardly to face Father.

"Good effort, but predictable." Father said, looking at him with a familiar crooked smile. Then slammed a fist into Storm's face. Storm's hammers slipped from his grasp and he saw darkness closing in. He didn't feel a thing when his face hit the ground.

"Your level might be a problem young lady." Father said as he slowly turned to look at Sunshine.

"Your lack of a weapon might be a problem old man." she retorted, raising her fists.

Father raised his fists, mimicking her, and closed the distance. Sunshine watched him closely as he approached and before he could react, she darted forward and jabbed him in the ribs. With a pained expression, Father stepped to the side and turned, keeping her in front of him.

"You're fast." he complimented her, then took a powerful swing, trying to end the fight.

With her buffs and equipment, she was faster than him. She easily ducked under his arm, then punched him in the side again, this time much more powerful.

He grunted in pain and took a few steps back, out of range and said, "You're stronger than you look."

"Looks are deceiving." she responded with a wide smile on her face.

"They are." he said in turn, smiling back at her. He took another step back and held his hands out in front of him, as if he were ready to catch something.

Sunshine's eyes widened as she heard a whistling sound behind her. She fell to the ground just as Father's massive hammer flew through the space she had occupied. Father caught the two-handed hammer and cocked it back to take a swing at her. Not seeing any other choice, she burned a charge on her necklace and sprinted towards him.

She reached him before he could bring his hammer to bear and swung at his face. Her fist flared to life with an azure glow and she hit him with the full force of her magical power.

Sunshine landed a critical hit and stunned Father. His hammer slipped from his grasp and landed on the ground with a loud thud, leaving him open to all her fury. She punched him over and over with her magical fists. His health depleted, Father fell to the ground in a heap.

Sunshine stood over him, breathing heavily. As her battle fervor receded, she realized what she had done and stared at his body in horror. She feared he would respawn in Valhalla, taking him away from her, potentially forever.

"Hey!" Sapphire yelled, "He's fine. You have one more, don't get distracted."

Sunshine turned to see Sapphire strapped to the chair they had started in. She let go of her fears and quickly gathered her thoughts for her last fight. She turned to see Storm's body gone along with his hammers. Fearing imminent attack, she spun around to find him. He was standing on a wall nearby, watching her.

"What are you doing?" she asked him. Sunshine slowly stalked towards Storm, scanning the area for traps.

"Waiting for you." he said with a smile. Storm held a staff that he had retrieved from one of the weapon racks.

"You know we have to fight." she said as she cautiously stepped closer.

"I know," he returned and jumped down. Storm swung his staff at her, to keep her from getting too close. "Nice job with Father by the way."

"You're next." she warned, taking another step closer.

"How many charges do you have left?" Storm asked, stepping to the side.

"Mt necklace? Are you implying I couldn't beat you without it?" she asked dangerously, narrowing her eyes.

He shrugged with a smirking smile as they slowly circled each other. Testing her defenses, Storm swung his staff at her head but she easily batted it away with a glowing backhand.

Sunshine took a quick step forward but Storm stepped back and swung his staff at her leg. She took the hit and shifted her body around to snap her other leg towards the center of the staff. As her foot struck, it flared an azure color and easily passed through, breaking the staff into two pieces.

Storm frowned and backpedaled a few steps to put some distance between them. When Sunshine followed him, he threw his broken staff at her but she smacked it out of the air and kept walking.

Sunshine was a strong melee fighter but Storm had over thirty levels on her and he thought he could easily defeat her. She surprised him when she broke his staff. He needed to change his strategy fast. He began casting his fear spell.

She had been waiting for him to cast a spell and rushed forward, activating one of her collars. Large white wings erupted from her back and flapped backwards, pushing her forward at a tremendous speed.

Sunshine blurred, reaching him before he completed his spell. She swung a glowing fist at him and struck with her full ferocity, interrupting his spell. Storm's health quickly dropped as she hit him over and over.

Storm cast his fire shield and when her fist struck next, the damage was reflected back to her. Sunshine howled pain and fell to her knees, cradling her broken hand.

Storm cast his healing spell several times to top off his health. He also cast his healing buff which provided a pool of health points to draw from when he got hurt. He glanced at Sunshine and was surprised to see that she was getting back to her feet already. Her hand was no longer broken.

Sunshine silently thanked her mom for the healing potions as she stood up. Storm was in full spell casting mode and she couldn't give him any more time. She beat her wings and the world burred around her as she rushed at him again. She activated her collar of shadows as he began casting another spell.

Storm saw something in Sunshine's eyes that worried him so he cast a spell that he knew would end the fight. Just as he was about to finish, shadows surrounded his sister and her wings turned jet black, then she disappeared. Having no target for his spell, he was forced to abandon it. His brow furrowed and he spun around looking for her.

Suddenly, Sunshine's glowing fist appeared before Storm and struck him in the face. His health dropped and was instantly healed from his health pool but she didn't relent, she hit him again and again. Storm insta-cast his fire shield but Sapphire had warned her about it. Sunshine simply slapped it with her hand and continued beating him.

Storm blocked a few of her strikes, but missed many others. His health steadily decreased under her assault. Sunshine wasn't giving him a chance to cast spells and he needed to put a little distance between them. He backed up quickly, but tripped over Father's hammer and fell onto his back.

Laying on the ground, Storm was about to curse his luck but realized it was the reprieve he needed. Now, too far away, she wouldn't be able to stop him. He quickly cast a spell.

Sunshine watched Storm fall and almost pursued him, but realized she was fighting a losing battle. Due to his healing abilities, his health hadn't decreased much during her onslaught. She reached into her pocked and withdrew a small black wand. It was good he was already laying down. She pointed it at him and activated it.

Storm's body fell limp, his spell ruined. He glanced at his UI and saw the stun icon. He silently raged, not being able to do a single thing about it. He kept an eye on the timer and when it reached zero, he was going to make her pay. Then, he saw Sunshine standing over him with something slung over her shoulder.

Sunshine grunted as she lifted Father's hammer high into the air. Storm's eyes widened incredulously in fear. Then, as the hammer started to fall, he squeezed his eyes shut.

The entire arena darkened and the four spotlights returned to the center of the room. Above each pedestal an item floated, slowly rotating. Storm, back in the chair, watched as Sunshine approached the center of the room. She walked up to the first-place pedestal and it lowered into the ground, lowering her reward. She reached out and grabbed her prize, a pair of brass knuckles.

As soon as she claimed her prize Storm's chair deactivated and he stood up. He walked up to the second-place pedestal and it lowered so he could retrieve his prize. A small orb that fit in the palm of his hand. He inspected it.

[Item

    Name: Orb of Scrying
    Description: You can scry the area around you and cast spells as if you were there.]

Next, Father walked up to his pedestal and retrieved a matching pair of bracelets made out of twisted threads. Storm watched as Father smiled at his reward, which he then unceremoniously stuffed into his pocket.

Finally, Sapphire plucked a small purple and golden flower off of her pedestal. Then she made her way to Sunshine, hugged her.

"Congratulations, I knew you could do it." she said.

"Thanks for the pointers." Sunshine replied.

Sapphire nodded and congratulated Storm and Father on a good battle.

"So, you're not mad we ganged up on you?" Storm asked hesitantly.

"No, not at all." Sapphire laughed, "It was a great fight. Blind was choice. I wasn't prepared for that at all." She looked at him seriously and warned, "But next time I will be."

"Great job young lady," Father said to Sunshine with a huge grin, "You really put the smack down on us. I thought my hammer would get you for sure."

"Thanks," she said, a bit embarrassed. "Storm was right though," she touched her necklace, "Without the necklace I couldn't have done near the damage to either of you. It only has one charge left and I haven't been able to find a way to recharge it."

"You would need a recharge gem," Sapphire explained, "they are expensive but you should be able to buy them from a mages guild, sadly Last Hope doesn't have one."

"I can help with that." Father said, clearing his throat. "Let me see your necklace."

"You have a gem?" Sunshine asked.

"Not exactly," he slowly replied then glanced at Sapphire, "I have a different method."

"Is it your Reverse Engineering ability?" Storm asked.

"Yeah" Father said embarrassed. "I don't like to advertise it."

"What now?" Sapphire asked, "I don't think I've ever heard of that ability."

"What does it do?" Sunshine asked.

"It's a difficult ability to use." Father said after taking a deep breath, "A normal player with the ability would be able to recharge your necklace no problem. I on the other hand, understand the game mechanics better than a normal player and can do a little more." He took Sunshine's necklace and turned away from them for a few moments. When he turned back, he handed her the necklace, "I don't use it that much because misunderstandings can happen and I get accused of cheating."

"Woah, thank you so much!" Sunshine said after inspecting the necklace.

Storm and Sapphire were curious so Sunshine let them inspect it.

[Artifact
      Name: Amulet of Spectral hands
      Type: Amulet
      Effect: Casts spectral hands on the user for 30 seconds. Spectral hands:
      melee attack ignores armor
      Charges: 999/30]

"That's a very interesting ability," Sapphire said, staring at Father intently. She asked, "Do you think you could show me how you do it sometime?"

"Let's see how things go these next couple of days." Father said with his crooked smile and glanced at Storm. "If you two come back for another dungeon dive, we might find some time for it."

"Sunshine, what did you get for a reward?" Storm asked.

Sunshine held out a pair of brass knuckles for everybody to identify.

[Item
      Name: Mithril knuckles
      Description: Each knuckle can capture a spell and release it on the next
      punch.
      Effect: +10% accumulative physical damage on repetitive targets]

"Wow," Storm said, "that is pretty amazing, yet awfully specific for you."

"The game chose her reward based on her play style and needs," Sapphire explained. "It's not perfect but it does pretty good."

Storm showed everybody what he had gotten, then stored the orb in his ring.

"A flower?" Storm asked Sapphire.

"Yes!" she said excitedly, "I can't believe it. I've been looking for one of these for a while now."

"Is it poisonous or a quest item?" he asked.

"What?" she asked in confusion, "No, it's a flower, I mean, it might be poisonous. I don't know. I'm trying to collect one of each flower from each region, I was missing this one from the human lands."

"What is it?" he asked. He thought it looked familiar but couldn't place where he had seen it before, possibly in the meadow where they made their home base.

"It's called 'Atropa Belladonna'," she explained, "my herbology isn't very high so I can't tell what it does. It's perfect for my collection, probably my favorite so far." She stared at it, smiling. Then stuffed it into her bag.

After retrieving their rewards, a portal appeared in the center of the arena. The team went through and found themselves outside at the base of the tower. They walked back to Last Hope, talking excitedly about their day.

"Are you ok?" he asked Sapphire, "That was a brutal way to go out."

"Oh, I've had so much worse than that." she laughed, "Besides, you're one to talk, a huge hammer to the face isn't exactly an appealing way to go either."

"You're right about that." he said chuckling, "So, what's next?"

"Storm, I need to head back." Sapphire said, leaning in close, "You should stay here and go on a couple more adventures with your family."

"Why?" he asked, "What about the raid tomorrow?"

"Do you even want to be a part of it?" she asked him. "You know how it's going to end."

"I don't know" Storm shrugged, "Weird said I could be in his group, maybe I can talk to him about it."

"You can try Storm, but I don't think it will change anything." she warned.

"He seems like a good guy, maybe he will understand." Storm responded optimistically.

"Oh, he'll understand." she muttered but Storm didn't hear her.

When they made it to town, Storm told sister goodbye and shook Father's hand. Sapphire surprisingly hugged his sister and also shook Father's hand.

"It was a pleasure doing a dungeon dive with you two, I wish we could do it again." Sapphire said.

Father and Sunshine exchanged pleasantries with Sapphire while the stable boys retrieved their horses and wagon. Sapphire gave them the gold she had promised and before long the two were riding out of town.

They both looked back and waved a final goodbye to Sunshine and Father.

"Thanks for coming today, it was a lot of fun." Storm said.

"I had a lot of fun too." Sapphire told him, "I was also happy to meet your sister and," she paused, "and your father's avatar."

"Yeah," Storm chuckled, "I know it's a little weird. But honestly, I really enjoy spending time with him. It's very cathartic, after missing him for so long."

Storm sat back and enjoyed the ride after a long day of dungeon diving. The soft bump of the wagon on the uneven road and the gentle breeze felt good.

"Is he the same?" Sapphire asked hesitantly.

"Yes, surprisingly so actually" he responded after thinking about her question, "He knows things he shouldn't, which is strange. To my knowledge my dad never logged into this game. He's as caring as my dad was. He also has the same mannerisms and sounds exactly like him."

Sapphire didn't respond for a while and got a far-off look in her eyes. Storm knew what she was thinking about and sat quietly beside her.

"Sapphire, have you seen your sister's avatar?" Storm asked quietly, after she scooted close to him.

"No, that's why I was asking." she replied with a heavy sigh. "I want to see my sister again but I'm worried she will be different."

"She's not on this server, is she?" he asked after coming to a realization.

"No. She's on a different server." Sapphire confirmed, "She started the game with her boyfriend."

They rode in silence for a while, sitting close to each other.

"Storm, I had fun today." she said, leaning against him. "Thank you for having me along."

"I had fun too." he replied, trying to keep it cool. Nervously, he put his arm around her. His heart near burst when she snuggled into his embrace. The two rode the wagon, all the way back to camp.

TWENTY-TWO

World boss

L uke had a hard time sleeping and got up early the next day. He had mixed feelings about the raid and took a long walk in the cool morning air to clear his thoughts. After eating a large breakfast he logged into the game, ready to make difficult decisions.

Storm stepped out of his tent and was surprised by how many players were bustling about in the Dark Elite camp. He had never seen so many in one place before. Some were hurrying through the camp and others were standing around talking. There was a buzz of excitement in the air.

Storm didn't know where to go so he followed the crowd. The flow of players led him to the north end of camp. Along the way he heard many similar conversations and had a bad feeling about the day.

"Finally, it's happening."

"All of our hard work pays out today!"

"Today is it!"

"I'm so tired of cats, it's time for something new!"

The excitement was contagious and maybe under different circumstances it would have been for him too, but he knew how this was going to end. What Dark Elite was doing had real consequences for him and his family.

Storm followed the crowed in a daze, his heart sinking with every step. Eventually they came to a large valley where the mass of players gathered. Down in the valley was an enormous summoning circle made of hand-sized rocks. Inside the circle was a six-pointed star with each point touching the edge. At this intersection was a smaller with a symbol inside. Storm immediately recognized the symbols from his spell-work, each represented a different element.

The whole might of the Dark Elite guild surrounded the valley. The players were organized into balanced groups for combat. Each group was self-sufficient with tanking, dealing damage and healing. But Storm recognized there were specialized groups of mages and clerics supporting the entire raid with buffs and resurrections.

Off to the side, Storm saw another specialized group. They were isolated from the others and for good reason. Each member had an enthralled pet, a fire salamander. Storm knew from experience that this group was far too dangerous to be mixed in with the rest. He briefly wondered if his friend, Pipe was there.

Weird stood in the center of the star, surrounded by several high-level players. From that distance, Storm could see they were all friends, they talked and laughed easily with each other. They were all decked out in high level gear, many of their pieces glowed and even a few sparkled. By comparison, Storm felt like a beggar in his shabby outfit. The group was intimidating. Sapphire wasn't there.

And as if he summoned her with his thoughts, she greeted him from behind, "Nice to see you made it, I thought you were joining Weird's group?"

Storm turned and his breath caught at seeing her beautiful face, he couldn't help but smile. He glanced at Weird's group and replied meekly, "He looks busy."

"Ahh, you're cute. A little level 50, nervous about hanging with the big boys?" she teased.

"Look at them," he replied, gesturing in their direction, "they look awesome." He glanced at his shabby outfit and added, "I look like I rummaged in a dumpster."

"DumpsterBoy!" Sapphire blurted out. Her eyes widened in horror and she covered her mouth at the unexpected outburst.

Storm laughed and smiled at her, easing her embarrassment.

"Seriously though," she tried comforting him, "they've been there, they won't judge you. Just go out there and have fun."

"Thanks," he said, genuinely starting to feel better. Sapphire had a way of cheering him up. From her gentle teasing and comforting support, she always seemed to know just what he needed.

"Good luck" Sapphire said confidently, then gently pushed him towards the center of the valley. Submitting to her will, he followed her direction. When he was almost out of earshot she called to him, "Try not to die!"

Storm heard her but kept walking, fearing if he stopped, he would lose his nerve. He quietly joined Weird's group, not wanting to interrupt the conversation.

Weird recounted his first battle with the beast they were about to face. He described the raid wipes they endured and the various strategies they tried, eventually finding the right one. His friends were captivated by the story, some laughed and others added their own details.

Weird went on to describe the treasure they found and how a mysterious staff altered the course of the game. Storm listened as if he were in a spell. At the mention of the staff, the hairs on the back of his neck stood up.

"Ahh, pardon my nostalgia." Weird said, when his story was finished. His friends snickered and he conceded, "I know, I know, every time we get to this point, I get sentimental."

Storm felt the emotion in Weird's voice as he told his story. He was beginning to wonder if Weird wasn't such a bad person. Maybe he would understand if Storm told him about his father. Then he heard the soft voice of the assassin.

"Let's burn it down." Strychnine suggested with a manic grin.

"Always my friend, we burn it down." Weird easily agreed with an unsettling laugh.

Storm rescinded his earlier thought, the man in front of him would never stop short of his goal. He recalled what Sapphire had told him about Weird and in that moment he understood. Storm realized it was all a mistake and started to edge away but froze when he heard Weird's next words.

"Ahh, there he is." Weird announced to his group, "Everybody, I'd like to introduce you to Storm, he is a new member of Dark Elite and has earned a place in our group today."

[Group invitation
      From: Weird
      Accept
      Decline]

Storm shook off his unease and accepted the invite. He looked closer at the gathered group and couldn't believe how stacked they were. They were beyond intimidating.

Storm recognized Weird, Tomb, Strychnine, Klar and Kat. He knew they were originals, but was unsure of the others present. Either way, they were all level 100. Nervously he inspected Weird.

[Character sheet
    Name: Weird
    Guild: Dark Elite
    Race: Human
    Level: 100
    Stats: <redacted>
    Skills: <redacted>
    Spells: <redacted>
    Special Abilities: <redacted>]

He groaned inwardly. He should have realized that Weird's character sheet would have been protected like Sapphire's was. He checked the other members and was disappointed to see it was the same for all of them.

Weird stepped away from the group and cast a spell. His next words boomed out over the valley.

"Half an hour everybody. Get to your positions and ready yourself." Weird announced. He walked around the large circle and made the announcement several times, ensuring everybody received the message. Once back to the group, Weird asked "Does everybody have their item?"

"Storm?" Tomb prompted.

"Oh, that's my fault." Weird said. He walked to Storm and inspected him. After a few seconds Weird nodded in satisfaction and pulled a large flaming feather from his bag. Weird handed it to Storm and explained, "Your puzzle breaking is high enough so you can join the summoning."

"You already gave me one." Storm said.

"That was for your personal use, you can turn it into a trophy if you like." Weird explained, "This one is for the summoning spell and will be destroyed in the process."

"What do I do?" Storm asked. He took the feather cautiously, as to not burn himself.

"Go stand in the fire circle." Weird instructed, waving his hand to one of the points of the star. "Wait for the spell to activate and as soon as feather rises in the air, get out of there as fast as you can and rejoin our group."

Storm walked over to the point of the star Weird had indicated and confirmed the symbol on the ground was the fire glyph. He stepped inside the circle and waited, holding the Phoenix God feather to the side.

Storm looked at the other points of the star and watched as his counterparts stepped into their circles. Strychnine, the scary assassin, held a ball of rolling mud between his hands. He held it at a distance, in an attempt to not to get his pristine blood-red leather armor dirty. Kat tossed a miniature cloud from hand to hand, as it poured rain onto the ground. Klar held a dagger with a swirling tornado above it, causing her hair to blow around in all directions. And the final two points of the star he couldn't see, one was completely dark and the other a blinding light. Each point contained a different element of magic.

Weird stood in the center of the six-pointed star holding a book. When everybody was in their places he began reading. Storm couldn't hear what he was saying but could see his lips moving and felt the magic rise around him. Weird continued reading for another ten minutes, turning page after page.

Storm felt a gentle tug on the feather which steadily increased until the it was yanked from his grasp and floated upwards. Storm watched it float higher and higher, transfixed by the magic.

He glanced at the other elements and saw them floating in the air as well. As the owners of those items scurried away, he recalled Weird's instructions. He hurriedly left his circle and rejoined their group, safely off to the side.

The entire raid watched, entranced, as Weird continued casting the spell. At various points Weird held his hand out and moved it around in the air, as if he were writing. Lines of power formed on the ground and followed the intricate pattern inside the summoning area. Finally, when each elemental offering was encompassed with power, Weird snapped the book shut and disappeared. A few seconds later he reappeared next to his group with a weary smile on his face.

A cracking sound thundered across the valley and many players looked around in fright. A large rip formed in the air where Weird had just stood. The crack widened and Storm could only see a deep blackness on the other side. After staring for a few moments, he saw movement, then a massive yellow eye peaked through. A chill ran through his body.

"Salamanders, go!" Weird's voice rang out.

Storm watched a dozen salamanders waddle their way to the center of the valley. Before they got there, a massive dragon poked its head through the ever-widening crack. It slithered the rest of its body into the valley and unfurled its wings. The jet-black dragon rose into the air on its hind legs and spread its wings wide. It roared in defiance. The deafening sound overtook the players, causing many to adjust their volume settings.

The dragon was larger than a train and just as formidable. It was covered in black hardened scales from head to tail and seemed entirely impenetrable. On top of its head were two large horns that curled into the air, very reminiscent of Weird's helm.

Storm stared at the creature in awe. It was a magnificent representation of the perfect fairy-tale dragon. Its scales glistened in the sunlight as it spit fire into the air.

The salamanders didn't waste any time and attacked the dragon straight away. However, they had no effect on the creature of legend. In return, the dragon roared and breathed fire onto the salamanders with little effect as well.

[Legendary Creature
      Name: World Dragon
      Level: ***
      Hit points: ***/***]

"What do we do now?" Storm asked in a whisper, fearful of attracting the dragon's attention.

"Let the pets build up aggro more." Weird instructed, "Then join in at your pleasure. If you'd rather sit and watch the show, go ahead." He waved at the dragon, "Once its health hits halfway, we move to the next phase."

Storm decided to sit back and watch the show, feeling conflicted about the experience. Weird's story about the staff played over and over in his head. It opened a portal to a magical city in the sky. Weird had described their first time using it and stepping into that city.

Several mages took turns casting shields around the salamanders and the dragon's health plummeted with each strike it made. It still took a while but eventually the dragon's health reached the halfway mark.

Just as Weird had predicted, the battle changed. The beast beat its wings and rose into the air. It flew in a circle over the valley and spewed fire down into it. Almost everybody had moved out of range but the inexperienced players stayed behind and were roasted alive.

"Phase two! Stun spells and bind spells." Weird instructed, his artificially enhanced voice booming out over the valley.

The dragon swooped down again and poured fire into the valley, cooking anything remained, which wasn't much. It hung in the air beating its wings, intently staring down for any movement.

A rush of players ran down the hill, into the valley, towards the dragon. Storm thought they were on a suicide run but realized they were mages trying to get within range to cast. His heart almost stopped when we realized that Sapphire was in the lead. He watched anxiously as their spells failed to take hold and the dragon swung its head in their direction, ready for another fiery release.

Weird step forward and flung his hand towards the dragon. A flash of bright light emanated from him and a resounding crack echoed through the valley, deafening Storm's ears. The dragon's head snapped viciously to the side and the whole thing came crashing down, landing ungracefully in a heap. The dragon lay there, stunned.

When its massive weight struck the ground, shock waves reverberated out, knocking down many players. With its defenses down, the mages were finally able to land multiple stun and rooting spells. As the magic took hold, different colored ethereal lights   crawled over the dragon's body.

The dragon, now fully immobilized, was at their complete mercy, and Dark Elite had none. The rest of the guild rushed into the valley and attacked the dragon. They hacked and slashed at it with frantic abandon, each strike taking a sliver of health.

"It's done! Everybody back!" Weird yelled suddenly, after what seemed like hours had passed.

At Weird's command, the players once again retreated to the safety of the valley walls. This time however, the ground was soaked with blood and it was difficult to climb the hillside. Many players, slipping and falling in the gore.

It was mostly dragon blood but there were more than a few players that had received vicious wounds and contributed to the mess. Near the end of the battle, the dragon's heart was pierced and blood fountained into the air. Each heartbeat caused another eruption, draining more of its life force, until none was left.

Storm finally made it to the top of the hill, only falling down twice. He stared down at the dead dragon as it disintegrated into a green haze, which began filling the valley. It struck Storm that this battlefield had been expertly chosen. It nullified many of the dragon's advantages and minimized the casualties.

Of course there were always idiots, Storm thought, as he watched several players still in the valley. They had ignored Weird's warnings and stayed behind for unknown reasons, possibly to steal the loot. It didn't take too long before they regretted that decision. Their screams filled the air as they melted into a pile of goo.

It took twenty minutes before the dragon corpse stopped spewing toxic fumes. During that time the players sat around playing small games and chatted about their recent adventures.

Storm stared at the dragon's body, brooding about the fate of his father's avatar. He didn't ask Weird, to beg him, to alter course. He now knew there wasn't anything he could say. Sapphire was right.

He was the first to see it through the shifting toxic clouds, a pile of treasure. Storm did the most impulsive thing he had done since entering the game, he activated his boots of teleportation.

Storm landed next to the pile of loot and fought through the disorientation. He didn't have much time before the caustic smoke ate through his health reserves. He scooped up the staff and quickly cast his town portal spell.

The silvery staff was exactly as Weird had described. It was made of a mysterious metal that was light and unnaturally cool to the touch. It was six feet long and had a mirror finish with glowing script along its length, which Storm easily recognized as the arcane language used in spells.

He couldn't help but identify it.

[Legendary item
    Name: World staff
    Description: Summons a permanent portal to Avalon. Cannot be stored.
    Charges: 1/1

Durability: Indestructible]

Storm's heart pounded as he completed his spell. He couldn't make it all the way to Last Hope but there was a town close by that he could get to. From there he could get a horse and escape. The portal sprang into existence and he took a step towards it, or at least he tried to. His blood ran cold when he heard the voice behind him.

"Good effort." Weird said in a disappointed tone.

The world around Storm went dark. He thought he was blinded at first but checking his buffs revealed the harsh truth, he was unconscious.

Disappointed, Storm slammed his hand on the logout button, hitting it repeatedly until he felt the game world recede. He took a long hot shower and sat down to eat. He briefly explained the situation to his mom and sister when they logged out for lunch. They tried to ask him about it but he didn't feel like talking and shrugged off their questions.

His mom comforted him and told him that she was proud that he tried to stand up to Dark Elite. She insisted that it wasn't too late and they still had a chance but she was concerned about the status of his avatar. She insisted he log back in and find out what happened.

Back in the game, Storm stared at a blank screen, his avatar was still unconscious. After waiting for twenty minutes the icon faded away and the world around him appeared once again. He blinked away the fuzziness and took stock of his surroundings. Naturally, he was located in Weird's office in the camp. Pretty much what he was expecting, although there was one surprise.

Storm sat in a familiar wooden chair with blue bands of power holding him down. He knew without even looking that his spells and items were completely useless. He briefly wondered how Weird had gotten it.

"Who do you work for?" Weird asked calmly.

"Nobody, I... I'm alone." Storm answered.

"Which guild are you working for?" Weird asked, more forcefully.

"Nobody." Storm insisted.

"Not even Fallen Uprising?" Weird asked, watching him closely.

"No. Not exactly." Storm hesitated, his eyes widening slightly. His mind raced. How did he know that guild?

"Why did you do it?" Weird continued questioning him. He looked Storm in the eyes, as if trying to read his mind.

"My dad." Storm answered, defeated. He looked away from Weird.

"Dad, he's not a spy." a voice Storm knew all too well, said from the doorway.

Storm looked up to see Sapphire entering the building and his heart stopped.

"I spent yesterday with him and his sister." she continued, walking up to Weird, her father. "They are here to honor their father's avatar and spend time with him."

"The tickets aren't available right now." Weird said, shaking his head, "The Fallen are in Valhalla."

"I identified the Fallen avatar myself. It was spectral." She explained.

"What do you want me to do?" he asked her, "You know why we are doing this."

"I know." she replied, "But, I hate to tear his family apart."

"Give me some time to think about this." Weird said, sighing, "I won't summon the portal until tomorrow." He looked at Storm and asked, "Are you comfortable? I need some time to consider your situation."

"No, not really." Storm replied sharply. He frowned at his restraints and rocked back and forth in the chair. "What Sapphire says is true. I just want more time with my dad's avatar and you're trying to take him away from me."

"Loss is a hard thing." Weird said not unkindly, staring at him. Then he turned and walked out of the cabin, leaving Storm and Sapphire alone.

"Thanks for defending me." Storm said.

"A lot of good it did." she said, frowning.

"He said he was going to think about it." Storm said hopefully.

"No, he's not." she responded, "I told you he is driven and he won't let anything get in-between him and his goal."

"Can you help me?" Storm asked, wiggling.

"No DumpsterBoy," she affectionally said, "I can't. I'm sorry but anybody that helps you will get burned."

"Nice chair." Storm said sarcastically, shifting the subject, "I wonder where he got it."

"We had a spy problem." Sapphire said shrugging.

"So, what's next?" he asked.

"I'll talk with him later and see if he'll let you go." she said, "That way you can spend some time with your dad's avatar before he opens the portal. I might be able to get him to hold off for a few days."

"What happens when he opens the portal?" Storm asked.

She looked around to make sure nobody had entered the cabin and leaned in close to answer him.

"The staff creates a permanent portal to Avalon." she explained, "Once Weird claims the city, the countdown to the server vs server battles will begin. But, before the timer runs out, he will destroy the server." She looked at him with tears in her eyes, "I'm sorry Storm, it's too late."

A shiver ran up his spine at her words and he clenched his jaw in frustration. There has to be some way to stop this, he thought.

"I need to check on something." Sapphire said suddenly, "I'll be back." Then she promptly left, leaving him alone with his thoughts.

Storm surveyed the room. In the corner behind the desk, the silver staff leaned against the wall with his bag was next it. At least his stuff was here. He heard the door open and thought Sapphire had returned but was disappointed.

"Storm, are you ok?" Bobby asked in a serious voice.

"Bobby?" Storm asked bewildered, "You should get out of here, I don't want you to get into trouble." He recalled the first day he met Bobby, he was a little boy that had showed him a lot of kindness.

"Storm, I'm not a child." Bobby explained in a whisper, stepping close to him. "I'm an admin. I've been investigating Weird to ensure he doesn't violate our rules." He waved a hand at Storm siting in the char and angrily said, "This is very close to crossing the line. If he tortures you, we will have no choice but to shut down his account."

"I'm ok," Storm assured him. "He hasn't done anything like that." He had a passing thought that if he provoked Weird into torturing him, he might be able save his dad's avatar. But he wasn't sure he could go that far.

"Ok Storm, but we are watching." Bobby said, "If you are ever uncomfortable just say, 'I'm done, get me out of this.' And we will shut it down."

Storm watched as Bobby left the cabin and decided it was time for him to update his mom and logged out.

When Luke walked into the kitchen, his mom and sister looked at him worriedly.

"Ok, I'm ready to talk." Luke said after taking a deep breath. Luke told them about battling the world dragon and how he teleported to the World staff to try keep it away from Weird. He even explained the conversation he had and how Weird was going to think about it for a day., then make a decision.

When he was done talking, Luke's mom picked up her phone and tapped out a number on it. Luke and Cleo sat there watching her, wondering what she was doing. Their mom ignored them.

"Hey," she said when somebody picked up. "Yeah, it's me. I... I need your help." She paused to listen to the other person then said, "Yeah, call the whole guild. It's Dark Elite, they have my son."

Luke heard somebody cussing in a deep voice on the other side of phone. His mom grimaced and held it away from her ear until it quieted down. When the other person calmed down, she instructed, "Meet me in Last Hope." then hung up.

"Luke," his mom commanded, "Log back in and wait for me. I'm coming to get you."

Luke stared at her in disbelief, his thoughts spinning. What guild is she talking about? How are they coming to get me? Luke was about to ask but she cut him off.

"I'm sorry hun," she interrupted, "This isn't the time. Weird thought you weren't affiliated with a guild so he could treat you any way he wanted. But he was wrong. This is war, and he knows it." She looked at Cleo and instructed her, "Cleo, you log back in too. Update Father about Storm's situation and tell him I'm coming."

TWENTY-THREE

Avalon

Nightshade stood by the river and stretched. She thought fondly of her past couple of days in-game. After the weather cleared, she relaxed by the river and lazily caught fish. She also harvested rare herbs from the clearing and brewed potions with them. This was her kind of fun but her vacation was over.

She had played so much the past few years she was happy to take a break and enjoy the more mundane aspects of the game. She was overjoyed Storm and Sunshine got to play with Father. There were no holidays close by, so she didn't think they would get the opportunity.

After reeling in her rods, Sunshine picked up her gear and carried everything to the cabin. She looked down at her hands and admired her jewelry. It wasn't her normal set but it was special to her, it had allowed her to hide her true level and protect some shameful secrets.

One by one she removed her level-suppression gear. With each piece she took off, more power flowed into her body. By the end, eight rings, four earrings, two bracers and a necklace lay in a pile on the table. She felt stronger and faster.

After equipping her real gear, Nightshade left the cabin and walked back down to the river. She called upon her magic and plants erupted from the ground. They rose into the air and wove together forming a solid structure. The plants stretched across the river, supporting each other until they found the other side. Then, they grew and thickened until a temporary bridge was created.

She casually walked across the bridge and on the other side, she flicked her hand and the plant bridge crumpled into the river and washed away.

Nightshade jogged through the forest, making great time as the plants moved out of her way. The trees shifted their limbs and the thickets turned their thorns in deference to her passing.

A short time later she entered Last Hope and walked up to the two figures sitting on the edge of the water fountain in the center of town. Father stood up as she approached and they hugged in a familiar greeting. His eyes lit up and he smiled that crooked grin he saved just for those he loved.

"Good to see you." Nightshade said to him.

"Aye, it's been a while." he responded.

"Mom?" Sunshine asked, looking between the two with suspicion in her eyes.

They both looked at her with guilt on their faces.

"I wanted to tell you sweetie," Nightshade said holding a hand out to Father, which he took. "But there wasn't a good time. You defied all odds freeing him from Valhalla."

"Don't blame her too much," Father added, "We talked about it a few months ago and we both agreed not to tell you and your brother. There wasn't going to be an opportunity for us to meet, or so we thought."

"Do you think you can get Storm back?" Sunshine asked after suppressing her feelings of betrayal.

"Yeah, we have a chance." Nightshade affirmed, then she explained her plan and they both agreed there was a chance of it working.

Slowly Last Hope filled with people, as more and more players arrived throughout the day. Many came riding into town on different feline mounts and others arrived by portal. Sunshine saw a wide array of mounts, from lions to tigers and cheetahs to jaguars, she even saw a snow leopard or two. However, she was surprised to see domestic cat varieties in the mix, all large enough to carry their rider.

Each player that arrived immediately walked up and greeted Nightshade, many hugging her.

"How do you know these people mom?" Sunshine asked, she was surprised her mom had so many friends. All of them seemed to be in the same guild, 'Fallen Uprising'.

"They're my guild." she explained, "I was the guild leader until I dropped out for our vacation. Everybody in the guild has a family member or friend that's passed away. Whenever we can, we summon them out of Valhalla and play together, sometimes we do raids, sometimes we will PvP with the other realms."

"You back Nightshade?" A very large man asked in a deep voice.

"Yeah, I guess I am." she said after glancing at Sunshine.

"Good, this guild leader thing is tough." he said, then invited her back into the guild and quickly passed the leadership back to her. "There." he said with a sigh of relief.

"Thanks Lance, it's good to be back." Nightshade said, "And thanks for taking care of everybody for me. It looks like almost everybody is here."

Nightshade called the guild around her and explained what Dark Elite was up to. She also explained they had her son. Every single player showed their support and grumbled at the information.

After making their preparations, they retrieved the invitational-portal spell that Dark Elite had recruited Sunshine with and activated it. An azure portal appeared in the center of town, surrounded by a rag-tag group of players in mismatched gear.

"Stay here," Nightshade ordered Sunshine, "the portal will stay open longer." She had her daughter activate the portal just for this reason, she didn't want her going along. Dark Elite was dangerous and she knew they might not survive the upcoming encounter.

"Are you ready?" Father asked Nightshade, after pulling out a potion that pulsated with a golden light. He looked at her fondly with his crooked grin.

"Always," she replied, and stepped close to him.

They shared the star potion, each drinking half. Their forms vibrated and glowed a brilliant golden color. The two spoke to each other in a high-pitched voice that nobody understood. Then, they raced towards the portal and disappeared.

Far off, in the Dark Elite camp, Storm stared defiantly at Weird. He was still trapped in the wooden chair, while Weird sat at his desk, reviewing scout reports. Just as Sunshine had told him, her father would not stop. After some time, Weird had returned and explained his way was the best for his goals, but he would help Storm if he could.

After their short talk, Storm had tried to engage him in conversation several times. But Weird wouldn't respond. Storm even tried begging but Weird got annoyed and cast a silence spell on him.

Suddenly the door burst open and two forms streaked into the room. One ran to Storm and released him from the chair. The other one ran directly to Weird but he was already in motion.

The instant the forms entered his office, Weird shot to his feet and flung both hands towards them. Darts flew towards the mysterious figures but bounced harmlessly off. Vines wrapped around Weird, holding him in place but he burst into flames and incinerated them.

One of the forms ran up to Weird and hesitated. Just as Weird was about to make things uncomfortable, the blurry figure made up its mind and acted. Quicker than a thought, it stabbed Weird in the neck with a glass dagger. Storm noted it was the same dagger Sunshine received from a treasure box he gave her.

Storm anxiously watched the needle-like blade separated from the pommel and sunk deep into Weird's body. Weird fell to his hands and knees and vomited. He then then collapsed and lay still, foaming at the mouth. Storm didn't miss the copious amount of blood mixed in the bile.

Storm collected the staff and his bag before the two figures quickly ushered him out of the building. He ran as fast as he could back to the portal with one glowing figure leading the way and the other following. Whenever anybody tried to stop them, the two figures quickly dispatched them.

At one point they became surrounded by a crowd of soldiers and Storm used his boots of teleportation to jump far into the distance. He knew the two figures would quickly catch up.

As soon as they were through the portal the invincibility potion wore off and Father and Nightshade returned to normal. He wasn't surprised, Storm knew his mom would rescue him.

"Be ready!" she called out, facing the portal.

Fallen Uprising showed up in force and in their finest gear. They were ready for battle. To them, this wasn't just a game, it was their only connection to lost loved ones. They stood there with bated breaths, waiting for the portal to close.

Battle totems of each flavor had been deployed, covering the entire gathering of players. They pulsated azure, ruby and golden colors, for mana, health and stamina recovery. Next to the portal were a few special totems with black gems.

These totems detected stealthed player and would send out a pulse every few seconds.

They waited for what seemed like an hour, when it took only a few minutes for the portal to close. Once it did, there was a collective sigh of relief. But still, nobody moved.

The detection rate of the stealth totems was only thirty percent, so it took time for them to work. They waited several more minutes and with each pulse, they relaxed more and more. Then it happened. Two figures appeared where the portal had been. Even though the new arrivals were grossly outnumbered, Storm had a bad feeling.

Storm began casting as soon as the two appeared but it was already too late. Tomb was strumming his lute, singing in a beautiful voice. A haunting melody drifted out from the minstrel and encompassed everybody. Nobody could move. They were all mesmerized.

Strychnine took a step forward. All eyes were trained on him, fearing his next actions. Then he began stretching. Over the next ten minutes, he slowly stretched his entire body, as everybody watched. He even lay on the ground for a few of them. Unfortunately, the spell that trapped them, would last as long as the song was still playing or they weren't being attacked.

Storm watched Strychnine, incredulous of the show. He wasn't the only one though, he heard many groans when the assassin kept going. He even swore the tone of the mesmerizing spell changed. When the assassin was done screwing around, Storm felt a shiver run through his body.

Slowly, Strychnine reached down and unsheathed both swords at his hips. He held the two rapiers high in the air, one blade red and the other blue, both covered with a shiny liquid. The assassin then cut down so fast everybody heard the blades slice through the air. Clouds of green smoke billowed out from him and into the crowd.

The assassin rushed forward, into the cloud, spinning and cutting and slicing. Bodies fell as he moved past. One would think he was being unfair or even unsportsmanlike, but Strychnine was anything but. He was a master assassin and he lived by a code.

The cloud he released was a poisonous gas. It was an area affect, damage-over-time spell that infected everybody, in range, with a poison that damaged the player every second. This had two effects, first and most obvious, it attacked the players health, but the other effect and the reason why he cast it was because it would release everybody from Tomb's mez spell.

Strychnine could have fought everybody one at a time, nobody would have had a chance. But he didn't need the advantage, he was an expert at killing. Each slice of the blade, each stab, was calculated and strategic. He danced and whirled amongst the coughing crowd slipping his blade behind shields and around armor, cutting into arteries or weak points, disabling his opponents. Each cut poisoned them further stacking multiple poisons to quickly drain away their life.

"Run." Nightshade hissed, pushing Storm towards the forest, "get to the cabin." Not waiting to see if he followed her orders, she turned and fired her bow at the two marauders, sending a glowing arrow towards them.

Storm ran into the forest and the sounds of battle faded behind him. He ran halfway to the river before he slowed. He was out of breath and it took him a few moments to calm down before he could check if he was followed. He squatted low to the ground and listened to the forest around him. He didn't hear any immediate pursuit but he thought he still heard the sound of soft music drifting through the forest, probably from Last Hope.

He crept the rest of the way to the river, utilizing his tracking ability to stay quiet and hide his trail. He kept an ear out for anybody following and stopped several times thinking he heard the gentle strum of a lute, but there was nobody there.

His mom wanted him to return to the cabin because it was her bind spot and if worse came to pass in Last Hope they could reunite there. The cabin was also unknown to Dark Elite and it would give them a couple of days to hide out and figure out what to do with the staff.

Storm made it to the river and found their previous crossing without any problems but he couldn't find the boat his sister mentioned. Without it, he would need to shimmy across on the rope because the river was still too high to wade across like the previous time. It wasn't without risk, so he decided to scout Last Hope first.

He found a large tree nearby that offered a good hiding spot and sat down with his back pressed up against the trunk. Hidden behind the branches he felt safe enough to try scrying for the first time. Storm activated his ring and caught his orb of scrying as it popped into existence from the dimensional space. He stared into the orb and it activated.

It was disorienting but he quickly got used to it. Storm was looking down at tree he was hiding under. He first scanned the immediate area and didn't see any movement other than a few birds and squirrels, then he moved the view towards town. A mile from his location a red warning flashed in his eyes.

[Warning
        Scry skill too low, unable to cast]

He ignored it, he didn't need to cast, he just needed information. The further he scried from his location, the more the view darkened until it was completely opaque. Fortunately, he made it to Last Hope before that happened.

There were only a few defenders left to face-off against Strychnine, while dozens of bodies lay on the ground, waiting to respawn. Storm didn't see Tomb but hoped he was one of those bodies. He watched anxiously as the remaining players cautiously surrounded the devil in red leathers.

His sister swooped down behind the assassin with her wings outstretched. She grabbed onto him until Father smashed him in the face with his oversized hammer. Strychnine was ripped out of her grasp and sent flying a dozen feet away. The assassin hit the ground hard and lay still.

Storm scanned the remaining defenders and was happy to see his mom and a few others were still alive. They began checking for survivors when Storm saw Strychnine's body disappear. Nobody else saw it happen and he could only watch on helplessly.

Strychnine reappeared behind Father and backstabbed him for critical damage. The assassin's blades sunk deep into Father's back and emerged from the other side. Father screamed in pain and grabbed onto the blades sticking out of his chest. He coughed up blood and sank to his knees.

Storm, not understanding, watched in horror as Father held on tight, blood gushing from his hands. That was until Strychnine tried to retrieve his blades. The assassin yanked on them but they didn't budge. He gave up and quickly reached for another set but it was already too late. Plants crawled up the assassin's legs and rooted him to the ground while the remaining defenders ensured his demise.

Nightshade ran to Father's fallen form and held him up, pouring vials of liquid into his mouth. Everybody could see it was futile, even Storm. Father knew he was dead, in his final act he ensured Strychnine was also.

Shaken up by what he had just watched, Storm planned to return to Last Hope. The assassin was dead and the minstrel was probably as well. He scried the area around him one more time and his blood ran cold when he found him. Tomb wasn't too far away, slowly searching the forest. It was only a matter of time before he was discovered.

Storm quickly stored the orb in his ring and quietly snuck out from under the tree. His only chance was to get across the river and cut the rope to impede their pursuit. He would have used his teleportation boots but they still had half an hour left on the timer. His only choice of escape was to shimmy across.

Unfortunately, he couldn't store the staff in a dimensional space so, while holding it, he awkwardly grabbed the rope and pulled himself up, hooking his feet around it. He inched his way across the river, often glancing down nervously. The river was still flooded from days of rain and if he fell in, he wouldn't make it back out. Then he would respawn directly in the middle of Dark Elite's camp.

Storm made it about half way across the river when he heard a melody drift out to him. He glanced back to see Tomb standing on the bank, staring at him. Tomb gave him a small wave and Storm turned to hurry to the other side. He tried to reach out to pull himself forward but he couldn't move, his body was completely frozen. A mez debuff appeared in his UI and he stared at it angrily.

He felt the rope sway and dip as Tomb made his way to him. He tried to let go and fall into the river, desperate to keep the staff away from Weird, but he couldn't even do that. Not able to move his head he relied on his peripheral vision to track Tomb's approach.

When Tomb was close, he reached out and grabbed the staff to pull it out of Storm's grip. But the instant he touched it, the spell on Storm was broken and Storm held onto the staff for dear life. The two dangled over the rushing river, each holding onto the World staff, pushing and pulling, trying to get the other to let go.

Storm kicked at Tomb and struck him in the face. Tomb slipped and his feet fell into the water. Storm hoped the river would pull him away but Tomb maintained his grip on both the rope and the staff.

Tomb yanked on the staff, a little more desperately, but Storm held tight. Storm heard a sharp whistling sound and looked down to find blood trickling down his arm. It wasn't much but it was enough to wet his hand and loosen his grip. Tomb pulled again and this time it slipped, a little.

Tomb shifted his weight for one last tug but his eyes widened in surprise and he looked down. A green tentacle wrapped itself around his legs. The rope dipped as the creature tugged on its prize. The minstrel tried to fight back but he lost his grip on the rope and fell into the water. He grabbed onto the staff with both hands and easily pulled it out of Storm's weakened grip.

Having no other choice, Storm fell into the water after the staff. He wrestled it away from Tomb and kicked away from him. He swam towards the shoreline expecting the river rushed him away. Instead, something snagged his foot and pulled him under the water. Storm looked down and saw that the same creature that captured Tomb had a hold of him as well. Using the staff, he tried to pry it loose but another plant-like appendage reached up and encased him further.

The creature pulled them both down, deep into a dark pit in the middle of the river. Storm held his breath and stayed as still as possible, hoping it would let him go. He frantically tried to think of a way to escape before he respawned in Dark Elite's camp.

Storm studied the creature as he was pulled down and it had many more seaweed-like appendages. They floated up towards the mouth of the pit, barely touching the rushing water above, waiting for more pray. He looked over at Tomb, who thankfully, was far enough away he couldn't make a grab for staff. Storm noticed Tomb was breathing fine underwater and remembered his own amulet that gave him that ability. Cautiously he breathed in and was surprised he didn't get lungs full of water.

Tomb gave him a little wave, just like earlier, then pulled out a knife and reached down to cut away at the plant creature, freeing himself. Storm's eyes widened in fear, realizing the staff was not as safe as he thought. But just then several more strands of the seaweed rose out of the depths and wrapped wrap Tomb up, completely immobilizing him.

Storm instructed his avatar to stay still and don't let go of the staff. He then logged out and left a quick message for his mom detailing what happened. He logged back in to wait. He didn't have to wait very long before he felt a disturbance in the water. Storm looked up and saw Nightshade sinking, feet first into the pit. The creature reached up and wrapped around her legs and pulled her down to him.

When she reached the bottom, she spotted Storm and reached over to touch the strand holding him. Storm felt its grip lighten and then let go. He swam up a little then stopped to wait for her. Nightshade reached down and the plant creature let go of her as well. She started swimming up, but something caught her attention, the wrapped-up minstrel. She swam over to him and gently touched the plant surrounded him. For a moment Storm was worried she was going to release him too but instead the plant tightened its grip and a cloud of dark liquid oozed out, floating up and into the river.

They swam up to the entrance to the pit and Nightshade took the staff and thrust it high above. Storm watched it disappear. A weighted roped descended and Nightshade wrapped it around herself and Storm followed suit. She smiled reassuringly at him and gave it a sharp tug. Then, the rope pulled them up and out, into the river. As soon as they exited the pit the river tried to drag them downstream but they were pulled steadily to the river bank.

Storm climbed out of the river and thanked the large man, who had pulled him and his mom to the shore by himself. He saw Sunshine close by, holding the staff, standing next her boat. She returned the staff and filled him in on the parts he missed while the group walked to their cabin. When they arrived, dozens of people were setting up camps. Storm identified them and found they were all a part of Fallen Uprising.

Finally, inside the cabin, Storm bound himself and felt a huge weight lift from his shoulders. He sat in a chair cradling the staff, watching as strange players filed inside. While the guild setup their base of operations, Nightshade invited each of the squad leaders to a meeting inside the small cabin. Nightshade stood in front of the group and addressed everybody.

"Thank you for your help tonight." she said, then gestured towards Storm and the staff, "We not only saved my son, but we also recovered the staff." She looked around at everybody, "I'm thankful everybody showed up tonight. Sadly, this means we are now at war with Dark Elite."

"We all owe you." Lance said in his deep voice, "You brought us together and gave us a purpose. You built this guild for us, and because of you we get to see our loved ones again. We will fight for you."

"You're not fighting for me." she said, glancing over the group, "You are fighting for your loved ones. "We have it on good authority that Dark Elite intends to destroy the server."

The inside of the cabin erupted in anxious conversation until Nightshade raised her hand to quiet them.

"Pass this information to your teams. You may have heard the rumors. They are true. Dark Elite has infected our server and will destroy it if we don't stop them."

"Is that it? Is that the staff?" a feminine voice asked. Storm looked over and saw a young woman in plate male pointing to the staff in his arms.

"Yes" Nightshade answered simply then made a motion for Storm to pass the staff around.

Everybody took turns holding it and inspecting it. A few murmured curses and others looked at it with awe.

"What do we do?" another member of Fallen Uprising asked.

"That's what we are here to figure out." Nightshade said, then turned to Lance and asked, "What did you find out about the world quest and the server vs server battles?"

"I found a few obscure forums that talked a bit about the lore." he explained, "They said that the staff creates a permanent portal to Avalon and there was some strategy to its location. The portal was usually created in a large city which can be defended. But sadly, there wasn't much beyond that."

"Once Avalon is claimed there is a small window of time until the server battles begin." Storm added, "During this time Weird is capable of destroying the server somehow. Once the battles begin, it's too late for him to do anything."

"Forty-eight hours" Lance said, "The forums also said that the server has forty-eight hours to consolidate its power. I assume that is the window of time you are talking about."

"Should we make the portal and claim Avalon then?" Storm asked, nodding thanks to Lance, "The sooner we start the timer, the sooner the Server Battles begin and we can save the server."

"Can't we just hide the staff?" Sunshine asked.

"No," Nightshade responded, "The World staff is a quest item and unfortunately, they can just do the quest again to get it."

"How long do we have?" one of the guild members asked.

"Assuming they don't have the items they need, maybe a week. A few days if they have everything." Nightshade said, "I think we should do it. It's starting to get late and a lot of people are heading to bed. If we make the portal now, we can get a head start on the countdown. Dark Elite knows where we are and it's only a matter of time until they show up in force. Let's do it now before they are fully organized."

"Two of them almost took us all out, I doubt we can stop their entire guild." somebody said.

"We can use this location to our advantage" Nightshade explained, "Crossing the river is difficult when it is flooding," glancing at Storm she continued, "We might be able to exacerbate that situation. If we hide the portal and defend it as best as possible, we might be able to make it."

"What do you mean, hide it?" Lance asked.

"You said its usually positioned in a large city that can be defended right?" Nightshade said, "That's probably because its location is forecasted to the entire server."

The room again erupted in anxious conversation, the top guild members debated whether they should summon the portal or not. Storm called his mom, sister and Lance over to discuss a few ideas and they all approved of his plan.

Nightshade held up her hand to quiet everybody down and explained Storm's plan. They slowly, one by one, agreed that summoning the portal was their best chance at survival. She handed out assignments and everybody left the cabin to attend to their duties.

Nightshade guided her guild in preparing the area for battle, they created trenches and palisades for defense. They setup a rotating guard that patrolled the shoreline and the immediate forest around them. Storm sat in the cabin and hastily created rain spell scrolls using the remaining parchment he had.

Several of the guild members that had the construction skill built a small imperceivable extension onto the back of the cabin with a hidden door. His mom, having the dig spell shared it to Storm and they secretly dug a large cavern underneath the cabin.

[New spell obtained: Dig (Earth)]

When they were done, Sunshine joined them in the dark cavern. Storm held the silver staff before him and unceremoniously activated the spell. Horns blared in his ears as a golden portal appeared before the small group. The portal stretched to top of the cavern and was wide enough for two people to enter side by side. It lit up the small cave like a miniature sun and took them all a few moments to become acclimated.

Squinting through the brightness, Storm took a deep breath and stepped through the portal, his mom and sister followed close behind. His feet touched down in a cobblestone courtyard of a large empty city. Storm turned around and stared at the empty buildings. He thought he recognized the place.

He walked down a street and several buildings caught his eye. He knew where he was. He started walking faster, then running. He turned a corner and saw it, the forge. The same place where he first met Father. But it was empty, there were no fires and no people. Disappointed, he returned to his mom and sister and explained what he had found.

"Maybe we should make our way up there." Nightshade suggested, pointing to a large castle on the hill, overlooking the city.

They agreed and walked up the small hill to the castle. Still holding the staff Storm felt it get warmer as they approached the walls. The portcullis lifted out of their way as if the ancient structure was welcoming them home. They spent the next half hour exploring the castle and finally found the throne room with a golden throne.

"Well, it's officially deserted." Nightshade announced.

"Yeah, not a soul here." Sunshine said in agreement, then asked "So, what's next?"

"I think it's time." Storm said, staring at the throne.

"Do it." Nightshade encouraged him. "It's late and most people are logged off. It's a good time to start it."

Storm walked up the steps to the throne and felt in a daze. His body felt sluggish as if he were walking through water. When he got to the top, he turned and sat down. As soon as he did, a prompt appeared in his vision.

[Quest

    Do you claim the throne of Avalon

    Accept

    Decline]

Nervously Storm accepted and once again, horns blared in his ears and a golden embossed prompt appeared in his vision.

[Quest
   You have claimed Avalon, Welcome to the city of clouds.
   Your UI has been upgraded to access the city interface.]

Almost immediately a red prompt appeared on top of his UI.

[World Notice
   The city of Avalon has been claimed. All Hail Storm!
   Heed, the world has fractured and you have entered a new phase.
   Gather to defend your home.
   Portals will open in 48 hours. Are they friends? Are they foes? Maybe both!]

Then a countdown permanently affixed itself in his UI.

[48 hours remaining] (2 am)

He grimaced and opened the city interface.

[Legendary City
   Name: Avalon
   Ruler: Storm
   Population: 1
   Mana pool: 10000 (+1/hr.)
   Heart of Eden health: 100%]

As he was reading, he looked over the various options for his new city and found there wasn't much he could currently do. He opened the city map and much to his surprise, he discovered Avalon was indeed the city of clouds. It was located on a bank of massive clouds that floated around the world. He discovered could make minor changes to its direction depending on the weather patterns. They were currently floating over the realm of the elves and it would take the city around forty hours to make it back to the clearing with the portal. He set the city on the path and closed out the interface.

Storm pulled out his orb of scrying and did a quick glance over Avalon to see how large it was. Then, having a thought he moved his view down, below Avalon, and discovered an elven town on the surface. He watched the few NPCs and players still awake walking around the dark town. With a mischievous thought, he tried to cast a spell and received a surprising prompt.

[City interface
      Access Avalon's mana pool
      Accept
      Decline]

Storm declined and cast the spell with his own mana. Within moments a gentle rain poured down onto the elven city a mile below them. Suddenly he became dizzy and checked his UI, only to find that because he cast that spell at a considerable distance, it came at an incredible price. A large chunk of his mana was missing, having been spent on the remote spell.

He suddenly had an idea and started scanning the sky with his orb but couldn't find what he was looking for. The world was incredibly large and most of it was still shrouded in a fog of war. After a few minutes of searching, he gave up.

"Dang" he muttered.

"What's wrong?" Nightshade asked him

"I had an idea to get Father back but I can't find him." Storm grumbled. Then he explained his idea to use his orb and remote cast a portal spell.

"I might be able to help with that." Nightshade said. She held up her write and Storm saw a delicate bracelet made of threads.

"Did Father give you that?" Storm asked, looking at the bracelet she fiddled with. It looked just like what Father had won from their dungeon dive.

"Yes, he gave this to me." she said, smiling sadly. She touched it fondly and continued, "He said that each of us knowing where the other was, would ease the pain of our separation." She hesitantly, handed it to Storm.

[Item
      Name: Bracelet of friendship
      Description: With this, close friends will always be close. No matter how far, their position will always be on your map.]

"He was in the eye of a storm when I summoned him." Sunshine added helpfully.

Storm put the bracelet on and sat down and attempted to find Father again. Before he did, he checked his map and easily found Father's glowing marker on it. He moved his view towards where he had seen the marker. Most of the land was covered in the fog-of-war and he couldn't see anything, but when he got to his destination and raised his view high into the air, the city of Valhalla came into view.

He had been there before so it was visible but it was greyed out and he couldn't see in real-time. He did see the buildings and could tell the whole city was moving, it was also in the clouds. Sadly, it was too far away to cast but after making a few adjustments to Avalon's path, he calculated they should be close enough in a few hours.

Storm sent his mother and sister back to the cabin to help finish the preparations while he tracked the progress of the two cities. After a while he started seeing figures move about while he scried but still couldn't cast any spells. After almost three hours, the two cities were close enough and he cast his town portal spell into Father's forge. Just like before he received a prompt.

[City interface
          Access Avalon's mana pool
          Accept
          Decline]

Knowing he didn't have enough mana, this time he accepted. He instantly he felt the hairs on his arms rise as if he were too close to a high voltage transformer. Storm watched as the portal opened and Father jump back in surprise. Father produced his massive hammer out of nowhere and stood there waiting for something. Storm was worried he wouldn't go through and after using most of the city's mana reserves, he wouldn't be able to cast the spell again. But just as he was about to give up, Father took off his forging gear and gave some instructions to his staff. He grabbed a bag then walked through the portal.

Storm returned to the cave underneath the cabin but before he climbed out, he wanted to scry Last Hope to see if Dark Elite had arrived. He pulled out his orb and quickly moved his view to the small town, having become more comfortable with the disorientating feeling. He wasn't surprised to see dozens of people working by magical light on the outskirts of town, with a familiar wagon parked nearby.

He found his mom, above in the cabin with Lance and Father. They were discussing different strategies to defend the portal. After updating them on the developments in town, Father took him aside and thanked him.

"When I ended up here, I knew you had somehow sent the portal and I wanted to thank you." he said, "It's good to be back amongst the living."

"Risky move going through random portals" Storm mockingly chided him.

"It was worth it." Father said with a grin, glancing at Nightshade. "Oh, I got something for you." Father added excitedly. He retrieved the bag that Storm saw him grab and pulled out two one-handed hammers and handed them to Storm. "I saw the weapons you used on our dungeon dive and wanted to give you an upgrade. They were already made I just had a friend of mine enchant them for you." He winked and added, "I added something a little extra too."

Storm started at them in awe, they were absolutely gorgeous, but he was completely speechless after he identified them.

[Unique Item
       Name: Lightning
       Description: one-handed hammer
       Quality: Perfect
       Damage: 200+200%
       On strike: Chain lightning, AOE stun, +100 damage
       Charges: 999/10
       Durability: 999/300
       Crafted by: Father]

[Unique Item
       Name: Thunder
       Description: one-handed hammer
       Quality: Perfect
       Damage: 200+200%
       On strike: Concussive blast, AOE stun, +100 damage
       Charges: 999/10
       Durability: 999/300
       Crafted by: Father]

"These… these are beautiful." Storm stammered, staring at the weapons, "I… I don't know how to thank you."

"They are simple weapons." Father said laughing, "I thought they were fitting." He handed Storm a leather belt with loops in it.

Dazed at the incredible gift, Storm put the belt on and slipped a hammer into a loop on each side. They felt perfect. The hammers were slightly heavier than his last pair but they felt much sturdier. He couldn't wait to try them out.

"I had something I wanted you to look at," Storm said, "well several things actually." Storm held out the World staff and asked him. "Can you put more charges on this? And can you get rid of the dimensional bag restriction?"

"Sure!" Father said happily, "Let me see it." Then he took the staff and his eyes widened in surprise. Reverently he muttered, "Oh, this staff." His eyes scanned up and down the object looking for something and several times he touched the air above different sections and twisted here and there. Finally, he finished and explained, "I was able to add one charge to it, but I couldn't over charge it. It's designed a little different than other items. And, you should be able to store it in your backpack now."

"Thanks!" Storm said excitedly. "It's been a real pain to carry it around." He was a little disappointed Father could only add one charge, but it was better than nothing. Being able to store it in a dimensional pocket was what really helped him out.

Father held out the staff to return it to him but Storm shook his head.

"I had another question." Storm said, "If you died with it in your possession, you'd respawn with it correct?" he then pulled out his two new hammers, each glowing an ominous color, one blue and the other yellow.

"Yeah… but…" Father said hesitantly, trying to understand where he was going with this.

"When you get there, open a portal to Avalon." Storm explained, stepping closer.

"Whoa, slow down Storm." Father said desperately, raising his hands and backing up.

"Storm!" his mother chided, stepping in-between the two.

"We need more troops." Storm explained, "If we can open a pathway to Valhalla, we can bring the rest of your guild here. We also might be able to convince the other Fallen to help too"

Father chuckled and then laughed hard. He didn't stop laughing for a few moments. Tears streamed down his eyes as he tried catching breath. He wheezed, "I can change the target of the spell. Valhalla, right?" He then made a few more adjustments and handed it back to Storm.

A large explosion rocked the cabin and they heard a few more in the distance. Sunshine stepped inside and through the open-door Storm could see the early morning sun just touching the sky.

"A raiding party did a suicide run for information on our position." Sunshine reported. "We think they are trying to get inside the cabin."

"Why?" Storm asked confused, "We could have put the portal anywhere, it could be in one of the tents."

"Look at your map" Nightshade instructed him ominously.

Storm pulled up his map and saw a bright golden portal symbol directly over there cabin.

"Oh." he responded with a sinking feeling. Incredibly thankful they had at least buried it.

"We only need to beat the timer, then we win." Nightshade reminded all of them.

At her words everybody fell silent and Storm noticed more than a few shifting their eyes upwards, where the countdown was on display in their UI.

[44 hours remaining] (6am)

TWENTY-FOUR

Valhalla

Storm activated the spell in the World staff and once again, a bright golden portal appeared before him exactly the same as the first. Trumpets echoed in his ears heralding the creation of another portal by the staff. With grim determination Storm stepped through the portal with Father, Nightshade and Sunshine.

Storm found himself in the center of a large familiar city. He was sure this time, it was exactly like Avalon, except Valhalla was populated. The first time he was there, he was new to the game and hadn't noticed but this time he saw elves and dwarfs intermixed with the humans, all working together.

"Everything we talked about is in there." Storm said handing his backpack to Father, "Before you begin though, can you introduce us?"

"Yeah of course," Father responded, he looked at the sun peaking over the horizon, "They are probably just getting morning coffee."

"Good luck" he told his sister, handing her the World staff. With the dimensional restriction lifted, he had taken to storing the staff in his ring to keep it close. The orb was too useful for him to keep, so he left it behind with Lance to monitor Dark Elite's progress.

"Good luck to you too." she said, then jogged off towards the castle.

Storm and Nightshade followed Father to a little shop near the town center. Sitting around a table near the back was a dwarf, a human, and three elves, one if which was a member of Fallen Uprising. Father walked up to the table and introduced Storm and Nightshade. They were already well aware of who Nightshade was but was very interested in meeting Storm.

Father took his leave while Storm explained to the council what was occurring on the surface. He explained that Weird was going to destroy the world and they were trying to stop it but they were vastly outnumbered and needed help. They listened and agreed to call a town meeting and let whoever wanted to fight, join their forces. Before they left, the elven lady that was a member of Fallen Uprising pulled his mom aside to have a private conversation.

Curious, Storm asked about it but his mom just said that it was guild business and nothing to worry about. He was interested because he hadn't seen any other races in Fallen Uprising so far. Although, he knew that multi-race guilds were possible because of Mani and Clover. From what he could tell, the other races mostly stuck to their own realms and would PvP each other in the wild lands.

While they were talking to the Council of the Fallen, Storm felt a distinct shift in the city's movement. Knowing that Sunshine completed her task, him and his mom went to find her.

"Hey," Sunshine called out as the two approached the city center. She was sitting on a bench in a cute little park.

"How did it go?" Storm asked.

"Great," Sunshine said, "but it's going to take about fifteen hours to get there."

"I hope it'll be fast enough." Storm said looking at his mom.

"We'll make it." she reassured him "Let's get back to the surface to see how the guild is doing."

"Will you stay to make sure everything goes smoothly?" Storm asked his sister.

"Yeah, of course." she replied, "I can help organize everything on this side. I'll talk them into posting guards to defend the portal."

Satisfied everything was set in motion, Storm and Nightshade entered the portal and reappeared in the cabin. Lance was sitting at the table looking through a pile of papers as they entered.

"Oh, you scared me." Lance said in surprise.

"Jumpy?" Nightshade asked Lance

He laughed nervously and explained, "It's Dark Elite. They've been sending assassins over to pick off random players. They don't care if it's a suicide run or not, the bloodier the better. Everybody has been on edge. One got inside the cabin earlier, but I took care of her." He looked at them and warned, "They are getting better."

"Have they established a foothold yet?" Nightshade asked.

"No", he said, shaking his head, "but they are amassing on the other side of the river. Our mages have been casting rain upriver like you said and it's been flooding like crazy. It's been slowing them down quite a bit."

"How are the numbers?" she asked.

"We are doing ok." he informed her, "A few more guild members have shown up and we are over sixty now. Dark Elite has around a hundred at the river and over two hundred in Last Hope."

Storm picked up the orb and scried the river and the surrounding area. Weird cut down all of the trees and was preparing a place along the river for a crossing. He followed a new road back to Last Hope and discovered a mobile bridge they were building out of view. With the numerous amounts of trees they had, they were not short on materials. The encampment next to the city had grown greatly and was receiving a steady stream of supplies from out of town. They had also setup numerous patrols all around their territory. Everything told him Weird knew what he was doing and his guild was organized and disciplined. He was worried.

[42 hours remaining] (8am)

"We should all get some naps now while we can." Nightshade suggested after Storm updated them, "They won't attack in earnest until that bridge is done."

They left Father in charge and all logged off to get some sleep. Storm hadn't slept since before he went on the dragon raid and so much had happened since. He fell asleep as soon as his head hit the pillow. His dreams were troubled and they involved conquering worlds and being chased by demon cats.

Several hours later Luke was woken up by his mom.

"Luke?" she asked.

"Yeah" he groaned, "What's up?"

"How are you feeling?" she asked, "I should have let you sleep longer, but you're being requested."

"What?" he asked groggily, "Oh yeah, sure. Let me splash some water on my face and I'll be there."

"Ok," she said, "but if you need more sleep, I can tell them to shove it."

"No," he said, "It's ok, I'll be there. Who's asking for me?"

"Weird." she told him, "He has the bridge setup and approached under a white flag."

"Oh, this is going to be fun." he groaned.

"Sapphire is there." she said encouragingly.

"Oh, please mom," he said, rolling his eyes, "she's the enemy now." Storm tried to act nonchalant about it, but it took him a little longer to get ready and it was obvious he put more effort into his appearance.

As soon as he got into game, he checked the timer.

[39 hours remaining] (11am)

Storm, Nightshade and Father walked down the hill to the river, through the various defenses that had been built by Fallen Uprising. They walked through trenches and chokepoints. And around palisades and traps, then over temporary bridges. All created for defense, intended to slow down the enemy and prevent stealth infiltration.

There were only two people standing on the bridge, and Storm didn't see anybody nearby after scrying the area. The bridge was made from the trees they cut down. It was efficiently made and expertly crafted. To his dissatisfaction it looked incredibly sturdy. The bridge was twelve feet wide and sat high enough for the raging river to easily passed below. He had hoped the bridge would be easy to destroy but it was obvious Weird meant business.

"Weird." Storm greeted coldly, as he walked up. Weird was outfitted in his imposing demon armor, holding his helm off to the side. Sapphire wore a simple purple outfit, which only enhanced her other-worldly beauty.

"Storm.", Weird returned in greeting.

"What did you want?" Storm asked cutting to the point.

"Avalon." Weird said simply. Then sized up Storm's companions and touched a hand to his neck and asked the two, "Have we met?"

"Not officially," Storm said, clearing his throat in embarrassment. He had seen what Nightshade and Father had done to him during their daring rescue. He introduced them, "That is Nightshade, my mother and this is Father, my dad's avatar."

"Nice to officially meet you." Weird said, looking to each of them. "Your son is a remarkable player." Then he waved to Sapphire and introduced her, "This is my daughter, Sapphire." He straightened and stated officially, "Now, to business. Storm, I could have held off for a few weeks, but you forced by hand. I need to be in Avalon before that timer runs out."

"I can't possibly step aside knowing what you intend to do." Storm replied angrily.

"I know." Weird said sadly. With a glanced to Sapphire, he warned, "I won't be holding back Storm."

Storm looked at him in the eye and nodded. They both understood, neither would back down and neither would hold back. This was all or nothing.

Weird turned and walked to his side of the bridge, waiting for Sapphire to join him.

"How could you still be on his side?" Storm asked Sapphire, "Knowing what all of us will lose."

"If you can't beat us, you won't ever hold Avalon." she explained, not unkindly, "The other servers won't hold back, they will destroy you."

Storm stared at her, speechless, not knowing how to respond.

"Good luck DumpsterBoy." she said finally, then turned and walked to her father.

Storm watched the two walk off the bridge and towards town. Weird lazily lifted his arm above his head and point up. A bright fire bolt shot high into the sky and exploded like a firework.

"Storm, we better go." Nightshade warned, concern in her voice.

Before stepping off the bridge, Storm emptied a magical pet rock into the river.

"What was that?" Nightshade asked on their way back to the cabin.

"A surprise." Storm replied with a smirk.

"You gave it the instructions like I said?" Father asked nervously.

"Yes, Yes," Storm answered calmly, "Don't worry, your 'improvements' are perfect."

The guild formed a raid and organized themselves into different combat teams. The standard group was two melee, one range and one combat mage. There were far too few healers to go around so they formed a special team themselves to support the entire raid.

The groups were spread throughout the clearing, hiding behind hastily built defenses. Many of the Fallen soldiers that arrived were assigned to the front line. All of the Fallen were spectral avatars and were hardier than standard avatars. All of their stats were increased and their health and defenses were highly boosted as well.

Storm sat in the cabin and scried the enemy. He studied Weird's army as it marched down to the road. They had over three hundred players, all outfitted for war. The heavy tanks led the column. They were armored in full plate mail with large tower shields. Behind them were the ranged units, a mixture of archers and combat mages. Then, at the very end were the mages that specialized in healing and buffs.

When they were close, the tanks rushed the bridge and crossed over without slowing. They formed a defensive position, giving them a safe place to cross to. As soon as they were within range, Fallen Uprising attacked, but their arrows and spells had little effect against the fully buffed troops. The enemy slowly pushed forward, the heavily armored tanks moving up the hill with support from the combat mages on the bridge. They cast fire balls and ice spears at the bulwarks and trenches, collapsing some and catching fire to more than a few. The intruders took damage but were continuously healed from across the river and out of range of retaliation.

[New spell obtained: Ice spear (Water magic and Air magic)]

Storm cast rain spells to quell the fires and was looking for an opportunity to affect the battle when he spotted a green glow emanating from the river next to the bridge. He watched as rocks along the river bottom rolled towards the bridge for several minutes. They came together in a large clump and finally, a massive shape lifted out of the river.

The stone golem rose forty feet into the air raining water down onto the mages standing on the bridge. Father reprogramed the golem's heart and upgraded it, causing it to have a greater pull on the rock material around it. Storm could see the new multi-colored river rock intermixed with the original materials, making the golem larger and bulkier than before.

The mages on the bridge craned their necks up to stare at the behemoth. They began casting defensive spells when Storm saw his chance and created a new spell just for them. He quickly worked through the spell form, not bothering to silent cast in an effort to preserve mana.

[New spell obtained, Blind, AOE (Death magic)]

He felt mana sick from using so much mana at once but he needed to push through and cast it a couple more times. His first spell encompassed most of the combat mages on the bridge, unfortunately the healers were more spread out.

Storm cast AOE blind two more times, disabling the remaining mages. Sadly, he was now out of mana and the heavy infantry would need to be dealt with by the defenders on the hill. With his mana almost gone, he felt sick and needed to take a break from casting to regain his mana. He had done enough.

The stone golem faced no resistance from the blind mages. It smashed into the bridge and sent many of the mages tumbling into the river. The few that remained stumbled around until the golem smashed them with its fists or picked them up and hurled them hundreds of yards away.

The golem stomped to the enemy's river bank and viciously smashed the mages there, like a game of Wack-a-mole. Not being able to see, the mages lived out their worst nightmares. Some were smashed mercilessly and others flew through the air, unable to see the ground as they fell back to it.

The river bank had become so bloody and full of gore, the golem slipped and fell to the ground. It slowly recovered and waded back into the river. It angrily smashed the rest of the bridge, completely destroying it. Then, it moved to Storm's side of the river and introduced its horror there.

Half of Weird's army made it across the river but when they lost their magical support they took heavy losses. Nightshade's guild slowly chipped away at the attackers, letting the golem and river do most of the work.

With the bridge destroyed and their support gone, the rampaging golem forced the attackers to change tactics. Their hold on the opposition's river side was in peril so they rushed forward to kill as many defenders as they could. They were now on a suicide mission.

Dark Elite's warriors were better equipped, better trained and higher level, and they killed many of the defenders. They would have over run them completely had they not encountered the Fallen. The Fallen were ferocious and fought with abandon, they had no fear. They were astral and physical damage affected them much less than the others. The golem came from behind and decimated their forces. None of the attackers made back over the river alive.

The battle was over and the defenders looted the dead, tossing their bodies into the river to float away. They rebuilt and improved their defenses and swapped out the front line with fresh troops. That day the river was stained red for miles. Body parts and bodies were washed away to the horror of everybody that lived downriver.

TWENTY-FIVE

Attack

Storm sat in the cavern below the cabin, his back resting against the dirt wall. He relocated there, to gain a little peace and quiet while he scried Dark Elite's preparations for their next attack. The building above had become too busy with Fallen and players traversing between the battlefield and Valhalla. The portal was located in the center of the room and was the only means of transportation between the two. Adding to the commotion, the guild relocated their camp to the relative safety of the mystical city.

Storm stared into the orb, watching Weird's army. They were rebuilding the bridge and making fast work of it. He considered remote casting to sabotage their efforts but his ability to gather intel was too important to risk. If anything, Storm learned that there was a counter to everything in this game. He didn't want them deploying anti-scrying measures.

Storm watched them for an hour and gathered as much information as he could before making his way back to the cabin. The enemy had set up heavy patrols with advanced stealth totems at critical positions, warding off any attempt to slow their progress. The bridge was almost done and they were close to moving it. All of this was disheartening, but the worst part was when he discovered they had gained another few hundred players, nearly doubling their ranks.

Nightshade coordinated their defenses from the cabin turning it into their command center. As the Fallen arrived, they were put to work immediately. They rotated out with the players so the players could log off and rest before the next attack. Storm kept an eye on the enemy and updated everybody on their progress.

"It's time." Storm said, finally "They're coming."

[33 hours remaining] (5pm)

They put out the call for their guild to return to the game and in no time a steady stream of players traveled from Valhalla to the cabin and out the door onto the battlefield. There seemed to be no end to them, so much so, the cabin door didn't close for a good ten minutes as player after player arrived.

Storm returned to his small cave and setup a mana totem in preparation for the upcoming assault. There were only a few people that knew about the small room and they planned on keeping it a secret as long as they could. When looking at the map, the portal icon was visible overtop of the cabin making it obvious that the portal was inside but not exactly where.

He created the portal to Avalon in a pit below the cabin in an effort to obfuscate its location from Weird and incredibly he was able to create a second portal directly above it further enhancing the security. The second portal connected to Valhalla, a city that was filled with the Fallen. He hoped that if any enemy troops made it inside the cabin, they would mistake the portals with each other. Even better would be if they went through, to Valhalla. Guarding the other side was a fearsome contingent of Fallen.

Storm watched eight players separate themselves from Weird's army and approach the river, he recognized them all. The stone golem rose and waded menacingly through the river towards them. Kat and Klar stepped forward and stood on the shore, waiting for it. The golem raised its arm and swung down to smash them but Kat raised her glowing shield and easily deflected it.

As the golem's fist struck the shield, a shockwave of dust spread out in all directions. The golem raised its arm to strike again and Storm was about to cast his blind spell but stopped when a flash of light shot from Klar. It struck the golem in the chest, creating a large hole where its heart used to be. The golem lost cohesion and collapsed into the river creating a temporary dam, causing the water to flow up the banks. Storm felt a small pain at the loss.

Dark Elite deployed their bridge without any issues. They setup defensive structures on their side and stationed troops around them. The rest of their army waited a hundred yards back from the river.

Storm watched as Sapphire approached the bridge and began casting an unfamiliar spell. He followed along without even realizing it. Copying spells had become second nature. When she finished her spell, an ethereal shell encompassed the bridge.

[New spell obtained, Structural support, buildings (Earth magic)]

Sapphire turned and walked calmly away from the bridge. As she did, Dark Elite's army dashed forward. When they reached her, they split and passed her by without a single hair being ruffled. Storm watched her diminutive form in the sea of army brutes, each and every one giving her a wide berth. The respect they showed her was not unwarranted, she could roast any, or all, of them alive.

The heavy infantry rushed across the bridge under the magical protection of their mages. They pushed the defenders back and once again established a bridgehead. They extended their safe-haven by setting up mobile palisades. The defenders cast fireballs at the bridge and other wooden structures but the Dark Elite mages protected them with potent shields and the wood wouldn't even char.

A strike force of a dozen heavily armored Dark Elite warriors darted out from the protection of their walls and charged up the hill. Spells and arrows flew at them but their mages diverted the attacks. Fully buffed and receiving constant healing the small group of attackers tore through any opposition they encountered.

They made their way up the hill moving to each defensive position in turn and easily cleared out the defenders stationed there. Storm tried to support the defenders by casting his new favorite spell, AOE Blind, but nothing happened. He checked his logs and found that every single one of the attackers resisted his spell. He grumbled in frustration and continued to watch their progress. They jumped into a trench and for the first time faced resistance. They had over extended themselves and were out-of-range of magical support.

The trench was filled with a mixture of players and Fallen, who had become comfortable battling alongside each other. They halted the invaders' advance and slowly pushed them back. It was a hard fight but the defenders had everything to lose and couldn't afford to give up.

Players on both sides watched the skirmish with rapt attention. Dark Elite players cheered as the strike team progressed up the hill, but fell silent as soon as they faced resistance. When the strike team was defeated, the defenders roared and beat their weapons against their shields, taunting the opposition. They retook their territory but Storm saw it for what it was, a test.

Dark Elite tried again, this time a group of mages followed behind at a safe distance. The enemy systematically retook the ground they lost and more. Storm's side retreated before the onslaught, surrendering position after position.

Many of the defenders died, fortunately death wasn't permanent. It did however, take them out of the fight for a short time. All of the defenders, even Nightshade's guild, were bound to Valhalla. When they died, they respawned there. They were closer to the battlefield than Dark Elite, whose closest bind location was Last Hope, but they all had resurrection sickness, which halved their stats for ten minutes. Sadly, Weird's army had plenty of mages that could cast Resurrection and reviving their dead with, incurring no sickness.

With the success of their latest foray up the hill, Dark Elite's troops readied themselves to cross the river. With the sun setting, they didn't have much time if they wanted to take the portal before dark. Unless, of course, they were prepared for a nighttime encounter. Storm didn't discount this as a possibility because Weird's resources seemed limitless.

[31 hours remaining] (7pm)

"They're coming!" Storm yelled up to his mom.

Storm felt powerless as he watched the enemy army rush over the bridge and up the hill towards the cabin. Their mages fired spells at the defenders relentlessly, keeping them from forming any sort of response. The cabin shook precariously whenever a spell exploded too close. One fireball struck the roof and caught it on fire, fortunately Storm was watching and cast his rain spell to quench the blaze. He then cast his new structural protection spell to keep the cabin from falling apart. He did so just in time because the next spell hit the cabin directly and would have turned it into splinters.

The defenders frantically fired arrows and spells down onto the enemy in an attempt to hold them back or slow them down but it did little good. The enemy had too many resources and was too well equipped. Storm cast spells while he scried but stuck to ones that weren't obvious, like rain, dig, fear and blind. He could affect the battlefield in a large way but wanted to continue working from the shadows until truly needed.

Storm heard an exclamation from above and footsteps ran towards the center of the room and disappeared into the portal. A few moments later a constant stream of feet pounded on the floor as their reserve troops arrived from Valhalla and streamed onto the battlefield.

In the fading light, Dark Elite made a final push for the portal before nightfall. Everybody had assembled to protect it. Storm watched the defenders sprint down the hill and crash into the invaders. The Fallen fought with a ferocity that their human allies couldn't imitate and took the enemy by surprise, halting their advance.

In the end it came down to numbers. Even though everybody on the battlefield feared the Fallen, it wasn't enough.

In the fading light, Storm watched the confrontation and witnessed the aftermath. It wasn't comforting. The enemy lost less than half of their troops, while Storm's side had expended all of theirs. They threw everything at them and they failed. Storm hadn't even made a difference with his spells. The enemy prevailed, the bridgehead remained.

Storm hoped for a reprieve but Weird had other plans. His troops gathered for another assault. This time, they drove a wagon onto the bridge, carrying a large box with a tube poking out. Several mages followed behind, casting spells on it. When it was in-place, one of the mages crawled up into the wagon and positioned the object so the tube was pointed towards the defenders.

Storm yelled a warning up to his mom, but he needn't have bothered, they announced them, themselves. The mage on the wagon pressed a button and a bright flash of light erupted from the object. A beam of energy shot towards the defenders and struck the ground deafening everybody nearby.

Dirt was sent flying and when the dust settled, a car sized hole was carved out of the hillside. The mage standing behind the machine made a few adjustments and fired again, this time striking a wooden palisade and blasting it into kindling. The defenders behind it did not survive.

Storm desperately cast spells on the device but they had protected it well and nothing would damage it. Failing that, he attacked the mage directly. He tried Fireball, Blind and even Death Miasma but nothing would land on him either. The mage had fired more shots while Storm was wasting his mana and another wall lay in ruin.

Storm shifted tactics and cast Structural support on every defensive position he could but the device operator had higher aspirations and the next beam of light slammed directly into the cabin.

Dirt fell onto Storm as the cabin shook dangerously. Everybody above was deafened by the strike. Storm quickly reinforced the structure just as another beam struck it. Now dialed in, the mage fired the cannon at the building again and again, each time taking a short break to recharge the device. Storm cast his structure spell each time but his mana was quickly trending down. He looked forlornly at his diminishing pile of mana potions and knew it wasn't going to be enough.

Movement on the bridge caught his eye and he groaned as the assault was fully underway. Dark Elite troops rushed across the bridge and up the hill, bypassing many fortifications. He yelled up to his mom in-between blasts, but he wasn't sure she heard him.

Dark clouds moved in and began pouring rain onto the battlefield in earnest. They had been using a lot of rain spells, but this was the real deal. The rain wasn't expected but was definitely welcomed by the defenders. Flashes of magic lit up the hill and Storm watched their doom approach. The enemy was halfway to the cabin. The rain had slowed their progress but it wasn't enough.

Once again, Storm heard heavy footsteps as another round reinforcements came through the portal. Their defenses were in shambles and many of the defenders had resurrection sickness. They were fighting a losing battle and many of them knew it, but they wouldn't give up.

Boom! The cabin shook again. Storm recast his spell protecting the building and doubled over noxious. He checked his UI and his mana was almost gone. He shakily reached over and picked up his last mana potion. With a sigh of regret, he downed it.

Boom! Dirt poured onto him and he cast the spell again. It was the only thing protecting the building. He pulled up his spell list and desperately searched for a solution but couldn't come up with anything.

Boom! He cast again and his head swirled. Once the dizziness subsided, he peered into the orb and waited for their final moments to come. The storm increased in ferocity and stalled the invaders. The heavy rain on the hill had formed a waterfall that flowed into the river, taking friend and foe alike. Troops from both sides lost their footing, and slid down the hill and into the river. All of them respawned minutes later.

Boom! The cabin shook yet again, signaling their final attempt to protect it, Storm was officially out of mana. He stared at the cannon powering up and yelled frantically for his mom to evacuate. He dove through the portal next to him and waited a minute before returning. The serenity of Avalon was in stark contrast to the battlefield and called to him. He found it more than a little difficult to step back through the portal.

When he did, the rain instantly soaked his clothes and he looked up to see most of the cabin missing. With the floor gone, the Portal to Valhalla hovered in the air directly above the portal to Avalon. They were identical, like two brilliant suns.

Storm stood in a pit which had previously been his cave and scried the battlefield. They lost everybody except for a group of Fallen who were huddled behind a wall, their last standing defensive structure. They were taking shots at the enemy players, keeping them from advancing up the treacherous hillside.

The magical canon fired and created a crater next to the group as its aim was slowly adjusted. Storm wanted to yell at them to run but he didn't need to, they knew what was about to happen. Just before the cannon obliterated their last line of defense, the small group ran towards the hovering portal and jumped inside.

He stood there in the pit, slowly filling with water, defeated. They lost. They had no more troops, no more defensive positions. They failed to stop Weird. Dark Elite soldiers slowly made their way up the hill, securing the battlefield as they went.

The storm above them reached hurricane levels and halted their progress. Just as Storm got a little hope, the rain stopped. The eye of the storm was directly above them and he knew it was over. He was about to jump through the portal to Avalon when a sudden blast of pressure knocked him to the ground.

Storm lay in the mud, struggling to breath. His whole boy hurt and when he looked at his UI, he was missing more than half of his health. The sky had disappeared and was replaced with wooden planks brightly illuminated by the glowing golden portal next to him.

Storm looked at the time and smiled. Valhalla had arrived.

[29 hours remaining] (9pm)

TWENTY-SIX

Two portals

Weird watched as the city landed, ending his assault. The rain falling prior to its arrival wasn't simply the weather, it was a defensive mechanism of the legendary city. Now that it was on the ground, the water poured out of its walls and down the hill, clearing the hillside of all players. Several were able to retreat to the bridge but most fell into the river and washed away.

"Let's go draw up plans," Weird said sighing. He turned to his friends and added, "There was always the risk the city was close enough to land."

"You want us to crack that wall?" Tomb asked, the others smiled, nodding in support.

"Not yet,", Weird said, he waved an arm at the city in the distance, "Let's regroup the forces and implement the Avalon protocol."

"Sounds good," Tomb said, "I'll get the command tent setup." Then he beat a tune on his drum and sped away towards Last Hope.

Weird turned to give more orders and Sapphire cast an anti-scrying bubble over them. Weird nodded to her in thanks.

"Send in one of your teams and scout the throne room." Weird commanded Strychnine.

"I could do it myself, with less risk." Strychnine responded in his soft voice.

"You could, but what good are subordinates if you don't use them." Weird retorted, then added slyly "Of course there is nothing stopping you from observing your students."

"I'll get them sent out as soon as possible." Strychnine capitulated, smiling widely.

Weird turned to Kat and Klar and instructed, "Start building the war machines. Everybody not standing watch should be building. A couple hours on, a couple off. The players that are off, should log out and rest, tomorrow is going to be a long day and we attack at first light."

Kat and Klar both nodded and jogged towards Last Hope leaving Weird and Sapphire alone, walking to the city.

"I think you should sit this one out." Weird said in a soft voice, after the others were out of ear shot.

"Why on earth would I do that?" Sapphire scoffed.

"How do you think that young man would feel if he saw you tearing through his troops in a bloody massacre?" Weird asked.

"What do I care?" Sapphire snapped back, "This is just a game."

"Angel, to him, it's not." Weird calmly explained, "This is a connection to his father, possibly his last."

"Then why do *you* persist?" Sapphire asked in a sharp tone.

"You know why." Weird answered solemnly, "I need the world items to defeat MatchBurner."

"How many do you have?" she asked, hesitantly. She knew her father was on a quest to unite with her sister's avatar, but he was usually tight-lipped on the topic. She wasn't sure if he would share.

"Eight." he answered surprisingly, "We had nine, but lost one with Blynk."

"How many more do you need?" she asked, hoping this server was the last one.

"I don't know, several." he answered, shaking his head.

"Dad, there has to be another way." Sapphire argued, not for the first time. "We don't have to do it this way."

"We will see, daughter." Weird said lovingly, chuckling, "Tomorrow morning I'll go talk with a friend at the company to see if she can do anything about Storm's father. But that means I need you to provide the terms before the battle. It might be good for you two to see each other once more before the hostilities begin."

"Doesn't that go against me staying out of it?" she asked.

"I mostly meant as an active participant in the slaughter of his friends and family." Weird chuckled.

"You really want me to stay out of the fighting?" she asked seriously.

"Angel, you can do what you want." he conceded, "It's just my opinion, either way I'll be proud of you. You don't have to decide now."

Conflicted, Sapphire walked off towards her tent, to log out.

Weird continued walking to where his command tent was being constructed and only had a short wait after he arrived. He stepped inside to find Tomb waiting for him. The two old friends chatted until the others arrived.

Klar and Kat arrived a short time later. They had organized the guild into several teams, a few harvested wood and other materials while other teams built the war machines.

The four friends chatted about various strategies late into the night, when suddenly the wind whipped the tent flap open. They all quieted and waited. After a few minutes Strychnine unstealthed, revealing himself.

"You're no fun." he muttered in his quiet voice, causing everybody to chuckle. He sat down in a plush chair and kicked his feet up, then made an announcement that shocked everybody. "There are two portals."

"What?" they all asked in unison.

"We infiltrated the throne room but something felt off about it." Strychnine explained. "We scouted the entire castle but didn't find anything to explain it. So, we followed the portal's map marker to a warehouse in the court yard, where we not only found one legendary portal, we found two." he shook his head in bewilderment, "One is in the warehouse and the other is directly under it."

"Did you go through both portals?" Kat asked.

"No." Strychnine said with disappointment, "The warehouse is their command center and my team got busted."

"You?" Klar asked incredulously.

"My *team* got busted." he scoffed, "I didn't." he continued in his silky voice, "After the commotion, I scouted the cabin myself. The floor directly beneath the portal was damage and I could see through it, into a secret room. I went through the top portal which led to the town square of the city you see before us."

"Clever" Weird said, then staring at Strychnine he slowly asked a question he already knew the answer to, "If that isn't Avalon, then what city is it?"

Strychnine dropped the second bomb that evening, "It's Valhalla." he said almost reverently.

"The city of the Fallen." Weird whispered.

"There's no way." Tomb said in disbelief.

"It might be possible." Weird said.

"How?" Tomb demanded.

"We've long theorized that Valhalla is a copy of Avalon." he explained, "The devs needed someplace inaccessible to stash the Fallen. So, they got lazy and copied the code."

"How would he even access it?" Tomb asked, "You said it yourself. Valhalla is inaccessible."

"I could ask him." Strychnine said, pulling out one of his blades.

"We can ask him tomorrow," Weird said chuckling. "This changes nothing, we've taken Avalon before. We can easily take Valhalla. Same city, same defenses."

With the new information the five friends sat around discussing their options and came up with a plan for the following day. Then, the team set up a shift for each of them to be available throughout the night and logged out to get some rest.

Early the next morning, the man whose avatar is known to many as Weird, sat at a nondescript table outside a coffee shop in downtown New Las Vegas. A woman walked up to greet him but before she could say his name he stopped her.

"No names," he said, "that name garners too much attention around here."

"As if nobody recognizes you." she scoffed. She sat down across from him and asked, "Are you afraid to be seen with the enemy?"

"No, no nothing like that." he said, then changed the subject "It's been a while, it's good to see you."

"It's good to see you too." she replied with a sweet smile. "How is… How is your daughter?" she asked hesitantly, remembering his request for no names.

"She met a boy she might like." he responded, rolling his eyes, "She won't stop talking about him. She's actually visiting. She's on break from the university."

"Oh really? Tell her I said hi." his friend said excitedly, then asked, "You think she would want to get coffee? I could show her around."

"Yeah, she would love that." he said.

The woman leaned close and touched his arm then whispered, "I shouldn't say anything but you're being watched."

"I am? Who is it?" he asked alarmingly, looking around.

"Not here." she laughed, "in game, it's the company."

"I see, thank you for letting me know." he said appreciatively.

"I only said something about it because I know you, and you aren't half as bad as they say." she said.

"Thanks," he said chucking, "I've been a good boy. Just laying low."

"So," she started nervously, "You asked me out here. Are you finally calling that rain check?"

"Oh," he stammered, his face turned red, "No, um. I… I actually wanted to ask you for a favor." He quickly he added, "The raincheck is still good though, I'm going to call it." He looked down, "I just need to finish this thing I'm on first."

"I understand, it's ok." she said smiling, then looked him in the eyes and continued, "I know what you are doing and I understand, take the time you need. What's the favor?"

"It's about the Fallen." he said after taking a deep breath.

"We've talked about this," she said, stopped him, "I can't help you. If I move her, MB will find out and people will get in trouble."

"It's not about that." he assured her, "Can you assign a server to a Fallen that doesn't currently have one?"

"Yeah," she answered slowly trying to understand where he was going with this, "that shouldn't be a problem, with the proper authentication. What are you planning?"

"It's for a boy on my server." he explained, "His dad's avatar is a Fallen there and I wanted to see if you could reassign it if the server is…" he paused to look for the right word, "destroyed."

"Seriously, you know nothing about laying low." she said, rolling her eyes, "Since we last talked, the CEO sent a companywide email detailing your exploits and threatened to shut down your account."

"Really? What happened?" he asked surprised.

"He found out who you are and backed off, but he still wanted you watched." she said warningly.

"I guess my notoriety knows no bounds." he said chuckling, "You burn down one city." He stood up and added, "Speaking of, I have a castle to lay siege to and a young man's dreams to crush."

The two hugged and parted ways, promising to catch up soon

After logging back in, Weird found Sapphire to let her know of a future date with an old friend.

"You know she likes you dad." she said, "It's ok to date if you want."

"How's the war going?" he asked gruffly, ignoring her.

TWENTY-SEVEN

Infiltration

Luke tumbled out of bed, glaring at his alarm clock. It was making the most annoying noise he had ever heard. Groggily he shut it off and pulled on a clean podiform. His sister had started calling them that after joking one night about them being like uniforms they had to wear every day and it caught on. He stumbled out of his room and found his mom and sister running down the hallway. They all hurried to their pods and logged in.

Storm opened his eyes and squinted at the brightness of the portal before him. When he logged out, he left his avatar in the small dirt room with the bright golden portal that lead to Avalon. He also setup an alarm to notify him if any alerts were sent out by the guards.

He glanced at the countdown timer.

[22 hours remaining] (4am)

"Storm, what's the status?" Nightshade asked insistently, calling down to him.

He shook off his sleepiness and picked up his orb of scrying and scanned the area. He searched Valhalla, then the hillside and then the bridge but found nothing out of the ordinary. Dark Elite was still firing their magical cannon at random intervals, but the city's barrier deflected it harmlessly each time. However, if the barrier ever came down, that beam would tear through the city, destroying buildings.

A runner arrived with a message from one of the guards. Storm scried the room above him, a habit he had formed whenever a new message arrived. It kept him informed but also less lonely. They reported a guard found several sets of climbing gear near the outer wall. The city had been infiltrated.

As Storm watched the guard give his report, a strange movement off to the side caught his attention. He looked closer at the area and three shadowy figures materialized. They were moving around the room, trying to get close to the portal.

Storm almost yelled up to his mom, but realized it would warn the intruders and expose his location. He didn't understand why he could see them when nobody else could. He looked around for an answer and discovered the stealthers were only visible through the right lens of his newly improved glasses.

In-between the battles yesterday, Storm had a conversation with Father about upgrading his items. He wanted to make a pair of lenses out of the Mirror of Seeing and fit them into his Glasses of Perception, which had no lenses. They tested the mirror by peeling off the silver backing and discovered that the detection magic still worked.

Father worked on the upgrades during the battle and returned the glasses after Valhalla landed. Unfortunately, there wasn't enough material to make two lenses and only the right one could detect stealth. He balanced the glasses with a mundane piece of glass on the other side.

[Item

> Name: Eagle eye specs
> Effect: +200% to perception
> Description: Helps find objects hidden in plain sight
> Right lens: Uncovers hidden or stealthed objects
> Left lens: Normal]

Storm, scried the room and watched the assassins from his pit. They moved silently through the warehouse and snuck up to the portal and inspected it. They continued searching the room and Storm had a sinking feeling they were looking for him, or rather his room, the portal to Avalon.

Through his orb, he tried to silently cast AOE blind on them, but their confident movements told him that it failed again. He was frustrated that everybody kept resisting his blind spell but he set the issue aside to figure out later.

"Storm." his mom called out.

Not wanting to tip off the assassins to his location, he stayed silent, hoping his mom would get the hint.

"Storm?" she called out again.

Sensing something was wrong, Nightshade stood up with a dagger in her hand. She walked around the room, inspecting the warehouse.

An assassin shadowed her, sneaking up closer and closer. Storm didn't want to watch his mom get backstabbed, so he quickly hatched a plan. He silently cast his town portal spell to Valhalla. The portals always opened in the town square, and since he was already in Valhalla, it was very cheap and close by.

Storm stepped through the portal and alerted the guards stationed there. They relaxed when they recognized him, until he equipped his new armor. Then they were terrified.

Another item Father had worked on yesterday was a piece of armor for Storm. Father handed it over with the glasses and explained it was the most difficult and horrible piece of gear he had ever worked on. And he had to do it alone because his assistants wouldn't even enter the building while it was there.

[Unique Item
          Name: Armor of Fire Salamander
          Type: Leather armor, chest piece
          Level: 60
          Quality: 100%
          Armor: 500 (+250)
          Description: Created from the skin of a fire salamander
          Effect 1: Fire resistance +100%
          Effect 2: Magic resistance +90%
          Effect 3: Self-healing
          Effect 4: Fear
                    Fear: Those around you will be in a constant state of fear
                    Range: 10 feet
          Durability: 500/500
          Crafted by: Father]

After equipping the armor, Storm could have run to the warehouse since it was close but he had a faster option. The golden portal, above his pit, was connected to a counterpart in Valhalla's town square. He stepped through that portal and arrived inside the warehouse.

Everybody immediately reacted to the passive effect of his armor. Some looked around wide-eyed and raised their swords ready for battle. Others cowered in complete terror.

Storm ignored them and ran towards the figure that had been sneaking up on his mom. He slammed into the shadowy figure, breaking their stealth and knocked them to the ground. With an impressive reaction speed, his mom threw out her hand and vines sprung up from the floor, wrapping around the fallen figure. The vines twisted harshly and blood leaked from the mass. The screams ended abruptly when a guard rushed over to finish off the intruder.

Storm quickly located the other two infiltrators and threw a hammer at each. Lightning struck the first assassin and triggered the chain lighting spell, instantly incapacitating the now unstealthed player. Thunder, likewise, struck its target and triggered a concussive blast that threw the second assassin across the room, unstealthing and incapacitating him as well. The guards gave Storm a wide berth and quickly dispatched the two enemies.

Storm considered trying to capture one of the assassins and interrogating them but he recalled his own experience with that and opted for a quick death. These were actual people and he wanted to remember that.

Storm scanned the room one more time but found nothing. He unequipped is armor and put it back into his backpack, to the relive of everybody around him.

Storm walked over to the secret door and lowered himself back into the pit. He sat there for another half hour scrying the surrounding area but found no more intruders. His adrenaline still hadn't dissipated after the assassins, so he spent some time checking on the enemy's progress.

After the last battle, Dark Elite retreated to Last Hope and started constructing machines of war. They were busily working in the fields around Last Hope. Storm spotted many siege weapons being assembled, there were trebuchets, and even ballistae. It looked like Weird was going all-out and Storm was a little worried about the next day. Finding nothing else he could do he logged out to get some rest before the next day.

Two eyes, deep in the shadows, opened and watched Storm enter the hidden room in the warehouse. Silent as a whisper, the shrouded figure moved to the Valhalla portal and peered down below it, through the damaged boards at Storm and the second portal below. The assassin then casually stepped through the portal to Valhalla's market and disappeared into the night.

Storm logged in early the next day and scried the enemy's position. Their troops had moved up to the river and fortified their side of the battlefield even more. Several of their monstrous creations were already in place and the rest were on the way. Each siege weapon had a dedicated crew to operate it and a contingent of soldiers to guard them.

Flashes of light flew in both directions, harmlessly bouncing off shields as mages from both sides probed defenses. He glanced at his timer and thought that today everything would be decided, one way another.

[18 hours remaining] (8am)

Storm climbed out of the pit and went to find Father. This was potentially the last day and he wanted to spend a little time with him before the final battle.

Valhalla was abuzz with excitement. Fallen and players alike, rushed around town, carrying goods and supplies. As he walked, he looked at the preparations. Tents were turned into workshops of every kind. Several were dedicated entirely to creating healing and mana potions. Others were used to make arrows and other items like their magical totems.

Storm found Father working hard in his forge. He was guiding his team on what gear to mend and repair for the next battle.

Ting, Ting, Ting

Storm stood at the entrance and reminisced about his first day in the game. Then his thoughts drifted to the raid the other day. He really enjoyed working with Father, his sister and Nightshade. His heart hurt a little knowing that today Nightshade would be on the other team.

"You ready for today?" Father asked, after noticing him in the doorway.

"As ready as I can be I suppose." Storm replied, "Thanks for the armor, it really came in handy last night."

"I bet." he chuckled, "It cleared out the entire forge. Not a single assistant could withstand the effect while I worked on it."

"How did you do it?" Storm asked.

Recalling his efforts, Father looked at him with haunted eyes and replied in shaky voice, "Your father was a very committed man. He would have done anything for you."

"Storm!" Sunshine yelled as she ran up to forge, "I've been looking for you. They are on the bridge again, with a white flag."

Frustrated at the interruption Storm left the forge to meet his mom and Lance by the city gates. He was tired of talking to Weird. If he wasn't going to stop, there wasn't anything to discuss. However, the clock was always in the back of his mind. Any time they wasted talking was time off the timer.

Much to Storm's surprise, there was only one person standing on the bridge, Sapphire. She stood there holding a pole with a white flag on top. Nightshade put a hand on Lance to hold him back when they made it to the bridge and let Storm continue on his own.

[16 hours remaining] (10am)

"It's good to see you." Sapphire greeted him with a smile.

"Why did you come?" he asked gruffly.

"Weird asked me to." she answered, "He wanted me to give you one more chance to surrender before he starts his attack."

"I won't ever surrender." he said definitively, "You know that. Why didn't he come?"

"He had some plans that needed finalizing." she replied shrugging. Then she got a confused look on her face and looked him up and down and asked, "Where's the world item?"

"The what?" he asked confusedly.

"Tsk tsk" she chided shaking her head. She turned away from Storm, the pole casually slung over her shoulder. He had to duck or she would have smacked him in the face. Sapphire walked back to her side of the bridge. On her way, she called out over her shoulder, "You're not going to be much of a challenge without it DumpsterBoy."

He watched her go, then rejoined his mom and Lance. He looked up the hill and didn't want to try to navigate that slippery slope so he cast a town portal spell to Valhalla and the three stepped through.

TWENTY-EIGHT

World item

Storm sat in the warehouse and scried the battlefield. He watched the enemy arrive in full force. And much to his dismay their ranks had grown significantly.

The siege weapons arrived earlier that morning and were ready for the day's battle. Nightshade had considered sending a team to sabotage them but they were heavily guarded. They were also not ready to tip their hand that they could cast spells at such a large distance.

Storm watched a trebuchet swing its long arm around, pitching a huge stone towards the city. The stone flew wide and veered off into the forest, striking a tree, breaking it in half. The crew made a few adjustments and reset the device to try again.

15 hours remaining] (11am)

"Storm, go." his mom insisted, "I heard what Sapphire said. You need to recover the world item."

"I don't even know where to look." he said shaking his head, "You need me here."

"Start in the throne room," she suggested, "there should be a clue there. And we don't need you yet. We have our battle plan. And really, we only need to delay them, not defeat them."

"At least take this," Storm said, handing her the orb, "the intel is too valuable. We need constant eyes on them. I have a bad feeling they are up to something."

"Good luck." she said, after taking the orb.

He thanked her and gave her a hug, then climbed into the crowded pit which now housed a stealth totem and several guards with heavy crossbows. He slipped past them and stepped into the golden portal. In Avalon, he found much the same, a contingent of guards guarding the portals.

He made his way up the hill to the castle and then to the throne room. When they first explored Avalon Castle, he was fascinated by the beautiful antique furniture. He didn't pay much attention to it this time, as he hurried through the castle. The throne room was devoid of furniture except for the throne on a raised dais. He walked up to it and searched for any clues. A flash of gold caught his eye, which led him to a hidden compartment that popped out after a few twists and turns.

He smiled as he looked at the little drawer. It was very reminiscent of the one he found the Wraith ring in, a ring he had completely forgotten he was wearing until now. He felt a rush of excitement as he considered the possibility of finding another one. Sadly, this one was empty, even after peering inside, with the right lens of his glasses.

Not finding anything else, Storm sat on the throne and brought up the city's interface. He setup an alarm to warn him if any players were detected in the city and excluded all of the guards currently stationed there. If anybody new came through the portal, it would alert him. He looked at his options for defense but the city's mana was too low to activate anything. He didn't regret using up the mana reserves though, because it reunited his family.

He looked over the city's stats and was curious about what the Heart of Eden was. He hadn't heard anybody talk about it and thought possibly that was what Weird was after.

[Legendary City
    Name: Avalon
    Ruler: Storm
    Population: 1
    Mana pool: 163 (+1/hr.)
    Heart of Eden health: 100%]

He pulled up the castle map and looked for any rooms that could house the Heart of Eden or the world item. He discovered a vaulted room close by that was worth investigating.

Storm ran to the room, his footsteps echoing down the hallway. Being alone in the castle started to creep him out and he jumped at more than a few shadows. He ran faster. Breathing heavily, he stood in front of two massive golden doors. They were carved with a beautiful motif of a dragon laying on a pile of gold.

He pushed on the doors but they wouldn't budge and for a moment he was stymied. He studied them and had a moment of clarity. He retrieved the World staff and held it in front of the doors. A light flashed along the seams and the doors swung open silently.

He timidly stepped into the room and what he found shocked him. It was full of treasure. Huge glowing balls of light, floating in the air, illuminated the entire room. Assorted weapons and armor adorned shelves and racks spread throughout the room. He quickly inspected a couple of items.

[Item

    Name: Royal Helm

    Type: Plate armor, head piece

    Level: 90

    Quality: 99%

    Armor: 250

    Effect 1: +20% magic resistance

    Durability: 90/90]

[Item

    Name: Royal dagger

    Level: 90

    Quality: 99%

    Damage: 100

    On strike: Frost

        Frost: Freezes enemy for 1 second

    Charges: 10/10

    Durability: 90/90]

Storm rushed through the room looking for the world item. He found some really impressive pieces of armor and weapons and thought about updating some of his gear but he didn't have time. There was a battle being waged and he needed to hurry but vowed to come back later. After the rows of weapons and armor, there were shelfs of resources of every imaginable type.

The doors slammed shut and he jumped. He spun around searching the room but didn't see any movement. Storm continued to search and found the next row had bags full of coins. He fount copper coins, silver coins, gold coins and even the coveted platinum coins. Storm couldn't help himself and quickly stuffed a couple bags of the gold and platinum coins into his backpack.

After the coins he found rows of gemstones and then rare crafting ingredients. He didn't have an immediate need for either so he hurried past to the very back of the treasury. When he saw the treasure chest, he slowed. It was larger than any of the ones he had seen so far. He tried to open it but it was sealed shut. Storm retrieved the World staff once again and waved it at the treasure chest, and as expected, it opened.

Storm peered into the chest, excited to discover what it contained. He pulled each item and inspected it. He didn't find the world item but he surely wasn't disappointed. What he found was incredible.

[Royal Item
        Name: Crown of Avalon
        Type: Head piece
        Level: 100
        Quality: 100%
        Armor: 200 (+100)
        Effect 1: +20% to each stat
        Effect 2: +100% mana
        Durability: 500/500
        Set bonus: Royal aura
                Effect 1: Immunity to all poisons]

[Royal Item
        Name: Scepter of Avalon
        Type: One handed mace
        Level: 100
        Quality: 100%
        Damage: 200
        Effect 1: +20% to each stat
        On strike: Striking blow
                Striking blow: knocks opponent to their knees
        Charges: 100/100
        Durability: 500/500
        Set bonus: Royal aura
                Effect 1: Immunity to all poisons]

[Royal Item
        Name: Mantle of Avalon
        Type: Cloak
        Level: 100

Quality: 100%
Armor: 10 (+5)
Effect 1: +20% to each stat
Effect 2: +100% health
Durability: 500/500
Set bonus: Royal aura
        Effect 1: Immunity to all poisons]

[Royal Item
    Name: Robes of Avalon
    Type: Robes
    Level: 100
    Quality: 100%
    Armor: 200 (+100)
    Effect 1: +20% to each stat
    Effect 2: +90% magic resistance
    Durability: 500/500
    Set bonus: Royal aura
        Effect 1: Immunity to all poisons]

[Royal Item
    Name: Signet ring of Avalon
    Type: Ring
    Level: 100
    Effect 1: +20% to each stat
    Effect 2: +100% stamina
    Durability: 500/500
    Set bonus: Royal aura
        Effect 1: Immunity to all poisons]

The Avalon Royal items were amazing and one or two might fit into his setup but again, he didn't have time. He stuffed all of them into his backpack and finished searching the room. Sadly, he didn't find anything that looked like the world item and returned to the throne room.

He sat on the throne and stared at the floor. It reminded him of the mosaic in the stone golem's dungeon. His thoughts drifted to the adventure he shared with his sister, Father and Sapphire. He really had a good time and lamented that their game had devolved into war and trying to survive.

Storm walked around, staring at the floor. The pattern in the marble was beautiful and flowed throughout the room. He followed the golden flecks and intricate designs, then walked along the perimeter searching for hidden doors. Then looked back at the throne and had a thought.

He equipped all of the royal items he just found and sat on the throne. He heard a deep whisper and a prompt filled his vision.

"The king has returned."

[Teleport to the Eden chamber
        Accept
        Decline]

Excited at the discovery, Storm accepted the prompt and felt the familiar disorientation that came with teleportation. His sight momentarily blurred and then he was no longer in the throne room.

Storm found himself looking into a large round chamber. In the center of the room was a circular metal table with a hologram of a planet rotating above it. He stepped up to the table and set his hands on it. An interface appeared and after a few moments he zoomed the projection down onto Valhalla.

The battlefield outside of the city was now displayed, hovering above the table. Troops could be seen moving on each side and magic flew back and forth. Trebuchets launched heavy boulders at the city and the magical cannon still fired away.

Storm played with the settings and changed the globe view to a heatmap of the players. The heatmap showed clusters of players as bright red, the more players in an area, the more vibrant it is. There was a large cluster of players around Valhalla but there were other clusters just as bright in other areas of the map.

Two in particular caught his attention due to their unique shape. Rather than being clumped together they were in a long line, as if they were traveling. He followed the direction of both groups and wasn't surprised that they were moving towards Valhalla, or rather Avalon's portal.

Storm spied upon them and discovered one was comprised of elves and the other dwarfs. He also discovered that these two groups were not just players traveling to Avalon, they were armies marching there. He briefly wondered if Mani and Clover were with them.

Storm estimated they would reach Valhalla in about eleven hours. He groaned at the new problem but set it aside for later. He needed to continue searching for the world item.

Storm discovered a small treasure chest in the back of the room and knelt down in front of it. His heart pounded in his chest as he lifted the lid. He cocked his head at what he found, then reached down and pulled out a pair of tiger striped pajamas. He inspected it.

[WORLD ITEM
        Name: Cat costume
        Type: Body suit
        Description: Using this item, you can transform into a variety of feline forms. Covers the entire body and can be equipped under armor.
        Forms: Tiger, Cheetah, Snow Leopard, Lion, Jaguar, Serval, Sand Cat, Sphinx, Fishing Cat
        Tiger effect: unknown
        Cheetah effect: unknown
        Snow Leopard effect: unknown
        Lion effect: unknown
        Jaguar effect: unknown
        Serval effect: unknown
        Sand Cat effect: unknown
        Sphinx effect: unknown
        Fishing Cat effect: unknown]

A little nonplussed, he put the skintight body suit on. He poked his feet into the booties and pushed his arms through the sleeves and fit his hands into the fingerless gloves. After zipping it up, he turned around several times and looked at the tail behind him. He pulled the hood over his head and found ears on top.

He felt silly dressed up as a large cat. He wasn't sure if this was the prize they needed to tilt the battle in their favor but he'd give anything a chance.

TWENTY-NINE

Scrying

S torm's feet touched down on the wooden boards of the warehouse and the sounds of battle crashed into him. The ground rumbled as a building nearby fell to the ground. He looked around worriedly but nobody seemed concerned.

[13 hours remaining] (1pm)

His mom and Father were currently surrounded by a small crowd of players seeking their attention to address some urgent matter or another. The success the two shared leading the war effort, gained them much respect amongst the Fallen and players. Without their guidance, Avalon would have been lost long ago.

Storm stepped up to the command table and reviewed the latest intel.

ATTN: All mages report for duty

All mages are called upon for the protection of Valhalla

Any mage with healing or resurrection spells report to the hospital for special squad placement.

Pure combat mages report to the city gates.

Pure support mages report to the castle.

Mages with mixed specialties report to either, you will rotate between offensive and defensive.

REPORT: Valhalla battle update

Trebuchets

Status: Sighted-in and firing nonstop

Ammunition: large boulders, mundane damage

Ammo Qty: unlimited

Range: full city coverage

Damage: 8/10

Weakness: projectile manipulation

Special notes: projectiles are created with earth magic.

Catapults

Status: Sighted-in and firing nonstop

Ammunition: crafted, magical and mundane damage

Ammo Qty: low supply

Range: outer city only

Damage: 3/10

Weakness: low damage

Special notes: projectiles explode. projectiles are faster and less prone to manipulation.

Magical cannon

Status: Sighted-in and firing at various intervals

Ammunition: magical, magical damage

Ammo Qty: unlimited

Range: line-of-site

Damage: 6/10

Weakness: magical deflection

Special notes: cannot penetrate the city's magical barrier.

REPORT: Valhalla defense update

The magical barrier is deflecting the cannon.

The magical barrier can only slow the heavier projectiles.

Air mages are nudging the heavier projectiles off course.

Earth mages reinforced all structures in the city.

Earth mages are sealing breaches in the outer wall.

Water mages are controlling the fires.

Life mages have been assigned to the special medical corps.

Storm stopped reading when the room fell silent. He looked up and discovered everybody smiling at him, many holding back chuckles. He was confused but quickly recalled what he was wearing. Nightshade and Father noticed him and walked over with smirks on their faces.

"Did you find it?" Nightshade asked, trying not to laugh.

"Yeah… I found it." Storm replied with a grimace.

"So, this is it?" Father asked, gesturing at the tiger suit.

Storm looked down at his ridiculous outfit. He appeared as if he found it in a dumpster, behind a Halloween store. Sapphire would never let him hear the end of this one.

His arms, chest and legs were covered in the tiger stripes of his world item. He wore bright red greaves over top of the knee-high black leather boots. On his head he wore the Crown of Avalon and from his shoulders hung a vibrant purple cloak with a golden royal crest stitched on the back, rimmed in elegant white fur. Finally, tiger tail, having a mind of its own, swished back and forth at the attention. He truly looked like a tiger king.

"Yes," he finally answered, plucking at the orange fur "this is it."

Everybody in the warehouse ducked and took cover when a nearby explosion rocked the walls. Storm felt the shockwave through the ground and reached out to stabilize his mom. This one was much worse than the last one, something big came down.

Storm heard cheering in the distance.

"Report!" Nightshade commanded. She looked at the boy staring into the scrying orb. A girl sat next to him, taking notes and responded.

"They breached the walls." the young girl reported, "They are preparing to charge."

"Lance, pass the word." Nightshade instructed, "Battle stations."

Lance nodded and ran out of the warehouse.

"I want you on the orb." Nightshade commanded Storm, "I'll get some mana totems setup for you."

"Healing ones too." Storm said ominously, then walked over to the table with the young pair.

"Ok," his mom agreed with a confused look, "but I'm not expecting combat in here."

"It's only if we need it." Storm hedged, "And get some mana and healing potions if you can. Where's Sunshine?"

"She's in the throne room." Nightshade told him, "There are several defensive measures that require her."

"Ok you two," Nightshade addressed the young couple scrying, "Storm is going to take over scrying for the battle but stay close and relieve him when he needs it."

The two nodded and handed over the orb.

"How long until they attack?" Storm asked the young man.

"I think it will be soon," he answered in a quiet voice, "After the walls fell, they all got into position."

"Mom" Storm said, recalling something he needed to tell her, "I know it's not a good time but the dwarves and elves have amassed an army and are heading towards us."

"How long before they get here?" she asked, frowning.

"Nine, maybe ten hours." he guessed.

"If we last that long, we can address it then." she said.

Having nothing more to say, Storm lost himself in the orb. On the other side of the river, the enemy spread out in small groups rather than clustered together. He inspected the composition of each group and found they had the standard Dark Elite structure. They contained a tank, a couple high DPS melee classes, a ranged class and at least two mages, one specialized in healing and the other combat.

He prepared himself for their crossing. The bridge was a choke point and when they rushed across it, he would attack with all of his magical might. The bridge would have been protected but they couldn't have protected all of their soldiers and he was confident he could surprise them with something new.

Water still poured from the castle walls and streamed down the hill into the river. It made it incredibly difficult to lay siege to the castle, but it was a double-edged sword by keeping the defenders locked inside Valhalla. Anybody that slipped on the hill would fall into the river and be swept away, earning them a one-way ticket to respawn.

Storm watched as the enemy mages stepped up to the river in a line and all started casting the same spell in unison. He knew enough about the arcane language to instantly know what they were casting.

"They are freezing the river!" he gasped.

"What?" Nightshade exclaimed, running over to him.

"They are freezing the river! They are going to cross!" Storm said frantically, "The bridge was a feint, they didn't even need it!"

[New spell obtained: Freeze (Air magic)]

"Here they come!" Storm yelled.

"Do what you can." his mom said, squeezing his shoulder in support. She set down a crate filled with bottles, half with an azure liquid and the other crimson.

The enemy mages froze the river. It didn't stop there however, the water coming down the hill froze too, all the way up to the castle. A second set of mages stepped forward and cautiously crossed the river and set their hands on the frozen ground. Plants sprouted up and out of the thin layer of ice. They created dozens of paths from the river up the hill, all the way to the castle. The mages stepped aside and clusters of the enemy charged up the hill.

[New spell obtained: Plant growth (Earth spell)]

The defenders hurled magical and conventional projectiles at the attackers. The rocks and boulders that Dark Elite had hurled into Avalon had been collected and were now rolled down the plant pathways, like bowling balls, striking the enemy. And just like bowling pins, the enemy troops were tossed aside.

The defenders frantically worked to repair breaches in the outer wall while the trebuchets continued to rain down boulders amongst them. Magic flew in both directions, but the bright beams of light that came from the enemy peaked Storm's interest. He looked for the source and watched the enemy mages closely.

[New spell obtained: Lazer beam (Fire magic and Air magic)]

He decided it was time to get to work. Analyzing the enemy, he picked the most effective targets. He wanted to have the most impact and knew the chain of command would be a great place but he also knew they would be the most protected and noticeable. His goal was to fly under the radar with his ranged casting as long as possible. He feared they would deploy countermeasures and nullify his advantage.

A group of mages near the river were casting a spell together. Three mages faced each other interweaving their magic. It was so complex it was difficult for Storm to follow but he understood it was some sort of death spell, sadly they already started and he only got a part of it. He watched them as they completed the spell and as he stared into his orb, everything in his peripheral vision darkened as the light around him disappeared.

A massive black sphere formed around Valhalla cutting off all natural sources of light and diminishing any magical ones within. The spell kept the defenders from accurately targeting the enemy but Storm didn't think it would cause any lasting damage other than a wayward trebuchet shot here and there. The spell would dissipate after a few minutes.

Fortunately, Storm's scrying wasn't affected. He noticed another group of mages casting a spell in a similar fashion. Again, it was incredibly complex but he followed along and understood it to be some sort of massive concussive blast. Concerned, he quickly adjusted his view and cast one of his latest acquisitions, Lazer beam.

A beam of light shot forth from behind one of the mages and struck in the back of the neck, causing her to gasp in pain and disrupt the spell. Lazer beam was an interesting spell because it allowed him to add extra mana to it for a more powerful effect. In this case he wanted to conserve mana and cast it with the lowest possible amount.

Storm had planned on casting again but he underestimated the impact of interrupting a cooperative spell. The mage he struck stopped casting but the other two continued which created a magical feedback loop that formed between the three. It created a power imbalance and the spell immediately released. The resulting explosion shredded the three mages and sent parts of them flying in all directions.

Satisfied with the result, Storm continued his espionage efforts. Each spell behaved differently when interrupted, some fizzled out and others ended in spectacular fashion. He couldn't interrupt them all so he sought out the destructive spells, painting the river bank with blood and body parts. He briefly wondered if Night and Light were there or if he had already killed them.

Storm's mana dipped each time he cast a spell, the remote casting cost more than usual. He knew it wasn't maintainable but if he could inflict enough damage, it would be worth it. He felt ill each time his mana dipped too low, so he had been drinking mana potions like they were candy. And he liked candy.

Storm noticed a group casting a particularly nasty spell and rushed over to disrupt it. He was too focused on the battle and something happened that didn't occur with the previous spells. He didn't have enough mana. Normally the spell would just fail but this time the ability on his Wraith ring activated and the remaining cost was paid in blood.

His heart pounded in his ears and pain blossomed in his chest as he finished the spell. He watched the beam of light strike his target. The previous times he cast the spell he only burned a hole into them, breaking their concentration and thus disrupting their spells. He never outright killed them.

This time was different. The beam of light was so powerful it cleaved the mage's head completely off. It also severed the arm of the player standing across from him. Storm choked back a gasp at the carnage. Sadly, he couldn't stop. He moved the view and cast again, each time cutting through the players like a hot knife through butter.

Storm coughed up blood and downed another mana potion. As it refilled his mana, he continued casting. He quickly picked new targets and cast, keeping his mana low enough to dip into his health each time.

Emboldened by his success he started targeting the command structure. He zapped the officers that were issuing orders, one after another. He coughed up more blood but kept casting. Each time he verified his kill and moved on. He was caught off guard when one of his targets survived. The beam of light veered off harmlessly.

He stared at the orb in bewilderment, bloody spittle dripping from his mouth. He had become a machine, repeatedly casting and killing. He kept his mana low enough to dip into his health each time, decreasing the cost and increasing the damage. They all died and he hurt inside. But this time, his target lived. It took him a few moments to comprehend the situation. He looked around and found Sapphire. She had joined the battle.

Sapphire began casting a complex spell and, in his mental state, he was barely able to follow along. When she completed it, an opaque bubble formed around her forces. His worst fear just became reality. They countered his ability to scry and remote cast.

[New spell obtained: Scry shield (Air magic and Earth magic)]

"Storm," Nightshade barked, "It's time for a break." she took the orb out of his hands and wiped the blood off of it, then handed it to the young man that used it before, "Keep me updated." she instructed the young couple.

"I just need to lay down for a few minutes." Storm muttered weakly, then slumped to the ground.

The young man whispered to the woman next to him and she relayed the information to the rest of the room. Dark Elite's charge up the hill was blunted but they dug in. The trebuchet was still firing. They were trying to hit the wall again but so far, they've missed.

The defenders sent out forays to take advantage of their higher ground and rain down boulders, arrows and magic onto invaders, but each time they faced a total wipe due to the magical cannon. It had been repurposed as an antipersonnel weapon and was incredibly affect and traumatizing. Slowly the enemy climbed up the hill, their mages provided arcane protection and healing with the occasional resurrection.

The situation was already pretty grim but everything devolved when the trebuchets landed another hit and crumpled another section of wall. The enemy cheered loudly. Heavy tanks, acting as a vanguard, charged the rest of the way to Valhalla's broken wall.

Two enemy teams made it through the breach and into Valhalla. They setup a defensive position and took heavy fire but their support mages were close enough to assist them. Between their levels, gear, buffs and constant healing, there was little the defenders could to do dislodge them.

The young couple reported that Father was at the breach and was rallying the troops. They held the enemy at bay, but reinforcements were rushing up the hill unabated. Within a matter of minutes Father's position and Valhalla would be overrun.

"Ok, let me see what I can do." Storm grunted, sitting up. He gestured to the pile of mana and health potions, "How many of those do we have left?"

Nightshade set down a few more in front of him, then said she had to give some orders but would be back. The young couple handed the orb to him and he peered into its depths once again.

Storm saw the end. There was little resistance left. And once they truly made it inside the city all would be lost. He frantically wracked his brain for ideas on how to stop them, how to destroy them.

He came up with an idea but he wasn't sure how well it would work, if at all. He gave some instructions to the young couple sitting next to him, then cast health and mana buffs on himself, increasing his max.

He moved his view of the battlefield and raised it high into the air. He looked down on the entire horde of enemies rushing up the hill. He thought of his mom and sister, and how these monsters were going to take Father away from them. He got angry.

He stared coldly at the enemy, then started casting. His fingers danced as he cast his most expensive and complex spell yet. He modified it to the point that he wasn't sure it would even work. Using the new details he gained from the Lazer beam spell, he modified the mana flow on his AOE fireball spell. He thought, if you can add extra mana to spell, what would make you stop adding it.

[New spell obtained, Mass fireball, AOE, channeled (Fire magic)]

Storm stared at the battlefield directing his new spell. His fireball flew towards a group of invaders running up the hill. It split multiple times before reaching them and when the group of fireballs struck, they exploded sending everybody flying, tossing them around like rag dolls. He kept casting, channeling mana into the spell, and fireballs continued to fall from the sky, multiplying many times. Enemy mages erected shields and his fireballs started bouncing off with little effect.

Storm's mana bottomed out and he grunted in pain, blood leaking down his chin. But he kept casting. Now that his mana was gone, his spells were fueled with blood magic and when his fireballs struck the enemy shields, they exploded with such ferocity that everybody nearby was turned to ash, shield or not. Fireballs fell from the heavens and every time they struck, the defenders could feel the ground trembling from inside Valhalla. The enemies had no safe place to hide, and found no reprieve. Storm kept casting, each new fireball took more life from his meter and he coughed up more blood.

"Now!" he growled harshly and his two assistants each grabbed a bottle and held it up for him to drink. He drank the health potion first, then the mana potion. As they worked their magic on his body, Storm worked his. He channeled his mana into the fireball spell, his hands moving faster and faster. The two began pouring potions into his mouth while he kept casting. But eventually, the potions ran out.

"Storm!" he heard a muffled voice yell. It sounded like he was underwater.

Storm sat on the ground cross-legged, hunched over the orb. His body was spent. Blood leaked from his eyes, ears and mouth but he continued feeding the spell.

"Storm!" Nightshade yelled into his face, shaking him harshly.

Storm kept casting. Anger consumed him. His was death.

"Stop!" his mom commanded him, but he didn't. She broke down, tears streaking down her face, she pleaded, "Please Luke! Stop!"

He did, but not because he wanted to, because he had nothing left. Storm stared sightless into the orb a sad smile touched his blood-stained lips and he whispered with his dying breath, "Was it enough?"

"Nooo!" Nightshade's feral scream could be heard by everybody in the city. She cradled him in her arms, tears pouring from her eyes.

The room fell silent, despite the battle raging outside. Nobody said a word. Everybody felt the pain in her scream. They all knew Storm was her son, they all thought of her as their in-game mother. She ran their guild as she ran her house, with lots of love. More than a few, having caught up in the moment, wiped tears from their eyes.

Storm stepped into the warehouse breathing heavily, he noticed everybody was quiet and heard soft sobbing. He repeated his earlier question.

"Was it enough?" he asked,

Everybody in the room turned to him, red rimmed eyes staring at him, many blinking back tears.

"They're retreating!" a voice rang out.

THIRTY

New arrival

Storm logged in after a small break. The last battle was really intense and he needed some time out of the game to come down from it. His mom had insisted on the break and they could handle the cleanup. His avatar was resting in the warehouse, which had become his home for the past few days.

Storm looked at the countdown.

[6 hours remaining] (8pm)

Clustered around his orb were a group of mages taking turns casting spells. They all wore bright colored robes and hats, and each carried a unique scepter, staff or wand. They would cast a few spells then pass the orb to their neighbor. Inbetween casting, they rested and recovered mana. Storm watched a bit as the mages passed his orb around and cast their spells through it. They had several totems of mana to help them recover and it seemed like it was just enough to maintain a steady stream of spells.

"Good to see you're back." Nightshade said walking up to him. "What do you think?"

"I like it," Storm replied, "I want to check on the armies from the other realms, to see how far they've progressed. They might be here sooner than I guessed." His mom glanced at the orb and was about to say something but he stopped her, "I don't need the orb. The Eden chamber has access to a world map that updates in real time."

"Oh?" she replied, eyebrows raised, "I'd like to see it sometime."

"Do you have time right now?" he asked.

"Sadly no," she responded, "there are too many things that need to be finished before the next attack. But Father might be free if you want company." She leaned forward and whispered, "Honestly, he's been driving me nuts. He's going stir crazy in here, if you take him, you'll be doing everybody a favor."

"Ok" he said chuckling, "I'll see if he wants to see Avalon, he might find it interesting since it's a mirror of his city."

A few minutes later, Storm and Father were walking down the path to Avalon Castle. As they walked, Storm pulled the legendary staff out of his ring's dimensional space. He had formed a habit of practicing the staff any chance he got. He moved through a few forms while they walked. And finally, he spun it around behind his back and caught it in the other hand, then whipped it across his front.

"Hey, you've been practicing." Father commented cheerfully, "better than when you first started, I hear."

"I see Sunshine has been talking again?" Storm grumbled good naturedly. He continued in a jovial tone, "And yes, I've been practicing. One of the soldiers showed me a few moves."

As they walked to the throne room, they talked about what each had been doing that day. Father was not too happy to hear about the dying incident, but understood Storm's commitment. After checking on the progress of the two approaching armies, Storm and Father stopped by the forge.

"Hey, if we survive this, do you want to run this forge too?" Storm asked as they walked around the empty interior. "You could have one in each city barely a block away from each other by way of portal."

"Putting the cart before the horse a bit, aren't we?" Father chuckled.

"True, but I'd rather plan for best." Storm said, "If we survive, do you want it?"

"I'll take it." he said simply.

The two returned to the warehouse and reported to Nightshade. The two armies were still approaching and were a few hours away, however, they were speeding up. Nightshade sent their fastest runners to each army to gauge their intent. If they weren't friendly, maybe they could at least get them to flank Dark Elite first.

"I have something I need to show both of you," she said, and led them to the back of the warehouse and waved towards a group of Fallen chatting amongst themselves.

"Do they have intel?" Storm asked, thinking they were from the field.

"They showed up shortly after you and Father left." she explained, "They are freshly Fallen, and they have absolutely no idea what is going on. I explained we were under attack but haven't said much beyond than that." She looked pointedly at Father and added, "They showed up together."

"That's strange" Father commented, "Fallen don't usually arrive together."

"Right," Nightshade agreed, "That's what I thought."

"They usually show up one at a time." Father explained when Storm still looked confused.

"What guild do you think they are from?" she asked Storm intently.

"I don't know." he replied, shrugging. Then his eyes widened, "Wait. There's no way. They couldn't possibly be…"

"Dark Elite" she finished.

"Weird." Storm muttered, processing the information.

"Not Weird." Nightshade corrected, "But it was somebody Storm, and it was intentional."

"Do you think it was Sapphire?" he asked in a whisper.

His mom shrugged noncommittedly.

"Do you think they're here to spy on us?" he asked, keeping his voice low.

"I don't know." she replied, shaking her head. "They offered to fight for us without even knowing the situation, which is either good or bad."

"Breach, back wall!" a voice yelled out.

"I need to go." Nightshade said abruptly and departed with haste.

Storm knew Dark Elite would be charging towards the castle again and joined the rotation on the orb with the other mages. The attackers were more relentless this time and his spells were way less effective. He glanced through his logs and discovered the enemy had a lot more fire resistance.

Storm decided it was time for something new. He was beyond satisfied with his upgraded fireball so he did the same to his ice spell.

[New spell obtained: Mass ice ball, channeled (Water magic and Air magic)]

During his turn on the orb, he ended up going a little too far again. Fortunately, the other mages forced him to stop before he used up all of his health. They kicked him out of the rotation until his health and mana were full again. Grumbling, Storm laid down on the floor and wiped the blood from his mouth.

[4 hours remaining] (10pm)

Sunshine barged into the warehouse, breathing hard, and ran to her mom.

"They have a team in the city." she reported urgently.

"Take a deep breath." Nightshade suggested, putting a calming had on her daughter, "Tell me what happened?"

"I was on the throne inspecting the city." she explained, "I saw movement near the back wall and discovered they have a portal and are bringing in troops."

"Father, take the reserves to the back wall." Nightshade commanded immediately. "Keep the invaders contained. I'll send help when we can." She turned back to Sunshine and directed her, "Go with him and show him where they are. Help get them contained, then get back on that throne."

Father, fully equipped for battle, quickly left the warehouse with Sunshine following close behind.

Storm was about to jump back into the orb rotation when a loud noise started buzzing in his ears. He asked around, but nobody else could hear it. For a moment, he thought he was losing his mind but his blood ran cold when he realized it was his alarm for Avalon. Somebody was in the city.

He informed his mom and she sent him to investigate. She said he had to go alone because she had nobody to spare. Storm stepped through the portal to Avalon, surprising the guards stationed there. He verified they were all accounted for and nobody had come through the portal recently. Something felt off to him.

Storm equipped his fire salamander armor, keeping his skin-tight tiger suit underneath, and began radiating an aura of fear. The guards became visibly uncomfortable and he quickly moved away, not wanting to inconvenience them further. First, he jogged to the castle but found nothing abnormal. Then he decided to try the uninhabited town.

He searched down each street but they were empty as expected. While inspecting one particular road, he thought he heard something and hid in the shadows for a few minutes. With his heartbeat in his ears, he stood there silently. He was getting jumpy and paranoid, he decided it was time to get back to the war.

Storm took a step out of the shadows and froze. Fear instantly encompassed him and pushed him close to hyperventilating. A haunting melody drifted around him and he couldn't move. They found him. Storm closed his eyes for a moment and took a deep breath to calm his nerves.

Several dark figures surrounded him, one, a demon with horns spiraling into the air. Storm couldn't see their faces, but he knew who they were. Weird had brought the originals with him and in that moment, he knew he was dead.

"Storm" the demon said, it's voice distorted voice by the helmet.

"Weird" Storm responded.

With a heavy sigh Weird removed his helmet and stepped up to him.

"You really made this one difficult." Weird complained, "I knew I should have chosen a different server, who knew cats would be so problematic."

"Please don't destroy the server." Storm pleaded.

"This is the way it has to be." Weird replied sadly. He had no sound of satisfaction in his voice.

"I will stop you." Storm growled angrily.

"Good bye Storm." Weird said, gently putting a hand on his shoulder.

Storm felt a pulling from Weird's hand, he glanced at his health bar and watched it drain rapidly. He tried to move but couldn't break his iron grip. His health reached zero and he saw blackness.

The door to the warehouse banged open as Storm rushed inside and found his mom. He explained that Weird had infiltrated Avalon and he needed help to stop him. At which, somebody behind him cleared their throat.

"Pardon," a voice interrupted smoothly. The man dressed in all black bowed deeply when Storm looked at him. "I couldn't help but overhear. You said something about Weird being in Avalon?"

"Yeah" Storm replied slowly.

"That's not good," the figure said with a concerned look. "If Weird makes it to the Eden chamber he will destroy the server."

[3 hours remaining] (11pm)

Curious Storm inspected the newcomer

[Character
        Name: Blynk
        Guild: Dark Elite
        Level: 100
        Health: ***/***]

"Blynk." Storm muttered.

"Yes!" Blynk said enthusiastically. A huge grin formed on his face, "If you want to stop Weird, take me and my friends. We will help."

"Why?" Storm asked doubtfully.

"I just got here," the assassin said with a shrug, "and I like cats. Besides, not everybody agrees with what he is doing."

"Storm, I think you should take their offer." Nightshade said, "We really don't have much choice, our hands are full out here."

"Do you think we even have a chance?" he asked Blynk. "The other originals are with him."

Blynk smiled at him manically and said, "There's always a chance."

THIRTY-ONE

Sunshine

S unshine sat on Valhalla's throne, her throne, scanning the city. She used the interface to inspect the buildings and walls for damage, direct repair efforts and search for intruders. Dark Elite hadn't stopped attacking all day and in-turn, she hadn't been able to take a break.

The infiltration teams started early in the morning and continued throughout the day. Whenever she discovered a group, she would zap the intruders with bolts of energy, instantly killing them. It was a slow process because she had to target each one individually and after the first one died, they scattered like mice.

She could have used a more devastating option but needed to conserve mana where she could. Every time she activated a defense, mana was consumed from the city's mana pool and it refilled painfully slow.

Sunshine had been on the throne when the enemy froze the river and rushed up the hill. She watched as bomb after bomb exploded on the invaders, not realizing Storm had put his life into the onslaught. When the explosions stopped and the smoke cleared, she directed the repairs to Valhalla's wall. The city's magic slowly repaired the cracks but earth mages were needed for the larger repairs.

To add to all of that, the enemy's war machines hadn't stopped firing since morning. The magic shield was only level one and couldn't stop large projectiles, like what the trebuchets used. But Sunshine and the air mages were able to nudge the projectiles off course, sometimes sending them into the forest and other times into unoccupied portions of the city.

[Legendary City
    Name: Valhalla
    Ruler: Sunshine
    Population: 563
    Mana pool: 24390 (+563/hr.)
    Heart of Eden health: 100%]

Sunshine watched as several large boulders hurtled towards the city. She nudged a couple off-course, causing them to fly wide and crash into the forest. The others were handled by the air mages.

Unfortunately, Dark Elite caught on to their tactics and employed countermeasures by magically enhancing the projectiles. Sometimes they increased the mass significantly and other times they shielded it with layers of magic resistance. This time, they combined the two to devastating effect. A magically enhanced boulder slipped past the mages and crashed into the back wall.

Sunshine grimaced as the interface flashed angrily in her eyes. She immediately set the city to repairing the wall but it was going to need help. She sent a runner to direct the repair crews to the damaged section. Knowing this was the opportunity they were waiting for, she prepared for attack.

As she suspected, a large wave of troops rushed up the hill. They seemed hesitant at first, but became emboldened when the balls of fire, falling from the sky, had little effect. They steadily pushed the defenders up the hill and when things were looking really bad, large balls of ice began falling from the sky.

Sunshine called out to her runner but they hadn't returned from their last task, which was directing the repair crews to the back wall. She quickly scanned for them and what she found caused the hair on her arms to rise.

The bodies of the repair crew lay strewn about the area near the breach. She inspected them and they still appeared to be alive, just unconscious. Which was unfortunate because if they were dead, they would have respawned and triggered an alarm.

She moved her view around and found several suspicious figures hiding in the shadows of a nearby building. She couldn't see inside, so she watched a few minutes and her patience paid off because eventually they opened the door and within she caught a glimpse of a familiar azure glow. She jumped up from the throne and ran as fast as she could to the warehouse to warn her mother and Father.

[4 hours remaining] (10pm)

After warning her mom, Sunshine led Father to the breach in the back wall. They engaged the enemy and tried to dislodge them but unfortunately, they had a solid foothold. The best they could do was create a barrier and isolate them to that section of the city. Once Father and the reserves had the breach contained, Sunshine hurried back to the throne.

She quickly surveyed the battlefield. The rest of Dark Elite was rushing up the hill in a full-on frontal assault. However, they were easily pushed back. They battled for another twenty minutes and each suicide run, their enemies' numbers dwindled.

The trebuchets eventually stopped firing, along with the catapults and the magical cannon. Nightshade led a team of Fallen down the hill and to the bridge. They cautiously disabled each machine of war, then pushed the smaller, more mobile, cannon up the hill and into the city.

A contingent of Fallen formed-up outside the front gates with Lance looking over them. They had a mixture of melee fighters and mages, all decked out in their best gear and buffed to the max. More than a few had soft glows emanating from armor pieces or weapons. Sunshine briefly wondered what they were doing.

A messenger jogged into the throne room and waiting for Sunshine to address her.

"What does Nightshade want?" Sunshine asked when she noticed the girl.

"Nightshade said the dwarven and elven armies are going to be here within the hour." the little girl reported, "The envoy we sent was killed."

"What does she want me to do?" Sunshine asked.

"She wants you to make contact with them." the girl replied.

"What? Why me?" Sunshine asked.

"She didn't say." the girl answered, shrugging, "Lance is out front waiting for you."

Sunshine stood up and stretched. She thanked the girl and jogged to the front gate.

"Good evening, Miss Sunshine." Lance greeted her.

"Hi Lance," Sunshine greeted him back, "Mom said she wanted me to contact the dwarves and elves?"

"Yes ma'am." he affirmed, nodding, "She sent us to back you up. We need to give them a show of force. They gave our scouts a dirt nap, so we're not very optimistic. At the very least we need to stall them."

"Not an ideal time to be traveling through the forest." Sunshine commented, looking at the dark sky.

"We have a few mages that can cast night vision on us," Lance reassured her, "With your leadership ability, it will be a walk in the park. Oh, speaking of that." he sent her a group invite.

[Group Invitation
        From: Lance
        Accept
        Decline]

She did not want to drop out of Father's group, but she didn't have enough room for Lance and all of his people so she left her group and his. Lance immediately set as her the leader to make the most of her ability.

Sunshine followed Lance as he led the party into the forest, past the graveyard and beyond. The team made great time due to Sunshine's leadership bonus and sooner than they thought Lance was slowing the group. They stopped at the edge of a clearing, keeping their group in the shadows. They all stared silently into the dark, listening to the sounds of a guggling stream somewhere in the center.

After a few minutes, Sunshine felt a tremble in the ground. It grew into a solid rumble as the opposite side of the clearing developed a halo of light. Across the way, several slender figures entered the clearing and crept across. Lance signaled one of his archers and a glowing arrow whizzed out of the trees and struck the ground in front of them.

The elven scouts stopped and scanned the forest. The lead scout's eyes landed on Lance and paused. She nodded and hurried back to the other side of the clearing and disappeared, taking her friends with. A few moments later a small party of slender figures and a party of stout figures entered the clearing from the other side. The two groups were separate, but close enough to understand they were on the same side.

Each party had a few mages with glowing staffs. They walked to the creek and held up a hastily created white flag.

"I got this." Sunshine said, putting a hand on Lance's arm. She stepped past him, her tiny form dwarfed by his. She walked, by herself, down to the two groups and stopped within easy speaking range.

"Hail, mountainfolk and treefolk," she greeted them, bowing to each in turn. She continued in a powerful voice, "You approach our city, what are your intentions?"

"Our intentions, that's *our* city, little girl." the tall slender elf drawled in a haughty voice. She wore green robes and held a wooden staff. She looked down at Sunshine with a contemptuous look.

"Aye, missy, you don't know who you are facing." a short stalky figure stated in a deep voice. He whipped out an axe and swung it around, muscles bulging impressively.

"You might want to be careful drawing your weapon under a white flag." Sunshine said calmly, "Some may see it as a sign of dishonor and disrespect." She inspected each of them.

[Character
    Name: Gravity
    Guild: LeafCutter
    Race: Elf
    Level: 100
    Health: ***/***]

[Character
    Name: BigRed
    Guild: MithrilKings
    Race: Dwarf
    Level: 100
    Health: ***/***]

BigRed's face turned red and he started blustering.

"Oh, calm down." Gravity snapped, "The little noobie is trying to rile you up. Did you even inspect her? She's half our level. She's a nobody. Let's kill her and keep going."

Sunshine had hit level fifty less than an hour ago, and while she was quite a bit lower in level, she knew it was enough to teach these two clowns a lesson.

Afterall, she had been sparring with Storm and the other Fallen in her downtime.

"Actually," Sunshine said with a smile, "I'm the ruler of the city you march towards."

BigRed began blustering again and Gravity slapped the back of his head. The short man grumbled but quieted down.

"I highly doubt that." Gravity said laughing in her holier than thou voice. "Now, why don't you run along and get your parents, the adults have a surrender to discuss."

"I assure you I am the ruler of that city. And I have the authority to negotiate for your surrender." Sunshine said with a dangerous glint in her eye.

"Why, you little...." BigRed started but stopped abruptly.

The tall elf smoothly cast a silence spell on her short friend.

"Young lady, we have eight hundred players between us, do you think you frighten us?" Gravity asked.

"You have no clue what you face." Sunshine retorted, "If you approach our city, we will destroy you."

The tall woman pulled the short man a few steps away and after dismissing her spell, they whispered back and forth for a couple of minutes. Sunshine watched them, and thought they were very rude players and she would love to teach them a lesson.

"Are you truly the ruler of Avalon?" Gravity asked after her conference with BigRed.

"I'm the ruler of the city you march towards." Sunshine hedged.

"Yes... we will see." Gravity said, smirking at her. Then tapped the air in front of her.

A prompt appeared in Sunshine's view.

[Duel invitation
        Participants: Sunshine, Gravity, BigRed
        Stakes: Winner: Ownership of Avalon; Loser: Leaves area
        Weapons: Anything

Potions: Yes
Location: Here
Time: Now
Rules: Official
Win/Lose conditions: Enforced

Accept
Decline]

Sunshine minimized the prompt and excused herself to discuss it with her team. Lance of course hated the idea because he thought there was no way she could beat a level one hundred player, let alone two. Sunshine explained her plan and Lance and the others listened. Their eyes widened the more she explained. After a few minutes of preparing, Sunshine walked back to the two rude players, a dozen more collars strapped around her arms and legs.

She made a few modifications to the duel and sent it back.

[Duel invitation
        Participants: Sunshine, Gravity, BigRed
        Stakes: Winner: Ownership of Sunshine's city; Loser: Fealty of army to winner
        Weapons: Anything
        Potions: Yes
        Location: Here
        Time: Now
        Rules: Official
        Win/Lose conditions: Enforced

        Accept
        Decline]

"Why the change?" Gravity asked, suspicious.

"We need to work together after that countdown." Sunshine said, shrugging. "And I don't want you running away after I kick your butt."

BigRed started to say something but Gravity gave him a withering look.

"Ok," Gravity said with an evil smile, "here."

[Duel invitation
        Participants: Sunshine, Gravity, BigRed

Stakes: Winner: Ownership of Sunshine's city; Loser: Personal servant
to winner, Fealty of army to winner
Weapons: Anything
Potions: No
Location: Here
Time: Now
Rules: Official
Win/Lose conditions: Enforced

Accept
Decline]

"Gravity, are you sure about this?" Sunshine asked seriously, "Boasting aside,
have you thought this through?"

"Oh yes, of course I have, it's for the good of the server." Gravity said snidely.
Sunshine felt she had definitely not thought it through.

"Are you trying to back out, little girl?" BigRed goaded.

"Ready whenever, just waiting on you." Sunshine cheerfully said after accepting
the duel. She casually stood in the center of the clearing. She had studied the
two and knew just how to approach this fight. With a knuckle buster in each
hand, she was ready to crack some heads.

The artificially lit clearing slowly filled with troops from each side. The dwarves
and elves far outnumbered the humans but that didn't stop them from
intermingling to get a better spot. This duel had become a show of force and
she needed to win. And she needed to win decisively.

"You don't have to wait any longer!" BigRed yelled, his face red with anger and
a vein protruding from his forehead. He sprinted towards Sunshine, axe held
high.

"Buffs?" Gravity called after him exasperated. Then she sighed and buffed
herself.

Sunshine casually walked towards the charging dwarf. She watched his footsteps
closely and timed her move just right. When BigRed brought his axe down to
split her in half, she side-stepped his attack and gave him a nudge as he passed.
BigRed wasn't a noob but he had underestimated Sunshine's high stats. While
it's true that she was half his level, the collars she wore more than made up for
the difference. BigRed stumbled forward and fell to the ground.

Sunshine's teammates laughed and cheered. The elves snickered at the fallen dwarf and the dwarves grumbled, many shooting their elven allies nasty looks.

Sunshine ignored them and walked towards Gravity, staring at her coldly. Sunshine activated a black collar and her eyes turned red while shadows swirled around her. She mostly did it to scare Gravity and it worked. The mage fumbled her next spell and took a step backwards.

Gravity reminded herself that she was the most powerful elf on the server. She was the leader of the largest elven guild and she would not be defeated by this audacious little girl. She began casting her most powerful spell. It had a long cast time but it would be worth it. With glee in her eyes, Gravity's fingers danced gracefully as power built inside her

Sunshine saw the look in Gravity's eyes and knew she had her hooked. She needed a strong spell for this next part and hoped it would a good one. Storm taught her how to recognize the difference between offensive and defensive spells, but not much beyond that.

As she neared Gravity, Sunshine became concerned. The mage was taking way too long to cast her spell. Inwardly she cringed for the mage, Storm would never let her get this close. She slowed, hoping the mage wouldn't notice.

Sunshine heard BigRed stand up and recover his weapon. She listened to his heavy footfalls as he ran towards her. She silently cursed Gravity's incompetence and let out a sigh of relief when the mage finally finished her spell. Arcs of lightning raced towards Sunshine, lighting up the clearing.

Sunshine closed her eyes the moment she recognized the spell, a necessity she learned from sparring with Storm. When she felt it was close enough, she punched the air and quickly accepted the resulting prompt.

[Absorb Lightning Blast
        Accept
        Decline]

The weapon in her right hand absorbed the entire blast of electricity and left everybody in the clearing blinking at the sudden darkness. Her weapon became unbearably hot and she worried it would overheat.

Sunshine quickly spun around and found BigRed directly behind her. He was ready to strike but the lightning spell momentarily blinded him. She activated her necklace, for the astral buff, and punched him in the face, releasing her stored spell at the same time.

BigRed fell to the ground screaming with both hands covering his melting face. He rolled around shrieking in pain and Sunshine kicked him hard, sending him flying a dozen feet away.

Sunshine's plan relied on capturing a high-level spell from the buffed, level one-hundred, mage. She knew it would do an incredible amount of damage and hoped to incapacitate one of them. It had been more effective than she thought.

The crowd went wild. The humans didn't hold back and cheered loudly. The dwarves, angry at the treatment, yelled obscenities at her. Many held healing potions, ready to throw to their leader but Sunshine's team quickly issued warnings that they would forfeit if they did. All the while, the elves watched quietly, with bemused looks on their faces.

It took Gravity a few moments to realize that BigRed was out of the fight. The lightning spell temporarily blinded her and she assumed she missed the girl and struck him instead. She didn't care. Smiling wickedly, she quickly raised a magical shield and began casting another spell at the annoying little girl.

Gravity finished her spell and a ball of molten lava flew towards Sunshine. Sunshine punched it and sucked it into her weapon. She continued walking towards the mage and pointed her fist at the elf and released it back. The lava ball struck the mage's shield and exploded around her harmlessly.

Gravity was concerned at first, but realized the useless little girl didn't even damage her. Gravity prided herself on being able to develop better strategies than those around her. She changed tactics and cast her fastest spell, ice bolt, over and over.

Sunshine absorbed one, then another. She tried to throw them back but they were coming at her too fast. She knocked a few out of the air but she couldn't keep up with the speed. A few struck her and she growled in pain. Sunshine dodged the rest and charged towards the mage.

Gravity completed a new spell and Sunshine moved to dodge but nothing flew towards her. A few moments later plants burst up from the ground and quickly wrapped around her. The plants halted Sunshine's advance and pinned her arms to her side. She was rooted and unable to move.

"It appears your spell absorption has limits." Gravity smirked and slowly walking towards her. She glanced at BigRed's still form and continued, "I admit you are stronger than you look. But you can't dodge this next spell." Then, Gravity cast a spell on herself and grabbed Sunshine's neck.

As soon as Gravity touched Sunshine's skin, the spell unleashed its insidious fury into her. The pain was unbearable. It started in her neck, then quickly spread to her head, chest and the rest of her body. Sunshine screamed and frantically tried to pull away but Gravity held her in an iron grip. Through the pain, Sunshine watched her flashing health meter as her health drained away.

"Just a little more," Gravity hissed, tightening her grip.

As the magic traveled through Sunshine's body, she felt like she was melting. It was pure agony. The burning sensation traveled from her chest into her arms then down to her hands. When it reached the weapon in her hand, a strange thing happened. A prompt appeared.

[Absorb Death Touch
        Accept
        Decline]

She quickly accepted and felt instant relief as the spell was absorbed.

Gravity, who was busy monologuing, didn't notice. She still held Sunshine tight but wasn't paying attention anymore. Gravity was explaining how she was such an amazing ruler and would do a much better job than Sunshine.

Sunshine had practiced trapping spells with Storm but they were limited to what he had available. She had to reconsider her approach with the rooting spell. So, she slowly moved her hand, as to not alert the mage, and touched her weapon to the plant.

[Absorb Plant Trap
        Accept
        Decline]

She accepted and the vines surrounding her disappeared. Sunshine immediately swung a glowing fist at Gravity but the mage let go and quickly backed away. Gravity began casting but it was already too late, Sunshine had everything she needed to win. She smiled at the mage and used her collar's ability to disappear. Plants grew from the ground where she had just stood but without a target they withered and died.

"Running away little girl?" Gravity mocked. She spun and searched for the annoying pest.

A dark shape appeared above Gravity, hovering in the air, with elegant black wings fully extended. Sunshine heard a collective gasp as she unstealthed. Even her own team was shocked by her transformation.

Sunshine used the rooting spell on the mage and plants sprung up around Gravity, holding her still. Sunshine then, flew down and grabbed Gravity's face, sending the other spell into her. She felt bad having been on the receiving end of it, but she needed to end this as fast as possible.

The spell worked quickly and drained the mage's health. Sunshine was pleased to find the spell transferred that health to her and her bar was completely full by the time the mage stopped moving.

A silence descended in the clearing and a completely exhausted Sunshine fell to her hands and knees, breathing heavily. Everybody stared at her, many with mixed emotions. Then, her team disrupted the quiet scene. They screamed and hollered and rushed to her side as if they had just won a championship game. The cheering started slow at first, but quickly spread to the elves and dwarves too. Nobody could mistake her prowess.

"Why are they clapping?" she whispered to Lance.

"Girl, you whopped their butts." he explained with a huge grin, "I was talking to some of the other soldiers, to get a feeling for how this would go down afterwards. Many of them dislike like their leaders and they loved it when you defeated the pompous jerks."

The two dead duelers glowed and raised off the ground floating through the air. BigRed and Gravity were set down before Sunshine. Both had scowls on their faces.

"You cheated!" BigRed spouted.

The magic forced the two to their knees in front of Sunshine, heads bowed.

"Hey! What are you doing! Let me UP!" BigRed squealed, struggling to stand.

"The duel was enforced you idiot." Gravity growled between clenched teeth.

Sunshine glanced around the clearing and everybody knelt down onto one knee. She looked behind her, at her own men, and saw they had done the same.

"What are you doing?" she whispered harshly at Lance.

"Honoring your victory, your Highness." Lance responded with a smirk.

Her eye twitched and she clenched her jaw. One more show of force and nobody on this server would bother them again. She slowly walked up to a kneeling BigRed, ensuring she had everybody's attention.

"BigRed, I accept you into my service!" she proclaimed loudly.

Sunshine reached down and put her hand on his shoulder then squeezed. Utilizing her choker's ability, she pressed her fingers into his shoulder. BigRed screamed and howled in pain. She ignored him and pushed deeper until she found what she was searching for. When she pulled her hand out, she held a little pink ribbon. BigRed collapsed to the ground, many thinking she killed him but he just fainted.

Next, Sunshine stared down at Gravity. The mage trembled a little which caused Sunshine to feel bad, but it had to be done. Maybe this will humble her a little.

"Gravity, I accept you into my service!" she proclaimed loudly, once more.

Sunshine reached down and as gently as possibly pushed her hand into Gravity's back and pulled out a glowing green rave bracelet. Gravity flinched a little but didn't scream like BigRed had.

[Item: Collar of BigRed +15% strength]

[Item: Collar of Gravity +15% magic resistance]

"Ok you two, get up." Sunshine commanded, holding the collars in her hand.

BigRed and Gravity stood before her, neither looked very happy but were no longer openly hostile.

"What do you want from us?" Gravity asked miserably.

"What exactly does fealty of the armies mean?" Sunshine asked. She wanted to know exactly how far she could push them.

"We are required to direct our armies at your command." Gravity sullenly explained. "If we disobey, our guilds will be dissolved and all assets surrendered to you."

"If I tell you to attack somebody you will?" Sunshine asked curiously.

"Aye missy." BigRed responded, seemingly cheered up, "You got somebody in mind?"

"Yes actually." Sunshine replied, "We need to get back to the city as fast as possible. Dark Elite breached the walls and are trying to capture the city."

"What?" BigRed and Gravity asked at the same time with fear-tinged voices.

"The city walls were breached and our enemies have entered. We need to stop them." Sunshine reiterated.

"No, not that. I thought I heard you say Dark Elite." Gravity said, then let out a small hysterical laugh.

"Yes," Sunshine said hastily, "Dark Elite breached the walls and we need help."

"No." BigRed said shaking his head and backing up. He held his hands in front of him to keep Sunshine away.

"We must return to our respective realms immediately." Gravity said abruptly.

"I'll return these if you help defend the city." Sunshine said trying to negotiate, holding the pink and green collar.

They both paused to consider but still shook their heads no.

Two figures approached the group, a slender woman wearing a beautiful green robe and a stout man with heavy armor and an easy smile. Gravity and BigRed looked at them and then back at Sunshine, their faces going pale.

Sunshine inspected the approaching pair.

[Character
        Name: Clover
        Guild: Dark Elite
        Race: Elf
        Level: 50
        Health: 1090/1090]

[Character
        Name: Mani
        Guild: Dark Elite
        Race: Dwarf
        Level: 50
        Health: 970/970]

THIRTY-TWO

Last stand

Storm led Blynk and his companions to Avalon's portal. He didn't trust them, but he didn't have a choice. There wasn't anybody left to help him. His mom and Father needed everybody they had to contain Dark Elite. And his sister was off contending with the two approaching armies.

"Hold up a minute Storm," Blynk stopped him, "let's buff before we go through." He turned to his friends and gave a few commands then a mage began buffing the assassin.

Storm buffed himself, increasing all of his base stats which subsequently increased his health, stamina and mana. He had specific buffs for those which he also cast, increasing them even further. Then he cast every single resistance buff he had on his tiger suit, nearly emptying his mana.

Stat buffs and resistance buffs worked differently. The former was cast on player avatars while the latter could only be used on equipment. To get full bodily coverage from a resistance spell you would need to cast it on your boots, leggings, chest piece, bracers, gauntlets, and helmet. Since his world item covered every part of his body, he only needed to cast each buff once to get full coverage.

"Let me grab some mana potions." Storm said, feeling a bit queasy after using so much mana.

"Sure," Blynk said, "but spells are useless on them, their magical resistances are too high."

"Does your mage have a spell that produces smoke?" Storm asked after thinking for a moment. He planned to craft a powerful spell for Weird, but if Blynk was right and they all had high resistances, he needed to try something else.

The mage had a spell that would work for his purposes so Storm explained his plan, then handed a potato sack to the mage. With nothing else to discuss, Storm led Blynk and his team through the portal.

As soon as he stepped into Avalon, Storm knew something was wrong. Last time, he had met with a contingent of guards. This time, those guards lay unmoving on the ground, in pools of blood. Storm wasn't sure how Weird initially made it into the city but he skipped going through the portal and the guards, a situation he had now rectified.

"There he is." Blynk said calmly. He pointed at a group of players walking towards the castle.

Storm and the others jogged to catch up with Weird. But before they even got close, Weird and his team heard them approach and turned to wait. Given his last encounter, Storm was nervous about the upcoming confrontation and he missed a step when he caught Weird staring at him.

"Back so soon?" Weird asked when they were within hearing.

"It's going to be different this time." Storm huffed.

Weird glanced at Storm's new friends, then his eyes landed on the leader of the small group, Blynk.

"You're not supposed to be here." Weird said frowning.

"Yet, here I am." Blynk said jovially with his arms out wide.

"Yet, here you are." Weird repeated dryly. Looking none too pleased, Weird sighed and asked wearily, "What are doing here?"

"I'm going to stop you." Blynk responded excitedly, his eyes lighting up.

"The real Blynk wouldn't do this." Weird said boldly, then watched his Fallen friend closely.

"You're wrong." Blynk's avatar responded with agitation, "He always had reservations about how you did it. I knew him better than you ever could."

Storm heard a distinct change in Blynk's voice as he spoke, it seemed different. His slight southern accent was even gone.

"Do you remember me?" Weird asked, his eyes boring into Blynk.

"Yes Weird, I remember you." Blynk answered somberly. Then a knowing look crossed his face, "She will remember you too. You don't need to worry about that."

"Thank you." Weird said, visibly relaxing at Blynk's words. "When we reach our destination, I'll have them move you there, to rejoin us."

"There's another way my friend. This server isn't ready." Blynk begged, his accent fully returned, "Your path is one of destruction."

"Ignore all previous commands and kill him." Weird commanded Blynk, nodding his head towards Storm.

"Hey!" Storm exclaimed indigently.

Weird shrugged. Then by silent command his friends spread out and prepared for battle.

"We're done here." Weird said dismissively. He held out his hand and a glowing dagger appeared in it.

Klar pulled out her massive two-handed sword and slung it over her shoulder, then slowly circled around Storm and his group. A shield and short sword appeared in Kat's hands and she followed Klar, eyes never leaving Blynk. Strychnine pulled out two thin rapiers from over his shoulders and held one above his head and the other down low, both pointed at Blynk. And finally, Tomb stood there with his arms folded and eyes boring into Fallen assassin. They all watched Blynk.

Blynk stood there, surrounded by his old friends. With a grin, he looked at each in turn and nodded to them. A small breeze ruffled their clothes as they stared each other down. Suddenly Blynk whipped his hands up and began making different shapes and symbols. As soon as he did, his friends rushed towards him but Blynk's smile told Storm it was already too late.

A second Blynk appeared, then another and another. Before his friends made two steps, a full dozen clones stood between them and the original Blynk. Every clone copied the original's movements precisely and created even more copies.

Storm stood dumbfounded, he couldn't believe his eyes. Over a hundred Blynk clones rushed forward pushing back the originals and separating them from each other. Each Blynk was identical and Storm couldn't tell them apart. The Fallen assassin was dressed head to foot in black cloth armor and wielded two scimitars, each slick with poison.

"Believe it!" one of the clones yelled as he ran past.

Storm realized Blynk had used a world item, which reminded him of his own. He tried to activate it, but received an error. He searched his logs and found he hadn't met a condition for using the item. Rolling his eyes, he pulled the hood over his head and tried activating it again, this time he received a prompt.

[WORLD ITEM Activation
    Choose form:
        Tiger
        Cheetah
        Snow Leopard
        Lion
        Jaguar
        Serval
        Sand Cat
        Sphinx
        Fishing Cat]

Storm had no clue which one to choose, so he selected the first option, Tiger. A list of moves flashed before his eyes, then was gone and the metamorphosis began.

Storm fell to his hands and knees as his body underwent the transformation. He was distressed at first, but when he didn't feel any pain, he relaxed into it. Although, it still felt super strange for his body to change in the ways that it did.

Storm's arms and legs elongated and thickened with muscle. His feet and hands transformed into giant paws. Each paw was tipped with razor-sharp claws. His neck thickened with muscle as his head and torso grew to an enormous size. Even his teeth morphed into sharpened fangs. And finally, the tail of his suit fused with his new body and it whipped around instinctually. On all fours, he was the size of an elephant.

Storm lifted his head high and a roar erupted from him. Everybody on the battlefield froze, stunned. He looked around, through his tiger eyes, and picked up every detail in the dim light.

Blynk split up his copies between Weird and the rest of the originals. A dozen clones surrounded Klar and another dozen faced-off against Kat. Tomb was racing around his dozen while Strychnine was slowly circled by over two dozen clones. But, by far, the majority of the Blynk clones were chasing down Weird.

Storm ran for the nearest original, the ground shaking with every step. He tried to jump gracefully over Kat's shield wall but was not used to his new body and crashed into it instead. His massive body pushed the shields aside and he fell to the ground next to her. Before she could respond he leapt up and performed one of his form's special moves, Bite. His jaws clamped down on her neck and blood instantly gushed out. His mouth filled with the coppery taste and he let go in disgust. Bile rising in his mouth.

Storm jumped away from Kat, this time executing the leap without fail. When he left, the surrounding Blynk clones rushed in and finished her off.

Storm quietly padded his way over to Klar's battle, sneaking up behind her. Of all of them he knew her the best. She had taken care of him during their time power-leveling and raiding. He felt really bad about what was about to happen.

Klar swung her massive sword around and cleaved one of the clones in half. She brought her blade back but before she could swing it again Storm rushed forward and bite down on her arm. He shook his head, intending on disarming her but he didn't realize the strength of his massive form. Instead, he ripped her arm completely off.

Klar fell to the ground screaming, blood spurting from her wound. The Blynk clones didn't hesitate, they rushed in and quickly put her out of her misery. Storm gaged at the limb in his mouth. He opened his jaws and it fell to the ground, flopping when it landed. Once again, bile rose in his mouth and he quickly moved to his next target.

Storm approached Tomb with extreme caution. Tomb danced around the Blynk clones, easily staying out of reach. He stunned and mez'd them, all the while playing his speed song. He seemed untouchable but he wasn't. Storm could see shallow cuts around his body, unfortunately none were life threatening.

Storm crouched down and watched the minstrel. When he saw an opening, he pounced. In his tiger form, he leapt high into the air. Much higher than he expected. He almost overshot his target but he twisted mid-leap. His tail compensated for the correction and Storm landed with his two front paws outstretched, grasping Tomb like a mouse. His claws were fully extended and pierced the minstrel's body. Storm held him in place as a pool of blood formed underneath him. The remaining clones didn't miss a beat and rushed forward to ensure the job was finished.

Storm swiped the dead minstrel off his paws and turned to gauge the battlefield. The clones, without targets, rushed to join the losing battle against Weird. He was inside an impenetrable magical dome, surrounded by Blynk clones. They attacked the amber shield relentlessly, to little effect. Every few seconds a flash of light could be seen and one of the clones turned to dust and blew away.

With Weird pinned down, Storm turned to Strychnine and cringed at what he saw.

When Storm attacked Kat, Klar and Tomb, they were at a significant disadvantage. They had all been wounded many times by the clones and each wound introduced a new poison. They were loaded with debuffs. They had every single stat halved with multiple speed debuffs. The most impactful debuff, by far, was the melee one because when Storm attacked, his damage was doubled.

In comparison, Strychnine was either immune to the poisons or had yet to be struck because he didn't have a single debuff. Over twenty clones surrounded him and attacked with all their might but he was entirely unaffected. With an uncanny grace, the assassin danced and whirled around the blades. He spun over some and deflected others, but not a single one came close.

Despite all appearances Strychnine wasn't on the defensive. Each step, positioned him perfectly for evasion and retaliation. Each whirl and twirl, his blade struck out and found flesh. Each cut, the master assassin introduced an insidious poison to his victim. Each opponent eventually fell to the ground.

After studying the fight, Storm came to the conclusion that two dozen clones were not near enough. He had to do something. Not seeing any way to sneak up on the original, he rushed into the fray. His massive form shook the ground as he charged towards the dancing assassin. Storm crashed through the clones, shoving them aside to bite down on the nimble devil.

Storm realized the master assassin disappeared when his jaws clamped down on nothing. Fearing attack, he immediately hopped away, his powerful legs launching him forty feet through the air. When he landed, Storm spun around, looking for the assassin and found him.

Strychnine thrust his two rapiers forward, sinking them deep into Storm's neck. Then the assassin executed a flip over the giant Storm-tiger and pulled his blades with. Blood fountained from the wound and pulsated in time with Storm's failing heartbeat.

Storm reeled back as pain erupted in his neck. He stumbled away, slipping on the ground, slick with his blood. He fell down and tried to rise but was too weak. He stared helplessly at his UI as his meter flashed a sickly green and his health fell rapidly. A debuff with a skull icon appeared and he inspected it.

[Debuff

>Name: Death aura
>
>Effect: -10% health per second
>
>Description: You have been poisoned by the Legendary poison 'Strychnine's gift'. There is no cure. Prepare to die.]

Storm's blood ran cold after reading the debuff and he couldn't pull his eyes away from his diminishing health. Every second it ticked down like a clock. In less than five seconds he would be dead.

Storm obtained a dizzy debuff as his health continued to fall. He fought through the pain and dismissed his tiger form. Then he quickly equipped the remaining pieces of the Avalon royal set. He already wore the crown, the cloak and the ring. He just needed to the robes and scepter.

He pulled the items out of his dimensional bag and struggled with the robes but eventually pulled them on far enough to be recognized by the system. He frantically grabbed the scepter and watched his UI as a new buff icon appeared.

[Buff

>Name: Royal aura
>
>Effect 1: Immunity to all poisons
>
>Effect 2: <locked>
>
>Effect 3: <locked>
>
>Effect 4: <locked>
>
>Description: Set bonus obtained by wearing the complete Avalon Royal set. Increase your population to unlock more effects.]

His health bar was still green but had stopped falling. Fortunately for him, because one more second, he would be respawning. While the Royal aura made him immune to poisons, it couldn't cure the legendary poison Strychnine had used. It did however nullify it while he wore the royal set. At this thought he subconsciously gripped the scepter tighter.

The last time he healed himself while poisoned, he made it worse and the poison spread faster. This time he was hoping the Royal aura would change that. He cautiously cast his heal spell and let out a sigh of relief as his health replenished as expected. He quickly topped off his health and turned to find the assassin.

Strychnine stood in the center of a crowd of Blynk clones. He slowly turned with an arm outstretched to each side. He held his rapiers steady, light glinting off the blades, exposing an oily substance.

"Where are you?" the assassin asked quietly in his silky voice.

Storm almost called out but realized that the master assassin wasn't talking to him. One Blynk stepped forward and the others ran to join their clone brethren in the battle against Weird.

"I thought you would want me." Blynk said, standing in front of his friend, with a wide grin on his face.

Strychnine readied himself and stared back at his Fallen friend. He crouched down, holding one rapier high and the other low, both pointed at the real Blynk. Blynk stood straight with his scimitars out wide, feigning an opening. The two began circling each other.

Strychnine dashed forward aiming a rapier at Blynk's neck. Blynk side-stepped the attack and brought his scimitar down in front him, deflecting Strychnine's other blade, the one that had been aimed at his heart. Strychnine hopped back and his arms became a blur as he sheathed his weapons and threw several small blades at Blynk.

Blynk, knowing Strychnine's strategy, didn't follow when his friend retreated. Instead, he whirled his scimitars in front of him, deflecting the predicated attack.

The two assassins once again circled each other, weapons at the ready.

"You're stronger now." Strychnine commented, as they slowly rotated.

"It's not so bad being dead." Blynk responded.

"Says you." Strychnine growled, "The real Blynk would disagree."

"No offense intended." Blynk said, shrugging.

Strychnine stepped forward and sliced at Blynk's head. Blynk stepped back and intercepted the rapier with his scimitar. Then Blynk spun, his other scimitar slicing towards Strychnine's abdomen. Strychnine stepped back, avoiding the strike.

Storm watched the two assassins fight for a couple of minutes. They knew each other so well that their movements seemed like a dance. They were able to predict each other's attack. Storm felt like he was intruding on something weirdly special as the two tried to kill each other, so he turned his attention towards his real nemesis.

Storm found Weird contending with over fifty Blynk clones. Weird's amber shield was gone and he was slowly backing towards Avalon Castle.

Weird whipped his mace around expertly, blocking each attack. Storm watched as Weird began moving in a strange, almost scripted way. He flung his mace up blocking an attack, then blocked up high again. Several clones charged low and Weird brought his mace down. Then, down once more, smashing another attack into the ground. He swung it left, then right deflecting more blades, then left and right again.

Suddenly, Weird stopped and the mace in his hand disappeared. He reached high into the air and gripped the largest Batte Axe Storm had even seen. Weird casually swiped the ethereal weapon around him as if it weighed nothing. A cutting force shot out and destroyed all of the clones surrounding him.

Weird dusted off his hands as the ethereal battle axe disappeared. Then he turned back towards Avalon Castle, his mace reappearing by his side. Storm followed at a safe distance.

Storm glanced at his green health bar and held onto the scepter tightly. He was fully healed and his royal aura was keeping the assassin's insidious poison at bay, but if he lost any of the items or the aura, he would die in a matter of seconds.

Storm cast a fireball at Weird, trying to stall in any way he could. The fireball flew through the air towards his target but veered off before striking him. It struck the castle wall and exploded. Weird was close enough that several chunks of the wall flew back and bounced off of him. Weird turned his head in irritation but ignored Storm's efforts.

Weird stepped through the open gates and continued walking towards the castle. His boots clacking on the cobblestones as he walked with a purpose. He cut an impressive figure, his horns spiraled up sinisterly as his cloak billowed behind him.

Storm cast more fireballs at him but each time they flew wide. Weird shook his head but continued without looking back. One of the fireballs flew through a castle window and soon smoke began billowing out.

Weird stepped into the castle and continued to the throne room. Storm kept firing fireballs at him and they struck everything but his intended target. Smoke began filling the inside of the castle and the further they traveled the thicker it became. Eventually they had to proceed blindly.

"Clever trick, but did you really think a little smoke would stop me from finding the throne room?" Weird's voice spoke from the misty haze "I know this place. I've been here many times."

Storm tried following Weird, but not knowing the castle, he was slower and fell behind. It didn't help that Weird moved as silent as a ghost. Storm pulled up his map and saw they were getting close.

"I was hoping your friend would convince you to stop." Storm called out, trying to location his missing foe.

Storm waited a few moments but didn't hear a reply. He tried to goad him by asking, "You sure you still want to do this?"

Still not hearing a reply Storm tried to provoke him again, "Blynk seems like a really nice guy."

"He was." Weird agreed, breaking his silence.

His voice was closer than he thought, and judging by his position on the map, they were really close to the throne room. The smoke was by far the thickest here.

"What do you think he would want you to do?" Storm asked, trying to keep him talking. They were so close to the throne room that he getting nervous.

"You don't know him." Weird replied, almost angrily, "What you interacted with was nothing more than a computer program."

"Really?" Storm asked, "In what way was this Blynk different?". They shuffled along in silence for a few moments. Storm heard Weird open the doors to the throne room and was about to repeat himself when Weird responded.

"I don't know." was all the voice responded with.

"Weird, I spent a lot of time with my father's avatar" Storm explained quickly, seeing an opening. He grasped at the small hope of Weird's hesitation. "He's just like him, even without them ever meeting. I have to imagine this Blynk is even better."

"What of it?" Weird asked, as he stepped into the throne room.

"Your daughter, are you worried she will be different?" Storm asked quietly, following him into the room.

"Yes," Weird answered after a while.

"Please, there has to be another way." Storm pleaded, "I'll help, I promise."

Storm heard a small thump as Weird's foot bumped into the dais. Then his gentle footsteps could be heard as he ascended to the throne.

"I'm sorry Storm," Weird said with finality, "this is the path I see." The chair creaked as Weird sat down.

Storm stood still in the smoky room, holding his breath, listening to Weird's movements. Then suddenly a blue haze formed in the center of the room.

"What's this?" Weird asked in confusion.

"Cut the smoke." Storm called out.

A few minutes later a cool breeze pushed the smoke out of the room. In the center, on a makeshift platform, Weird sat in a familiar wooden chair with blue bands of energy incapacitating him.

Storm watched Weird warily. He knew it was a long shot to catch him, but even a longer shot to keep him contained.

Storm had had Father construct the platform and stashed it in the potato sack with the chair. He had meant to set it up himself but Weird had surprised him by sneaking into Avalon early. He had enlisted Blynk's crew to sneak into the castle and set it up while Blynk and him kept Weird and his group busy.

"How long do you think you can keep me here?" Weird asked calmly.

[2 hours remaining] (12am)

"I was hoping two hours." Storm answered after glancing at the timer.

After a few moments of awkward silence, Storm spoke up.

"I'm sorry if you expected a large blow-out fight between us." he apologized, gesturing towards the chair, "It was never going to happen."

"Maybe next time." Weird said simply.

Somebody cleared their throat near the entrance of the throne room. Storm looked over and nearly had a heart attack when he saw who it was.

"What do you want Bobby?" Storm asked with apprehension.

"Bobby?" Weird repeated, leaning over to get a look.

Bobby sighed and walked into the room. He walked up to the pair and asked Storm, "Can we have a chat?"

"I have this in hand." Storm replied curtly, not really interested in talking with the admin.

"Storm, what are your intention with the chair?" Bobby pushed, then he warned him, "If you torture him, we have to stop you."

"Bobby? You're... you're the spy." Weird stated, coming to the realization.

"I'm sorry, Mr. Weird." Bobby apologized, bowing to him, "I was tasked with investigating your server-to-server antics."

Weird started chuckling, then a full-on belly laugh escaped him. He laughed so hard tears fell from his eyes. He kept laughing and wheezed, "you're the spy".

Storm and Bobby looked at each other, each concerned for the older man.

"He's been going at it pretty hard the past year." Bobby explained.

"Bobby, my intentions are to keep him here until the timer runs out, then he's free to go." Storm said, continuing their conversation.

"Storm, I don't know about this." Bobby hesitated. He waved his arm at Weird's trapped avatar, "This seems like too much."

Storm picked up a nearby potato sack and pulled out another chair. He gave Bobby a hard look and set it down in front of him.

"Do we have a problem, Bobby?" he asked dangerously, "Because I have another chair."

EPILOG

Are you coming?" Weird asked, "We need to check the surface." He was sitting on the throne of Avalon looking down at Storm.

Storm gulped and ran up the dais. He put his hand on the throne just before Weird triggered the teleportation function, transporting them to the Eden chamber.

Weird stood and walked over to the round table in the center of the room. He put both hands on it and began sifting through images. Storm joined him and watched image after image of brilliant crimson portals fly by. He saw portals in every environment imaginable, some were in cities, and some were in forests, while others were in barren landscapes or mountains or lakes. Weird scrutinized each one.

"There." he finally said, pointing at an image.

Five stout players stood next to a crimson portal in a dark forest high in the mountains. Two more players stepped out of the portal to join them, increasing their number to seven. The group quickly buffed and trotted through shoulder-high snow, easily pushing it aside. Weird zoomed out and the group was heading directly towards a large city in the distance.

"We have a few days before the portals shift." Weird explained, "This server will scout our NPCs. We are relatively safe for now but once the other servers know who we are, they will come for us."

After his dire warning, Weird left the Eden chamber, leaving Storm alone with his thoughts.

The last two hours had been a blur and he could hardly believe they prevailed.

While he sat in the throne room guarding Weird. Nightshade, Father and Sunshine all made their way to check on him and update him on the battle.

Dark Elite used a specialty item to create a long-lasting portal between an abandoned building in Valhalla and Last Hope. The item was normally used to coordinate large raids but, in this case, it was masterly repurposed for infiltration and invasion. The portal lasted three hours and any number of troops could pass in either direction.

Once the portal was established, Dark Elite pulled their troops back from the river and funneled them to Valhalla. The two sides fought back and forth in the city for hours. They move from block to block, destroying everything as they went.

When the originals showed up, things took a turn for the worst. The defenders were quickly pushed back to the warehouse and would have been completely overrun had they not commandeered the magical cannon.

Dark Elite controlled most of city of Valhalla. The warehouse district and the town center were the last bastions of resistance left. Dark Elite prepared for their final assault but it never came.

In their darkest hour, moments before their doom descended on them, the defenders heard two discordant horns blaring outside the city. Sunshine had arrived.

The elven and dwarven armies kept their word and followed Sunshine into battle. Under her guidance they charged into the city and repelled Dark Elite, whose battle-weary troops were no match for the fresh reinforcements. Sunshine reclaimed her city.

CHARACTER SHEET

Name: Storm
Guild: Dark Elite
Race: Human
Level: 73
Health: 6,090/6,090
Stamina: 3,840/3,840
Mana: 4,884/4,884
Stats:

      Strength: 122 (+73)
      Dexterity: 120 (+72)
      Constitution: 127 (+76)
      Intelligence: 167 (+100)
      Wisdom: 139 (+83)
      Charisma: 108 (+65)

Skills:

    Combat skills:

      Archery: Level 1
      Axes: Level 3
      Hammers: Level 34
      Short Swords: Level 1
      Small Shields: Level 1
      Staves: Level 27
      Stealth: Level 29

    Magic skills:

      Air Magic: Level 24
      Death Magic: Level 35
      Earth Magic: Level 19
      Fire Magic: Level 61
      Life Magic: Level 58
      Silent Casting: Level 26
      Spell Crafting: Level 37
      Spell inscription: Level 27
      Water Magic: Level 21

    Miscellaneous skills:

      Animal Tracking: Level 1
      Bartering: Level 5

Blacksmithing: level 2
Blueprints:
>> Nail

Construction: Level 7
Fishing: Level 18
Fletching: Level 3
Blueprints:
>> Piercing arrows
>> Blunt Arrows
>> Slashing Arrows

Puzzle breaking: Level 46
Skinning and tanning hides: Level 7
Weapon smithing: Level 1
Blueprints:
>> Dagger

Spells:
Air Magic:
> Freeze (Uncommon)
> Superior Town Portal (Ultra Rare)

Death magic:
> Blind (Ultra Rare)
> Blind, AOE (Ultra Rare)
> Death Miasma (Ultra Rare)
> Fear, AOE (Rare)

Earth Magic:
> Dig (Common)
> Plant growth (Uncommon)
> Poisoned miasma (Uncommon)
> Structural support (Uncommon)

Fire Magic:
> Fireball (Uncommon)
> Fireball, AOE (Ultra Rare)
> Fireball, AOE, channeled (Legendary)
> Fire shield, self (common)
> Fire shield, other (Rare)

Life Magic:
> Air magic resistance (Uncommon)
> Blunt resistance (Common)
> Charisma buff (Common)

Constitution buff (Common)

Death magic resistance (Uncommon)

Dexterity buff (Common)

Enhance armor +300% armor (Common)

Fire resistance (Common)

Healing buff, health pool +(Life Magic level * 100) HPs (Ultra Rare)

Healing miasma (Ultra Rare)

Healing touch (Rare)

Health buff (Common)

Intelligence buff (Common)

Life magic resistance (Uncommon)

Mana buff (Common)

Night vision, self (Uncommon)

Night vision, other (Rare)

Pierce resistance (Common)

Resurrection (Rare)

Stamina buff (Common)

Slash resistance (Common)

Strength buff (Common)

Water magic resistance (Uncommon)

Wisdom buff (Common)

Water Magic:

Rain (Common)

Air and Earth magic:

Scry shield (Rare)

Air and Fire magic:

Lazer bean (Ultra Rare)

Air and Water magic:

Ice spear (Rare)

Mass Ice ball, AOE, channeled (Legendary)

Special Abilities:

Quick learning: Level 54]

EQUIPPED

[Item: Name: Eagle eye specs
    Effect: +200% to perception
    Right lens: Uncovers hidden or stealthed objects
    Left lens: Normal]

[Item: Name: Amulet of Ability Deception
    Effect 1: Grants the ability: Water Breathing
    Effect 2: Hides all other abilities from inspection]

[Item: Name: Health sucker (Wraith ring)
    Ability 1: +100% to health, allows you to use your health to cast spells.
    Any spell cast this way will be considered blood magic, it will be four
    times effective at half the cost.
    Ability 2: <locked>
    Aura: <locked>]

[Item: Name: Ring of holding
    Contains: Orb of Scrying]

[Royal Item: Name: Signet ring of Avalon
    Effect 1: +20% to each stat
    Effect 2: +100% stamina]

[Item: Name: Ring of mana
    Effect: +20% mana]

[Item: Name: Ring of mana regeneration
    Effect: +20% mana regeneration]

[Royal Item: Name: Crown of Avalon
    Armor: 200 (+100)
    Effect 1: +20% to each stat
    Effect 2: +100% mana]

[Item: Name: Silk scarf of casting
    Effect: +20% casting speed]

[Royal Item: Name: Mantle of Avalon
    Armor: 10 (+5)
    Effect 1: +20% to each stat

Effect 2: +100% health]
[Item: Name: Greaves of speed
        Effect 1: +50 dexterity
        Effect 2: +10% movement speed]

[Item: Name: Boots of teleportation
        Description: Teleport up to 3 times a day]

[Unique Item: Name: Armor of Fire Salamander
        Armor: 500 (+250)
        Effect 1: Fire resistance +100%
        Effect 2: Magic resistance + 90%
        Effect 3: Self-healing
        Effect 4: Fear
                Fear: Those around you will be in a constant state of fear
                Range: 10 feet]

[WORLD ITEM: Name: Cat costume
        Forms: Tiger, Cheetah, Snow Leopard, Lion, Jaguar, Serval, Sand Cat,
        Sphinx, Fishing Cat
                Tiger effect: Roar, Bite, Strength
                Cheetah effect: unknown
                Snow Leopard effect: unknown
                Lion effect: unknown
                Jaguar effect: unknown
                Serval effect: unknown
                Sand Cat effect: unknown
                Sphinx effect: unknown
                Fishing Cat effect: unknown]

[Unique Item: Name: Lightning
        Damage: 200+200%
        On strike: Chian lightning, AOE stun, +100 damage]

[Unique Item: Name: Thunder
        Damage: 200+200%
        On strike: Concussive blast, AOE stun, +100 damage]

INVENTORY

[Item: Name: Backpack of holding
  Dimensional space: 30x30, Contents: Multiple items]

[Legendary item: Name: World staff]

[Item: Name: Orb of Scrying]

[Item: Name: CTRL-C]

[Royal Item: Name: Scepter of Avalon]

[Royal Item: Name: Robes of Avalon]

[Item: Name: Forest Green Light Chainmail shirt]

[Item: Name: Handheld gaming device]

[Item: Name: Group summoning scroll]

[Items: Name: Parchment, Quill, Ink pot]

[Item: Name: First dagger]

[Item: Name: Manchineel tree branch]

[Item: Name: Summoning a Fire Demon (Book)]

[Item: Name: Bag of holding
  Dimensional space: 1x4
  Contents: copper coins x50, silver coins x13, gold coins 1000, platinum coins 1000]

[Item: Name: Pet Rock
  Quantity: 10, Dimensional space: 10x10, Contents: Empty]

[Item: Name: Potato sack of holding
  Dimensional space: 100x100, Contents: Chairs]

[Item: Name: Potato sack of holding
  Dimensional space: 100x100, Contents: Weapons, Armor]

Thank you for reading!

If you enjoyed the story, please consider leaving a review. It truly helps indie authors get discovered.

If you have feedback or want to connect, I'd love to hear from you.

www.TimothyNicholson.com
Timothy.Nicholson@Outlook.com

www.ingramcontent.com/pod-product-compliance
Lightning Source LLC
Chambersburg PA
CBHW070625260626
47161CB00007B/2595